FAE

DAUGHTERS OF ELTERA — BOOK ONE

CASSANDRA FAYE

Text copyright © 2015 Jennifer Bene / Cassandra Faye

All Rights Reserved

No part of this book may be reproduced in any form or by any electronic or mechanical means including information storage and retrieval systems, without permission in writing from the author. The only exception is by a reviewer, who may quote short excerpts in a review.

This book is a work of fiction. Names, characters, places, and incidents either are products of the author's imagination or are used fictitiously. Any resemblance to actual persons, living or dead, events, or locales is entirely coincidental.

ISBN (e-book): 978-1-946722-02-7

ISBN (original paperback): 978-1-946722-01-0

ISBN (new paperback): 978-1-946722-42-3

Cover design by Eris Adderly. http://erisadderly.com/cover-designs-by-eris-adderly/

❊ Created with Vellum

I have so many people to thank for their help in bringing the first book in my Daughters of Eltera series to life. Fae has been a work of many years as I worked to find myself as an author, never forgetting about this draft sitting on a shelf collecting dust.

So, first, thanks to my best friends Sarah and Blake for listening to me talk about Fae and Kiernan and the Faeoihn for hours, and never once complaining, but always being some of my biggest cheerleaders.

Second, major thanks to my editor (the Brit who shall not be named) and my author friend Myra Danvers for putting in hours and hours of work editing the drafts of this book, you guys are amazing.

Third, I have to thank all the men and women in The Erotic Collective for inspiring me to believe I could publish in the first place, specifically, Tara Crescent (my publishing guru).

And last, but most definitely not least, I have to thank you, the reader. Without your tweets, Facebook comments, emails, reviews, and general support for my other books I likely would have never gained the courage to publish something so close to my little author heart.

Now I'll shut up and let you enjoy Fae's story.

PROLOGUE

THREE YEARS AGO

Suyhay Market, Bangkok, Thailand

"Are we going to be okay?"

Again, with that damn question. The pixie with the wide violet eyes and iridescent wings just wouldn't stop *talking*.

Fae was doing her best to stay detached from the people around her, but the insistent whispering of the frightened girl was difficult to ignore. Rolling her shoulders she tried to ease the pressure on her arms from being cuffed to the wall.

What do you even to say to a question like that?

Fae knew the girl wanted to be comforted, wanted to feel better, but how could she do that without lying? It just wasn't possible. The girl repeated the question again, straining herself even more to get closer. With a little growl, Fae made herself answer.

"Stay quiet, obey them, and you'll probably make it through alive." Fae didn't look over at the pixie, keeping her eyes trained on the bolted door on the opposite wall – she didn't want to get dragged into a conversation. *Couldn't* get dragged into one. She had to focus.

It had only taken twenty-two years to be back in this dump. The third Wednesday of every month was unique in the Suyhay Slave Market, because amidst their normal stock of women and men were those from their 'special collection'. Supernatural creatures collected from a variety of places and planes of existence that were carted into their white tiled storage area in chains, and cages, and boxes, to be sold to anyone with the money to buy them.

It really, really sucked.

Muffled crying was echoing around the room and grating on Fae's nerves. But there was nothing she could do about it, not while chained to a fucking wall in a room warded against magic. Not even Eltera's healing gifts could get in here.

"What are they doing with us? Why are we all here? I want to go home." The pixie had her arms fully extended, the chains taut from her to the wall, to get as close to her as possible. The girl shivered, pale blue skin damp with sweat and the chill in the air wasn't exactly keeping her warm, but she was so intent on Fae she didn't seem to notice. "I want to go home, please," she whispered, her violet eyes slightly glassy and unfocused, "Can't I just go home?"

Fae dropped her head back against the wall, squeezing her eyes shut as if that could block out the sound of the girl's desperate pleas. "No. They aren't going to let you go home." She twisted her body again trying to relieve the strain on her shoulders. If they were going to leave her here for hours, the least they could have done was cuff her arms in front of her or give her enough chain to sit comfortably. With a sigh she continued, "Listen. You're going to go home with whomever buys you today, and if you're lucky they'll want you just because you're a pixie, and you'll be some party trick."

The girl shifted, a bundle of nervous energy. "And – and if I'm not lucky?"

No one here was lucky.

"You'll be a house slave, or a bed slave." Fae's voice was flat and tired. It took a moment to realize it was so much quieter nearby. Looking around she could see wide eyes of various colors staring at her, too many future slaves listening to her. Listening to the knowledge she'd gained from too many years of being bought and sold. Part of her wanted to comfort them, but there was nothing more to say. The truth was the kindest thing to give them. The girl didn't ask any more questions, there wasn't a need to elaborate, and the pixie finally shrank away, curling her wings tight to her back.

The grating sound of metal on metal filled the room before the heavy door was thrown back. The thing that stood in the opening was tall, bald, broad-chested, and dumb. All Durgha were dumb, but this one looked like he might have traded some of his IQ points for a few more muscles at some point in his life. He scanned the room until his dull, black eyes lit on Fae and he started walking over.

Fae whispered her final comment to the pixie. "Also, if you want to survive? Don't act like me."

Leaning heavily against the wall to look weak and tired, Fae waited for the chains to be unlocked. It took a moment longer for the idiot to find the right key and remove the cuffs.

"Up," he grunted. Monosyllabic and everything. He was a half-step above a caveman, which was perfect for her. When his hand landed on her shoulder Fae brought her elbow up into his face. The crunch of his nose and the sudden spray of blood took him by surprise and he roared in pain. Rolling to the side Fae popped up a few feet away from him, lunging forward to deliver a well-placed kick to his groin. The Durgha dropped to his knees, groaning but lucid enough to reach for her. Fae reared back and kicked him in the face, sending him bloody and moaning to the tiled floor. Various creatures in chains called out to her, called out for help, for rescue, for *freedom* – but she couldn't help them. There wasn't time.

Turning around she ran out the open door into the hallway with concrete covering the floor and walls. She'd only been in it once before, but she remembered the way out to the streets was to the right. Running full speed she skidded around a corner. Already, she could hear loud voices and heavy footfalls behind her. This was her only chance. No master meant no commands, no commands meant no curse to stop her from escaping. The slap of her bare feet across the floor increased as she pushed herself. Now that she was out of the warded room, she could feel Eltera's power allowing her to keep going even when her lungs were on fire.

"Dammit, where is it?" Fae hissed out loud to herself as she turned the next corner and saw the large metal door with a window in it. There was light from the street pouring in.

Shouts echoed up the hall from behind her and she kept moving. Slamming into the door at full speed she grabbed the handle and yanked hard. The door didn't budge.

"No!" she screamed and started yanking on the door harder. "No, no, no, no, no!" The low voices of several Durgha were getting closer. Time had run out. Taking a deep breath Fae slammed her fist into the glass of the small window at the top of the door. It cracked, but didn't break, though her wrist may have. Pounding footsteps were in the hallway now, and she struck again. More cracks, another wave of pain from her hand. Yelling again, she slammed her fist into the window and was rewarded with pieces of the small window slicing into her hand as she pulled it back.

Reaching an arm through the new opening she scrambled for the handle, grasping. Her fingertips couldn't reach it.

The warm air from outside filtered in and she angled her head so she could see a small scrap of the sky beyond the roof. There was freedom. So close, but so impossibly far on the other side of the thick steel door. Large arms wrapped around her waist and yanked her back – away from the sky, away from freedom, away from hope. She screamed as the glass sliced her arm, and slammed her foot down onto the toes of the first Durgha that grabbed her. He howled in her ear and released his hold enough for her to drop out of his grasp. Landing on her side, she kicked both feet into the nearest leg she could see, a sickening pop and the accompanying yell from the behemoth signaling victory.

Won't be chasing anyone now, will you?

Scrambling backwards, Fae pushed herself to standing and ducked a windmill swing by one of the Durgha. They always relied on their strength, no skill whatsoever. The punch she returned to his stomach didn't do more than knock some air out of him, but she had to try. What she wouldn't do for a weapon in this situation. The crushing grasp of one of the Durgha pinned her arms to her sides, but he lifted her up so she couldn't kick him. She *could* kick the idiot standing in front of her though, and connecting her heel with his face was satisfying, even more so when he roared and spit out a tooth. He lunged forward at her, but stopped short when a voice echoed down the hallway filled with panic.

"Stop! Don't hurt her dammit, we have to sell her today! You fools, do *not* hurt her!" The grating, high-pitched voice of Panupong seemed to cut through the rage in the

Durghas' faces as they turned towards him. He was the auctioneer, and some kind of middle-management at the Suyhay market. Cheeks red and eyes bulging as he approached, Panupong's breaths rattled in his chest. His large belly heaved up and down as he tried to catch his breath. Fae wished he was close enough to kick.

Panupong had been there two days prior to greet and accept her from her former master who had sold her to cover his outrageous gambling debts. That master hadn't been terrible, just foolish. Fae had hated Panupong from the first moment she'd laid eyes on him. He was only concerned with money and not the welfare of any of the beings he sold. Clucking his tongue, he looked her over, and groaned at the sight of her. "Look at this, she's a mess!"

Fae hissed through clenched teeth, "You could always let me go." Panupong stepped forward, ignoring her, and Fae kicked out again, narrowly missing him before he jumped back.

He scowled. "Put her on the ground. Hold her down. We're going to have to sedate her or no one is going to spend anything on her." Fae arched her back and kicked her legs, trying to twist away from the Durgha's arms, but it just made him tighten his grasp further making it difficult to breathe. The one with the busted mouth grabbed her legs and pinned them to his side and they dropped her to the ground. Quickly adjusting the grip on her arms the Durgha pinned them to the floor at her sides. Fae strained against both of them, but there was no budging now. Panupong stepped forward, sweat dripping off his round face. His hands shook as he opened a small case and took out a syringe full of a liquid with a faint blue color.

Fuck. Dreamland.

Fae shook her head and started to plead. "Don't. You don't need to give me that." She knew she wouldn't be able to do anything, no chance for another escape attempt, if they injected her with it. It would make her so loopy she'd barely be able to stand, and eventually she'd just go to sleep as it took effect.

Panupong reached under the Durgha leaning over her and brushed her auburn hair out of her face, sweeping it away from the sweat on her forehead. "You made this choice when you tried to run. Now be a good girl and hold still." He ran his thumb over the crook of her elbow looking for a good vein. It was pointless she still tensed up. He injected her quickly with a sharp stab, and the drug flooded her veins sending her head spinning seconds later. She tried to focus on what she wanted to do.

Escape.

She had no master, had no commands to follow.

This was her only chance to get away.

She felt their hands let go of her, and she tried to get up, to run, but rolling to her side was all she managed. Her mind was so fuzzy, so full of warmth, and she felt a sense of calm wash over her. She could hear them talking, but it was hard to focus on a single thought. Then one of the

Durgha lifted her up and tossed her over his shoulder. A few minutes later a rough washcloth was scrubbing the blood off her arms and thin bandages were being wrapped over the cuts. A new tank top and cheap black cotton shorts replaced the bloody ones, but there was nothing they could do to make her look like an obedient little slave. Every inch of her screamed disobedient, and she didn't bother stifling the giggle that bubbled out of her. Panupong glared and left the room in a huff, mumbling as he did. She didn't care. It was hard to care about anything as the Dreamland stormed through her bloodstream. It was one of the few drugs on the planet that effected beings like her, which only made her hate it more.

When they were satisfied, Fae was shuffled into the hallway, a heavy hand placed on her shoulder by one of the Durgha. It was difficult to stay standing under the weight of the drug. Trying to think, or talk, or move took so much effort that she resembled a zombie as he moved her around. She knew on some deep level that she wouldn't feel normal again until the morning, but that was little comfort in the moment.

The Durgha stopped her outside a pair of large swinging doors that were left over from the time when this place was a meat packing warehouse. The auction took place in what had been the central packing floor, a large space that now only witnessed these weekly auctions. Fae leaned against the wall, fighting to keep her eyes open, and the Durgha only used his hand to keep her somewhat upright. There was the murmuring of a lot of people talking inside the doors, but none of it was clear.

She knew she should fight, that she should try to run, but her body wouldn't respond. It took all of her effort to stay still against the wall as the room curved around her, making her feel off-balance and uneasy.

After a few moments the Durgha banged his fist against the swinging door. Above the din Panupong's irritating voice rose up, "Many apologies for the delay, we are now moving back to lot twelve." As he spoke the Durgha pushed Fae through the doors, she stumbled once as she stepped up onto the raised platform to face the thirty or so people sitting in metal folding chairs. Panupong's smile was so wide his cheeks must have hurt, and even through the effects of the drug Fae really wanted to hit him and wipe that stupid grin away. The Durgha pressed down on her shoulder until Fae dropped into a kneel in the middle of the platform.

"Here we have a treat for you. A female from a race called the Fae-oh-een." Panupong annunciated carefully and then cleared his throat to speak louder. "One of only a hundred or so god-touched beings originally part of a warrior cult worshipping the goddess Eltera."

'It's not a cult', Fae thought to herself. She wanted to scream at him, correct him, explain her purpose. Their real purpose.

But that was pointless.

Fae leaned forward and put her hands on her knees. Her stomach was starting to turn from the dose of Dreamland. Panupong looked her over and continued, "She looks quite young, but is actually immortal so she will look like this forever – her exact age is unknown. Other things to know, the Faeoihn can receive almost anything other than a fatal wound and at dawn every day will be healed and good as new. Think of it! Punish her however you like, enact any fantasy, and she will be fresh in the morning. Can you really put a price on something this magnificent?" Panupong was pointing at her, but Fae had slumped forward as the drug thumped through her veins. *Sure*, she could heal, in another ten hours or so, but for now he'd drugged her into uselessness. He gestured at the Durgha to straighten her up with a nervous flick of his hand. The mammoth grabbed her shoulder and pulled her back into a sitting kneel. When her head was still hanging down the beast lifted it up by holding onto her hair. Once her face was visible again, Panupong smiled back at the crowd, "If that isn't enough, the Faeoihn are required to obey! Once a master is identified, magic-formed control bands ensure an obedient creature by delivering pain when direct commands are not followed! Delightful, yes?" Panupong gave himself a little round of applause, but no one else joined him.

He laughed nervously, as he looked over at her again.

Fae was barely conscious and didn't exactly look appealing in old clothes, half-covered in bandages, and almost unconscious from the drugs required to control her.

Yeah, she was a real prize.

"Time for the auction!" Panupong started the bidding with a desperate voice and a surprising number of hands went up. As the auction continued Fae drifted in and out of consciousness, the haze of the Dreamland had completely engulfed her. The speed of the auction began to slow until there were just two bidders left. Fae forced her eyes open when she heard him saying the same bid numbers over and over. She could see a green skinned woman with a cruel face, and a dark haired man wearing sunglasses – both raising their hands to bid.

They were both looking directly at her and not Panupong.

A few more bids were thrown out, and the higher pitch of Panupong's voice hinted that it must be getting good, but she couldn't focus enough on the numbers he said. There was muttering among the group and then the loud clap of Panupong's hands echoed through the room like thunder. When Fae opened her eyes one last time a slow smile appeared on the dark haired man's face, and the middle-management peon of the Suyhay Market spoke with clear delight.

"Sold."

CHAPTER ONE

PRESENT

RÁJ MANOR, CALEDON, ONTARIO

"ARE YOU SERIOUSLY EXCITED ABOUT THIS?" Caridee sounded shocked as her head jerked around.

Irena was perched on top of a cabinet, her legs hanging over and her iridescent wings fluttering madly above her. "Of course! We never get to decorate. Master always brings in some *company* to do it." Irena's voice was reaching pixie-shrill as it sped up, "Usually the dinner parties are all boring, but we get to do it this time! Lights, and floral arrangements, and ribbons and table settings!" She rocketed off the top of the cabinet and did a loop before landing on her toes in front of Caridee, her wings flicking rapidly. "He's going to use *my* flowers, Cari!" Irena's energy was impossible to ignore, and several of the girls who had been sleeping this early in the morning were drifting out of their nooks, rubbing their eyes and yawning as Irena's voice shook them all awake.

"You crazy!" Caridee threw up her hands, her Latin accent thicker in the morning hours. With a sigh she sat down on a floor pillow and began braiding her wavy, dark hair as Irena pranced around her.

Fae was stretching, still coming down from the high of Eltera's healing touch, which woke her at dawn every day. It had been over two thousand years since she had seen her, but Fae knew Eltera loved her – why else would she risk everything to heal her every morning whether she needed it or not? Watching Irena's excitement brought a small smile to Fae's face, but she knew it wasn't exciting for everyone. It was Juliet's first dinner party, and although she was almost her normal bubbly self, Fae could tell she was nervous as she fidgeted and forced smiles for Irena.

"I'll help you, Irena! With all of it!" Juliet's loud voice effectively woke up anyone who was still sleeping. She was quickly giggling with Irena and talking about various flowers in her French accent, as some of the girls mumbled about preferring quiet in the morning. Irena popped her head up and looked at Fae, her short, dark blue hair was floating around her head in a poof.

"Fae! Will you help too?" Her smile was huge, but Fae was not getting roped into crazy pixie decorator mode.

"I help with growing the flowers, not arranging them into pretty decorations. I think I'll leave that to you two."

There were a few chuckles around the room as several of the girls found spots on the floor to stretch and talk before Lena addressed them all. Some of them had curled back up on the large floor pillows, eyes drifting closed now that Hurricane Irena was in a controlled state of planning and designing her decoration scheme. They had to find their happiness where they could get it, and this version of Irena was much better than the frightened pixie that had accompanied Fae from the Suyhay Market years ago. Irena wasn't her real name, but her true name had been so difficult to pronounce that Nikola had simply renamed her. She didn't seem to mind it though and watching her come out of her frightened shell to become this loud-mouthed, hyper, little pixie had been great. She was great with supporting any new girls too. When Juliet had arrived a couple of months before, Irena had taken her under her wing quickly, and now they were always together if possible.

Looking stern and carrying her usual clipboard, Lena came from the door leading to the showers. She was already perfectly put together, her dark hair drawn back into an artistic bun that allowed a few strands of hair to frame her face. Now in her early forties, she was just as beautiful as many of the younger girls, but would probably look even better if she ever *smiled*. The cheap linen sheath dress clung to her curves in all the right ways. The pale green color and low cut neckline didn't detract from the air of professionalism she somehow maintained.

It was really annoying that she wore the same uniform as the rest of the girls without looking like a servant.

Lena tapped a pen on the clipboard to get everyone's attention, but when that didn't stop the chatter between Irena and Juliet, she cleared her throat. Juliet nudged Irena and they both snapped to attention, staring at Lena with wide eyes. The girls who had been lying down sat up, shaking off the remnants of sleep.

As the matron of all the girls, Lena demanded respect.

"Good morning. As you all know, tomorrow night is the Winter Dinner. Master will have many guests and it is our responsibility to get the house ready." Lena looked down at her clipboard and checked something off. The adoration in her voice as she said the word 'master' was nauseating. "I have your assignments for the day prepared. Be sure to get yours from me before you leave the female section. Tomorrow night will be white dress, but today you may choose any other color." With that she clapped her hands together twice, and the sound of several locks being undone came from the double doors that led to their area.

As a door opened, one of the house guards stood outside with the keys as Alec, the cook, pushed in a metal cart covered in plates of food. Alec was one of the male servants. Fae wasn't sure how he had arrived there, but he was a nice guy and a great cook and was the unofficial head of the kitchens.

"Morning, girls!" Alec gave a bright smile as he wheeled the cart to a stop. "I've got an egg white and veggie omelet, with some shredded chicken on top, and some orange juice to wash it down. Really tasty, so come grab a plate!" As each of the girls stepped up he handed them a plate, a glass, and each grabbed a fork from the cart before sitting down to eat. Some of the girls chatted with him and smiled, eating the omelet while standing next to the cart. One of the girls, Ebere, grabbed two plates and sat beside Fae. Without a word, she set the plate and fork in front of Fae and began eating her own omelet. Fae sighed and leaned back on her hands, ignoring the plate. It was sweet that Ebere was trying to look out for her, but unnecessary.

"Eat, Fae," Ebere whispered at her.

Fae shook her head and watched everyone else eat. Ebere was an Ethiopian girl with beautiful dark skin, and she was one of the kindest girls in the house. At only nineteen, she still went out of her way to protect the others whenever she could – and on *that* point Fae and Ebere agreed. They were always watching out for the weaker among them. On protecting Fae though, they always disagreed.

Ebere sighed and leaned forward, grabbing Fae's plate of omelet and sliding it onto her own.

"No! Ebere, give that to me." Fae reached for the plate, but Ebere's long arms moved it away.

"If you won't eat it, I will." Ebere whispered back. Fae reached across her again, only to have Ebere hold it out of her reach.

"You can't have two doses of it right now, give it back." Fae spoke through clenched teeth, but Ebere just shrugged one elegant shoulder and picked up her fork.

When Ebere moved the plate back in front of her to take a bite, Fae lunged forward, snatched it from her, and stood up. More than a dozen sets of eyes watched her, and with a sigh, Fae walked up to Alec's cart and set the full plate onto the top shelf.

"Fae, you have to eat it." Alec's handsome face looked strained, staring at the food still on the plate.

"I'm not going around today drugged, only to get dosed in the morning again when all the effects disappear." Fae pointed at the plate and smiled. "But it looks great, Alec."

"Bu- but, I'll have to report it. I'll have to tell him you didn't eat it." Alec looked really distressed, and Fae hated to do it to him, but she wasn't eating any food with Oblivion in it. Not when it wouldn't matter.

It was bullshit anyway.

The drug made you warm, and maybe a little hyper at lower doses. It was hard to sleep on it, but at its full dose it would make you feel really, well, *friendly*. The build-up technique didn't work for Fae though, it would just burn away at dawn when Eltera healed her and there was no way she was dealing with side-effects all day for no reason.

"That's on me, not you. You brought the food, you told me to eat it. You can't do anything else. So, I'm going to take a shower." Fae turned, walking past the other girls, and headed for the massive bathroom. At the door Lena scowled at her, open disgust showing on her face.

"You're a fool, Fae."

"Love you too, Lena!" Fae called over her shoulder, blowing her a kiss. Lena was Nikola's lapdog, he had taken her from somewhere in Czechoslovakia when she was only sixteen. She had been with him ever since.

Stripping off the dress she'd slept in, Fae tossed it into the laundry basket and stepped into the showers. A large open room with showerheads spaced along the wall, each one boasted a shampoo, conditioner, and body wash dispenser beneath it. Flipping the lever to hot, Fae stepped underneath it and her shoulders relaxed under the water. Of all the modern inventions, showers were her favorite; instant hot water on demand was a luxury that hadn't been common just a hundred years ago. As she let the shower relax her muscles she reminded herself that today would be filled with cleaning and organizing to prepare for the party, but in two days it would be over. The guests would arrive and leave, and everything would return to relative normalcy.

Caridee stepped beneath the showerhead right next to her. "You really are an idiot."

"Thanks for the vote of confidence, Cari," she muttered, and Cari huffed as she began to carefully shower while keeping her hair out of the water, her braid wound on top of her head and pinned carefully. Fae ignored her, focusing on the relaxation of shampooing her hair and the scent of vanilla that started to fill the showers.

"He's going to be mad at you. Why can't you just do what you're supposed to? You make it difficult, it's *you*. Whatever you are, it make you crazy." Caridee finished washing and shut the water off a little harder than necessary. Most of the other girls were filing in to grab showers so she started mumbling to herself in Spanish and walked out. Not that it mattered, since Fae understood every muttered comment and curse. Rolling her eyes, Fae washed the last of the soap out of her hair and turned off the water. When had Fae ever made it easy for any of her masters? That was *never* going to happen.

It was way too cold in most of the house to let her hair stay wet so she used the hair dryer. Her hair went from a dark brown while wet, to auburn heavily tinted with red as it dried. Grabbing a pale purple dress she tugged it over her head and stepped out of the bathroom to find Lena waiting, still scowling. Fae flashed her a big smile just to irritate her. "What are the chores for today, Lena?"

Lena glared before looking down the list on the clipboard. "East wing, upper-floor bedroom preparation. Clean them, put new linens on the beds, make sure each bathroom is stocked." A sharp checkmark was made on the clipboard, and Fae gave a mocking salute as she walked towards the exit. Lena called after her. "Oh, Fae! Butler will be around for checks, so it would be a good idea to actually *do* your work."

"I always do my work, Lena, and you're doing a great job with your whole standing around and making checkmarks thing." Before Lena could respond Fae stepped into the hallway, past the guard on duty, leaving Lena sputtering in her mute anger.

Fae had to go down the north stairs to get to the central part of the house, and then move through the large foyer to climb the east stairs. Ráj Manor was expansive, and of the twenty-five bedrooms in the house, twelve of them were in the upper floor of the East wing. It would be a long day, and since Lena had made sure no one was assigned with her, Fae would be doing it all on her own. *Bitch.*

Four bedrooms in, already sore from leaning over beds and cleaning the floors, Butler found her. She wasn't quite sure if it was his last name, or his title, even after several years in Nikola's house. He sneered at her from the doorway as she tucked sheets in.

"Doing the bare minimum, I see." Butler was trying to goad her into a reaction, but she just stood up silently and waited to see what he wanted. He finally broke their staring contest and spoke. "Nikola wants to see you. Immediately. He's in his office." Butler was like all of the guards in the house, an ex-military man with a few screws loose. Except Butler was chief among them in the crazy department, and Fae tried to tread lightly around him since it was rarely worth the consequences to make him angry. As soon as she could, she nodded and walked past him towards her master.

Nikola's study was part office, and part library on the second floor of the house. It was a large room with a wall of windows at the back overlooking the gardens and walls of books on either side. The dark oak doors were cracked open when she got there. She looked down before she walked in to find the bands of light around each of her wrists that always appeared in his presence, humming and waiting for his command.

It was a disheartening reminder of what she was.

Stepping in between the open doors, she started to move towards the center of the room to kneel as Nikola required. Walking across the thick carpets that lined the room, she felt the bands buzz against her skin a moment before she felt a sharp pain in her side. Fae cried out as her muscles locked up and she hit the floor hard. When the pain faded she looked up to see Nikola standing next to her holding a stun gun in his hand.

'Why?' she asked in her head as he moved quietly over to a table near the wall of books and set the weapon down, rubbing his hands together as he walked back to her. Fae rolled over onto her back, the pain was gone but the place where the stun gun had touched her was tingling and her muscles weren't quite ready to respond yet.

"So, I understand you feel you're too good for the food I provide you?" He had a thick, Eastern European accent, and always sounded calm and relaxed, which made her wish he'd just scream at her.

"No, Master, I-"

Nikola pressed his foot down over her neck, cutting off her air.

She tried to arch her back off the floor to ease the pressure, but it didn't work.

"Stay still." The hum of the bands turned into a painful ache, which amplified quickly for every moment she disobeyed, so Fae stilled, even though spots were starting to appear before her eyes. "I don't like being lied to, you know that. Alec and Lena have already reported that you refused the food I provided this morning. Now let's try this again, were you too good for the food I provided?"

Fae's vision was fading, so she gave in and nodded. Instantly the pressure on her neck released and she took a gasping breath, coughing against the strain in her throat. Nikola still looked calm and professional in his suit, unruffled by the situation. He stepped in front of her and leaned against the front of his desk, waiting a moment for her to catch her breath.

"Sit up and kneel, Fae." The bands hummed again, an ache beginning to rush up her arms before she rolled to her stomach to push herself up into a kneel. She was still dizzy from the stun gun and the near suffocation, so she was leaning heavily on her hands as she forced deep breaths. Nikola sighed, "Look at me, and tell me why you refused the food I provided."

She lifted her head to look at him knowing he was not going to like her answer. "It was drugged, Master."

Nikola gripped the front of the desk, knuckles white, but his voice remained calm and steady, his dark eyes intent on Fae's. "I'm aware of that. I always do this to make the dinners more pleasant for everyone. You haven't explained why you would refuse what I provided you."

The intensity of his stare was making her uncomfortable, and the low hum of the bands was distracting. "Master, I know you will have to dose me tomorrow for the dinner, and since the build-up does not work on me I thought I would be more effective in my chores today if I were not drugged."

"And whose choice is that to make?" His voice was cold and precise, and his bored facial expression didn't change.

"Yours, Master," Fae whispered, before gritting her teeth so she didn't try to keep defending herself.

"Good. Now that we're on the same page…" Nikola took a small vial of clear liquid out of his jacket pocket. "You're going to take the Oblivion, and you're not going to defy me in front of the other girls ever again." Turning the vial over in his hand, he tossed it to Fae who caught it and held it in her lap.

"Master, I –" Nikola raised his hand and cut her off.

"Stop. Drink the vial. Now." He had put his will behind the command and the bands reacted quickly, aching pain crawling under her skin. Fae doubled over as the pain burst in her chest, feeling like her ribs were trying to collapse in on themselves. It was hard to breathe through the pain, but the amount in the vial was a large dose and she really, *really* did not want to drink it.

Nikola stepped forward, walking around her slowly. "It's only going to get worse the longer you fight this, and in the end you will still drink it." Fae gasped as the pain increased, sure that her bones were cracking, and the golden light of the bands had increased so it was visible through her eyelids. Nikola sighed and leaned down, pulling Fae back up by her hair. Another wave of pain came and her body arched.

"Drink. It."

Fae's thumb popped the lid off the vial and she brought it to her mouth. The moment she swallowed it Nikola let go of her hair, and the pain abruptly ended. The relief from it was a sense of euphoria all on its own and she brushed her cheek to find it wet with tears. She quickly wiped her cheeks off and took a deep, steadying breath. She'd given in. Again.

Weak.

Nikola was standing in front of her as he held out his hand for the vial, which she returned to him wordlessly. When she looked up to meet his eyes, he delivered a sharp backhand. It wasn't hard enough to do more than make her cheek sting, but it almost surprised her. She'd obeyed him and it hadn't mattered. It never did.

"Do not embarrass me any further, slave." His voice still sounded bored with the situation as he continued. "You will behave like the perfect servant tomorrow, or it won't matter how much my guests want to meet you. I'll give you to the guards for the evening. Understood?"

Fae nodded, and the bands hummed in response to his command. Nikola turned back to his desk.

"Good. Get back to work."

CHAPTER TWO

SEATTLE, WASHINGTON

KIERNAN SHUT the lid on the observation glass, and sat back in the chair at his desk thinking over everything he'd seen. The glass allowed him to see any of the Faeoihn assigned to him, but he only ever seemed to find himself watching Fae. *Why her?* Other than going out in the city when he had to for errands, he spent most of his time with the observation glass open on his desk. Showing her.

It was, honestly, getting a little weird.

He was lost in his own thoughts about everything that had happened that morning when Cole appeared in his living room with a loud pop and dropped himself onto the couch. "Kiernan, that's it, I am taking you out of this damn house. You don't get to be Mr. Hermit anymore." When he didn't respond Cole shouted, "Hey!"

He snagged an apple from the table and threw it at Kiernan. It narrowly missed him and bounced off the window behind him, and Kiernan glared at him.

"What the hell, Cole?!" He leaned down and picked up the apple, throwing it swiftly back at the man's head, but Cole caught it with irritating finesse.

"Man, you didn't even notice I showed up. I could have come in swinging a battle axe, and you wouldn't have done anything about it!" He stood up and walked over to where Kiernan sat, his eyes catching the box.

For a moment Kiernan almost regretted reconnecting with the man that was like a brother to him. He'd successfully avoided him, and all of the Laochra, for almost two hundred years – but with the digital age it was much harder to hide, and much harder to ignore Cole's pleas for contact. Regardless, he'd missed him. No matter how annoying he was.

With a roll of his eyes, he spoke. "I noticed you, I'm just not in the mood for your shit. Anyway, I would have kicked your ass. You don't handle axes well."

"You *wish* you could kick my ass." Cole scoffed, and started messing with a small stone egg sitting on the edge of the glass desk. "So, what were you doing?"

"My job." Kiernan mumbled. Cole raised an eyebrow at that and switched to tossing the stone egg from hand to hand. "Do you ever stop messing with things, Cole? Put it down."

Cole threw the egg up high and caught it close to the

floor, just to be a dick, before finally setting it back down. "Well, I only stopped by because you haven't been to base in a while, or to my cabin. Not checking in looks bad even if you're *supposedly* doing your job." Cole put emphasis on the word 'supposedly', adding finger quotes in the air. "Especially after your little vacation for the last two hundred years."

"I said I'm not in the mood for this."

"When are you *ever* in the mood these days? You went from badass, bloodthirsty warrior just a few centuries ago," Cole spun a finger in the air to indicate the clean, modern apartment around them, "to this guy."

Looking over his shoulder out of the floor-to-ceiling window behind him, he could see the bay and the cloudy, cold skies he loved, but today the view wasn't helping. He couldn't get Fae's antics from the morning out of his head. She was definitely stupid – he couldn't argue with the others who kept telling her that – but he kept watching her. *Just her.* She was interesting, too interesting to ignore, and had been for over a hundred years. Kiernan had gone from avoiding his monitoring duties, barely paying attention to the Faeoihn under his watch, to monitoring Fae almost daily with rare check-ins on the others.

Cole was still ranting about epic battles long past when Kiernan turned his head back around.

"Cole, shut up." He stood up and walked around it past Cole. His friend just followed him as he headed towards his bedroom.

"So what was happening?" Cole indicated the other room

with his thumb, "I saw the box out on your desk and I know you were watching one of them."

"It doesn't matter." Kiernan leaned over and started looking for a book on one of his shelves, running his fingers along their spines.

"That's true, but I never used to see you watch them, now the last few times I've been over the glass is always out."

"I don't watch all the time." *Lie.* "This one is just interesting. Kind of feisty." *Truth.* Kiernan had found and opened a book, but wasn't really reading anything in it. It just gave him the option to not look at Cole.

"A lot of them are like that. Eltera didn't choose the weak ones for her special little army. That's why Gormahn chose their punishment. What better way to make a bunch of girls who are playing at war recognize their rightful place than by cursing them to serve in it?" Cole laughed a little, "It's really smart when you think about it. Way worse than just having us kill them that day."

Kiernan looked up at Cole, controlling the reaction on his face. He had blocked out most of those early years and didn't want to hear Cole's version of events, "Yeah, that's true. I guess I just haven't noticed it before." He tucked the book back into the shelf, "Listen, I don't really want to talk about the job. What did you want?"

Cole rubbed his hands together, grinning from ear to ear. "I was thinking we could go hunting! Get you out of this house and back in the mix. Personally, I've always wanted to kill another big cat. I think a skin would look great spread out in front of my fireplace. Impress the ladies when I bring them home."

"Nothing you do will impress the ladies once they're home with you." Kiernan grinned and Cole dropped his mouth open, making a dramatic stabbing motion at his heart in response.

"Oh, Kiernan, you wound me."

"You're obnoxious, Cole, but yeah, hunting sounds fine." *Fine?* He used to love hunting, looked forward to it and would bother Cole to go with *him*. Kiernan thought about the dinner party, and couldn't understand why instead of going on a hunt he really wanted to stay and see what happened. Cole was right, he had been cooped up with the observation glass too long. He had to get out of the house, and being on a hunting trip with Cole would ensure he couldn't cave to the temptation to check in on her again. *Perfect.* "How long do you want to be gone?"

"Eryn and I were thinking two or three days? If we get bored we can just pop back."

"Wait, Eryn is going?" Kiernan worked to hide his reaction.

"He's fine, Kiernan. Plus we'll be somewhere in Southeast Asia, it's not exactly civilized out there in the jungle. If he goes nuts, we'll clean it up, and just so you remember we used to have to clean up after *you*." Cole pointed at Kiernan, another of his infectious grins spreading across his face.

"This sounds like a *great* trip." Kiernan laid the sarcasm on thick, but Cole seemed unfazed.

"Also, picture this… we're not using any of these fancy new guns. Bow hunting only for us." That grabbed Kiernan's interest, and Cole saw it as he mimed drawing back a bow. "I knew I'd get you with that."

"Okay," he put his hands up in surrender, "you've convinced me." Kiernan figured this was the best thing he could be doing, and getting to dust off some of his skills would be useful. Also, if he didn't give in, Cole would just keep bothering him. "When would you want to leave?"

"Let's head back to base now!"

"Alright, I'm just going to grab a shower. I doubt we'll get one when we're out there, and I prefer being clean." Kiernan pulled his shirt off over his head, and Cole cursed.

"What the -? Are you an idiot?!" Cole was suddenly right next to him, grabbing his left arm. Dark, thorny vines coiled up Kiernan's arm starting from his palm and stopping just short of his shoulder.

"It's okay, Cole, I just haven't taken care of it yet." Kiernan pulled his arm away with a sharp jerk.

"Haven't taken care of it? If you wait much longer it will *kill* you." Cole's eyes were tracing the vines that looked like they were tattooed on Kiernan's skin, and he noted how close they were to Gormahn's mark, the black sword pointing down, over his heart. Kiernan turned around and ran a hand through his hair in frustration. He hadn't meant for Cole to see the vines, it was just further evidence that Kiernan wasn't obeying Gormahn's command anymore. It was the last thing he needed another Laochra to report back – but there were just some things that he couldn't stomach anymore.

"So what do you want me to do to fix it, Cole?" Kiernan's memories made him nauseous. "Want me to go and slaughter a village? Kill some soldier just for not listening to his commanding officer? Hurt some woman for not listening to her husband?"

"If you have to, yes! That's *exactly* what I want you to do! Gormahn was pretty clear with the rules when he created us. Make sure the Faeoihn are suffering, keep the wars going, and punish those who break his laws." Cole snapped his fingers in front of Kiernan's face. "You can find someone, somewhere, who is being insubordinate, or showing cowardice or disobedience." Kiernan didn't respond. "Come *on*, Gormahn just wants you to deliver some justice!"

Justice.

Kiernan clenched his fist and bit down so he didn't yell at Cole about what Gormahn called *justice*. The strong were not meant to prey on the weak; they were supposed to protect them. There had been a time in Kiernan's life when he had lived the right way, before Gormahn had taken him. Gormahn had twisted all of their beliefs and a lot of the others still followed him blindly. Except Kiernan wasn't blind anymore, but revealing that to Cole wasn't going to help him stay free of the rest of them to figure out who he really was. Who he'd become in the last century, where more mattered than just the sound of a battle cry and a sword leaving its sheath.

"Alright, Cole. You tell me, how do *you* take care of the vines?" Kiernan really hoped that Cole's answer didn't change how he felt about him. He had so few people he still talked to that losing Cole's friendship wouldn't be a small loss after millenia together.

Cole grinned. "There's a few military schools near where I live in Virginia, a lot of the guys there sneak out against their commanding officer's orders and go drinking at the local bars. I get into a bar fight every couple of weeks; sometimes send one to the hospital. They learn their lesson, I'm doing my job of appeasing Gormahn's command, the vines recede, and I'm confirmed as a complete and total badass. Ta-da!" Cole spread his arms out, and then began bowing to an invisible crowd.

Kiernan couldn't help but smirk a little at Cole's ridiculousness. "I might be able to do something like that, as long as those kids don't die."

"They're fine, they just don't forget the lesson. Don't worry though, I'll help you remember how to have a bar brawl before we go tiger hunting." Cole winked and Kiernan shoved him in a friendly way. Cole punched him in the shoulder in return.

"I taught you how to fight, remember?" He grinned and Cole rolled his eyes, but Kiernan continued, "And the hunt sounds good." He needed it, needed to be away from this apartment and the observation glass for a few days. Getting the vines back under control was necessary too, as much as he dreaded it. Kiernan looked down and tugged on a belt loop on his jeans. "But, unless you want to see me naked, I suggest you leave and I'll meet you back at base in an hour or so."

Raising his hands in surrender Cole backed up, "Alright, alright. Just know that I'd only suggest you doing anything because I don't want you to fucking *die*. We've had each other's backs for too many lifetimes, okay?"

Kiernan nodded back, and Cole disappeared. It always took Kiernan a second to process the whole popping in and out thing, so he blinked and rubbed a hand over his face. One of the few advantages of having a god own you was that the god had to give you some level of power to keep you alive. Gormahn had claimed them so he could raise his own army to destroy Eltera's Faeoihn. They got to heal, they got to move themselves at will, and they got to give up everything that made them human.

Lucky, lucky.

Staring into the mirror in his bathroom, Kiernan rubbed his hand across the vines on his arm. He shook his head, and gripped the edge of the counter as his urge to check the observation glass came back.

"You can't do anything, so stop obsessing." Kiernan met his own eyes in the mirror; the iris and the pupil were so dark they were impossible to tell apart, like all of the Laochra. "Just stop thinking about her." He closed his eyes, trying to think of anything else, but all he could see was her face. Her beautiful, perfect – "Fuck."

Yeah, he really needed to go hunting.

CHAPTER THREE

Ráj Manor, Caledon, Ontario

By the time Fae walked back to the upper floor of the East wing the bands of light on her wrists had faded to a dim ghostly outline, but her throat only hurt worse. Especially when she swallowed. At least it would be gone in the morning, like everything else. A blank slate, like every other day, so he, or Butler, or one of the guards could do something new. As Fae moved down the hall, Ebere walked out of one of the bedrooms holding a large basket full of sheets on one hip.

As soon as the other girl saw her she started shaking her head and murmuring to herself as she approached. "Fae... your neck." Her long fingers reached out and touched the tender skin, and Fae fought the urge to jerk back. She hated being touched, but she forced a smile for the kindness the girl was showing.

"I'm guessing it looks great?" Fae tilted her head and Ebere stepped back so she could finally breathe again.

"It's already bruising. What did you do?" Her forehead was creased with concern.

"Nikola -", Ebere grimaced at the use of his name, so Fae corrected herself, "Sorry, *Master* heard about my little breakfast boycott. He disagreed with my decision."

Ebere made a tsk'ing sound. "I told you to eat it."

"Yeah, I know, but I didn't want to deal with the drug today. I made a choice. There were consequences." Fae shrugged and stepped towards the next room she needed to clean.

"I already did that one," Ebere nodded her head at the door behind her, "and this one. I came upstairs to bring you fresh sheets, and you weren't here. I figured something had happened, so I tried to help."

"What's going to happen in laundry if Butler does a check?" Fae crossed her arms, not wanting to be responsible for someone else's punishment.

"Mei-Li will tell him I'm running sheets up to the bedrooms". She shook the basket she was carrying for emphasis and grinned. "And I am. See?"

Fae smiled back, if that was true it was going to be nice to have the help since she had lost time that morning. It would also be nice to be done when Lena decided to check the rooms. "Alright then, which room is next?"

Ebere stepped across the hall and opened the next room,

setting down the basket of fresh sheets at the doorway. They got to work pulling the old sheets off the queen sized bed. Ebere's eyes were glued to the bands of light that were barely visible in the dim light of the bedroom. For a second Fae thought she'd ignore them like everyone did, but then she spoke. "Those things are on your wrists again."

"Yeah, it's because I was around Master." Fae wadded the sheets up and stepped into the hall, leaving them in a pile before grabbing new sheets from the basket of clean ones.

"Do they hurt?" Ebere spoke quietly, keeping her eyes on the bed as they fluffed out the sheets. No one really asked these types of questions in the female section. You just didn't ask about punishments, or scars, or prismatic wings, or glowing bands. A few girls had asked her one on one in the last years, and it seemed being alone made Ebere brave enough to ask for herself.

Fae sighed, hating the itching heat that was starting to crawl under her skin as the Oblivion took effect. She didn't want to explain the bands, but lying would be worse. "They only hurt if I don't obey him, they're tied to his commands."

"Do they hurt right now?"

"No." Fae started tucking the sheet in on her side, tempted to ask Ebere to drop it but too grateful for her help to snap at her.

"Then why would you disobey him at all?" Ebere pulled the new sheets across the bed, and when Fae looked up at her she realized it was an innocent question. She wasn't judging her. It was just that she couldn't imagine consciously choosing pain over obedience.

Then again, Ebere hadn't served for two thousand fucking years.

"Because it's my choice. My choice to obey or not. I'd have gone crazy years ago if I just said 'yes sir' or 'no sir' all the time, my life wouldn't be mine anymore. At least this way *I'm* making the choice, not them, and the consequences are mine." Fae surprised herself with the stream of words that had just left her. She *never* talked this much and usually shut this kind of conversation down. The Oblivion was really starting to affect her – *great*.

"But you could have a much easier life, without so many consequences, if you just did what he asked."

"He never *asks*, Ebere. He commands. There's a big difference." Fae turned to check the bathroom as they continued the routine. Bed linens, bathroom, towels – rinse and repeat.

"Okay, I get that, but don't you always end up doing what he tells you anyway? Because of those things?" Ebere pointed at her wrists and Fae was grateful the bands had faded away. She hated the attention they brought from the others, and the constant reminder they were of her own failures. Reminders of the ways they had all failed Eltera.

"Ebere, how long have you been a slave?" The question came out harsher than Fae had meant it to and Ebere straightened up for a moment before returning to wiping down the shower.

"Almost four years," she mumbled.

"How did it happen?" Fae almost bit down on her own tongue. It wasn't a good question to ask. It wasn't tactful to make Ebere talk about it. It was sort of an unspoken rule not to ask about any of the *before*, but Ebere had opened the door asking about the bands and the drug was making Fae talkative for once. They were silent for so long that Fae was about to apologize and tell her to forget it, but then Ebere started speaking quietly.

"I was sixteen and... and my family needed money. I heard about this job in the city, and so I went. When I arrived they said it was housework for a family. I would stay with them and clean their house, only once I went... they never let me leave." Ebere stepped out of the shower and wiped down the mirror. "They did not pay me, and they said if I tried to run they would kill me and my family. I had four younger sisters, and I didn't want anything to happen to them, so I stayed, and I did not try to run away." Fae shook her head as she listened. Her story wasn't unique, it was similar to others she had heard from girls all over the world in recent years, one of the traffickers' best traps. "I was there only a year before they sold me to a market in Cairo, that is where Master bought me. I have been here since then."

"I'm sorry, Ebere." Fae said it on reflex, but Ebere just shrugged and walked towards the next room. Just as they started working again she spoke up.

"What about you? How long have you been serving?"

Fae tried to stifle the giggle that bubbled up, but it only came out in a loud laugh, and once she started she couldn't stop. Ebere was just staring at her as she lost it, and she ended up clutching her sides as she sat down on the floor. It had been so long since she'd laughed like this, years, *decades* since her cheeks had hurt from laughing.

Oh yeah, the drug was definitely in full swing.

Ebere stepped in front of her and touched her forehead, looking into her eyes. "Are you serious? Your pupils are huge, and you're sweating like crazy. Master gave you the Oblivion didn't he?"

Fae tried to control her smile as her laughter wound down and she patted Ebere's hand. "I told you he disagreed with my decision."

"It looks like a full dose though." Ebere was staring at her, her brow furrowed in concern.

"It probably was, but it doesn't matter I'll be fine." Fae pushed herself to her feet and felt a little dizzy before she grabbed the bedpost and steadied herself, the last of the giggles fading away with the hint of nausea.

"You'll be fine in the morning when you light up. *Right now* you haven't eaten and you got a full dose of Oblivion —"

"I will be fine. Just let it go, okay?" Fae cut her off and shook off the dizziness to get back to work. Ebere stood with her arms crossed on the other side of the bed, ignoring the sheet that Fae had tossed across to her.

"Tell me your story." She pointed at the sheet on the bed. "Tell me your story while we finish these rooms and I'll stay and help and ...and I won't bring up the Oblivion again."

"You don't want to hear my story, Ebere." Fae smoothed her side of the bed, but then Ebere ripped the sheet out of her hands, ruining her efforts.

"Yes. Yes, I do. *Everyone* wants to know but everyone is terrified to ask. Now you know mine and I want to know yours." Ebere held tight to the sheet as Fae tried to pull it back, and part of her wanted to attack the girl for making the task more difficult. She hated being cornered, hated being forced to do anything. Her whole fucking life was being forced to do things, and now this girl who had lived the tiniest fraction of Fae's life was trying to bully her into telling a pointless story. It took a deep breath and a silent prayer to Eltera before she could speak again.

"I'm sorry I asked about your past, but there's no point in telling you my story. Now, can I have the sheet back?"

"What do you mean there's no point? I'm here helping you, we have six rooms left, just tell me your damn story!" Ebere had actually raised her voice, she'd actually *cursed*.

"There's no point in telling you my story, because you won't believe it. My story is a myth, it's a fucking fairy tale, a legend that I doubt my own people even remember. It's a waste of –"

"Then tell me the fairy tale!" The girl threw the wadded up sheet at her and Fae caught it. "You spend all your time with this giant wall around you, and you're nice to everyone, and you do things for us, but you don't let us in. You won't be our friend, and what else do we have but each other? Stop trying so hard to be alone and just tell me your story so I can *understand*!"

"You're not going to believe me." Fae clenched her jaw, her fingers tightening in the sheet as she remembered the times in her past she'd tried to explain what she was, and how she'd come to be. The ones who'd called her a liar, the ones who had beat her, demanded she repent, commanded her to deny Eltera. All she had anymore was faith. Faith and the bands to remind her that Eltera was still out there – somewhere.

"I think you might be surprised what I will believe from a girl who lights up like she's filled with fire every morning." Ebere gestured at her, "And I've seen those things on your wrists before. I've seen you in pain, but I didn't understand why until today. Until you *told* me the bands reacted to his commands and hurt you. I'm still here, still ready to help you finish these rooms, and I'm not running away. I just want to understand more about you."

"So you can tell the others?" The anger was bleeding out of Fae, replaced by the shimmery buzz of the Oblivion in her system. It was hard to maintain anger for long while bordering on some kind of euphoric high.

"If you don't want me to tell anyone, I won't."

Fae laughed a little to herself. "It doesn't matter. Tell all of them. Tell them all about the god-touched warrior who failed her goddess and ended up on her knees for eternity."

"Fae?" Ebere's voice was much softer now, and when she looked up at her she once again looked like the beautiful, friendly girl that Fae liked to sit with. "I'm listening. Just tell me."

"Alright, fine." Fae fluffed out the sheet and this time Ebere caught it and helped her get back to straightening the room. The last thing any of them needed was Butler checking in before they were done.

Thinking of her past was like opening a locked room that she had long ago barricaded with heavy furniture and chains and nailed up boards. It was the stuff that normally tore her to shreds on the inside, but with the Oblivion burning her up and making her feel fuzzy and light the memories didn't seem to cut as sharply. She swallowed the bitter taste in her mouth and steeled herself to talk about it.

"You're not going to believe me, but here it goes. First, I'm over two thousand years old," Fae glanced up to see Ebere's mouth hanging open and she shook her head, "and no, I don't know my exact age. I haven't exactly kept track. I do know that I spent fifty-three years as a warrior for my goddess, Eltera, and for the seventeen years before that I was just a daughter."

"And since then?"

"I've been a slave." The complete shock on Ebere's face

slowly morphed into that pained look of pity that Fae hated, and she stopped her before she launched into some long apology for things she had no power over. For things she hadn't even been alive for. "You said you wanted to hear the story."

"I do, it's just –"

"Okay, then listen." She cut her off again, trying to figure out where to start. How to explain how she'd found herself on that battlefield the day everything had changed. "I guess I'll start at the beginning... I can tell you my mother never wanted me. Pregnancy was very hard on her, and she almost died giving birth to my middle sister, but my father wanted a son very badly and so after my two older sisters he convinced her to try again, hoping for a son. Instead? I was born. She hated him for making her have another child, and so on the day of my birth my mother told him I was his responsibility, even though I was a daughter. Surprisingly, my father was just fine with that."

"He was a great man. As soon as I could walk he took me with him everywhere. He worshipped all of our gods, of course, but he was a man of nature and his chosen goddess was Eltera because she was nature – life and death, ends and beginnings, and he loved the balance that worshipping her represented. He taught me how to help things grow. What plants to eat and not eat, which ones healed, which ones hurt, and how to make sacrifices to the gods." Her memories burst forth from the room she'd kept them in, and she was overwhelmed by the bearded face of her father, laughing and singing. Her sisters laughing, her eldest sister's little boy. Even the way her mother would hum as she tended the sheep, it all came back like a whirlwind. The image that stuck was of her father's excited face as he woke her on the last day she'd ever see him. Fae cleared her throat, "And one day, after being so faithful to Eltera his entire life, Eltera spoke to my father."

"What did she say?" Ebere was rapt with attention, and Fae couldn't help but smile at the bittersweet memories as she let herself sink into them, no matter how painful.

• • •

It was shortly after dawn when her father woke her. She had her face shoved into the wool and deer skins that formed her bed and she groaned as he shook her shoulder.

"Neala." His deep voice roused her, speaking her name with the softest tones. When she turned over he was smiling broadly through his beard, and his dark hair was hanging in curtains above her. "I have had a vision." The old language rolled off his tongue like music.

She sat up and turned to face him, excitement waking her even though the chill air would have usually made her burrow back into bed, "A vision?"

"Yes! Eltera appeared to me in a dream, she has asked us to come to her in the southern woods tonight." Her father was obviously glowing with pride, but the idea that their goddess, *the* Eltera, would have spoken with him was almost beyond comprehension. He shook her shoulder gently and tugged her off the bed. "We must hurry. It will take the day to travel there."

"Wait! What has she asked of us?" Neala's head was spinning. She couldn't fathom seeing Eltera, the goddess she had grown up learning so much about, worshipping, praying to. Every ancient story of her and her power, every blessing requested when one of the sheep was lambing – to see her was a dream made real.

"To come to her, she says she has great plans for us." He clapped his hands together, his infectious grin making her smile as well, "Come now, get up and prepare for the journey."

Checking to make sure her father had not woken her mother, she got up and grabbed her wool cloak to follow him. He was putting some dried venison into a bag, and she handed him his cloak, which she knew he would forget without her getting it for him. He smiled and took it, and then pointed at the pot of porridge on the hearth. He had scooped some out into a bowl already so she started eating. "How long will we be gone?"

"Only Eltera knows that, but are you not a little excited, my girl?" He asked and she nodded quickly. "Good! Finish up so we can leave." He stepped outside into the damp morning air.

She could feel the draft and knew it was cold so she pulled the cloak on and left the bowl near the porridge before following him outside with only a brief glance back at her mother, still asleep.

"Let's go," he said with a broad smile. Breathing in the

mist that floated over the ground, he started walking south out of the village and she followed, keeping pace with him. She turned back to look at their small home, and it felt strangely like a goodbye, but she turned back to catch up with her father. They had an easy silence between them formed in years of walking the woods together, of watching the animals and looking for plants. As the sun rose it grew light, but the gray skies stayed. It was beautiful in its own way, the swirl of the clouds above them making patterns she could look for through the trees. They talked a few times about different herbs they needed to gather, some for cooking and others for healing, making a mental list of what to watch for. In the excitement to get to the place chosen for the meeting, they didn't even stop to eat but chewed the venison while they walked. In the evening they finally came to a stop, their excitement about the possibilities of what could happen the only thing keeping the exhaustion at bay.

"Is this it?" Neala's eyes scanned the meadow they had stepped into; all soft green grasses with large stones that had been placed in a circle surrounding a larger flat stone in the center. The fading sunlight filtered through the trees leaving them in twilight. Her father nodded and pointed across at two people sitting on the ground. It was another man with a girl near her own age.

"Eltera must have asked others to come." He reached over and rubbed her back, giving her his warm grin that split his beard and showed his teeth. "The important thing is we are here to see whatever will happen." Over the next hour the meadow grew dark and two other pairs appeared, both a man with a girl. Quick conversation among them confirmed that Eltera had asked them to come and the girls were the daughters of the men.

They were talking together when the earth started to shake beneath their feet, a loud rumbling filling the air just before a bright burst of light filled the meadow. Neala grabbed onto her father to keep her footing, panicked gasps moving through the group. As the earth calmed the light faded to reveal Eltera standing behind the stone in the center that resembled a large table. She had the most perfect, elegant features. She was beyond beautiful, standing over eight feet tall with long brown hair that fell to her waist, and a deep green dress edged with gold designs wrapped around her. A soft golden glow came off of her skin, lighting the ground around her. It was actually *her*. A goddess. Everyone had fallen silent, staring in awe, but she just smiled.

"You have all come. I am humbled by your dedication and your faith." Eltera's voice rang out, echoing loudly across the meadow, musical and strong. "What I ask of you today is no small gift, but it will change the future of all of your lands. It will allow your people the opportunity to thrive without fear, to live fully, and to prosper." When no one responded Eltera smiled, and it reminded Neala of what it felt like to stand in sunlight. "For what I ask, you must have faith in me and my hope for all of you."

"We do, Eltera. Our faith in you carried us here, as it has carried us always." Neala's father spoke powerfully, his deep voice carrying easily. The other men quickly nodded, speaking their own affirmations. Eltera's eyes turned to the girls, and her smile grew.

"And what of you, young ones? Do you have faith in me?" Each of the girls nodded and stepped forward a little, stumbling over their words to confirm their faith.

"Good. Come to the stone and kneel before it." Eltera waved her hand and small balls of light appeared around them, lighting the area. The girls stepped up and knelt down, and Eltera turned her eyes to the men. "And you, my faithful, stand behind your daughters." They obeyed, and her father placed his broad hand on her shoulder, squeezing it gently to confirm he was there. Power hummed in the air, and it smelled like the air after a lightning strike.

Scalded and thrumming with tension that seemed to buzz under Neala's skin.

Eltera took a slow breath as she walked in front of them on the other side of the table. Her voice was solemn when she began to speak, "There is a darkness on the people of this land. Hatred and violence and war taint what could be a great and powerful people. I have promised that my faithful can undo this darkness, can free the people of this land to be prosperous once again. I have promised that peace is possible. But to do this, I need warriors. I need *your* strength to fight this darkness back, for I cannot do it myself. Not directly." Her pacing paused, and she stood across from them. Neala almost shivered with the pulse of power coming from the goddess. It was almost making her dizzy to be this close, and then Eltera made eye contact with her. The shocking, unreal blue of the goddess' eyes was like the sky on the clearest day of summer.

"I need you. I need each of you to give yourselves over to me, so that together we can lead the land into the light again." Eltera waved a hand again and before each of the girls a stone knife appeared on the table with a clatter. One of the girls yelped in surprise, and her father started to speak but stopped himself when Eltera began speaking again. "Tonight, I ask each of you for your mortal lives, and to my faithful I ask for the sacrifice to leave your daughters in my care."

There were gasps, and a few mumbled words between father and child, but neither Neala nor her father moved at all. Some part of her had known when she left that morning that she wouldn't be back. It had all felt strangely surreal, and now, in the presence of Eltera, it felt *right*. Neala was about to reach for the knife when Eltera raised a hand.

"I swear that you will live, young ones, but you must have faith. If you are ready to join me and take on this task, simply hand the knife to your fathers. They know what is required to make a sacrifice to the gods." Eltera clasped her hands and waited. Power rolled off her in waves of golden light, but her face was calm and gentle. Neala almost smiled, because while the other girls may not have been allowed to attend sacrifices – she had. Her father had taught her everything he could, and she had never been excluded simply because she was a girl. There was no doubt in her mind what would happen when she handed her father the knife.

Taking off her cloak Neala turned around and set it at her father's feet, and he looked down at her and held her chin in his hands. His eyes were shining in the lights Eltera had formed, but no tears fell. Leaning down he spoke in her ear, "My daughter, my lovely Neala... you are the one I waited for. I knew that I was meant to have another child, but I did not know that Eltera would bring me you. You have grown to be a beautiful woman, a woman with strength of spirit and of heart. I do not think even Eltera knows fully how much of a gift I give her today. For the rest of my days... I will be less for *you* made my heart whole. I love you, my girl." With that he kissed her forehead, and Neala tried to hold back the tears, to be strong like him, but a few fell anyway.

She wanted to respond, to speak all the feelings in her heart, but when her mouth opened to speak no words could match his and so she simply nodded and whispered, "And I love *you*, father." Straightening her back, she swallowed and turned back to face Eltera. She was the first to take up the knife in front of her; the edge was so sharp that the light caught it in a thin line. Looking across the stone table at Eltera, she handed the knife over her shoulder to her father. Eltera looked into her eyes and nodded once as Neala lifted her chin and her father placed the stone knife at her neck. The pain was a flicker inside her, a weakening flame.

There was a rush of warmth down her front, a rumble in the earth beneath her, and then everything went dark.

• • •

Ebere was frozen, her mouth slack, as she watched Fae refold the towels and stack them. "Wait! Fae! He killed you? Your father *killed* you?!"

"Not exactly." Fae shrugged, trying to forget the sound of her real name in her father's voice that echoed in her memories. She wasn't that girl anymore. She hadn't been that girl in a long time. "I did die, and he did hold the blade that took that life from me, but he did it to let me be reborn as Faeoihn. Eltera explained it to us when we woke. When our lifeblood spilled over the stone and into the earth, it became a part of her. It was a sacrifice *to* her. She had the choice to accept our death as a sacrifice, or return our life to us, and so she let our life pass through her and return. Except when it came back to us there was, there *is*, a part of Eltera in us too. It made us god-touched and changed us into this," Fae gestured at herself, and she knew what Ebere saw. A young woman, fit and healthy, long auburn hair, with smooth, pale skin. In a crowd, no one would ever pick her to be the ex-warrior of an ancient goddess.

"So you can't die?" Ebere's question snapped her attention back.

"I can, it's just very difficult to kill me. The day she brought us back we were renewed – no more scars, in perfect health, and immortal at the age we were then. And every morning since that day her power has returned at dawn to renew us again."

"That's when you glow, right? That's her?"

"Yes." Fae tried to suppress the ache in her chest when

she thought of that sweet warmth, the smell of earth that flooded her when the power came.

"So, wait, what happened after? How did you get those bands? Did you stop the darkness she talked about?" Ebere wasn't laughing at her, or mocking her, she was actually interested.

"I don't know why you want to know this, or why I'm agreeing to tell you."

"This is the best story I've heard in years, and you're drugged, probably overdosed since you chose not to eat anything and you made our Master so mad. But, please, don't stop now. I'm listening." The girl smiled a little and gestured for her to continue.

"Well, you're taking advantage of this situation." Fae muttered, and Ebere just laughed quietly. Now that she'd started telling the story, the rest of it unwound like a scroll, waiting to be told. The words seemed to leap to her tongue, and with a sigh she started again. At least it was distracting her from the heat in her skin and the monotonous cleaning of the rooms. "Okay, well, we woke up at dawn the next day, glowing with her power, amazed with just being alive. There were only three of us. The fourth girl hadn't gone through with it, which Eltera seemed to be saddened by, and she had made them leave before she brought us back. Once we were awake we realized we were stronger, swifter, and just *better* than before. The clearing was empty, and when we asked about our fathers Eltera told us that we didn't belong to them anymore. We were *her* daughters, and she would name us her Faeoihn."

"Is that why your name is Fae? Did you have another name?" Ebere asked.

"I am Faeoihn, and Fae is the only name I have anymore."

"But –"

"No, Ebere." Fae flinched, hating the hollow place the memory of her father's voice speaking her name had created inside her. Neala was the name of the girl in the forest picking berries and gathering herbs with her father. Fae was the name of the woman, of the slave, she was now.

"I'm sorry, I didn't mean..." Ebere sighed, "Please continue the story? What happened to your father? Do you know?"

"I don't know for sure, but Eltera told us our families would always be blessed for giving us up. She said we had a new family now, and she gathered all the new Faeoihn together in a hidden part of the land where no one else lived. We totaled a hundred and seven fledgling warriors on that first new day. She trained us herself to be the strongest possible so we could carry out her mission. For a year we fought and bled together as sisters until we were fearless with our weapon of choice."

"Weapon of choice? You chose a weapon? Which one?" Ebere rapid fired questions, and it made Fae smile a little.

"The sword. Anyway, when she felt we were ready, she sent us to our first battle. She wanted us to make the sides stop fighting. It was one between two villages who disputed grazing lands for their livestock. We arrived in a flash of light, which sent some of them running, and then fought the remainder of both sides until they surrendered. Each man that fell before us we gave the same choice: return to your family and your village to live peacefully, or die that day. Almost all of them chose to return to their families; it was where they wanted to be anyway. As we continued to fight, the word spread that anyone taking up arms would call the Faeoihn to them. By the end of it all there were almost fifty years of relative peace in our lands. Villages started to work out their disputes by talking it through instead of going to war. Farming near the coasts prospered. Populations grew with the additional available food, and villages were stronger because all of their men were there, and *alive*."

"It sounds amazing." The girl was leaning against the wall, holding an unfolded towel. Fae snagged it and Ebere smiled at her, "We only have two rooms left, you better finish this by then."

"I will, but you're not going to like the end." Fae shrugged, "Honestly, for a while it was perfect. Everything was. I spent each day with my sisters, Eltera was with us often and anytime we were around her it – it was like standing in sunlight. Warm and pure. In the last years we didn't even have to go anywhere, there was no more fighting within the boundaries of Eltera's control." Fae swallowed, turning away from Ebere so she didn't have to watch her as she told the last of it. "What we didn't know was that the god of war, Gormahn, was furious over the peace. Furious with Eltera for making it happen. He formed an army that he called the *Laochra*," she fought the urge to break the glass in her hand that she was wiping down as rage flooded her with the memory of them. Instead, she carefully laid it back by the sink and continued speaking. "Laochra ironically meant 'heroes' in our language, but they weren't heroes. These were brutal, evil men who swept through villages and left them burned and the people terrified or dead. We had no choice but to meet them in battle before they could do more destruction."

That battle, the last battle, was something Fae couldn't forget if she tried; and she had tried. She had tried for so long to forget. But the memories were always waiting just under the surface, and not even the blissful blur of the Oblivion could erase the pain they caused.

• • •

There had been more than two days of fighting. The Faeoihn, her sisters, were used to mortal opponents who tired over time, but the Laochra never seemed to. They fought with a bloodlust that left them beyond reason. One of her sisters had tried to talk with one of them, offering them the normal bargain of returning to his family but he had only spit at her and used the moment of distraction to sweep her legs out from under her. If Neala hadn't blocked his downswing, Tara would have died. Their fighting had turned the ground to mud. The grass had been churned away by the combination of hundreds of feet, the rain the day before, and the spilled blood leaving a slick mess to fight in.

Neala was fighting a monster with a battle-axe, his blows landing hard against her sword and forcing her backward. She had managed a small cut on his side, but the pain didn't seem to register in him and she knew her exhaustion was slowing her blocks. One of her sisters appeared out of the melee and charged into his side, knocking him away.

"Thank you, Kiera! Have you slain any of them?" Neala was breathing heavily, letting her sword rest in the ground to give her muscles a quick break. The other Faeoihn, one of her best friends, shook her head.

"I could have sworn I gave one a mortal wound, but he kept fighting. Have you looked at them closely? Their eyes are black as night, I believe death itself is inside them. Nothing else could explain this." Kiera carried a long staff with blades in either end; a wicked weapon if one knew how to use it. Neala shook her head, this was the third day and with both sides healing the battle could go on forever.

Looking across the field, all of her sisters were caught in fights with the Laochra, and some were doing well, while others were falling back. One took a sword to her side and fell, but before the Laochra could deal the deathblow his sword was caught by another Faeoihn's blade. They all healed at dawn, but the Laochra seemed to just steadily heal over time. Unfortunately, it seemed that this was keeping them stronger on the field than the Faeoihn, and it was only a matter of time before they started to buckle. They were outnumbered, exhausted, wounded, and hungry. Neala's eyes turned to the skies and she whispered a prayer to their goddess before looking back to Kiera.

"Eltera will come, I know it, she will stop this madness.

Move!" Neala grabbed the other Faeoihn and pulled her forward, bringing her sword up to block the downward blow of the rushing Laochra. He stepped back and swung his sword again, but Fae knocked it aside and delivered a deep cut to his thigh on her downward swing. When he fell she brought her sword up to deliver what she hoped was a deathblow, but a bright light suddenly blinded her. It was followed quickly by a loud clap of thunder that boomed across the field and shook the ground beneath her feet hard enough to knock her off balance. As the light faded, it revealed Gormahn and Eltera standing on a raised hill in the middle of the battle. Their voices rang out in argument, silencing both sides of the melee almost instantly.

"Return your Laochra to their homes!" Eltera shouted at Gormahn who stood a head above her. He only laughed, and his deep voice was rough when he responded.

"Yield the field, and perhaps they won't slaughter all of your Faeoihn." Gormahn raised his sword high and the Laochra roared back at him.

"Let these lands have peace, Gormahn. Imagine what they can do if we give them the peace in which to do it!" Eltera was insistent, and Neala couldn't pull her eyes away. It seemed that both armies felt the same way. No one was fighting anymore, as they all waited for their leaders, their gods, to act.

"Peace is the harbor for the weak, Eltera." Gormahn's growl rumbled through the ground, and he brought up his sword to attack her. Eltera spun her staff in the way and blocked the attack, the Laochra yelled again in support of their god. The Faeoihn cheered for their goddess, and the skies lit with lightning as their power clashed.

"Peace is a harbor for their future!" Eltera screamed and they both moved faster than normal eyes could track. While Eltera attacked fiercely, Gormahn countered each blow and pressed her back with his own. Both the Faeoihn and the Laochra began cheering and calling out to their god. Both gods glowed brightly, which was enhanced by the red of the setting sun and it made the sight of their battle all the more awe-inspiring. Booms of thunder and bright flashes in the sky above them seemed to be timed with their strikes. The world itself was reacting to their power being released on the earth. Gormahn brought his sword around in a hard swing, and Eltera blocked it with her staff but the force of it buckled her arms and his blade dug into her shoulder. She only let out a short groan before she switched the staff to her other arm to continue the fight.

"Surrender to me, Eltera, and I will let your Faeoihn live. I swear it." Gormahn swung his sword again and Eltera barely blocked it. She stepped back and he swung again, this time the blow of his sword wrenched the staff out of her hand. A roar went up from the Laochra across the field, and Neala tensed. Disbelief froze her in place as Gormahn laid his sword against Eltera's neck, and the goddess kneeled down in defeat. "Surrender." His voice was deafening, and Neala shook her head slowly. Silently pleading, praying.

They had failed her.

They hadn't fought hard enough, they hadn't been strong enough, hadn't been *good* enough to win – and so she had stepped in. The goddess of nature had challenged the god of war directly, and now she had lost.

No. Impossible. It wasn't possible. Neala's mind raced, trying to think of something that could be done, but then Eltera's voice rang out with words that broke something deep inside her.

"Alright Gormahn, I surrender. I accept your offer and your sworn promise not to kill my Faeoihn." Eltera put her hands up in front of her. She was surrendering, actually surrendering. Gormahn held out his hand and two large gold manacles appeared, linked by a golden chain.

"I assure you, my Laochra will not kill them." Gormahn grinned, and clasped the manacles around Eltera's wrists. Across the field the Faeoihn screamed in unison, golden bands of light appeared around each of their wrists, the curse in the manacles latching itself onto all who were linked to Eltera. Pain shot through Neala and she collapsed to the ground crying out as incomparable pain paralyzed her. It was like her bones were breaking and melting from the terrible heat that rushed through every inch of her.

"No!" Eltera's shout echoed across the field, intermingling with the other shouts from the Faeoihn. Neala craned her neck to see Gormahn lift Eltera's chains high. Tears blurred her vision as she bit down on the scream that wanted to escape her lips.

"My Laochra! We have won!" Gormahn's voice shook the ground as he bellowed. "Take the Faeoihn as your spoils of war, and celebrate their defeat!" The Laochra cheered, and Gormahn looked down at Eltera, lowering his voice. His words imprinting themselves on each Faeoihn, "They won't die, Eltera. They will serve forever."

A fist wound into her hair and craned her head back until she could see the bloody smile of the Laochra above her. She wanted to fight as he pushed her to her back, but the golden tendrils of pain were dragging through her like knives. It was hard to tell the different pains apart as he hit her, cursed her for the cut to his leg, and then pushed her thighs apart.

Across the field there were whimpers and screams, and Neala's joined the other Faeoihn.

• • •

Fae swallowed and bundled up the sheets from the last rooms. Ebere was silent, grabbing another bundle of sheets from the earlier rooms. The memory of that day usually sent her into a rage, but it was more of a dull twist of an old knife under the weight of the Oblivion. For a moment she wondered if Ebere would ever make eye contact with her again, but then she stepped up and just shook her head. "So from then on you've been a slave? For all these years?" Fae nodded, and they both turned towards the stairs. "With the Laochra?"

"No. Gormahn let them keep us for a month or so, but then he wanted them on the march. He wanted them to bring war back to our people. He also didn't like that we were all with each other, my sisters and I comforted each other, and did our best to protect each other." Fae got quiet as she passed by a set of guards before continuing to the back of the house with the bundles of sheets. "So, he had them scatter us across the world. No two Faeoihn in the same place. I ended up in Rome."

"Rome? That must have been amazing!" Ebere seemed to actually be impressed as they neared the laundry. Fae almost laughed out loud.

"The Romans were terrible to non-citizens and, let's just say I never saw much of the great city." Fae stated it matter-of-factly, and didn't leave it open to questions, not wanting to remember her time there any more than her time with the Laochra in their keep.

"I'm sorry, Fae. I didn't mean –" Ebere swallowed, "I couldn't imagine being like this, being a slave, for so long."

"Well, I've served in a lot of places, and I'm fortunate that part of Eltera's gift with us was a knowledge of language. Otherwise, it would have been a nightmare to be scattered like that."

"So, you learn languages fast?"

"Try instantly. It hurts like a bitch, like a cold headache. But then I know it." Fae tilted her head at her, "What language did you speak before you learned English?"

"Amharic, but I learned a lot of English before I left school to work. It wasn't hard to pick up the rest of it."

"Say something in Amharic." Fae braced herself outside the laundry, as Ebere gave her a critical look and then spoke.

"Amarenya techiyallesh?" Ebere's words made her flinch as Eltera's gift flared to life inside her. The headache pierced through her temples and Fae gasped as the words echoed in her mind: *Do you speak Amharic?*

The pain started to fade and Fae shook her head and replied in perfect Amharic, "*Now I do.*"

Ebere looked shocked and then covered her mouth as she started laughing. "How have you not shared this with all of us?"

"I kind of like listening to what Caridee has to say about me when she thinks I don't speak Spanish." Fae grinned and Ebere laughed again.

"I'm curious about what she says too, so I'll keep this a secret as long as you'll fill me in."

"Deal." Fae was smiling as they turned the corner, but she felt short of breath when she finally dropped the sheets in the laundry room, and her skin was coated in sweat. She leaned against the wall and both Ebere and Mei-Li moved in front of her.

"You need to eat, Fae." Ebere pushed the hair back from Fae's forehead so it would stop sticking. "You need water too. You're overheating. The evening meal is soon, you should just stay down here with us." Fae sat down hard. Her heart was racing and she still felt giddy even though she had decided to tell Ebere about her father, Eltera, the

Faeoihn, Gormahn and the battle. Normally if she talked about Gormahn and his Laochra she was angry all over again, but the Oblivion was muting all of that. Instead, right now she felt detached. She could think about the faces of her fellow Faeoihn, she could remember the last day she saw Eltera, and she didn't want to fall apart over it. The anger was still there, she could feel it simmering, but it was a distant murmur in the white noise of the drug.

"Thanks, Ebere." Fae forced a smile for her. Mei-Li, Ebere, and another girl named Sobeska continued loading the washers and dryers. They spent the rest of their time folding on the floor or running things around the house.

AN HOUR or so later Fae woke up to a sharp boot kick to her ribs. She gasped, wincing as her eyes opened, and she heard Ebere's voice scream off to her left, "Sir! Please!"

"What the fuck are you doing down here?" The gruff voice belonged to Butler and Fae looked up at him as she crossed an arm over her stomach and used the other to push herself up. She didn't even remember falling asleep, but the Oblivion was still raging in her system. Unfortunately, it didn't do anything to dull the pain – it just made her care a little less about it.

"She brought us laundry! From the East wing!" Mei-Li spoke up this time and Butler just sneered at them before grabbing Fae by the hair and pulling her to her feet. She stumbled as he yanked her towards him, but his grip on her kept her upright.

"Tell me, Fae, where are you supposed to be?" The sinister tone of his voice almost sounded happy as he asked. She wanted to just tell him to punish her, to get it over with, but no, he had to make a point first.

"Upstairs. East wing." She gritted her teeth to stifle the smart-ass comments she wanted to make, because she really doubted Butler was supposed to be looking for her. Nikola had already delivered a punishment for her defiance that morning and it was unlikely he'd given Butler permission to hunt her down again.

"Why aren't you there?"

"I brought the laundry down." As soon as she answered, the other girls started speaking to back her up but Butler just snapped his fingers to silence them.

"What should you have done once the laundry was delivered?" His lips brushed against her ear as he leaned close to her, and a shudder moved through her.

"I should have gone back upstairs, sir."

"That's right," he growled out the words and then shoved her forward, bending her over one of the machines. He lifted the hem of her dress, and someone started to plead with him as he held her down by her hair.

"Sir! Please, it's -"

"Shut up! The next girl that talks gets twice what Fae here is getting for leaving her assigned area." The sound of his belt unbuckling made her flinch in preparation. An instant later the leather cut through the air and the first lash across her ass was a bright spike of pain inside the delirium of the Oblivion. The next line of fire went across the tops of her thighs, and she bit down hard to stay silent.

I've had worse. I've had worse. This is nothing.

It was the mantra that got her through so much, and even as he laid line after line across her ass, she swallowed the little yelps that tried to slip by. It was a searing heat that broke through the warm fuzz that had filled her and replaced it with the aftershocks of each blow. She refused to beg for him, to let him hear her plead, because she knew that's what he loved most. The last few were as hard as he could deliver, and she pressed her cheek hard against the metal, gripping the back of the machine and pushing out breaths to fight the urge to cry. Her skin felt blistered. Even the slight shifting of her muscles revealed how bruised she was, and she knew he reveled in punishing her because he never got in trouble for it. Who cared what he did to her when she was a blank slate the following morning?

It was probably why Butler had hunted her down.

Even if she had been upstairs he would have found some small error, some tiny mistake to punish her for. As the pounding of her heart in her ears faded, she could hear sniffling from the other end of the laundry room on top of Butler's harsh breathing.

"Get on your knees," he released his grip on her and

stepped back. Fae stood up carefully and knelt even more gently, keeping her ass off her heels. She could see that Butler's cock was hard in his pants, and she tried to ignore the three girls huddled together in the corner of her eye. "Go on, slut, you know what to do."

"Mei-Li! Sobeska! Ebere!" Lena's irritating voice rang out from the hallway, "Do you girls not understand what time it is? If you miss -" her words stopped short as she stepped into the doorway, and Fae hated the blush that flooded her cheeks. Lena took in the scene, and then tried to stifle the smile on her lips. "Ah, Butler, sir, I didn't know you were here. I didn't mean to interrupt you."

"No interruption, I was just reminding Fae of the house rules, and the consequences of breaking them." His fingers wound in her hair and he pulled her forward until he rubbed her cheek against the front of his pants. She clenched her fists tight to keep herself from doing something incredibly stupid. Like twisting his balls until he screamed like a girl, or breaking every finger of his hand and then driving a coat hanger through his abdomen as she spit in his face.

"Of course, sir. The other girls are late for the evening meal, would you mind if I took them with me?" Lena spoke so sweetly as she pointedly ignored Fae on the floor.

"Go ahead, I'll give this one her dinner personally." Butler's voice made her shudder, but she took relief in the fact that the other girls wouldn't be here for what would happen.

"No! It's my fault! I -" Ebere started to speak and Fae jerked away from Butler's grip and shouted at her.

"Shut up, Ebere! Go with Lena!" Fae hated the hurt look that passed over the girl's face, but if it meant she'd be safe and back in the female quarters, it was worth it. Butler slapped her hard for pulling away, and Fae swallowed against the urge to cry. She didn't even touch her cheek because she didn't want him to know how much it had hurt. Glancing up through her hair she saw Ebere standing with her fists balled at her sides.

"Come on, Eb." Sobeska took her arm and pulled her past Fae, and Mei-Li followed them. Lena turned back and grabbed the doorknob as they all stepped outside.

"Sorry for the interruption, sir. Hopefully with your guidance she'll learn some manners." Lena smiled and Fae growled at her as she shut the door and left them alone.

"I don't think you're capable of learning manners, whore." Butler grabbed her chin and yanked her head up painfully. "Are you?"

"No." Fae kept her eyes on his as they widened slightly in surprise and then narrowed as his rage filled him.

She had never obeyed, and she wasn't going to start now.

"That's *no sir*." He hissed it through his teeth and she pushed down the urge to spit in his face.

"No, sir." She growled the words back at him and he returned his fingers to her hair, straightening up above her.

"I agree, you're not capable of being anything more than the slut you were made to be. Now, you're going to do your best as you suck my cock, or after I come in your throat I'll just go talk to Nikola about what you did when you finished your chores." His fist tightened in her hair, "And I'll check the security footage to see who helped you finish all those rooms, because I *know* you didn't do them alone. Then I'll have you watch as they get exactly what they've earned."

Ebere.

He knew exactly who had been helping her. Hell, Ebere had tried to confess to him. She wasn't going to let Butler go after her too. Fae reached up and swiftly undid the button on his pants and tugged the zipper down. Then she slipped her fingers into the band on his boxers and paused, "I'll do whatever you want, sir."

"Show me." He pulled her head forward and she yanked his pants down.

"Yes, sir."

CHAPTER FOUR

RANNOCH MOOR, SCOTLAND

APPEARING in the middle of Gormahn's great hall was disorienting, because from the moment Kiernan arrived he was overwhelmed with the light of the fires and the sound of people shouting over each other and laughing. As his head adjusted to the sudden change of scenery, Kiernan lifted the duffel bag he held over his shoulder.

"Kiernan!" Phelan clapped him on the back hard enough to knock the air out of him. A big man with red hair and a thick beard on his face, he looked like he should be at a modern day renaissance fair with his kilt and a broadsword strapped to his back. Some of the Laochra hadn't been too interested in updating themselves to modern times, and Phelan looked several centuries behind and proud of it.

"Hail, Phelan. It's been a long time." Kiernan gave him a smile and gripped his shoulder.

"A long time? That's what you say after over a hundred years?" Phelan's bellowing laugh shook the rafters and drew the attention of others who were eating and drinking and gambling.

"I've been out seeing what the world has to offer. It's changed a lot in the last century, you know. They have technological marvels you wouldn't believe, but you'd have to actually *leave here* to see them."

"I leave to fight, and return to celebrate!" Several of the men cheered at Phelan's response, and he gave a belly laugh and returned to drinking.

Kiernan turned around, taking in the huge hall he had been avoiding for more than a century. Gormahn was not interested in modern conveniences, and the huge castle that served as the base of the Laochra could have been pulled out of ancient Europe. There were even rushes on the floor, and a pair of huge wolfhounds running the length of the hall snatching at scraps thrown down.

Gormahn had only acknowledged modern technologies in one way – the base was hidden from humans by his power.

On late nights, when he woke up in a cold sweat, Kiernan often that it might have been the effort it took to keep it hidden that had his hold finally waning. It could also just be the way the world had mostly forgotten him and the rest of his pantheon – either way Kiernan didn't care. He had woken up from that vision of blood and gore, and he did everything he could not to return here where it lived.

Shaking his head at the men around him, he walked to the end of the room where the doorway to the sleeping quarters was. A lot of the Laochra had found places of their own out in the world, but some refused to leave the base, and all of them still acted like the days of conquest were alive and well. It was strange how much it bothered Kiernan that they still wallowed in their bloodlust, and he knew living like this only made them worse.

Sitting in a chair against the wall Kiernan settled his duffel bag across his lap and waited. He watched the Laochra cheering, and drinking, and singing, and drinking some more. Some of them waved him over, but he just held his hand up to say he was fine and remained where he was. It was almost two hours later when Eryn swaggered in through the door from the sleeping quarters. Kiernan tucked the book he had started reading under one thigh as he took in the form of his old friend. Eryn was in a black t-shirt and cargo pants, his long hair was pulled back into a pony tail with just a single braid trailing from his temple. He grinned when he saw Kiernan, but the smile didn't reach his eyes. It never did.

Kiernan had really hoped Cole would appear first.

"Ah, there you are Kiernan. Cole said you'd be coming." His voice was bored, and he didn't even meet Kiernan's gaze. Instead, he looked over the hall and roared out a cheer that was echoed back by several of the groups who then toasted their general. Eryn's viciousness had long ago earned him the respect of the Laochra and had provided him the place of honor as their unofficial general. Right hand to Gormahn.

"Cole told me to meet you both here, but I've been here for a couple of hours." Eryn turned his eyes back to him, looking over Kiernan's jeans, converse shoes, and vintage Mariners shirt. Kiernan raised an eyebrow at Eryn's long evaluation of him, suddenly nervous that his mental changes were written all over him like war paint. It wouldn't do well for Eryn to already be curious about him.

"I was meeting with Gormahn. I'm sure he'd be interested in seeing you since you decided to return to base." Eryn finally met Kiernan's eyes, and it made his stomach clench. Although Eryn looked about nineteen, his eyes told a different story. The black revealed a cold, calculating individual devoid of empathy. Just the thought of seeing Gormahn face to face made Kiernan sick, especially if it was just he and Eryn in the room. He had a feeling Gormahn would somehow know everything and that he would realize his grip on Kiernan was slipping.

Who knew what he'd do then?

Kiernan kept his voice light, and didn't look away from Eryn even though he was going out of his way to make Kiernan uncomfortable. "If he wants to see me, sure. Have you seen Cole though? Little prick said he'd meet me here." He crossed his long legs in front of him, trying to look casual under the harsh stare of the man. Showing any kind of weakness in this moment would make Eryn go for blood, and he would likely drag

Kiernan in front of Gormahn just to see what would happen.

"I don't know where he is. Cole is unpredictable as always. Are you sure you're going to be able to handle the hunt? From what I understand you're out of practice." Eryn crossed his arms and Kiernan laughed, leaning back in the chair.

"Is that what Cole says about me? I think he's just jealous that I've always been better than him, he knows I'll come home with the first kill." With that Eryn gave his first real smile, and Kiernan could remember how exhilarating it had been to go into battle with Eryn and receive that smile before the charge.

When it came to war, Eryn was a pureblood killer. He had no hesitation, no regret, and he actually *enjoyed* it. Modern psychiatrists would probably have a field day categorizing him while he told them about what it was like to fight until his arms were coated in blood.

Then he'd probably kill the psychiatrists.

Kiernan had loved it as well once, had roared into battle at Eryn's right hand – and now he just wanted to distance himself from all of it. From all of them. Staring at the man who had once been his friend, he felt like he had come upon a wolf while walking in the woods and he had to be careful with how he moved away so he didn't get taken down. Eryn stared at him, evaluating, weighing his answers and the relaxed posture that Kiernan forced himself to hold.

"I've missed this." He tried to lie smoothly, but the words

settled heavy in his stomach. "It feels good to be back around the men, to know we'll be out again. I forgot how good it felt."

Eryn's smile finally soaked into the rest of his body and he relaxed a little. "It's been a little boring since you decided to enter the world, Kiernan. I haven't done a midnight raid in too long. Does that mean you're coming back to us?"

"Maybe. It's easy to lose track of time in these walls, and there's so much changing in the human world right now, I've enjoyed being there for all of it as well." Kiernan shrugged and Eryn nodded.

"True, but many of the men used to look up to you, and I know they'd like to have you back."

Kiernan felt the pressure to stay, and he was about to respond when Cole's voice shouted across the room.

"Hello, everyone!" His words were followed almost immediately by a yell. Cole had appeared at the side of the room on top of one of the long tables, and he'd landed square in the middle of a game of cards. One of the men grabbed his feet and jerked him off the table and onto the floor. Cole jumped back up, and ended up laughing with the man a minute later.

"And the fool has arrived." Kiernan muttered and grinned as he stood up with the duffel, tucking his Discworld book back into the side pocket.

"I heard that!" Cole sauntered over with a pack on his shoulder, his hair was mussed and his shirt was wrinkled.

"I was busy enjoying some time with a lady friend before our manly trip." Kiernan rolled his eyes and Eryn just chuckled.

"So that took five minutes, what happened to the other two hours?" Eryn grinned at Cole, and Cole started mocking him. Watching them mess with each other made Kiernan remember what it had been like to be a part of the group, and he missed it. He couldn't help but miss the camaraderie. This hunt was going to be good for him, it would help him center himself, and maybe keep him from wasting away in his apartment staring at a girl inside a glass.

It only took about thirty minutes for them to grab Eryn's bags and collect some well-made bows and combat knives for their hunt.

Eryn pulled out a map and pointed at a section of South Asia, "This is where we're headed. I'll take us there because I scouted it a few weeks back." Kiernan barely had time to nod before Eryn placed a hand on each of their shoulders and the world blinked out of existence for a second, and then the deep green of the jungle faded in. The air was muggy but clean; there wasn't a trace of exhaust or industry in the air. It was how the earth had been meant to look, and smell, and feel. Raw and real. Eryn and Cole seemed to be enjoying it too, looking up through the canopy at the sky. Cole immediately started walking forward, Eryn followed him, and Kiernan brought up the rear as they pushed their way through the thick undergrowth.

"Mind if I show you where I was planning to camp? Or

would you like to wander the jungle for a while?" Eryn whispered, his accent showing up even though he wasn't speaking their ancient tongue. Cole stepped aside and bowed with a flourish, making room for Eryn to walk by. As he passed Eryn shoved Cole's head to the side and the weight of his pack almost toppled him. Kiernan grabbed him and stifled a laugh.

"I'm pretty sure I can find a clearing." Cole hissed out the words, glaring at the back of Eryn's head.

"Sure you could, and would it also be near water and in good hunting territory? Oh, and be on higher ground so we'll be dry?" Eryn grinned and Cole ground his teeth, but he was still smiling. They all had more energy now that they were out in the wild with a purpose. The march wasn't long before they broke through into an open space about fifteen feet across, the canopy was thin above and provided more light for them to set up camp. As they worked, Cole nudged Kiernan.

"Are you glad you came out? You have to admit this is better than your sissy apartment."

"Yes, I'm glad I came, but just because my apartment is clean doesn't make it sissy. I'm taking advantage of all of the modern conveniences the mortals have come up with." He threw a stick at Cole and nailed him in the back of the head. "By the way, you live in a house, it's not like you're roughing it like the old days either."

"It's a *cabin*." Cole emphasized his term for it. The nice place was nestled in the low mountains of Virginia and was too pretty to be called just a cabin.

"It's got running water doesn't it? Electricity? You have a fucking television, Cole." Kiernan rolled his eyes at Cole's huffing and puffing over being called out.

"Oh, shove it." Eryn laughed. "Both of you have given in to luxury. Made yourselves a couple of princes over there in America. You should come back to the days of straw beds and cooking over an actual fire, hearing the wind howl through the cracks in the walls." Eryn was smiling as he started to clean his bow off and make sure it was ready.

"I think sleeping in the mud with you two over the next day or so will be enough for me. I like air conditioning, and I like my bed." Kiernan grabbed a protein bar from his bag to chew on.

"I spend more time outside than Kiernan does in his sixth floor apartment in Seattle. It would take him a couple of hours just to get to the woods. I walk out my back door and boom, I'm there." Cole zipped his pack back up. "And, for the record, I like my microwave and watching fights on pay-per view." They all laughed.

"Some of the modern inventions are helpful, I admit that. But we've lost the freedom. We used to be able to come across any village and take what we wanted, food or women or livestock, and burn the rest. The known world quaked at the mention of the Laochra." Eryn shrugged, "We were like gods among men, and blood and fear were our bread and water."

Kiernan's memories of those times when Gormahn's power over them was total were scattered images and short clips of violence that he tried not to think about. Eryn seemed to remember everything so clearly and he reveled in it.

"There are parts of the world where we can still do that." Cole said, and Kiernan hid the flinch the words brought.

"Yeah, but they're shrinking. Every year man gains control over another part of the land. They talk of peace like it's some great destiny, and they deny the fact that we're all just animals walking upright. We need the blood and the violence to survive, and the weak either serve the strong or die beneath our heels. This *civilization* they crave does nothing but mask our true natures." Eryn's cold, matter-of-fact voice sent chills down Kiernan's back. He was a zealot for Gormahn's vision of the world, one where man gave in to its true nature. Where everyone took what they wanted because they could, where the strong overwhelmed the weak. Kiernan had been a part of that vision, but he knew deep down that he wasn't anymore. He recognized the responsibility of the strong to protect the weak, and he wanted to do that, he wanted to be *that* person. The realization surprised him. If he wanted that, what did it mean for him? If he didn't want to be Laochra, to stand for Gormahn's beliefs, then what was he? Who was he?

"Kiernan, man, you've got to stop zoning out." Cole was waving a hand in front of his face. "I'm seriously worried you're going to end up something's dinner."

Kiernan kicked his leg out and swept Cole's feet out from under him, he hit the ground hard and Kiernan laid the combat knife against his throat. "I'll be just fine, Cole."

Removing the knife to the sound of Eryn's laughter, Kiernan stood up and pulled Cole to standing.

"You didn't have to make the point so bluntly." Cole rubbed his back, grimacing, and Kiernan just grinned at him.

Eryn's eyes grew wild as he lifted the bow to his shoulder, his smile widening to a manic level. "Enough joking boys, let's hunt."

CHAPTER FIVE

Ráj Manor, Caledon, Ontario

Fae woke the next morning in the warm glow of Eltera's power. Her body lit up like always, a shimmering golden light that emanated from her skin, and she tried to focus on it and make it last. Just as the power was cresting, the lingering exhaustion inside her fading, Ebere appeared in the entryway to the little nook she occupied. Fae sighed and pushed herself into a sitting position, crossing her legs on her cot.

Each of them had one of these little nooks, barely eight feet by four feet. Enough room for their tiny beds, and a few scavenged items that they claimed as possessions. All Fae had in hers was a white stone with a hole in it that she'd found working in the garden, and a battered copy of *Brave New World* that made its way around the girls at random.

"Morning, Fae..." Ebere whispered and sat down against the doorframe. She was twisting her fingers together, her eyes occasionally flicking to the fading light on Fae's skin before returning to her nails.

Fae dropped her head back against the wall and blew out a breath, and mumbled, "Morning."

"Look, I'm really so-"

"No." Fae cut her apology off instantly, and Ebere slapped the floor beside her.

"Damn you, Fae!" Ebere hissed, trying to stay quiet enough to not wake the other girls, "You should have let me take part of the punishment! It was my choice to help you. I didn't wake you when I saw you had fallen asleep and -"

Fae started laughing bitterly to herself, shaking her head at Ebere who started stumbling over her words in her anger. Instead of letting the girl continue to founder, Fae started talking. "You really don't get it, Eb. Butler was *looking* for me. He didn't accidentally stumble on me in the fucking laundry. He tried to find me upstairs, and when he couldn't he watched the security footage to see where I went. You were trying so hard to confess, to get him to punish you instead, but he already knew you'd helped me and he didn't care."

"But... but *why*? Why come after only you when he knew that I'd helped you? Why not me?" Ebere's earnest confusion came out in the stress of her voice.

"Because *you* wouldn't heal by the party tonight." Fae

extended her arm, the fading aura of light still visible even in the dimmed lamps from the main room. "He wanted to hurt someone, and he needed someone that Master wouldn't be upset about. Lena probably assigned me to the East wing because she knew it was impossible for one person to finish in that time, especially knowing that Master was going to punish me for the breakfast thing once she and Alec reported it."

"...and when you didn't finish Butler could do a check and deliver his own punishment." Ebere sighed and rubbed her hands across her face. "That *bitch*. I – I'm so angry, that's even more of a reason why I should have taken part of it. They can't set you up like that, I mean, my God, Fae, you can't keep that up!"

"I've been doing it -"

"For two thousand years. Yeah, I get it." Ebere threw her hands up. "I get it, okay? You're the product of some ancient goddess' messed up plan for peace, and maybe you were originally supposed to protect people – but you have to *stop*, Fae. Stop trying to protect all of us, just stop. Protect yourself for once!"

"I don't need protecting, *you* do. All of you do." Fae felt like she was pleading with the girl to come to her senses. "Trust me, I can handle it. I'm fine, okay?"

"No, it's not okay. You have to stop throwing yourself in the line of fire, because I know it hurts just as much regardless of whether or not you're *fine* in the morning." She muttered under her breath and then continued, "I don't want you to get hurt anymore. Not for me, not for any of us. Promise me you'll stop. Please, Fae, please promise me you'll stop."

She tried to fight back the tears that suddenly burned the corner of her eyes. How long had it been since someone, *anyone*, had actually cared about her? Cared enough to lecture her like she was a child? She was a *hundred* times this girl's age and Ebere was talking to her like a little sister. It was so unexpected that for once, Fae was at a loss for what to do for a moment. It all made a smile creep across her lips. "I can't promise I'll stop, Eb. I've spent too many lifetimes using myself as the shield, but I can try."

"Promise me you'll try then." Ebere shifted closer to the bed, moving to her knees so they were almost face to face. Then she reached up and grabbed Fae's hand in a tight grip and Fae saw the threat of tears in the other girl's eyes - *that* almost undid her completely. "*Please*, just promise me you'll try and take care of yourself."

"Okay. I promise." The words choked out as Fae fought the emotion down, and Ebere gripped her hand once more before she stood.

"Okay then." She nodded and stepped towards the door, but then she looked back and said, "I like you, Fae, and I think we could be close. We could be great friends. You could have a lot of friends if you – if you'd just let *someone* in. While you're trying to take care of yourself, think about that."

Fae opened her mouth to respond, but Ebere had already slipped back into the main room to wander back to her own nook. The girl's words were a heavy weight inside her. She'd had friends before, she'd cared about mortals, loved them like family – and then they had died. That was the trouble with mortals, they died.

'But how's your life going without any friends?' Her mind piped up, and Fae cursed herself.

The walls she'd built up around her had kept her numb. Numb to the things they did to her, numb to her past, numb to the suffering of the women and men around her. It had let her survive – but surviving wasn't *living*.

"Eltera?" Fae whispered into the dark, looking up at the ceiling and trying to focus on the images of the goddess burned into her memory. A few tears slipped out and she pushed them off her cheeks as she steeled herself to pray. "I don't know what you'd tell me to do. I don't know if any of what I've done has been right, or if you can even see us anymore. I know –" her voice broke as more tears slipped down her cheeks and she brushed them away quickly. Sniffling and clenching her fists in her lap she continued. "I *know* this was not in your plan, and I would never blame you for this curse. I know that this was my fault, *our* fault for failing you in the battle, but I don't know what to do. I don't know what to *do*, Eltera, and no matter what I just feel like I'm continuing to fail you. I feel if I were just stronger, if I were just braver, I could handle this with grace. I could bear this burden *and* continue to help others, to protect the weak – but what if I can't?"

There was a dull ache in the center of her chest as she tried to stop the tears. She was speaking in the old language, and she knew even if one of the girls was listening they wouldn't understand the words, but the sniffling and the hitch in her voice was obvious to anyone who cared to eavesdrop. Fae knew if she hadn't cracked open the door on her past the day before that Ebere's words wouldn't have hit her so hard. The words wouldn't have summoned images of her Faeoihn sisters smiling, and laughing, and joking with her about being so damn serious. She wouldn't be thinking of all the ones she'd helped over the centuries, and she wouldn't be haunted by the ones she'd lost.

Fae brushed her thumb over the pale blue veins in her wrist. Her skin was once more just skin. No light, no power thrumming inside her – just skin. Her eyes moved back to the ceiling, wondering for the millionth time if Eltera could hear her, "What if – what if I'm doing the wrong thing? Would you give me a sign? Would you tell me to stop? To lay down my arms, stop fighting, and submit? Please, *please Eltera*, just give me a sign?"

She fell silent, and the quiet of the female quarters rolled in to fill the space her prayers had vacated. There was the blurred sound of more than a dozen girls breathing, shifting in their beds, the dull white noise of the heat coming on – and nothing else.

No golden light, no scent of rain or earth, no claps of thunder.

Nothing.

Fae tried to stifle the tears as they overtook her. She felt so alone. She *was* alone, but Ebere was trying to reach out. Others had tried too and she had been kind, but kept them all at a distance. These fragile little mortal lives that would only hurt her in the long run if she cared, but what could they be to her in the mean time if she let them in?

'Friends', Ebere's words echoed in her mind.

They could be friends, if she would just let them. If she would just let them in, if she'd actually talk to them, give them real answers, maybe her days wouldn't feel so hollow. As Fae curled back up on her side, she sniffled again and the edge of her mouth ticked up a bit. Yes, Ebere wanted to be her friend, but if she was her friend then there was no way that Fae could do what she'd asked; friends *protected* each other. It didn't mean Fae couldn't try and be more careful with herself, but she wouldn't give up on helping these girls.

As soon as she'd been able to get out of the female quarters she'd found Irena and followed her, because she'd needed to be around the pixie's bright energy after her heavy morning. Watching Irena and Juliet hanging their decorations and fluffing up their bouquets around the house was an easy distraction. Strands of lights were hung throughout the house, woven together with garlands over doorways and down the stairs. How long it had taken for Irena to do it all, Fae wasn't sure, but it did look impressive. Juliet's eyes were fever bright as she kept up with the pixie, a mix of the third dose of Oblivion and her own excitement over the decorations.

"Can you believe how beautiful it all is? It reminds me of Christmas!" Juliet was giggling and excited as Irena swooped down and landed next to her, they hugged each other tightly and bounced up and down laughing.

"It's perfect! Just how I imagined it!" Irena's wings were twitching with her infinite supply of energy. "Fae, you love it right? Tell me you love it."

"I love it." Fae smiled, glad to see her happy on the day of a dinner party. Maybe Nikola would let her decorate for each of them; that would be a bright spot to look forward to. Irena was still staring at her, impatiently waiting for more comments, and Fae scrambled to fill the void. "Ummm, it's *gorgeous*, Irena, magical. The white flowers and the evergreens, it really looks like a winter festival. You positively transformed the house." That seemed to satisfy the pixie who was fluttering about six inches off the floor in her pride.

"Juliet weaved the lights in all of the garlands!" Irena grinned, and Juliet blushed and high fived her.

"It was all your idea, but it was fun."

Just as they were all giggling, Butler stepped into the foyer from the huge parlor room and closed the double doors behind him. They went silent as he stared at them, and then he tilted his head, "I believe you are all supposed to be getting ready for this evening."

"Yes, sir," they all mumbled.

"Then get upstairs and do it," he growled. Juliet and Irena immediately clasped hands and rushed towards the north stairs to get back to the female quarters. As Fae stepped past Butler he held out his hand to stop her. "I've been asked to watch you tonight. I suggest you do nothing foolish, but if you do," he paused, a smirk lifting the corner of his mouth, "I'll be there to make sure you regret it."

"Thanks, Butler," Fae muttered. She couldn't feel the punishment from the day before anymore, but she remembered it completely.

"Sir," he corrected her.

"Thank you... sir," she muttered, and he nodded. Fae clenched her jaw and walked past him, jogging to catch up with Irena and Juliet. Those two were inseparable and still whispering about their decoration scheme as they topped the stairs. The din of noise coming through the doors to the female quarters was loud, and the guard at the door opened it as they approached.

Then the three of them stepped into chaos.

All of the girls were talking in a hodgepodge of accents in a relatively small space, some were sitting on the floor while others twisted and shaped their hair into various styles that matched them best. Others were applying make-up to each other, or filing their nails, or applying clear polish. Nikola wanted to show off his collection to his guests at the party, and Lena wanted to make sure they were perfect. She was red-faced when she saw the three of them standing awkwardly near the door.

"Irena! Fae! Juliet! You are *late!*" She hurried over and pushed them towards the showers. "Hurry and shower so we can get you ready. You only have an hour. Remember, white dresses, and make sure one of the twins does your make up." She snapped her fingers and turned back into the room to go yell at someone else, probably about eye liner or lip gloss.

The important things in life.

The three of them showered fast and when they were drying off, the twins, Sobeska and Zofie, stepped in the doorway with big smiles. They already looked gorgeous with their dark hair falling in waves and their olive skin shimmering under the light thanks to the lavender powder they brushed on. Small crystals had been clamped into their hair and the effect was that they both looked like winter nymphs.

Fae grabbed one of the white dresses and Zofie laughed and grabbed her hand to pull her into the main area again as she tried to pull it on. "You're lucky you are so beautiful already, otherwise I may not have time to fix you." Her Eastern European accent was still thick, like she and her sister just refused to lose it.

"I didn't realize how late it was Zofie, sorry." Fae actually did feel bad that Zofie was rushing to get her ready. She didn't make a peep as the girl tore a hair brush through her tangles and dried it as much as possible. Zofie twisted two small braids from the front of her hair around the sides to bring them together in the back, weaving little white flowers into the braid. A few clamped crystals in the rest of her hair finished it. Then came the make-up which Zofie used to draw attention to her blue eyes with heavy liner. Finally, a sparkling lavender powder was lightly dusted on her arms, legs, and across her neck and chest. It made them all look ethereal as they lined up in the room. Every shade of skin tone, tall and short, curvy and straight – they were beautiful. As was expected. Lena seemed almost on the verge of tears she was so happy when she looked them over. Somehow in all the chaos Lena had done her own makeup as well, and she looked completely put together as always.

Fae really hated that about her.

"Remember girls, you represent our Master tonight. This is your chance to shine and make his guests feel welcome. Each of these guests contributes to his success, and *his* success is yours." Fae rolled her eyes as Lena clapped her hands. "Alright, come on, follow me."

She knocked on the door and the guard outside unlocked it and let them all out. They followed Lena down the stairs and arranged themselves in the foyer in a curved line against the entrance to the parlor. A moment later Nikola came down the main stairs from his study, talking to Butler on the way down. He was in a finely tailored, but somewhat casual suit. His dark hair was graying at the temples, and he still had a tan from his latest trip. He looked handsome. It was frustrating that under the crisp appearance he was so cruel and uncaring. He smiled when he saw them all, but it was without feeling as he opened his arms wide.

"Lena, you've outdone yourself. They look perfect, and my guests will be so happy." She stepped up to him, and he rested his hand in the small of her back and placed a kiss in her hair. She was radioactive with joy and her smile was so wide her cheeks must have hurt.

"It's nothing, Master. We're delighted to make the evening a success." Lena's voice was syrupy sweet and Fae had to fight the urge to throw up, or strangle her. Both urges were relatively strong if she was honest, but she didn't get the chance. The bands were already humming against her skin with him so close, silently reminding her to not do anything stupid so soon after she'd assured Ebere she'd try.

Nikola stepped away from Lena to address everyone. "My girls, tonight is my Winter Dinner and my guests will be expecting the level of entertainment my house normally provides. You will serve dinner and then take your Oblivion. We will celebrate the evening in the parlor room. My expectation is that everyone is on their best, and most *friendly*, behavior. Any disobedience will be dealt with swiftly." He pulled his sleeve up to check the time on his watch, and then let it fall back while he scanned the line. "The guests will be arriving soon. Fae and Sobeska, you will be at the front door greeting and taking coats to hang up. Juliet, you don't have experience in table service so you'll spend the evening entertaining the guards." There was a gasp from Irena, and Juliet looked around confused and wide-eyed.

"*What?*" Juliet whispered to Irena, "What does that mean?" Her panicked voice was a knife twisting in Fae's stomach. *He couldn't give her to the guards.*

"Master -" Fae spoke up, but Nikola raised his hand.

"No, Fae."

"But Master! Please, no!" Irena was panicking, which was making Juliet even more frightened. They were holding hands tightly and Juliet kept whispering questions at Irena, who was so fixated on Nikola that she wasn't answering. A few of the other girls started muttering to each other, and Paloma on the other side of Juliet started rubbing her back to try and calm her.

"SILENCE!" Butler yelled over the noise, and Nikola nodded to him in thanks as everyone went quiet.

"I am not interested in your arguments. I have decided that Juliet will be with the guards. The rest of you will serve drinks and hors d'oeuvres as the guests arrive." Nikola's voice was level and almost too low to hear over Irena and Juliet's hitched breathing. Fae glanced at Ebere and flinched before she took a step forward and the bands of light lit up brightly, drawing everyone's attention.

"Please, Master, I can take her place." Fae spoke softly, and kept her eyes down even though her stomach was doing flips.

Nikola stepped up to her and grabbed her chin, tilting it so she was looking up at him. "I have already made my decision. I did not ask for a volunteer, but if you're so eager I'll make sure you get time with them this week." He leaned forward so he was speaking in her ear, his words taking on the edge of a command that the bands hummed in response to, "You will be the highest example of obedience tonight or I'll make sure you suffer for it. Remember that." Nikola dropped his hand from her and walked back towards the center of the foyer. The buzz of the bands started to hurt, so Fae stepped back in line and looked at the floor, gritting her teeth against the urge to argue further.

Butler walked up and grabbed Juliet's arm, but Irena started crying and held on to her hand even as Butler started to pull her away. Paloma finally grabbed Irena's arm and made her let go, wrapping her arms around Irena to calm her down as she whispered in her ear. Juliet locked eyes with Fae as she passed by, and it was clear she was shaking with fear. No one had told her this was a possibility because Nikola hadn't done it in so long, but they should have prepared her anyway. They should have let her know all the possibilities so they could help her. As Fae watched, Butler handed Juliet a vial of the Oblivion and Fae relaxed slightly.

Whatever happened at least she'd be high as a kite for it.

"I expect you all to be on your best behavior. Don't disappoint me." Nikola nodded to Lena who looked mortified at having lost control of the girls in front of him. He walked back up the stairs, clearly not ready to join the party quite yet, and she spun on them. Lena's eyes were furious when she stormed over to the group. All of the girls had collapsed around Irena, talking to her quietly as they tried to soothe her, but she was still crying. Sobeska was trying to salvage her make-up by brushing her thumbs underneath Irena's eyes to sweep away the tears and the melting eye liner.

"What is wrong with you girls? All of you!" Lena was hissing her words at them, trying not to disturb Nikola. "You *never* argue with our Master."

"Shut up, Lena." Fae moved her aside with a glare, her bands still brightly lit. With Nikola's command they probably wouldn't fade all evening as they enforced his command, and she felt sure that's what he wanted. Reaching Irena, Fae leaned down a little to meet the pixie's eyes. "Listen to me. Juliet is going to be fine, she's strong. Butler gave her the Oblivion, I saw it myself, and she'll be fine." Irena started to nod along with Fae's words. "But you have to pull it together," Fae looked around at the group of faces, "we all do, or this night is going to be much worse." A few of the girls straightened up, and Lena glared bitterly at her. Ebere and Mei-Li had stayed calm and simply nodded. Irena finished wiping her face, and Sobeska moved in front of Fae to evaluate Irena's make-up again.

"I need to touch up her eyes." Sobeska sounded just like Zofie, but tended to be more outspoken, otherwise they were identical. Lena just threw up her hands and nodded, and they ran back towards the stairs.

By the time the first guest arrived everyone had their friendly masks on, all big smiles and flirty winks and perfect make-up. Fae and Sobeska were welcoming everyone that came in and alternating between hanging their coats in the closet under the stairs. The guests were milling around the huge tiled foyer talking to the girls and each other while the chandelier above sent sparkling light down. The wine and liquor were already flowing and the guests were mainly talking about their jobs in industry, and government, and their side businesses. Some of the girls were good at making the guests feel welcome; Annika with her blonde hair and long legs was sultry even when she wasn't trying. When she tried? The men melted around her. Others, like Caridee, were smiling and laughing but carefully avoided their touches however she could.

Once all of the guests had arrived, Sobeska and Fae were just standing near the entrance smiling at the guests. Fae's bands were still lit up and one of the guests was staring at her, focused intently on the circles of light.

He finally got the courage to approach her. "What are those?" He asked, pointing at her wrists.

Fae contemplated being sarcastic, but the bands buzzed against her skin in warning. She made her voice polite instead. "They are the mark of a curse, sir."

"A curse, like, a *real* curse?" His eyes went wide with interest. "So you're one of Nikola's special ones?"

"I believe I am, sir." Fae gave him a smile, hoping he would move on, but he was too intrigued.

"So what are you?" He motioned his hand toward Irena. "It's clear she's some kind of fairy –" *Pixie*. "– but you look human."

"That's because I was human once, and now I'm Faeoihn." She tried her best to respond in a submissive tone as she explained herself. He mouthed the word to himself and took a drink.

"And that means?" He asked, eyes drifting down the length of her body.

"That I'm immortal." *That* grabbed his attention and his eyes snapped back to her face.

"So you can't die?"

"Not easily, sir." She responded with a small smile just as Butler clapped his hands together near the entrance to the dining room, and gradually the conversations stopped.

"If you'll come to the dining room, Nikola will be joining you in a moment. But don't worry, the girls will be back soon." He gave one of his practiced smiles, which always looked weird on his face, as if it had been plastered on. The men handed back their empty glasses and set their napkins onto the serving trays. The man next to her gave her what he probably thought was a seductive wink and headed towards the dining room. As soon as they had all funneled into the dining room, the girls headed to the kitchen. Irena found her way to Fae's side and grabbed her hand, interlocking her fingers in a deathgrip, Fae squeezed her hand back as they stepped through the doors.

The kitchen was chaotic, Alec was talking over his shoulder at the two other guys cooking, trying to get the first course finished. When he turned back he noticed the girls and gave his winning smile, pushing his hand through his blond hair as he walked over to them.

"Hey ladies, everyone ready for tonight?" There were some nods. "Just remember to be as quiet as possible so you don't interrupt them, and set the plates down and pick up the last ones from their left. We have sixteen guests, plus Master, and there are seventeen of you so that works out perfectly. Who set the table this morning?" Mei-Li and a girl named Blithe raised their hands, and Alec rewarded them with another grin. "It looks wonderful, ladies! Now I just need you to wait for Butler to begin service." They could all hear when Nikola entered the dining room as there was a round of applause. Nikola's voice carried back through the short hall to the kitchen.

"Good evening and welcome. For many of you this is your first time to Ráj Manor, but if our relationships continue to be productive it will likely not be your last. Tonight celebrates all of the advantageous business ventures we have taken on this past year, and all of the ones you *will* help me with next year." There were some polite laughs as Nikola paused. "As a thank you to all of you, for the duration of the evening everything that is mine - is yours." This brought a quick cheer, and then Butler pushed open the door to the kitchen.

"Begin service." Butler snapped his fingers and everyone moved. Plating was a whirlwind and they all had to move calmly and quietly into the dining room to serve the courses, refill glasses, make more drinks, and get out of the way of the conversations and plans for next year. As they were setting plates down, hands slid up their thighs, occasionally slipping between their pussy lips to delve inside them. Fingers pinched their asses or tweaked a nipple. Each course ended with half the girls flushed as they stepped back into the kitchen, and they all tried to grab some food from the cooks. Dinner took a little over two hours before dessert was finished and the guests were enjoying drinks around the table. All the girls had gathered back in the kitchen and Alec brought out a tray of shot glasses from the industrial fridge filled about halfway with clear liquid.

Oblivion.

"Alright ladies, it's time." He lifted a glass for himself off the tray, and a larger one that was filled to the brim. He handed the full one across the cooking island to Fae, and all of the other girls grabbed a glass and held it. Almost everyone's cheeks were already flushed from the doses they had received and this final dose would push them all over the edge for the party. Alec lifted his glass up in the air. "To an easy night, and may the morning come quickly!"

The girls all repeated it, raising their glasses, and then everyone drank. The Oblivion didn't taste like anything, it was like drinking water, but the second it hit the stomach it grew warm like a shot of alcohol. The drug had been designed by someone with intimate knowledge of *special* beings along with two others – Dreamland and Torment. Oblivion was the only one that mortals could tolerate though, and once the slave trade had got their hands on it, it had spread like wild fire. It was a twisted kindness, because it would make anyone feel a little invincible, a little brave, a little wild. At low levels it would make them hot, and the heat would spread out to their limbs and made their mind fuzzy. When they built them up, or when Fae took a dose as large as she'd just drank, it was much stronger. It made you want to laugh, and dance, and after a while it made you want to climb into bed with the nearest option as the heat focused between your thighs and became a pounding need.

"Good luck tonight." Ebere had stepped up right behind Fae, and she snapped her head up from looking into the empty glass, waiting for the heat to wash over her.

"You too, Eb, keep yourself safe." Fae smiled and Ebere gripped her hand.

"How about you focus on keeping yourself safe tonight, eh?" She grinned before letting go and turning around to face Butler who had stepped back into the kitchen. Just as he clapped his hands together and held the door open for them, heat blossomed in Fae's belly and spiraled up her back.

It was time for the party.

CHAPTER SIX

Ráj Manor, Caledon, Ontario

Walking across the cold tile of the foyer felt good on Fae's feet. Her skin was flushed from the Oblivion and the heat made her contemplate what laying down in the foot of snow outside would feel like. There was music coming from the closed doors to the parlor, mostly instrumental with a heavy bass line that could be felt through the floor. As the group of slaves got closer to the doors, Butler opened one side and hypnotic wordless vocals could be heard intermingled with the music.

The parlor was a huge room with a wall of windows along the front of the house, and fire reflected in the windows from the large fireplace. It was all dark wood and expensive leather chairs and couches. Thick curtains hung by the windows, but they were pulled away so that the snow could be seen outside. Most of the guests had removed their jackets and were lounging around the room in their button-downs. Some had already rolled their sleeves up to adjust to the warmth of the room, but for those high on Oblivion the heat was dizzying. Fae's blood flushed in her cheeks as the guests turned like wolves catching the scent of sheep.

She took deep, steadying breaths to try and counter the early effects of the Oblivion. Her skin was breaking out in a sheen of sweat, her pulse was pounding just under her skin, and even the brush of the dress against her body had her tingling like static rushing over her.

Dim lamps had been placed around the room, but they allowed for plenty of dark corners. The pool table in one corner was being set up for a game and cigars were being passed out to the guests.

Caridee found her favorite place behind the bar in the corner, swaying to the beat as the Oblivion took its hold. She was already leaning across the bar to smile at the guest in front of her before she made his drink. The best way to get the night over was to dive in, so Fae walked forward until one of the men at the pool table waved her over. She let the false smile slip over her lips, letting her hips roll as she walked towards him.

"Hello." She tilted her head as she stopped next to him. He tucked a strand of her hair behind her ear and smiled. He was a larger man with curly dark hair and Fae didn't resist the urge to return the favor, reaching forward to run her hand through his hair. The brief contact was already sending static-like tingles across her skin.

"Want to help us play?" he asked and Fae smiled. "I'll take that smile as a yes. Rack it up!"

Fae grabbed a pool cue and watched as the other man set up the game. For a moment she considered breaking the cue and killing the four men standing around the table, way before Nikola could stop her with a direct command. It would be exhilarating to do it, to feel the rush of battle again, but it would be a short-lived victory followed by so much pain – and it was the exact opposite of what Ebere had asked her to do. So, Fae pushed the temptation away and she soon found herself swaying to the beat in the music, humming along to the melody. The curly haired man snaked his arm around her waist and the Oblivion made it so the touch sent a flush through her skin, overriding her normal instinct to pull away. He spoke softly, "What's your name?"

"Fae, sir," she replied with a bit of a slur to her words, and it made her laugh.

He grinned and ran his thumb across her cheek. "I like how you look when you laugh. You're beautiful." His touch was too gentle, and his words were too kind. Her stomach twisted as his hand ran down her back, and she lifted the pool cue in her hands. The Oblivion hadn't progressed enough yet, and she wanted to put him off until the drug was raging in her system.

"Mind if I play?" she asked. He stepped back from her and gestured towards the table with a grin watching as she leaned over to line up a shot. He didn't seem to mind after several rounds of play that Fae was beating him badly, he was drinking glasses of brandy and making sure he got the best view whenever she bent over to hit the cue ball. After she missed a shot she laughed and stepped back to let him play.

"I was beginning to think you were going to clear the table. Glad I didn't put money down on this game." He winked at her as he lined up a shot, and she grinned at him. Then Caridee made her jump when she appeared next to her with a glass of wine held out.

Fae arched an eyebrow at the girl who had never been her biggest fan, but Caridee sighed. "It'll make it all the more fuzzy, and who doesn't love wine? What other time do you get to drink some?" Caridee hissed and pushed the glass into her hand. It was a deep red and with one taste she knew it was expensive. When Fae took a sip Caridee smiled at her and danced her way back to the bar. It made Fae grin that it was Nikola's wine and he couldn't keep her from drinking it tonight without causing a scene, and it seemed to be an olive branch from Caridee. Maybe they could be friends too, or at least friendlier than they had been.

"I am definitely not as good as you are with a cue." The man's hands returned and rested on her hips as his lips moved against her neck. She rolled her eyes at the double entendre, but she was focused on checking on the girls around the room. Everyone seemed fine because the guests were playing nice - for now.

A thin thread of panic rose up inside her as the guy pulled her back to a chair and into his lap, but finishing the glass of wine burned it away and she settled against him.

"I'm Andrew, by the way," he whispered in her ear. She really didn't care about his name, or about him in general, but she smiled anyway and set the wine glass on the floor by the chair. Of the choices in the room for the night, he seemed nice.

"Hi, Andrew." She looked into his eyes, a soft brown that were watery from how much he'd had to drink. He traced his thumb over her bottom lip and then gently kissed her, the sweet taste of brandy lingering on his lips as she kissed him back. Even with the Oblivion in her system there was no heat to the kiss, but her body responded.

Her pussy clenched as he pulled her tighter against him, and she contemplated straddling him to get a little friction to feed the liquid heat growing inside her. His hand trailed down her arm until his fingertips were resting inside the bands of light, and he suddenly broke the kiss and looked down at the skin of her wrist where the bands glowed.

"It's weird, I can actually feel this humming in my fingers. Do you feel that?" he asked with boyish excitement, and she smiled even though it was an incredibly stupid question since the bands were *on* her wrists.

"Yes, I feel it." She watched as he was mesmerized by the light suspended in a wide band around her wrist, moving his fingertips in and out of the light. "Are they always there?"

"Only when Master is near, or if he gives me a command," Fae answered and his hand stilled and he looked away from her, taking another drink from his glass. Drinking wasn't going to suddenly make it okay that he had accepted Nikola's invitation, or that he had tracked down one of the two non-mortals in the house. No matter what he felt, his curiosity would likely get the best of him and overrule any moral ideas he thought he had – this guy wasn't a knight in shining armor.

"I'm sor-" Andrew looked penitent, but his eyes were still staring at her lips when there was a harsh tap on her shoulder and Fae turned to find Irena with her violet eyes wide. Fae knew that look, and knew that Irena was moments from an all-out scene.

Fae turned back to Andrew with a smile. "Let me get you a drink refill?"

He gave a lopsided smile and handed her his glass, sighing as Fae slipped off his lap to talk to Irena. Moving towards the nearest corner Irena gripped Fae's arm tightly, her pupils were dilated from the Oblivion, and her pale blue skin was coated in sweat.

"Fae, you need to do something, I know you can do something." Irena was out of it, the Oblivion was a big dose for a tiny pixie and she was babbling and talking fast. "Alec said – Alec, he said that he heard Juliet fighting them in the guards' quarters. He said he could hear her screaming!"

Way to be helpful, Alec, like Irena needed to know that.

"What do you want me to do, Irena?" Fae was trying to think straight through her own mental haze. It's not like she could just walk out of the parlor and grab Juliet from the guards with a 'please and thank you'.

"Please, Fae. Help her? You're much stronger than her, I know you can do it. Promise me, promise me you'll help, promise you'll keep her safe." Irena was out of her mind, and definitely not thinking straight, but she was begging and people were starting to stare. It was the inverse of what Ebere had pleaded with her over that morning. Fae tried to take a steadying breath, tried to push back the heat inside her, and tried to *think*.

Her head felt like it was full of cotton, and Irena's panicked whimpering was too distracting. Others were looking, and soon Butler or Nikola would notice and that would be worse.

"Listen, I'll do what I can. I'll do something." *Sure. Something.* "But you have to stay safe, don't do anything stupid." Fae whispered and Irena nodded, and her bottom lip quivered like she was about to cry. Fae shook her head. "Go on, I promise it will be okay."

It was foolish to promise something she couldn't guarantee, but she couldn't say no to Irena. She hadn't been able to ignore the pixie in the Suyhay Market, and it had been a futile effort to try since.

Turning away, Fae headed to the bar to get more brandy for Andrew. Why couldn't tonight have gone smoothly? Everything would have worked out fine if Nikola hadn't sent Juliet to the guards. The guilt at betraying Ebere's tentative friendship on the very day she'd told the girl she'd try to do better was gnawing at her, turning her stomach. Even worse, she really had no idea what to do.

Fae asked Caridee for more brandy, and as she was

waiting her eyes landed on a large glass decanter of wine on the bar top. When they had told her not to do anything stupid, they had probably meant exactly what she was thinking. Which is exactly why it would probably work.

Fuck it.

"Here goes nothing..." Fae whispered to herself.

Taking the brandy from Caridee in one hand she grabbed the decanter by its narrow neck with the other. Turning to walk back to Andrew she watched him smile at her from across the room. He seemed so nice, he would have made the evening easy, but she had to try and keep at least one promise tonight. *Sorry, Ebere.*

She smiled back at Andrew before tripping herself against a thick carpet on the floor. The glass decanter slammed into the ground and shattered into slivers of glass, the dark red of the wine seeping into the carpet. That was probably a very expensive 'accident' because the carpet likely wouldn't recover. It took a second for Fae to realize that the sharp pain in her hand was a sliver of the glass. She sat up and pressed on the edge of the cut so she could pull the glass out, hissing as it slid from her skin.

The music was still playing, but other than a few random giggles from the girls around the room it had gone eerily quiet.

Fae gasped as her hair was suddenly wrenched up and back, and she brought her hands up to ease the pull as she met Nikola's eyes. His face was calm but his eyes were furious, and Fae's stomach dropped to her toes. *Shit.* The group finally reacted and several of the men cheered, calling out to Nikola in their drunken excitement at the show that was about to commence.

"Nikola! Look at your rug!" One of the guests sitting on a couch, with Mei-Li in his lap, was laughing loudly. "What are you going to do about that?"

"I'm sure Nikola knows how to keep these girls in line. Don't you Nikola?" another of them called out and he was cheered on by a few others. They were Romans calling for blood. *Entertainment.* His fist tightened in her hair and she lifted herself onto her toes trying to relax his hold. The men were laughing and hooting, their cries filling her ears. Nikola pushed her forward and she stepped onto a piece of glass and screamed at the sudden pain.

He leaned his head down by her ear and spoke quietly through his teeth. "I told you not to embarrass me, Fae, and if you thought this little incident was going to get you to Juliet you were *wrong.*" She was standing on her left foot, barely on her toes on her right to avoid pressing the glass in further, as his grip in her hair made her wobble. The comments and suggestions from the guests were growing into a loud roar, and then Andrew's face came into view in front of Nikola.

He spoke quietly so the other guests couldn't hear. "Hey, Nikola, I'm sorry, that's my fault. I asked her for the wine. I should have guessed she was too drunk to carry it all."

Oh, Andrew, you're not helping.

Nikola pulled Fae's head back towards him, which shifted her more off balance and she whimpered at the strain.

"Don't let her fool you, Andrew. Gods don't make their pets clumsy." He pulled her back further and her right foot came down, pressing the glass in sharply. She yelped and he spoke directly into her ear, "Isn't that right?"

Fae clenched her jaw against the urge to respond, or beg, or scream. There was a cheer from the guests and random applause, and Andrew was still trying to talk but he couldn't be heard over the group and Nikola wasn't listening anyway. Nikola pulled Fae to the side again and she stumbled trying to keep her foot up. He moved her to the middle of the ruined rug and raised his voice so everyone could hear him as he issued the command. "Down."

The bands on Fae's wrists lit up brightly and she cried out as the pain shot up her arms and her knees hit the floor in response. Nikola finally let go of her hair and stood next to her. The relief at not being on her foot was short as an old oak chair with slats on the back was placed in front of her. Butler was leaning on the chair, grinning, and the fact that he actually looked *happy* made Fae sick. *What did they have planned?*

"Give me your hands, slut." He leaned over the back and pulled Fae's arms through the slats, zip-tying her wrists together before she had the chance to decide if she wanted to fight. Panic seeped in under the haze of the Oblivion, and she pulled her arms back hard against the slats. It just served to hurt her wrists, and she let out a little frustrated scream that she'd been so stupid. She jerked back again, but Nikola pressed her arms down against the seat of the chair and shook his head, a silent command not to even try and break the plastic strips. He stepped back from the chair and Butler turned to the group of guests. Fae's eyes tracked him as he raised his arms to the sound of their hollering cheers – and unwound a whip.

"No!" Irena screamed from across the room, "Don't! Don't, please -"

"Stop, Irena!" Fae shouted at her and stared at her wrists through the slats. The last thing Fae needed was for Irena to get in trouble too. *Just one more time to be a failed shield.* She was glad she couldn't see Ebere from where she was. Fae's heart was pounding against her ribs and her stomach churned when Butler stepped behind her.

The whip cracked overhead and she jumped, which brought cheers and laughs from the guests. Gritting her teeth she tried to slow her heart rate down to prepare for the first actual blow. Then Butler walked up behind her and Fae felt the chill of a knife against her skin just before she heard the fabric of her dress rip down the back.

"I told you I'd make you regret it if you did anything, and I am going to enjoy this so much. Feel free to scream for me." He brushed the whip across her back before he stepped away from her, and Fae tried to shut out his words. She was trying to breathe, and trying to think through the haze of Oblivion to remember what it felt like to get whipped. It had been years, and all she could remember was that it was a sharp pain, and that it hurt. A lot.

There was a loud cheer a second before a line of vicious fire went down her back. Fae caught the scream in her mouth and bit down to swallow it and tears pricked her eyes.

Okay, so it did more than hurt.

The pain didn't really fade, but spread out from the thin line it was at first. The cheers got louder and a second line of fire criss-crossed with the first. Fae jerked forward against the chair, but she kept the cry quiet through tightly closed lips. She clenched her fists on the other side of the slats, her one palm slick with blood, and put her forehead down against the seat. The cheers were a constant, bloodthirsty roar. Somewhere between the third and fifth strikes, Fae found herself crying out into the cushion of the seat. Her back was a web of searing pain and the ache spread all over her ribcage, making her bow away from the lash and lift herself off the chair. He paused until she returned to position, and she bit her tongue to keep from begging.

Butler began again and Fae started seeing spots behind her eyes. She was hoping she'd pass out soon but eight, nine, and then ten came and she was still conscious. The twelfth lash landed and it somehow hurt worse than before and she screamed into her arm, hiding her face from the room so she couldn't see the rabid looks of the guests as they roared out their encouragement.

"Enough." Nikola's voice was a boom to her right, and her

ears were ringing from the pain. She felt a hand run down her back and it burned so much her muscles locked up. Butler lifted her head with one hand and showed her his palm, a bright red streak of blood painted across it.

"That's mine," she whispered and Butler laughed. Fae was delirious from the Oblivion, and the pain, and the exhaustion creeping up on her as the adrenaline fled. The words had slipped from her lips more out of surprise that he had actually whipped her hard enough to bleed, but her brain wouldn't get into gear. Her body just wanted to shut down, the heat in her skin making her nauseous now as the pain throbbed with the beat of her pulse. She felt her hands cut free and she slid to the floor next to the chair hoping she'd pass out soon.

Feet crowded around her, the chair was pulled away and she tried to curl in a ball. Instead of leaving her on the floor, someone hoisted her up into their arms, and she screamed weakly when their arms rubbed against her back. She opened her eyes, but couldn't see the man's face as he had turned away, then she heard Butler speak with laughter in his voice.

"You sure you want her? She's going to ruin your bed."

Above her there was a laugh, and a muffled, "Yes, I'm sure." The words sounded far away, and then pain pierced her as the man adjusted her in his arms. Her whimper was ignored, and then she felt them moving, saw the glittering lights of the chandelier grow closer as they moved up the staircase. Fae tried to sit up, but the arms just shifted her back towards the chest she was against and her back argued at the movements. A few more steps and she was in a dark room, being dropped onto the bed. She gasped at the pain from the lashes, and then the door slammed shut and the figure of the guest moved towards her.

Fae propped herself on her elbows and almost opened her mouth to beg. If she'd just listened to Ebere, it wouldn't have happened. The pain would remind her of that. It would make her remember, and with the way her head was swimming she wouldn't be conscious long anyway.

CHAPTER SEVEN

Ráj Manor, Caledon, Ontario

Fae had been awake longer than she'd hoped, but when dawn came she took a deep breath and took in the scent of clean rain and earth that meant Eltera was with her. Her eyes opened to a soft golden glow coming from her skin and she could feel the tingling warmth of her skin knitting itself back together.

"Eltera?" Fae whispered out into the darkness of the room and sat up. It felt like Eltera was just out of sight, that if she turned her head she'd catch her standing next to her, her warm hands on Fae's back healing her. Looking down she felt the tingle move across her hand and underneath the dried blood that filled her palm she knew the skin was whole again. Lifting her right foot, she watched as a shard of glass was pushed out, and the skin knit back together behind it. Wrapping her arms around herself Fae leaned forward, trying to hold on to Eltera's scent, the feeling of her presence as every inch of her was renewed underneath the evidence of her punishment.

Fae took another breath but the scent of rain was already fading, replaced by a copper tang. The pale glow still coming from her skin revealed the dried blood from where she had slept. The guest in the bed rolled over and she pushed away the flashes of memory of him on top of her. Andrew had been brave enough to try and talk Nikola down from punishing her, but once the damage was done he hadn't been brave enough to pick her up off the floor.

So much for his knighthood.

Her skin was itchy where the blood had dried and all she wanted was a shower. Grabbing the blanket at the foot of the bed, Fae wrapped it around herself and slipped silently out into the hall.

By the time she was halfway to the female quarters the glow of her skin had faded completely. Alone again, without Eltera. Turning the corner into their hall she saw the guard sitting in a chair by their door. He grinned as she approached but opened the door without a word. She wasn't in the mood to fight with anyone so she simply ignored his obvious glee and walked inside, heading directly to the showers. When she dropped the blanket to the floor someone gasped behind her and Fae flinched. All she wanted to do was get under the hot water and forget.

Yeah, as if she ever forgot anything.

"Oh, Fae..." Mei-Li was standing in the doorway with her mouth open. "There's so much blood." Fae didn't know how to respond, didn't know what she wanted from her, so she just stepped into the showers, turned one on, and moved under it before it was warm.

The icy water at her feet turned red as it started washing it all away, and she clenched her teeth hard to keep them from chattering. Mei-Li's dark eyes were still staring from the entrance to the showers, her pin-straight black hair twisted up into a knot on the top of her head. Her petite features pinched with concern as she spoke, "Are you okay?"

"Of course I am. It's all healed." The water had turned a pink color as Fae scrubbed her skin, the blood was under her nails though and that was harder to get clean. She pried the crystals out of her hair and dropped them to the floor of the shower, not wanting to look at them.

"I know that, but I still want to know if *you* are okay." Mei-Li crossed her arms and waited. She was a tiny thing from China but she had steel in her spine and wouldn't back down. Most people didn't realize that the smallest of them was one of the strongest, and Fae respected that in her, but it didn't mean she wanted to talk things out.

"You tell me, are *you* okay after last night?" Fae asked and finally turned to look at her.

Mei-Li shrugged one delicate shoulder. "I'm hungover from the Oblivion. Last night wasn't easy, but I'll survive like I always do."

Fae huffed out a breath and rinsed her hair one more

time to check that the water was clear before flipping it off. She couldn't help but give a hint of a smile as she stepped by Mei-Li to grab a towel. The girl was strong.

"Same here, Mei, I'll survive like I always do." Fae spoke as she stepped up to the long counter. At her comment Mei-Li shook her head and hopped up onto the bathroom counter.

"It's weird to see your back look so normal after... that. The last time I saw someone use a whip it took more than a month for the girl to heal."

"Good thing I'm not normal." Fae pulled a green dress over her head to cover up her back, and grabbed a fresh towel to continue drying her hair. Mei-Li made a noise in her throat and then leaned back against the mirror to watch her. Part of Fae wanted to reach out to her, to show her she was willing to be her friend, to try and recapture the feeling she'd had talking to Ebere – but there was just too much weighing her down from the night before. Mei-Li seemed stuck in her own head anyway, and it was an easy silence after a few minutes.

Fae had started drying her hair when she heard a few of the girls yelling in the main room, and Mei-Li snapped to attention as well, her dark eyes going wide. Turning off the dryer they both hurried into the central area to see the girls crowding around something on the floor. Above the din of voices she could hear Irena's high pitched voice saying Juliet's name over and over.

Oh no.

No, no, no, no.

Caridee turned around from the edge of the group, her hair was a mess and her eye makeup had smeared into raccoon eyes. "Can you help her?" Caridee shifted to the side and grabbed the girl's shoulder in front of her to clear a path to Juliet who was lying on the floor covered in a thin blanket from one of their cots. Fae knelt down next to her and felt for a pulse, it was faint but still there. There were bruises *everywhere*, and her lip was split. Something inside Fae twisted with the dark thought that her own actions might have made it worse for the girl. Nikola had probably told the guards to hurt Juliet, told them to do it to make a point, but he couldn't have wanted *this*.

"Why isn't she awake? They just – they just came in here and dropped her, but she won't wake up." Irena's words came between sobs, her violet eyes desperate for Fae to give her some kind of answer.

"I don't know." Fae ran her fingers along Juliet's scalp, but she couldn't feel any cuts or bumps. She sighed, "I don't feel a head injury." Turning Juliet's face towards her, she patted her cheek and repeated her name a few times. The girl's blonde hair was greasy, and her face was a little swollen with bruises. Shifting the blanket to the side Fae could see that there was a wide dark bruise in her midsection. Fae pushed on it gently and Juliet groaned and Fae sat back and covered her up again. "I think the injury is inside. They might have hit or kicked her, broken a rib and punctured something. Fuck, I'm not a doctor, Irena, I can't fix it. They need to call someone." Irena broke into sobs again and Ebere started rubbing her back. Fae was worried she would see judgment or irritation in Ebere's face, but there wasn't any of that. The girl looked concerned – for Juliet, for her, for all of them.

"I'm so sorry, Fae, I'm so sorry for last night. I just didn't want her to get hurt, and she's hurt anyway, and Butler hurt you too, he hurt you so much -" Irena couldn't catch her breath between the crying anymore and gave up on trying to talk.

Fae looked up, trying to figure out what they could do, when she saw Lena standing at the door; the woman's face was pale as she stared at Juliet on the floor. With a quick squeeze to Irena's shoulder she stood up and moved out of the group towards Lena.

Locking eyes with the matron of their little group, Fae grabbed her arm and dug her fingers in as she hissed under her breath. "Do you see what they did? Is *this* what you think Nikola wanted?" Lena's face soured at the use of Nikola's name, but Fae continued without correcting herself. "Someone needs to go to him and tell him that Juliet needs the doctor. No matter what, he's not going to want to lose one of us."

"You think *I* should do it?" Lena looked shocked, then her eyes moved down to where Fae held her arm and she pulled it away. "I'm not going to demand *anything* of Master. He will make the appropriate decision. This is his house."

"And what if he doesn't *know*, Lena? You'd let her fucking die because you don't want to bother him during breakfast?" Fae asked with disgust in her voice and Lena glared before turning on her heel and storming away from her. She cursed under her breath and grabbed her hair as she looked back at the girls all crowded around the small form of Juliet. She had planned on keeping a low profile for the next few weeks, letting Nikola and Butler forget about their frustrations with her. She'd wanted to actually *try* and take care of herself, but it looked like that wasn't going to be possible. Fae turned to the doors and knocked loudly, and the girls all looked up at her as the guard opened the door.

"What do you want?" The guard at the door sneered.

"We need the doctor for Juliet. I need to speak to Master so he can call." Fae said it with more confidence than she felt at the moment, but there was no way she'd trust the guards to deliver the message themselves. They'd be much more concerned about keeping it from Nikola than admitting what they'd done.

The guard glanced over Fae's shoulder and smiled. "I'm sure she's just fine. We weren't too rough."

Fae clenched her fists to resist the urge to drop him and crush his throat. She had to take a breath and remember that attacking him would just keep the doctor away longer. Swallowing her anger and her pride, she spoke as calmly as she could. "Please, sir, may I speak to Master?"

"That would be up to Butler, sweetheart." The guard was trying to get under her skin on purpose, but Fae just gritted her teeth and dug her nails into her palms.

"Then may I *please* speak with Butler, sir?"

"Maybe. After last night I think Butler will be happy you

want to spend some more time with him. I'll go tell him you miss him." The man grinned and Fae wanted to hit him and break bone, and then keep hitting him for Juliet, but she forced herself to nod and step back so the guard could shut the door. The girls behind her were quiet for a moment, but Sobeska finally spoke up.

"Fae... what *exactly* are you going to do?"

"I'm going to offer Nikola what he wants if he'll get the doctor for Juliet."

"Which is?" Sobeska asked.

"My obedience." No one responded to that. They could all think of a hundred times Fae had done something to be defiant, and it was clear Nikola wouldn't take it from her anymore. He'd used Butler to make that point loud and clear.

Everyone sat quietly around Juliet while they waited for Butler to arrive, and each minute that passed had Fae more on edge with concern. Irena was trying to comb Juliet's hair with her fingers, and a few times Juliet groaned, but she stayed asleep – which under the circumstances was probably best. When the door finally opened everyone jumped. Butler was standing in the doorway and his eyes locked onto Fae immediately.

"Come outside, Fae." He snapped his fingers, and Ebere grabbed Irena to make her stay seated when she started to stand. Fae nodded at Ebere in thanks, and held a hand out to Irena to make sure she stayed. Walking out the door she found herself in the middle of two guards and Butler. "You asked for me?" Butler crossed his arms and didn't hide the self-satisfied smirk on his face as the door to their quarters shut.

"Juliet needs the doctor. I just need to talk to Master, sir." Fae tried to speak as respectfully as she could manage.

Butler grabbed Fae's hand and looked at her palm, running his thumb across where the glass had cut it. "All better I see." Fae tried to tug her hand back but Butler tightened his grip and twisted her hand to the side, which sent a shock of pain up her arm. Butler tilted his head watching Fae's face change as she fought to suppress her reaction. "Why would I want to take you to Nikola this early in the morning?"

"He'll want to know how bad she is, he needs to call the doctor, sir. If you don't want me to go, *you* ask him." She growled the words out and Butler twisted her wrist harder making her bite back the cry.

"Don't tell me what to do, whore." He bent her wrist a little farther and for a second she thought he might actually break it, but then he let go. She clenched her jaw so she wouldn't respond hastily again, after all, she still needed his help. "Are you sure you want Nikola to see you again this quickly? He might ask me to give you another *lesson*." The idea made her nervous and sick, but there wasn't much of a choice.

"Yes, sir. I'm sure." Fae cradled her wrist against her chest, keeping herself calm by focusing on her breathing, and trying her best to ignore his comments. When she looked up at him, Butler made her stomach lurch with the way he looked at her.

"Alright then, since you're sure, let's go." He turned on his heel and Fae followed. One of the guards remained behind at the door but the other guard followed her. They moved down the stairs and ended up with Butler standing in front of the doors to the parlor. Fae's heart was racing at the mere idea of walking back in that room, especially with *him*, and Butler could see her discomfort so he just stood by the door waiting. "Anytime you're ready, Fae. Unless you want to go back upstairs?"

Fae glared at him and stepped toward the door. He knocked on it and from inside came Nikola's voice telling him to come in. When Butler opened the door he went directly to Nikola and leaned closed to whisper to him. Fae slipped inside the door and stood at the entry, noticing that the room had not been cleaned yet. The remnants of the decanter were still on the rug, catching the firelight and twinkling against the dark weave. The heavy oak chair was still sitting to the side and Fae's heart rate increased even further looking at it. Nikola's eyes finally lifted to hers, and his face was unreadable as he nodded to Butler.

"Kneel here." Nikola pointed at the floor in front of the fireplace. He had been sitting in one of the chairs facing the fire, which had been renewed at some point in the night because it was still blazing. Fae's bands lit up brightly in response, but she walked over and knelt without argument. "So you're concerned about Juliet?"

He sat on the arm of one of the chairs and looked at her, and she dropped her head down to stare at the pattern in the carpet. Butler's presence to her right made her want to shudder. Her mouth always got her into trouble, so Fae stayed silent and just nodded, because making him mad at this point wasn't going to help. His voice gave nothing away, and it left her unsure of how to react.

There wasn't a hint of concern, or irritation, or lingering anger from the night before as he spoke. "Alright, explain why."

"Yes, Master. Thank you, Master." She swallowed. "Juliet is hurt. Badly. I think she could be bleeding internally. We need the doctor here to help her." She peeked up through her hair and watched as Nikola looked over at Butler. Nikola spoke quietly to him as he stepped up, and then Butler left the room. When he turned back he clasped his hands together.

"You know, Fae, you revealed something interesting to me yesterday." A chill went down Fae's spine and she looked up at him. "You don't seem to care what I do to you, after all you're perfectly fine today. Yesterday's pain seems to already be forgotten as you come to me and tell me what I need to do about the property in my house."

"Master, that's not -" She started to argue, but he raised a hand to stop her.

"You may not care about yourself, however you seem to be *very* concerned about what happens to the other girls in this house. You even chose to be the one to come to me this morning, which just puts you at risk again."

"Master, I swear to you, if you will just help Juliet I will be perfect from now on, for as long as you will have me in your house you will never have trouble from me. I will do *anything* you ask of me." Nikola chuckled at her pleas and it made Fae feel cold inside.

"You clearly don't understand our relationship. You will obey me because you have to, and I will continue to do whatever I see fit with *my* property." The door opened and Butler came in carrying Juliet. He walked past Fae and laid her down in front of Nikola on the brick before the fireplace. Nikola nodded to Butler and continued with a cold smile. "From now on, if you choose to disobey me, in any way, I'll pick one of the girls to take whatever punishment I would consider for you. At the same rate I would have it delivered to you."

Fae didn't know how to respond. Her mind was racing with the possibilities, the damage that her behavior could do to the girls she wanted to help – but as long as she was *perfectly* obedient they should still be okay. She could swallow her pride and submit for the next twenty or thirty years, however long he wanted to keep her around. She could obey. She could do that for them. "Yes, Master. I understand and I *will* obey you. I swear it."

Nikola gestured to Butler who turned and left the room, shutting the doors behind him. Hopefully he was being sent for the doctor. Relief started to move through her because Juliet was still unconscious and didn't look any better. The sooner the doctor came, the better.

"I know you will, Fae." His words pulled her eyes back to him, and she watched as Nikola walked over to a desk in the corner and pulled open a drawer. He took something out and then walked back over to the fireplace with his back to Fae. "I know for sure you're going to obey me, because I'm going to make you understand just how serious I am." When he turned around he was holding a sleek black handgun, and he stepped forward next to Juliet and aimed it down at her head. Everything inside Fae snapped to attention, panic hitting her like a tidal wave.

"No, Master!" Fae screamed. Her instinct to stand up and get to Juliet was shut down by the bands on her wrists that sent pain up her arms as soon as she tried to defy the command he'd delivered. She was stuck where she was, unable to move closer to protect her. All she could do was plead with him from afar. "*Please*, Master, please don't hurt her. I swear, I swear I'll do whatever you ask. I'll serve every guest you bring without argument. I'll do anything to make you happy with me, just please don't hurt her!"

Nikola didn't even look at Fae, even when she started begging, repeating '*no*' over and over, louder and louder. His body shifted right before the ear shattering pop of the gun going off made Fae jump and cover her ears. When she looked again she could see blood pooling under Juliet, dark and shining in the firelight as it spread slowly.

It was unreal for a moment, an impossible reality that he had killed one of his own slaves, but it was true. It was true, and as the idea settled deep inside her – she screamed. A long wail that ripped at her throat.

She'd broken her promise to Ebere by taking action, then broken her promise to Irena when she'd failed to protect Juliet. And now her defiance had led to this, and the realization that it was her fault hurt. It hurt more than the curse coiling its vicious tongue through her body as she tried to move forward again and the bands lit up. The pain arced across her back forcing another cry out of her that turned into a scream. The emptiness in her chest was a hole. Juliet was dead because Nikola had wanted to hurt *her*, and he had. All of her pain and frustration and rage at herself came out in an unending scream as Nikola stepped back from the body, brushing at the fine spray of blood across his shirt.

"*Why*, why would you do that? I swore I would obey. I promised!" Her breath caught in her chest when the pain in her bands increased, and she leaned forward onto the floor trying to fight through it. She choked on a sob and screamed at him, "WHAT DID YOU WANT FROM ME?!"

Nikola was calmly ignoring her as he turned to set the gun on the mantle when a wind suddenly ripped through the room, sending papers flying and causing the fire to hiss and crackle. He looked up to check the windows just in time to see them explode outwards. Fae gasped, the wind became a howl in its ferocity, and then she looked down to see her skin glowing a soft gold.

What the-?

The bands were so bright they were casting a shadow behind her, and she swallowed the next sob and turned to glare at Nikola again. Bracing her hands against the floor she tried to stand once more, but the pain made her collapse as her bones felt like they were cracking under the strain of her effort.

"Stop, Fae. Whatever you're doing, stop *immediately*." His will was in the command, but as the room shook and the wind howled, pulling at the curtains against the walls, she didn't care. She tried to lift one knee, to get her foot on the floor so she could push herself up through the pain, and Nikola's eyes widened in fear. It was too intense to even scream, her lungs were empty, and her head was dizzy from the effort. Fae looked up at him as he lifted the gun to point it at her, and she wanted to laugh. She still couldn't believe he had shot Juliet, and if she could only speak through the pain she'd tell him to go ahead and try to shoot her. Maybe it would kill her.

"I never should have wasted the money on you." He growled the words, and his other hand came up to steady the gun. He was actually going to shoot her. He narrowed his eyes and she prepared herself, but instead of a gunshot the flames behind him leaped high and bowed out of the fireplace like crashing waves. They paused for a moment in the air as Nikola turned to look at the fire, and his mouth opened in shock just as the waves collapsed and surrounded him.

Nikola started screaming and Fae finally stopped trying to stand. His body was engulfed, a twisted shadow inside the fire as he went quiet, and then he stumbled backward into the wall, which caught fire. The fire wasn't fading at all, it seemed to cling to him like a horrifying aura that Fae couldn't tear her eyes from, and then his body tumbled forward slowly before falling behind the chair.

Suddenly, the bands on her wrists disappeared and the pain stopped like a switch had been flipped, leaving her dizzy for a moment in relief. A buzzing euphoria at the absence of it made her bend over her knees as she caught her breath.

Nikola was dead, and Fae was free.

The fire was already spreading up the chair, and across one of the carpets. Fae could feel the wet of the tears on her cheeks as she crawled across the carpet to touch Juliet's neck. No pulse. Of course there was no pulse. Fae choked out a sob. "This wasn't how it was supposed to be. This wasn't meant to happen, Juliet."

She was supposed to fix it, to make everything okay so they were safe. So they were all safe.

There was a loud banging coming from the doors, and when Fae looked over at them she could see the edges of the doors glowing a soft gold. From the other side was Butler's voice yelling to break the doors down.

Run.

The word echoed inside her, and she stifled the sobs in her chest, locking the guilt away so she could think. Fae gave Juliet one more glance before she stood up. The fire was spreading up the wall, roaring against the ceiling and Fae backed away from it. There was no way to get to Irena or any of the girls, not from this room. The only way out for her now was through the windows. Running over to them she hopped up onto the windowsill and slipped out the window.

She gasped as her bare legs went through a foot of snow that had built up against the house. Pushing through the bushes that scratched at her arms she tumbled out onto the front lawn. Although the cold was painful she had to hurry, they'd be through the doors soon, or someone would see her out front. Moving across the snow covered turf she started to run as best she could, pulling her legs high out of the snow. Her breaths were puffing out in clouds around her, and she couldn't really feel her feet anymore, or her hands. The realization was far away though, she just had to run, to get as far from those girls as she could so no one would get hurt because of her again.

That was the greatest gift she could give them.

Juliet was dead, but Nikola was dead too. If she were there they'd only use the other girls to punish her, and she couldn't handle that on her conscience. She couldn't have another of their deaths to remember.

CHAPTER EIGHT

Rannoch Moor, Scotland

The roar of laughter slowed down and Cole picked up his story again, "So there's Kiernan, waist deep in the river getting his grooming routine on, and this beauty comes walking along the other side of the river." Cole planted his foot on the ribcage of the massive tiger that spanned the length of one of the tables, and one of the guys shook Kiernan's shoulders while laughing loudly in his ear. "So we hear Kiernan whispering at us, '*Hey! Guys! There's a tiger!*' and I open my eyes to see his ass, *naked*, running around our camp trying to find his bow." Cole scrubbed his face in a dramatic way, "I'll never forget that image in all of my days!"

"Like you looked so hot with your face in the mud? I woke this idiot up half drowning in a puddle! And I put on my fucking pants, Cole." Kiernan shouted over the others, which only renewed the laughter from the group of Laochra who had gathered to see their trophies.

"Yeah, yeah. Anyway, so he grabs his bow and runs back to the bank of the river - and there she is just drinking. She stretches herself out like she *wants* to get shot, just waiting for him. Kiernan pulls back the bow and POW down she goes." More hands reached forward to clap Kiernan on the back and he took a big drink of his beer, which sloshed over as he got bumped again by the crowd. Eryn was sitting on the other side of the table and he stood, the group growing quieter to listen to him.

"She wasn't down for the count though! No way. Kiernan fords across the river, half-swimming and gets to her and she starts hissing and roaring at him, swipes at him with one of those huge claws." Eryn raised his glass in a toast. "And he leans over her and slits her throat with his knife!" A roar of cheers rose up and Eryn's grin split his face, showing his teeth.

His own smile was false, hollow.

It had been a fantastic trip, but Eryn was just as vicious as ever and Kiernan couldn't be a part of the vision Eryn had for the world. He tipped his beer back and finished it, showing the empty mug to the group. Standing up he headed back to refill his drink from a barrel that had been brought out in celebration of their kill. As he stepped away a few of the guys gripped his shoulder, or slapped him on the back and he made himself smile at them. His stomach was turning though, a feeling of dread pooling in his chest as he opened the tap. His arm suddenly burned and he pulled up his sleeve to see the vines progress towards his shoulder. The pitstop at the bar in Virginia on their way back had been enough to move the vines back to his elbow, but not enough to push them back completely.

What the hell was happening?

He headed towards the sleeping areas and hissed as the burn in his skin faded. He couldn't shake the feeling that the vines were a warning, that it was something important, and not just his normal lack of action. Kiernan rubbed the ends of the vines on his arm and tugged his sleeve down as Fae's face popped into his mind. He froze for a moment as her sad smile filled his head and pushed away all thought of the hunt, of the other Laochra waiting to celebrate with him. He just needed to check in on the observation glass and then he could come back. He could come right back, and no one would even notice.

Hopefully.

Focusing on his apartment he felt himself reappear and waited a second until everything came into perspective.

"Alright, what's going on..." he muttered to himself, shaking his head at his sudden paranoia as he moved his desk and flipped open the box holding the glass. He touched the edge of it, thinking of Fae. Light flickered in the glass and then the image came into focus. He saw her walking in the snow, bright sunlight making it sparkle around her like diamonds. He frowned as he tried to squint and saw the thin, sleeveless dress she had on.

Why would she be outside? Half naked? In the middle of winter?

What the fuck had happened?

Sliding his finger counterclockwise around the glass time moved backwards, images flickering until he saw fire fill the glass. He paused a second before moving it back even further to get back to the dinner party he knew had happened over the days he was gone; when he saw the whip he stopped and let it move forward. His heart rate increased as he watched, and he found himself digging his free hand into the desk as anger took him over. He wanted to find the man who had held the whip, the one called Butler, and kill him slowly. Very slowly. Then there was the one who'd picked her up off the floor, bleeding, and taken her to his room to-

Kiernan cursed loudly and forced himself to speed up the time, not having the stomach to watch what he did. Moving forward he finally saw the other young girl die, and then he had *no idea* what he saw inside the glass. The windows blew inward, her master was pointing the gun at her, and then the fire came to life and took Nikola into it. Then Fae was running, out into the snow.

In Canada. In only a dress.

Shit.

When he removed his hand from the edge of the glass it snapped back to real time, only now there were three black clad figures coming towards her in the snow. He slammed the box shut and stepped back focusing on the image of her face.

He felt the frigid air hit him before he recognized he had moved, and when his eyes came into focus he was only a few feet in front of her next to the road, standing shin deep in snow. Fae had one of the men clad in black in some kind of arm hold, and she drove her knee into his stomach hard. Then when he bent over she snapped his arm over her knee. Kiernan could hear the bone break from several feet away and the scream from the guy only confirmed it. Brutally efficient.

"What the hell?!" one of the other guys shouted in a thick accent, and when Kiernan looked over both of the other men were staring wide-eyed at him. Shifting away from the man on the ground Fae kicked the guy with the accent in the chest before turning to look over her shoulder. Her lips parted in surprise and her brow furrowed as she finally saw him – and Kiernan was struck still.

Her eyes were an even paler blue than he thought and her hair was filled with fiery red strands that caught the sunlight. Her cheeks were flushed from the cold, the exertion of the fight, and trudging through the snow. He watched her turn back just in time to see the last man reaching for her and she side-stepped him, knocking his arm away from her. She was more beautiful than he could have ever thought watching her from afar, and watching her move fluidly as she fought, with her breath coming out in clouds in the air around her, was mesmerizing.

"You fucking bitch! You broke my arm! Travis grab her!" The guy with the injured arm had pulled a stun gun out of a pocket in his pants with his good arm, and that finally snapped Kiernan out of his daze. The one called Travis turned to respond but Kiernan caught him in the jaw with a right hook that sent him down into the snow.

What was he doing?

Travis tried to get up and Kiernan leaned down to deliver another two punches, which dazed the man sufficiently to stay down.

"Who the hell is *he*?" The last guy circling Fae pointed at Kiernan, and Fae glanced at him, her brows pulling together again. The injured one with the stun gun lunged for her, but she jumped out of the way. Kiernan took a few steps towards her, ready to step in if the guy went for her with the weapon, but she obviously didn't need his help.

Her arms and legs were bare, and from what he had seen when she had kicked the guy she was barefoot. She was cold, she *had* to be cold because it was very, very cold here.

He needed to fix that.

The guy with the broken arm lunged for her, but Fae had been waiting and smoothly moved to the side, grabbing his vest and shoving him towards the last man. When the stun gun made contact there was a crackle of electricity, the other man yelled and hit the snow and the injured man screamed and grabbed his arm as he landed badly. Before the men could react again, Kiernan rushed forward and placed his hand on her shoulder. He focused back on his apartment, and with one last blast of frigid air he shifted and they were in his living room dripping snow onto the tile.

"What the -" Fae's eyes grew wide as she stumbled back from him, trying to catch her balance against the edge of his couch. She looked around wildly. "How- Who? What the hell just happened? Who - *what* are you?" Fae held a hand out in front of her in an effort to get some space from him, and all the color fled her cheeks. He knew the nausea she felt, it had taken him years to adjust to the instant movement from one place to another.

"Sit down, the effects will fade soon. I just need a minute to think." Kiernan sighed and pushed a hand through his hair, gripping it at the root.

"No. You need to tell me what the *hell* you are and how you got me here." She was still bracing a hand against the couch, but every line of her body was ready to fight. He tried to tear his eyes from her curves, from the very short hem of that dress, and focused on the impossibility of what he'd seen in the glass.

"I can't believe you did that." Kiernan was muttering to himself and suddenly turned around to face her again, raising his voice at her, "How did you even kill Nikola? That shouldn't even be *possible!*"

"How do you even know he's dead?" Fae's voice was serious, and she stood up straighter.

"I watched it happen!" His head spun as he remembered the eerie way the fire had moved, the way she had glowed with the power of the gods. He felt angry all of a sudden, like she'd somehow lied to him all these years. "You've *never* been able to do that before. Moved fire? Blew out those windows? What the fuck, Fae!" Kiernan put his hands in his hair again so he wouldn't grab for her. He started to pace around the edge of his living room. Fae started moving around the front of the couch taking slow steps back from him, and he was somewhat grateful for the additional space between them.

"What do you mean you watched me? How do you even *know* me?" Fae's voice had grown quiet, and he turned to face her, those blue eyes evaluating him in a way that made his cock twitch in his pants.

"Of course I watched you, it's my freaking job, Fae." He laughed as the bitterness of that statement hit home. He growled as he pointed at her. "The other Laochra will *kill* you if they find out you killed your master. Do you have any idea what you've done?"

Fae stilled and Kiernan pushed out a breath of air, his hands clenching in his hair as he tried to *think*. But he couldn't think, because she was here. In front of him. In his freaking apartment. This was so stupid, so very stupid. Suddenly, Fae jumped up on the couch and grabbed one of Kiernan's swords that hung on the wall above it.

"Oh gods." He groaned. For a second Kiernan regretted keeping his weapons sharpened, because this wasn't going to go well. Drawing the sword from the scabbard she stepped off the couch and stomped towards him, he raised his hands, about to try and reason with her when she swung it hard at him. Kiernan barely ducked it before hitting the wall behind him as he threw himself backwards.

"Are you insane?!" Kiernan shouted at her as Fae brought the sword back around. He picked up a small table to block the blow, and the little statue that had been on it shattered on the tile. Fae pressed Kiernan backwards, striking at his legs and his head, each blow he caught with the table. His anger flickered inside him and he yelled again, "Stop it, Fae, stop!"

"You're Laochra?! How dare you *touch* me, how dare you even *speak* to me, you bastard son of Gormahn!" Fae screamed back and surprised him with a hard kick in the stomach before bringing the sword around again. This time Kiernan was slower to block it and it almost cut into his side. Rage flared inside him.

Son of Gormahn? He was no son of Gormahn.

Kiernan stepped back quickly to get some breathing room from her range with the sword. There was a battle axe hung like art inside a black picture frame next to him, and every piece of him demanded he grab it and show her how he could fight. He gripped the hilt, then he imagined himself swinging the wide blade into her ribs and he released it instantly. A wave of nausea hit him, and he barely got the table up in time to block another blow.

"Listen! If I didn't take you from there, those guards would have taken you back to Butler, and you know he would have claimed you. You *know* what he would have done to you." He tried to reason with her as he blocked yet another attack. She was moving the blade incredibly fast and it was wearing him to keep up without a weapon of his own to counter and press her back.

"A Laochra wouldn't care about that!" She kicked for his knee and he barely avoided it.

"Fae, stop! Would you just talk to me?" he pleaded, and Fae responded by bringing the sword down hard in a two-handed swing meant to separate his shoulder, but Kiernan caught it in the butchered legs of the table and it stuck. When Fae tried to pull it back he saw that it wasn't moving and he twisted the table to wrench the sword out of her hands. Once it was free he threw the table and the sword behind him down the hall to his bedroom. "Okay, now st-" Fae spun and caught him in the side with a kick, but he grabbed her foot while it was still up and yanked her forward off balance. Catching her he threw her to the ground and avoided a head-butt as he pinned her.

Fae screamed even louder in frustration, "Get off me, you filthy fucking son of Gormahn!" He grabbed her wrists and slammed them to the tile above her head, bracing his knees on either side of her as she squirmed under him.

"STOP CALLING ME THAT!" He roared in her face, and she spit at him, screaming again.

"You *are* a filthy, disgusting, son of Gormahn! His vile power is inside y –" Kiernan cut her off by grabbing her throat, and she coughed as he tightened his grip. The darkness swelled inside him, a cold power roaring like the rush of the ocean in his ears. Her eyes closed as she tried to twist away from him, but that wasn't possible. She wasn't a match for him. Her body was strong, he could feel that, and he wanted to feel a lot more of it. It wouldn't be difficult, to shift himself and push her thighs apart,. and –

What the fuck was he doing?

Kiernan released her throat and she coughed and sputtered, tears sliding down her temples as she jerked hard against his grip on her wrists. He wanted to let her go, he wanted to get off her and get some space, because the ideas that had crossed his thoughts were –

'*Vile?*' his mind offered, and he was almost sick. Yes, vile, because Gormahn's power *was* inside him, and he was Laochra, and he was tainted - and she... she wasn't.

"Get off me, Laochra!" Even as her voice cracked from the strain of her shouting she glared at him. He could hear her feet slipping on the tile as she tried to get the leverage to knock him off her, but he was too far back on her thighs for her to manage it. He was a little impressed, now that his head was his own again, how she was managing to still be so brave. She stilled suddenly and hissed at him, leaning her head up to meet his eyes, "You, and all your bastard brethren, should have died screaming."

The viciousness of her words almost felt like a slap, but he just shrugged a shoulder as he took in her blue eyes up close. "I can't really argue that."

Her brows pulled together for a second as confusion passed over her, and then she arched her back as much as she could and let out an ear splitting scream. He slapped his hand over her mouth, trying to be gentle this time, but if he didn't get her to stop soon the neighbors were going to call the police, and this was not something easy to explain.

No, officer, I'm not attacking a woman in my apartment. She's actually not human, and no, I can't really let you in to check or I'll have to kill you, or she might kill you, it's complicated.

Yeah, this was going so well.

"Listen to me!" Kiernan pressed his hand over her mouth and shook her a little, but her eyes were still blazing and her cheeks were flushed red in anger. He groaned, "Okay, listen, I'm sorry I choked you, but I'm not going to hurt you again. I promise, and I'd prefer if you wouldn't hurt me either. Just nod if you understand and you'll be quiet."

For a long minute she just stared at him, dragging in harsh breaths through her nose, and then she gave one curt nod. As he lifted his hand she licked her lips and he tried to ignore the weight of his cock in his pants, knowing she could probably feel it and that wasn't helping him much at all. He was about to apologize for his idiotic body, when she spoke again, much calmer this time.

"Why? Why would you *not* hurt me?"

Kiernan sighed. It was a reasonable question, but he never would have even raised a hand to her if she hadn't come after him first.

"I don't want to hurt you, that's why." Fae rolled her eyes and tried to twist her arms away from him, but he just pressed her wrists down more firmly. "Stop it! If I'd really wanted to hurt you I could have just let those guards take you to Butler. Right?"

"Then what *are* you going to do with me?" Fae was still fuming, her breath huffing out quickly.

"I don't know." Kiernan's head was pounding. He still hadn't even thought through what was happening yet, and he needed some fucking space. He needed her body not to be pressed against his, and he needed his own body to get with the program and calm down.

"Are you going to take me back there?"

No.

The answer popped into his head, but that didn't make sense. It was *stupid*, because taking her back would be the easiest solution to this. Everything all cleaned up, nice and neat – except, even the idea of handing her over to Butler made Kiernan's skin crawl and that dark part of him wake up for totally different reasons. His brain wasn't working right, so he gave the only answer he could, "I don't know."

Fae's brows came together again as she stared up at him. "So you're going to keep me here?"

"I'm not sure," he mumbled. Fae rolled her eyes at that.

"What the fuck do you want with me then?" Fae tugged on her wrists again to punctuate the question and Kiernan eased off.

"Nothing. I don't want anything."

"Yeah, right." Fae arched her back and jerked her arms hard, which broke Kiernan's loose hold on her wrists. Twisting her body she threw him off her and kicked both feet into his stomach. He shouted in surprise but in an instant she had flipped over, and was running flat out to his bedroom, grabbing the sword from the floor on the way. He tried to scramble after her, but she slammed the door and he heard the little mechanism on the handle flip that locked it. When he got there, Kiernan's fist banged into the door and he growled in frustration.

"Fae, dammit, I am *not* going to hurt you. Open the door!" She wasn't responding, and he had to take a slow breath to calm down. The door to his bedroom was thick and he really didn't want to break it down, or shift into the room and terrify her further. Also, none of that would really sell his whole 'not wanting to hurt her' claim.

"Kiernan! You here?" Cole's voice rang out from the living room, and his heart went into triple time. Things were only going from bad to worse.

"Stay in there and stay quiet, *please*, for both our sakes." Kiernan pressed his head against the door and talked as loudly as he dared before walking back to the living room, which didn't exactly look normal as Cole and Eryn both turned to him. The shattered statue was on the floor, the scabbard from the sword was sticking out from under his television stand, and there was water scattered across the floor from the melting snow.

Oh yeah, this looked *great*.

"Hey man, you just disappeared." Cole looked concerned,

although he was thankfully a little drunk. Kiernan smiled and shrugged a shoulder which made his side ache where Fae had kicked him, she might have cracked a rib.

"I felt like I forgot something here, wanted to come check on it. And anyway, I'm not in the mood to get obliterated with the guys." Kiernan tried to act casual and steady his breathing as Eryn was looking around the room. He watched as his eyes landed on the shattered statue, Kiernan's damp jeans, and the puddle of water next to his boots.

"And you decided to what? Walk through water on your way back? And destroy whatever that was?" Eryn pushed a piece of the statue with the toe of his boot.

"Actually I made a pit stop back in the jungle to make sure I hadn't left anything behind, ended up stepping in the river when I tried to wash my shoes off, and wasn't focused when I came back here so I bumped into the statue." Kiernan choked out a laugh which sounded as fake as his story, "I'm an idiot, what can I say?"

Eryn's face didn't change, and his expression was guarded and serious as his eyes scanned the room. Cole stumbled forward and put an arm around Kiernan.

"Who cares, would you please come back and finish drinking with us? You're still standing and that's not right. You had the biggest kill of the trip!" Cole swayed and pulled on Kiernan to keep himself steady.

"I went with you so you could have a tiger skin rug for your cabin, remember? The kill's all yours." Kiernan waved a hand across his apartment which was in blacks, whites, and grays. "It doesn't really go with my style."

"Okay, fine, but come drink with us at least." Cole was whining and Eryn was watching him closely - he didn't have a choice. Kiernan tightened his jaw and finally nodded.

"Alright, I'll meet you there. I need to change my jeans and clean up this crap, alright? I'll be there in fifteen." Cole cheered and Eryn nodded, finally moving his eyes back to Kiernan.

"See you there. Soon." Eryn placed a hand on Cole's shoulder, Cole gave a fake salute, and then they both disappeared.

Turning around, Kiernan pushed a hand through his hair again and tried to breathe. His heart was pounding, and the clock was ticking as he walked back to the door to his bedroom. This time he knocked on it and waited.

"Fae, come on." He called through the door, trying to remember if he had a spare key for the door anywhere, when it suddenly cracked a little. Kiernan waited to see if it would open further, but it didn't so he pushed it with one hand and it swung open to reveal Fae in that way too short green dress holding his sword like she was ready to kill him. Somehow that just translated to him being unable to move his eyes from her legs and her hips.

Maybe he did have a death wish.

"You didn't tell them about me." When Fae spoke in a normal voice, not on the verge of panic, or screaming viciously at him, it was soft and almost lyrical. He could hear the hint of their old accent, but it was completely overrun by the random languages she had spoken since.

"I told you, I don't want to hurt you, and they would have definitely hurt you. If Gormahn found out about your master, he'd have them - he'd have us - kill you." Kiernan spoke seriously, and Fae adjusted her grip on the sword before slowly lowering it. Not that it meant much, she could kill him just as easily with it resting at her side.

"Okay. So why don't you kill me?" Her words were so honest that he flinched.

"I don't want to."

"*Right*, and what are they going to do about it if they find out I'm here?" Fae's brows came together as she stared at him.

"Probably kill you, and me as well, but like I said, I am still not going to hurt you." Kiernan took a step back from her to show he wasn't going to rush her or try to disarm her.

"So you keep saying." She shifted her weight from side to side, obviously making a decision. "I guess I'm willing to listen to you, but if you touch me again I'll kill you. And if I don't like what I hear, I'm gone, and you *will* let me leave." She brushed a strand of hair back behind her ear and let the tip of the sword rest against the floor. Her back was straight and even though he'd already bested her once that morning, she was still defiant, skilled, and holding a weapon - so he nodded in agreement to her terms.

"I want to talk to you about this, I want to explain myself, but if I don't go back with them they're going to come back here, and I can't risk them finding you. I won't be gone long though, and there's food in the kitchen and you can watch TV." Kiernan had turned back towards the living room when he paused, "You know what a TV is right?" Fae rolled her eyes and swung the sword up to rest on her shoulder.

"Of course I know what a TV is, I'm not an idiot, and I've seen them before." Fae responded bitingly and Kiernan put his hands up and walked down the hallway. He turned away from her before the smile tugged at his lips. She was so damn feisty.

"Okay, well, here it is." He picked up one of several remotes on the TV stand and started pressing buttons and telling her about the surround sound and satellite and his blu-ray player. Finally, he noticed the confusion on her face and stopped and handed her one remote which she leaned forward to take from his hand. "Just use this one to browse the channels, up and down, volume, up and down."

"Thanks." Fae smiled with bitter sarcasm and stepped back from him again. With a sigh Kiernan turned to head back to his bedroom to change, but he stopped.

"Listen, please don't leave while I'm gone. I want to talk about this, and anyway, in what you're wearing you'd attract a lot of attention. This is a big city, and I don't know who you'd run into, or if someone might lay a claim to you."

"Where am I?" Fae looked past him out the windows at the gray skies.

"Seattle, Washington. In the US. Will you stay inside? Will you wait for me to come back?" Kiernan kind of felt like he was pleading with her, especially when Fae didn't respond for a moment, but finally she nodded.

"I'll stay inside until you return. As far as other people," she shrugged, "I can handle myself." Fae was looking out the window, and Kiernan didn't know how to respond so he just gave her a thumbs up, *which was weird*, and headed back to his bedroom to change.

Why couldn't he act normal around her? And what the fuck had happened to him when he'd pinned her?

Shutting the bedroom door, he kicked off his boots and grabbed a new pair of jeans and a clean shirt. He had a bruise forming on his side where Fae had landed the kick, but even if the ribs were cracked they'd heal soon enough. He pulled on the fresh clothes and tried not to think of the dark side of himself. It had been so long since that part of him had surfaced, decades, and he worked hard to keep it at bay.

He worked hard to be as human as possible.

Shoving his feet into some Converse, he focused on the great hall and tried not to think about Fae. Just a few hours and he could come back – and now he really wanted to come back. Wanted to sit and talk with her and explain himself.

He just hoped she was still here when he did.

CHAPTER NINE

SEATTLE, WASHINGTON

As soon as she was sure he'd really left, Fae started to wander his apartment. She wasn't exactly sure what she was looking for – answers on why he had helped her? A secret room full of torture devices? Sadistic trophies earned over a lifetime of rampant killing and pillaging? A manifesto outlining his evil plan?

She didn't find anything interesting.

It was sparse and extremely well organized, a place for everything, and everything in its place. Bookshelves full of normal books. Pantry full of normal food. Pristine, modern desk with a neat stack of unopened envelopes – all irritatingly addressed to *Resident*.

In all her thousands of years serving, Fae had never

known a man to be this precise. This tidy. The order was unnerving. And not at all what she'd expected to see from a Laochra.

Everything was perfect, except for his bed, which was a chaotic knot of sheets.

Fae had even taken a few steps out his front door and into the hallway before going back inside. It was pointless to go out right now. She had no idea what kind of city Seattle was, she had no money, and she wasn't exactly dressed to walk around in public without attracting attention. So, now Fae was on the couch with her legs tucked under her, staring at another animated movie on the television.

This was her grand dream of escape come to life. Sitting in a Laochra's apartment like a good little girl, waiting for him to return, and watching movies.

For the past *seven* hours.

According to the Laochra, *'not being gone long'* meant hours and hours. She was frustrated with herself because she hadn't even asked his name before he'd left, then again she *had* tried her best to kill him, and he - he was so... odd. She had watched him reach for the axe, a heavy weapon that would have been hard to defend against with the strength he would be able to put behind it, but he hadn't taken it off the wall. To push him, she'd tried to go for a harder attack, but her sword had lodged itself in the damaged wood of the little table. Then he'd disarmed her and put her on the floor.

"Idiot," she grumbled to herself, chastising herself for

the tenth time since he'd left. For her *weakness*. He could have done whatever he wanted with her on the floor under him, and having those pitch black eyes above her had brought back memories of the battlefield. She'd lost it, cursing him and his kind, and called him a son of Gormahn. Well, more accurately, a filthy bastard son of Gormahn, but *that* had been what set him off. Not her attacking him with a sword, not the kick she'd landed.

Fae dropped her head back on the couch and blew out a breath.

"Why did that set you off? Of all things?" She laid her arm over her eyes and groaned. "And why, Mr. *Resident*, did you even fucking rescue me?"

And beyond that, why had he left her, alone, in what was obviously his home, with a lot of very sharp weapons?

Her fingers trailed over the hilt of the sword on the couch beside her as the questions whirled around in her head. Too many unanswered questions after a day that had already been a nightmare.

At least the movies were entertaining.

She knew about television, and she'd even had the chance to watch it sometimes, but she'd never had the opportunity to just immerse herself in it and in all the little worlds the screen displayed. She was as attached to the characters in the movies as she usually got to characters in books. The little Stitch character in the current movie was a chaotic little blue thing, but he was sweet and was currently trying to save the little girl, Lilo, from aliens. It seemed silly to be so emotional about it, but Fae was totally invested.

To her right was a strange whooshing sound, and where there had been empty space one moment, the next he was standing next to his desk shuffling a bunch of paper and plastic shopping bags in his hands. She jumped, tensing as she dragged the sword back onto her lap to be ready.

"Fae! It's me, I'm back." He was loud, rustling the bags and calling out to her.

"I can see you." She rolled her eyes.

"Oh, uh, hi. Listen, I brought –" The Laochra started talking and she shushed him, cutting him off.

"You've been gone for eight hours, whatever you want to tell me can wait ten minutes for me to finish this." Fae was irritated with him as she pointed at the television screen, because she couldn't hear it over all the noise he was making. She noticed his eyes fall to the sword before stepping toward the television to see Stitch attacking a spaceship. His eyebrows went up and he looked back at her, his mouth opening and then shutting. With a shrug, he dropped the bags by the television and walked into the kitchen.

"You know that's for kids, right?"

Fae shushed him again and he went quiet, opening and shutting cabinets. She watched the end of the movie, once more drawn in by the way that everything came together so perfectly. The bad guys lost, the little blue alien had a family – *Ohana. Nobody gets left behind. Happily ever after.*

The real world never worked like that.

As the credits started rolling to the music, the Laochra appeared in the doorway to his kitchen. Fae untucked her legs and kept her grip on the sword as he stood still holding a glass of water. His eyes went to the sword again and he pointed at it. "Are you really going to hold onto that the entire time you're here?"

"Yes."

He shrugged and stepped into the living room, nudging the bags with the toe of his shoe. "Listen, I'm sorry it took me so long to get back. I had to act like everything was normal, and that meant drinking with them until they started to pass out. Which took a while." The Laochra took a drink of the water. "But I stopped at some stores and grabbed you some clothes."

"Playing dress up with me already?" Fae was irritated, frustrated with not knowing what he wanted from her. She wasn't stupid, and she was pretty sure this act would end soon enough.

"Uh, no? I just figured you wouldn't want to stay in that." He sighed. "If you don't want the clothes you don't have to take them. I was just trying to help." She narrowed her eyes at him for a moment, waiting for there to be some flicker of that other side of him, some alternate reason for him to bring her clothes. Then Fae looked down at the dress Nikola had made her wear, the same style she'd worn for three years in his house. A shudder went through her as she remembered him standing over Juliet, and she clenched her jaw.

No, she didn't want to stay in this any longer than she had to.

She stood up and let the blanket fall off her lap, but she kept the sword in her hand. "Okay. I'll change, and then you'll explain what you want?"

His brow furrowed and he started to look around the room, eventually looking out the window behind his desk. "I don't *want* anything, but we do need to talk. You can use my room to change. I'll stay out here." Fae stepped towards the bags and he moved back to give her room. She started to grab the bags and had to tuck the sword under one arm to grab them all. The Laochra suddenly reached forward and gently touched her arm, and she jumped. She was about to rip her arm out of his hand when his thumb traced lightly over the bruises. "I did that, didn't I?"

"Yes," Fae replied in confusion as she watched him stare at the pale little bruises on the sides of her wrist. Before his touch could make her any more uncomfortable, she spoke up again. "I've had worse, and to be honest, I think you might have more bruises than me." She smiled a bit, and he didn't argue with that as his eyes lifted to hers. Then he seemed to realize he was touching her and he jerked his hand back like she'd burned him.

"Well, I'm sorry. For your wrists, and your neck. I should have never – I wouldn't have -"

"It's okay, I *was* trying to kill you." Fae shifted her weight from one foot to the other, uncomfortable with his apology and the weird, surreal reality of talking to a Laochra like he was a normal person. She was about to reach for the clothes again, when she stopped herself. "One thing though... So, you know who I am, but before I go change could you tell me what *your* name is?" The Laochra's eyes widened and he looked up at her as if he just realized he hadn't introduced himself.

What an idiot.

"It's Kiernan, just call me Kiernan." He stumbled through the sentence when he talked and then took another sip of water, giving her a half smile.

"Kiernan," she repeated, "Got it." Fae nodded and grabbed the bags of clothes, tucking the sword under her arm. Then she walked backwards a few steps toward the hallway to his room. When he didn't start to follow her she turned and walked the rest of the way to his room where she shut and locked the door.

"Kiernan." Fae muttered the name to herself as she dropped the bags to the floor. It was a nice name, and it fit him. She was confused for a moment as she started to pull the clothes out. She'd expected dresses, short skirts, and items that barely counted as garments at all. Instead she pulled out jeans in a couple of sizes, some soft sweaters, some normal long-sleeved shirts, and a whole bag of socks and undergarments. In one of the bags were three boxes of shoes in different sizes, she found a pair that was a little loose but she was able to get the laces tight enough that they wouldn't slide off. The shoes matched the ones he wore.

"He must only know where to find this kind," she muttered to herself and then took them back off to get dressed. After slipping on a pair of jeans she tugged a dark gray sweater on and instantly felt warmer.

She stepped into his bathroom and was surprised at how normal she looked. Slaves didn't dress like this or look like this. *People* looked like this. Normal people. She tugged her fingers through her tangled hair, and then gave up as she was only making it frizzy. Sitting down on the floor she decided to put on the shoes again in case she wanted to leave, because whether or not she had a temporary peace with this Laochra, this *Kiernan* – she'd made no promises to stay after their conversation.

With a deep breath she grabbed the sword again and walked back into the living room, Kiernan had flipped the TV off and was sitting in a big black chair to the side. He was still drinking the water and rubbing his head when he noticed her coming in and looked up. His mouth opened a little and he stared at her like he had that morning when he'd first appeared near her in the snow.

"You look -" Kiernan stopped himself and cleared his throat, sitting up in the chair before saying, "I mean, they fit? It all fits?" Fae nodded and shifted in the shoes a little before she sat down on the couch as far from him as possible.

"The shoes are a little big, but everything else works." Fae leaned the sword against her leg and stared at him. "So, start. Explain all this to me."

Kiernan shoved his hand through his hair.

Now that she had a moment, she looked him over. His hair was a dark brown and cut in a modern style, and he kept himself clean-shaven and dressed casually. Right now he was in jeans, a pair of black shoes that matched hers, and a long-sleeved blue shirt that read, 'My other shirt is chainmail'. She almost smiled at that because she imagined he owned chainmail somewhere judging by the weapons he had decorating his walls.

"Yeah, I don't really know how to do that." Kiernan sat back and sighed. Fae lifted an eyebrow at him, a little annoyed that now that it was time to talk he seemed to be avoiding it.

"Let's start with, how did you know where I was?"

"I can see any of my charges in this observation glass I have." He motioned over her shoulder to the desk by the window. "It's over there, in a box." Fae's heart pounded in her chest as she turned around.

"You can see other Faeoihn?" She asked, looking back at him. Kiernan nodded and Fae stood up and walked over to the desk, and he jumped up and walked after her. "Show me." Her hands were shaking as she opened the lid of the box and looked at the concave disc of glass inside that was about six inches across. It was nestled inside the wood box on some cloth, but nothing was visible in it.

"I don't think that's a good idea, Fae." His voice was somber, but it just irritated her.

"Why? I haven't seen one of my sisters in a millennium and you think it's a *bad* idea?" Fae shoved the box towards him across the desk. "Make it work."

"Listen, you don't know what could be happening, you don't want to see that." His words brought up a lot of images in flashes that made her stomach twist, but it didn't deter her. Whatever was happening with her sisters, she wanted to see one of them. She had to.

"Do it." Fae adjusted her grip on the hilt of the sword and pointed at the box. Kiernan grumbled and placed a finger on the edge of the glass. The center lit up for a second and then suddenly it was like Fae was looking through a window at a young woman. Her light hair was pulled up into a bun and she was wearing a t-shirt and jeans, but Fae still recognized her. Aleine. She could see her talking, but she couldn't hear her. "I can't hear anything, make it so I can hear it."

"Just touch the box." Kiernan pointed at it, and Fae rested the sword against the desk and pulled the box back towards her so she could see more easily and as soon as her hands touched it Aleine's voice came through as if she were right next to her. She was talking to someone across the room, saying something about wanting to sleep. Another woman's voice started screaming at her about being grateful and then she came into view and slapped Aleine. Anger bubbled up inside Fae, but Kiernan reached over and slammed the lid shut before picking the box up.

"Give it back! Let me see her again!" Fae reached for it

and Kiernan stepped back and shook his head, his expression grim.

"You don't want to see. Trust me, Fae." Kiernan looked down at the box, avoiding Fae's eyes.

"Then go get her, dammit, go get her like you did with me!" That snapped his head up.

"It's not the same thing, your master was dead, hers is alive. *If* I could even bring her here it would only hurt her because the curse would pull her back, and it would attract even more attention to us."

"I don't care, go get her!" Fae slammed her hand onto the desk, and Kiernan walked back into the living room away from her. "Go get her, Kiernan!" Fae shouted at him, using his name for the first time. He set the box down on the end table by his chair, and she stomped over to him leaving the sword against the desk.

"You don't understand. If I go get her, Gormahn's curse will just activate the bands and hurt her and keep hurting her until she's returned to her master. The *only* reason I was able to get you was because you were unclaimed, and you still haven't explained how that happened." Fae's chest hurt thinking about Aleine, trapped wherever she was. She hadn't seen her in years, and they hadn't been close like Keira and she had been, but she didn't want her to suffer. She didn't want any of her sisters to suffer.

"Kill her master then, and bring her here." Fae said it seriously, and Kiernan scoffed at that idea.

"You're not the only one Gormahn has control over, Fae."

"Oh, that's right. You're a son of Gormahn." She sneered the words at him, angry that he seemed to pick and choose who he'd save, but she wasn't prepared for the flare of rage in his eyes when he looked up at her.

"Please stop calling me that." His words were polite, but his voice had a cold edge that made her want to go back and pick up the sword again. She had said it on purpose, to irritate him, but she didn't want to fight him. Not yet, at least.

"I don't understand why it bothers you so much. Gormahn made you, just like Eltera made me. I am a daughter of Eltera, and you -"

"Gormahn didn't *make* me. He stole me." Kiernan growled under his breath, looking away for a minute, but then he turned back to her, "Regardless, I am forbidden from harming any of the masters. I can't do what you're asking. If I did try to kill him I'd be the one to die, not him." That caught Fae's attention and she took a step back towards the couch, and Kiernan dropped into the chair again.

"What do you mean?" She asked, and Kiernan immediately pushed up his left sleeve, where dark vines were visible on his skin like tattoos. He pulled it up as high as it would go on his arm, around his elbow, and the vines continued upwards.

"This is how Gormahn controls us. These vines are just the visual representation of a poison Gormahn gave all of the Laochra. If we disobey him, the poison gets closer to our hearts. If it reaches it, we die." Fae's eyes trailed the thick vines, and although she didn't exactly feel bad for him at least he had a reason for why he wouldn't save Aleine. As she stared at the vines she realized that they were actually visible at his wrist and seemed to spring from his left palm.

"So you can't go get her?" Fae was digging her nails into her palms in frustration at the constant futility of her situation, and Kiernan shook his head.

"If I went, it wouldn't help her, and it could draw attention to you, and I already said I don't want to see you hurt."

"And why exactly *is* that?"

"I just don't." His response was curt, but she just laughed under her breath.

"You haven't helped me for two millennia, why the sudden interest in my safety?"

"I have tried to help you. When you were at that auction a few years ago there was a woman that almost bought you. She was really sadistic, Fae, you have no idea. She had *killed* the last few girls she bought and she wanted you because you wouldn't die as easily. I had the guy who handles our creative accounting mess with her bank accounts so she would stop bidding, and trust me that request was *not* easy to explain. Before that, there was that guy in Vietnam who was pimping you and those other girls out for political favors. How do you think his enemies found him?" Kiernan was speaking quietly, staring at his hands.

Fae couldn't think of a way to respond to him. Those memories were still too fresh, and she didn't want to think about any of it. Instead, she just sat down on the edge of the couch on the end closest to him.

He took a breath and looked up at her, "My turn for a question, how did you kill Nikola?"

"I don't know." Fae crossed her arms over her chest, and he scoffed.

"Really, Fae? Just tell me."

"I really don't know. I'm not keeping some secret, I actually have no idea. It's never happened to any of my masters before, and there have been others who deserved it more. Even though he killed Juliet, others have done so much worse. Repeatedly. If I could do it, why didn't I do it before now?" Fae stared at him, and Kiernan sighed and put his head in his hands.

"That's true. But what if it's a new thing? Some new skill?"

"If it is, I don't know how to control it. If I could I would have killed you this morning." Fae shrugged, and the expression on his face was priceless for a moment.

"Wow. Thanks for the honesty." Kiernan chuckled a little, and Fae smiled at the sarcasm.

"No problem. My turn again, you said Gormahn controls you with those vines." Fae tucked her legs under her on the couch and Kiernan flinched, staring at her shoes on the fabric. Noticing it she pulled them off and dropped them to the floor one at a time. He just sighed, and she wanted to laugh at him. Who knew a big, bad warrior would be worried about clean furniture? Once his couch was safe, Kiernan gestured for her to ask her question. "Well, what did you mean by that? Exactly how does he control you, and why are you so pissy when I refer to him? Didn't you worship him?"

"That's way more than one question, but fine." He leaned back in the chair, rubbing his thumb into the center of his left palm. "I worshipped Gormahn the same way I worshipped all the gods. I honored them, I made sacrifices, I prayed – but I wasn't a warrior. When Gormahn found me and decided he wanted me to be a part of the Laochra, I remember that he told me I had the chance to be truly great. To be a *hero*." He laughed to himself as if he'd told a joke. "I told him I was good where I was, happy. I had some land to farm and was doing fine, but he said that destiny wasn't a choice and he grabbed my hand and stabbed this black stick into it." Kiernan ran his hand over the vines, "It was incredibly painful, and I tried to get away from him, but... he's a god. Found out later it was a branch from a poisonous tree called the Ebon Oak, something that grows where the gods live. It let him get into my head, and it was like his thoughts were my thoughts. He *changed* me into what he wanted."

"So he stabs you with a stick and you join his bloodthirsty army and start pillaging our land?" Fae crossed her arms, because the story sounded plausible, but it didn't make sense. Gormahn had to have his own followers, just like Eltera had. No one really knew anything about the Laochra other than their viciousness. Fae had only heard about them through stories that moved through their people and that Eltera said they had to be destroyed. No one had known how they were created.

"Basically." Kiernan tore his gaze away from his palm, and the furrow between his brows made his features even stronger. "When he stuck me with it, he also gave me some of his power. So I heal much faster than normal, I'm stronger, faster. I had the instinct to fight. But, that's the last memory I have of a mortal life, standing in a field, in shock at being in the presence of a god – and then pain. The first thousand years under his control are nothing but scattered images of war and violence, because he never let us rest."

"So you don't remember the battle?" Fae tilted her head and Kiernan stared at the floor when she asked it. Fae's own memories of the battle were fresh in her mind after her conversation with Ebere. Even worse were the memories of what had happened after the battle was done.

"I remember parts of it."

"Well, I remember *all* of it. Do you at least remember which one of us you took from the field?" Fae couldn't keep the anger out of her voice, and Kiernan put his head in his hands and remained silent. Fae grabbed her shoe off the floor and threw it at him. It bounced off his shoulder, but Kiernan didn't lift his head. "Answer me, dammit! I remember who took me. I don't know his name, but I remember his face. He gave me a battlefield for a marriage bed, and then sold me to a fucking Roman when Gormahn had you rip us all away from each other. So, which one of us did you take, Kiernan? What was her name? Did you even find out? Where did you leave her? Tell me!"

"I don't remember, Fae!" Kiernan yelled at her, and it made her jump. He stood up, pacing away from her. Rubbing his face with one hand as he stared at the wall by his front door. "I really don't remember, and the things I can remember in the last two thousand years make me sick. It's like having nightmares except they're all real and I actually did them. They keep me up at night, this shit I've done haunts me, and I deserve it. I have to live with that, and I can't even remember *everything* I did."

"All of this is just so convenient. You didn't *want* to join Gormahn, he *made* you, he *poisoned* you, and now you can't even remember? I thought we were doing the whole honesty thing." Fae thought about leaving right then. She didn't want to believe him about the poison or the forgetting. How could anyone *forget* things like that? They were seared into her memory with complete clarity, even things she wished she could forget. Things she wanted to erase.

"I wouldn't have left if I could have stopped it." Kiernan's fists were clenched at his sides, and she could see the tension in his shoulders.

"Why not, Kiernan? What was better than being a warrior for Gormahn? What could have possibly been better than taking whatever you wanted, doing whatever you wanted, and getting away with it with a fucking god at your back?" Fae was furious and laying the bitter sarcasm on thick, and Kiernan just stood there with his back to her. She was about to throw her other shoe at him when he spoke softly.

"My family."

The anger bled out of her fast as she stared at him, her mouth opening to speak, but she couldn't think of what to say. *He'd had a family?* All of the Faeoihn who had been taken didn't have a family of their own. Although it wouldn't have been weird for her to have found a husband and had children by her age, she had been waiting and her father hadn't pressured her. He had always said she would know when she met the right one for her, and it hadn't happened. Similar things were true for her sisters.

She finally found her tongue and asked, "You had a wife?" He nodded. "Did you have children?" He nodded again, and that made a sour place appear in her stomach. To lose your spouse would be bad enough, but to lose a child? She couldn't imagine.

"I had a wife named Branna, and a son named Lann. I only had four years with them before Gormahn took me from them."

"What happened to them?"

"I don't know." Kiernan's voice seemed hollow, and he still hadn't turned around. "I can't remember what happened after Gormahn took me. I don't know if we went back and destroyed the village I lived in, I don't know if they lived to old age, or died in the chaos the Laochra wrought, and trust me, I think about it a lot. I think about whether or not I could have held the sword myself." Fae flinched and realized how badly she wanted to comfort him, because while terrible things had happened in her long life – Eltera had made sure her family was safe and prosperous. *Blessed*. There was no need to even say what Gormahn could have done to ensure his Laochra had no ties to humanity.

"I'm sorry." Fae spoke softly, but he didn't even acknowledge it.

"My turn." Kiernan's voice was strained, and he was still talking to the wall. "Why haven't you given up, Fae? Why haven't you just stopped fighting all this and either resigned yourself to it or ended it?" When he turned around his face was flushed, and his eyes didn't quite find her face.

"Eltera hasn't given up, so I won't give up."

"He'll never let her go, Fae. All of this will never end. Never."

Fae gritted her teeth against the urge to scream at him. He had been stolen from his life, from his family. He didn't know what it meant to pledge your life voluntarily, to do it without fear, to do it with *faith*. He wasn't going to convince her of anything. She'd suffered for this long, so the idea of an eternity like this wasn't unrealistic, she just usually tried not to think about it.

If Kiernan had already resigned himself to his life, to his curse, that was his choice.

"Someday she'll be free, Kiernan, I believe that, I have to. One day she will gather all of the Faeoihn up and we'll all live together again. Safe and sound." When it came out of her mouth it seemed naïve, but she still believed it was true.

"How can you believe that, Fae? After everything that's been done to you, *how* do you still believe in any of it?" His face scrunched up with the depth of his frustration and confusion, but she just smiled.

"I have faith in *her*, that's how. Eltera's power comes every morning and heals me. Every. Single. Morning. In more than two thousand years she's never missed a sunrise. I don't know what it costs her to do that, but it lets me know she's there. It lets me know she's out there, somewhere, and that she still knows I'm alive. I couldn't leave her to suffer alone, just to end my own pain." Fae looked down to see her fists clenched from the passion of her speech, and she made herself relax her hands. "My turn again. Have you seen Eltera?"

"Yes." Kiernan nodded, but he was still staring at the floor, or the wall, or the ceiling, and not her.

"How was she?"

"It's been more than a hundred years, but she always looked fine when I saw her. But, you know, she's a goddess." Kiernan clenched his teeth for a second, and then he seemed to make a decision. "I probably shouldn't tell you this, but I know that that from our reports, the ones we write about you guys, Gormahn finds out what happens to you all and he makes Eltera watch his favorites so she knows you're suffering. I think that's the worst thing he does to her, worse than hurting her in any other way." His voice trailed off and Fae's stomach knotted up. To imagine everything that Eltera could have seen – it wasn't good.

"I just – I miss her." Fae leaned forward and wrapped her arms around herself. She hadn't meant to say it out loud, but it had spilled out, and Kiernan finally looked at her again.

"I'm sorry, Fae." He walked towards her and knelt down in front of her. Fae looked down at him and met his dark eyes as he continued talking, "I'm sorry for everything. Everything you've gone through, everything that's happened. I didn't always do my job, and I wasn't always watching, but from what I did see, if that's been your life since – since Gormahn... I'm just sorry."

Fae didn't know how to respond to that, he seemed sincere and almost as if it hurt him to think of everything that had happened to her. She thought for a minute, staring at him, that in all her life no one had ever apologized who actually had a hand in her suffering. He'd had every opportunity to hurt her, to send her back to Butler, to send her *anywhere*, and instead he had bought her clothes and kept his distance. He hadn't told his friends about her.

"I believe you." Fae said it flatly and Kiernan's face registered surprise. She hadn't accepted the apology, but she hadn't rejected it and he realized that. He reached forward and ran a finger lightly across the bruises on one of her wrists.

"I swear I'll never hurt you, not even accidentally, ever

again." Kiernan seemed to be promising himself more than her, and Fae couldn't respond to that so she just nodded. He seemed so sincere, but it was hard to believe anyone. Especially a Laochra. Everyone gave in to the temptation of the bands eventually.

"How am I supposed to trust you?" Fae tilted her head as she looked down at him.

"You're not. At least, not until I've earned it." He pushed himself up to standing and looked around the room, taking a deep breath. She could respect that answer, and she was glad he knew that pretty words were not going to do it. He looked back at her, a serious expression on his face. "You know what we need after a day like today?"

"What?" Fae arched an eyebrow up at him.

"A drink." He held his arms out like it was an obvious answer. That made her laugh, and the laughter soothed some raw place inside her that had been torn open.

"Haven't you been drinking all day?" The smile disappeared from her face but she looked back to him. He shrugged a shoulder and walked to a coat closet.

"Yeah, but it wasn't here, and we both need a drink after all this. Don't you want to go out and see the city? Feel normal for a bit?" Fae was itching to leave the apartment, to see other people, and walk around without worrying someone was going to yank her proverbial leash – and she really wanted to drink until the memory of Juliet was fuzzy and distant.

"Yes, I do." She nodded and stood up. Kiernan gave a grin

that transformed his face, it made him look young and mischievous, and – she had to admit – good. Fae forced herself to look at the floor and tried to quell the uneasy feeling in her stomach about him.

He clapped his hands, a new energy filling him up. "Then put on your shoes, and let's go."

CHAPTER TEN

SEATTLE, WASHINGTON

WATCHING Fae step out onto the street was quite a sight. When she walked out the front door of Kiernan's building, her eyes widened at all of the Christmas lights in the trees and the big bows around some of the street lamps. He already felt better about their disaster of a talk just seeing her enjoy the sights of the city, outside and free for the first time in gods knew how many decades.

"It's so beautiful." Fae turned her head around to look at the lights as they headed down the street, the red strands in her hair catching the light at random. His heavy coat was slung around her shoulders, dwarfing her and hiding her incredible curves. He kept them on track as she took in the city with wide-eyes, occasionally gasping and muttering to herself, spinning in place to look up at a building, or staring across the street at other couples heading back from the bar district. He cleared his throat trying to think of something, *anything*, to say to her after the difficult conversation they'd had.

"Yeah, I always love this time of year, it's Christmas time for them. It's a Christian holiday, and they celebrate by -" Kiernan started to explain, but Fae looked at him like he was stupid.

"I know what Christmas is, Kiernan. I may not have been out in the world and free all this time, but you'd be surprised that people actually *talk* to me about things. Slaves may not see much of the world, but we're not blind." She had shoved her hands inside the pockets and was lifting her shoulders against the breeze, her auburn hair whipping around her face.

"Sorry. I guess if you have a question, ask me." He shut his mouth, obviously failing at the casual conversation thing. He wanted a drink even more now. Stopping in front of one of his favorite bars, he opened the door and Fae stepped in before him. It was crowded and Kiernan realized it was a Saturday night, which meant *a lot* of mortals packed in. Fae was frozen at the door, her eyes widening as she looked at all of the people crammed into the room. There were low tables on the left side of the bar for eating and higher pub tables on the right side around the bar, but she wasn't moving forward.

Maybe this had been a mistake.

He gently touched her elbow, and he noticed she didn't jump for once. Raising his voice over all of the noise he pointed at the bar and asked, "Do you want to get a drink?"

Fae nodded and followed him as he pushed his way through the people, and when he got to the bar he was glad he was tall because he could just lean over the hipster that had snagged a stool. The guy turned to give him a glare, but when he saw Kiernan he switched on a nervous smile and leaned out of his way. When the young girl behind the bar noticed him she grinned.

"What can I get you?" Her perky voice was on the edge of annoying, but he smiled back. The way she was pushing her chest out was more comical than attractive, but he was used to it. He'd always figured his almost black eyes would scare off the mortals, but instead they seemed to be drawn to him. Like they all had a fucking death wish. Kiernan turned back to see Fae hidden behind him, so he tugged her elbow gently so she stepped in front of him to the bar and he could give her a little bubble of breathing room by shielding her. The bartender's face fell when she saw Fae, and she suddenly wasn't so friendly anymore.

"Okay, Fae, what do you want?" He raised his voice and talked close to her ear so she could hear him.

"Depends. Are we drinking just a little, or are we drinking a lot?" She looked up at him and he let out a sudden laugh.

"After everything that's happened today, let's go with a lot."

Fae craned her neck trying to read all of the bottles lining the walls, but she quickly gave up. "Let's go with scotch then, whatever they have."

Kiernan smiled and turned back to the bartender who was leaning across the bar, now directly in front of him. Her low cut top didn't leave much to the imagination and her plastic smile was back on her face. He was tempted to tell her to stop trying so hard, that it was a waste of time, but it was pointless. A glance to the side and he could see that Fae was annoyed with the bartender's antics because she rolled her eyes. "You heard her, do you have any Glenlivet? It's a scotch. Eighteen or twenty-one?"

The bartender sighed at the lack of attention and walked along the wall of bottles for a minute or two until she found a bottle. She brought it back to them and sat two glasses on the bar a little harder than necessary. "We have the twenty-one, single or double?" Kiernan shook his head.

"I'll just take the bottle." He handed across his credit card and the bartender took it and asked him to wait. He watched her walk down the length of the bar and grab a male bartender and come back. The guy took the card from the girl and started talking to Kiernan while his eyes were glued to Fae.

"Hey man, you know how much a whole bottle is?"

"It's fine." Kiernan answered, and the guy shrugged and rung it up at the register along the wall and came back to hand the card to Kiernan. As he was tucking his card back in his wallet, the bartender leaned across the bar with his hand extended towards Fae.

"I'm David by the way, if you need anything else just ask for me." He gave a charming smile and added, "I'd be happy to give you anything you need." Fae smirked at him and shook his hand once, but she didn't offer her name or any other response. Kiernan grabbed the bottle in one hand and the two glasses in the other, glancing at the bartender who shrugged and grinned before heading back down the bar.

"Let's grab a seat." Sitting down at one of the tall tables he set the bottle and the two glasses down, opened it, and poured an inch or so of the amber liquid into each glass. Fae was staring into hers, still hunched inside the huge coat. "You know you can take off the coat if you want?" Fae shrugged it off and gave him a small smile, before she swirled the scotch in the glass, her eyes flickering around the room.

Her shoulders were tense and he was going to suggest they just leave, but then she sat up taller and spoke. "So do you come here a lot?" she asked, and Kiernan laughed. Fae furrowed her brow, frowning at him, "What?"

"That's sort of a pick-up line. Like, something you'd say if you wanted to take me home." A blush crept across Fae's cheeks and she glared at him. It made him grin, but he tried to stifle it.

"Not what I meant, at all."

"I know, it just caught me off guard, but yeah when I'm in town I like to come here." Kiernan took another sip of the scotch. "So, are you okay? With the crowd? If not we can leave."

Fae nodded and finally took a drink. "I'm fine with it, just not used to it." She licked her lips and inhaled slowly over the glass. How she'd developed a taste for scotch in her time as a slave would *have* to be a topic of conversation. "So how long have you been watching me in that glass of yours? The whole time, or do the Laochra take shifts?"

"You've been assigned to me since we started the monitoring, probably fifteen hundred years ago now. At first, Gormahn just let the curse do his work for him, but then somehow he found out one of you had been free, without a master, for over a hundred years." Kiernan stared at the bottle, speaking quietly so other tables couldn't hear him. "That's when some of us were assigned charges. Not all of the Laochra monitor, and I've got four of you I'm responsible for. But, honestly? It was only a couple hundred years ago that I did more than just react if you got free somehow, same with the others. That's rarely happened though, so I didn't really observe as often as I should have according to Gormahn. He wants quarterly reports on what's happening, but I turn mine in about half as often." Kiernan couldn't tell if it was a good thing or a bad thing that he'd ignored his job as one of the monitors. What was worse - watching and not doing anything, or not caring enough to know what was happening? He poured himself another drink.

"So, what changed two hundred years ago?" Fae finished her first glass and waited for him to pour another. When he sat the bottle down again, he leaned back from the table.

He shrugged, "I don't know." Fae sighed and finished her glass, reaching for the bottle and glancing at the others in the bar. She let out a little huff under her breath as she poured. "I really don't, Fae. I have some theories that Gormahn's power is waning, or that he's not spending so much of his power keeping us under his control, but I don't actually know anything. All I know is that I've slowly felt more like who I think I really am, or who I was before."

"And who do you think you really are?"

"Hopefully a better man than I have been with Gormahn."

She nodded and finished her glass again, pouring herself some more. "Well, I hope so as well. Since I'm trapped with you," Fae mumbled into her drink, and Kiernan felt a panic in his chest at the idea that she thought he had kidnapped her – which he kind of had. *Shit.* He was about to start explaining when Fae smiled. Her smile stopped his heart from racing, and it felt like it almost stopped altogether. Her voice was a little playful when she continued, "I'm kidding... sort of."

"Oh." Kiernan swallowed against his suddenly dry throat. "Look, I just want you safe, and it might be hard to believe, but I think I'm your best bet on that for now. I know we started out on a bad -"

"It's fine, Kiernan. I stayed in your apartment all day because I needed to know more about what you are, *who* you are. And now that I know a little more," Fae shrugged, "I'm not against staying with you for a bit, until I can figure out what comes next."

"I wish I could say I had some ideas on that front, but –" He blew out a breath. "This is *complicated* to say the least."

"What's the risk that your friends will show back up?"

"Not very high." Kiernan refilled his glass, smiling to himself at the fact that he didn't need to try and act mortal around her. Knocking back scotch this fast would lay out most humans, but he was barely feeling a buzz. Looking at Fae, it seemed to be true for her too. There were some advantages to being touched by the gods. "I haven't really seen either of them in a while, I sort of disappeared a while back and Cole only recently started reaching back out to me. The hunt we were on was my attempt to figure out what the fuck is going on with me."

"And what *is* going on with you?" Fae narrowed her eyes at him, leaning forward on the table to evaluate him like she may be able to answer the question herself.

"I wish I knew." Kiernan felt his lips tick up in a smile. "I do have to say I like this version of myself a lot better than the dark one."

"The dark one?"

He laughed under his breath. "Uh, yeah, it's kind of the phrase I use for the side of myself that I feel is Gormahn's influence. It's like this darkness living inside me, and if I'm not careful it just takes over."

Fae was staring at him in silence for a minute, her blue

eyes boring into him until he felt like a butterfly pinned to a board. "You're right. About the dark one."

"Huh?"

"I saw it in you." Fae pointed at him with the hand holding her glass as she leaned back from the table. "When we fought, and I called you a so-... the thing you asked me not to call you, I saw the darkness in you. You had been in control, and then the person I'd been talking to was just *gone*. It was in your eyes."

"My eyes are black. What do you mean it was in my eyes?" Kiernan was surprised that she even believed him. He'd tried to talk to Cole about it once and he'd stared at him like he was crazy, but she not only agreed with him, she said she'd *seen* the dark one.

"They looked different. Right now I can see you, Kiernan, the person. When you choked me, it wasn't you. Not the guy talking to me right now anyway." Fae shrugged like it was the most normal thing in the world to talk to him about having different sides to himself, one of which had tried to *kill* her.

"I can't believe you believe me." He shook his head and she smiled over the glass at her lips.

"You're kidding, right? After everything that's happened in my life, in my very long, very fucked up life, why *wouldn't* I believe that someone created by a god could have some bad side-effects?" Fae licked her lips. "The gods don't always think everything through."

"Eltera seems to have done a good job, except for betting

against Gormahn." Kiernan tilted his glass towards her. "*That* probably could have been handled better. But other than that, what has Eltera done?"

"Let's just say that for the first fifty years after the curse, Eltera's healing gift was a little too *thorough*. As in, I was a maiden again at dawn every day?" Fae finished her glass in a single swig as the drink Kiernan had been taking almost made him choke. He started coughing and she grinned at him, completely amused by his discomfort.

"Okay, so, yeah, that was a mistake."

"Absolutely. She figured it out though, and it hasn't happened again." Now that Fae had somewhat warmed up to the bar she was watching everyone around her, listening to their conversations and twisting in her seat to track some as they left. He leaned back to let her enjoy herself, wondering if she'd ever had the chance to just observe mortals who had no idea who or what she was. It was probably a unique feeling for her. Fae suddenly turned back to him, excitement threading in her voice, "Let's do a *toast*."

"What?"

"A toast. Those people over there just did it." Fae raised her glass up above the table, and Kiernan followed suit as she announced at a high volume, "To being immortal, and better days ahead!" Kiernan rubbed a hand across his face, and he didn't repeat it as he just clinked his glass against hers. She grinned and finished it. He could tell she was finally getting a little buzzed, because she was much more animated and that gorgeous smile wasn't fading.

He grinned at her. "You probably shouldn't announce things like that out loud, people will think you're crazy."

Fae shrugged. "Who cares?"

"You're not afraid of them carting you off? Putting you in an asylum somewhere?" Kiernan tilted the bottle of scotch over his glass again.

"Fear never gets anyone anywhere. I learned a long time ago to let it go. You may feel it, but if you let it change what you do you're giving yourself up to it."

"Good point." Kiernan raised his glass again. "Well, I have a toast too. To your freedom." Fae arched an eyebrow at him before she seemed to believe he was sincere and raised her own glass.

"For however long it lasts." Fae added, and they both drank.

They started small talk about what they enjoyed and both quickly uncovered that they liked to read, which led to favorite authors and books. They both avoided talk of Nikola or Juliet, of their pasts, of Eltera or Gormahn, and instead listed books they wished everyone would read. Kiernan was halfway through a story about trying to buy a book with a gold coin once, when a group of guys walked up to their table laughing loudly. Most of the bottle was gone and Kiernan felt pretty good as the haze of the alcohol numbed the edges of his nerves from the last few days. Fae actually seemed to be enjoying herself, if the smile lighting up her face was any indication. It was her smile that distracted him from the group that stopped by their table, but when he realized they weren't moving on he looked over at the guy standing next to him.

"Hey man, you guys looked like you were having fun so my friends and I decided to join you. You cool with that?" The guy was young and overly confident. A few of the others gave greetings and one of them leaned on the back of Fae's chair. She hadn't reacted to the group and was currently staring off into the crowd, ignoring them completely. Just as Kiernan was about to respond and explain that they didn't want or need the company the guy leaned down to whisper, "So, is she yours? Cause she's hot."

"No, she's not *mine*." Kiernan answered out loud so Fae could hear while he stared at the guy. He caught Fae's head as she turned around in his peripheral vision.

"Well, that's good to know!" He laughed and leaned on their table locking eyes with Fae. "Hey baby girl, I'm Jared. How about you let me buy you a drink?"

"No, thanks." Fae's voice was flat and cold and her smile was gone. Jared made a wounded sound.

"Oh come on, beautiful, give me five minutes. You'll love me once you get to know me, trust me." He reached forward and put his hand on her arm and tugged once, and that was all Kiernan needed. He grabbed the front of Jared's shirt and pushed him back. Jared's eyes widened before he caught his balance and shoved Kiernan's hands away from him.

"Hey! It's not my fault you got friend-zoned, asshole. Give the girl a chance to get to know someone else!" His friends drunkenly cheered and dissolved into laughter.

"She said no. Move on." Kiernan was trying to keep an eye on Fae, but Jared put his hands on Kiernan's chest and shoved him back.

"Why don't *you* move on, man? She's clearly not interested in you, and maybe she'd like to come home with me." Out of the corner of his eye he saw Fae move as she slid from her chair. One of Jared's friends dropped a hand on her shoulder, laughing loudly. He said something about her coming to hang out with them, but stopped suddenly when Fae grabbed the hand on her shoulder and twisted it violently. In a moment the guy was bent over with his arm twisted up behind his back, he went from laughing to crying out in pain in a matter of seconds. The ghostly outline of the bands had appeared on her wrists. Someone was focusing on her hard enough to tempt the curse. *Damn.* The guy she held started cussing at her and she brought her knee up sharply into his stomach and then let go of his arm so he dropped to the floor. He watched as her eyes found the bands at her wrists and her fists clenched.

"What the hell?! You little bi-" Another of the guys stepped forward and tried to grab Fae, and when his arm went around her she shifted and flipped the guy over her shoulder, and he landed hard on top of his friend.

She didn't need his protection.

Kiernan grinned, grabbing the back of Jared's shirt as he went for Fae. He was pretty sure Jared was the one who wanted Fae, and it wasn't going to happen. When Jared turned he tried to throw a punch, but Kiernan dodged his flailing arm easily and responded with two hits to the guy's midsection. Jared bent over, wrapping his arms around his stomach, so Kiernan just kneed him in the face which sent him to the floor cupping his hands over his bleeding nose. Kiernan turned around to see Fae duck under a wide swing from the last idiot, and then David, the bartender, was grabbing the guy from behind.

"Trying to hit a girl? What the hell is wrong with you?" The guy was slurring his words as he tried to explain that Fae had attacked *them*. David wasn't listening and locked eyes with Kiernan. "You guys better go before someone calls the cops. As far as I'm concerned, I didn't see anything but these guys trying to start a fight with a customer."

Kiernan stepped over the men on the ground and clapped David on the shoulder. "Thanks. I appreciate it." Fae was hiding her arms under the coat she had pulled off the back of the chair to keep the bands hidden. Shifting her in front of him, Kiernan moved toward the exit. When they hit the cool air outside he took a deep breath and looked over at Fae to find her smiling broadly. "What are you smiling for?"

"Are you kidding? That was the most fun I've had in years!" She grinned and bounced up and down, pulling the bottle of scotch from under the coat. "Plus, I brought this with us so we could finish it." Kiernan laughed and she joined him, her voice echoing off the buildings around them.

"Everything okay?" He gestured to the bands and she nodded.

"I'm fine, it could have been worse. The curse could sense him, and he could have made a claim, but you didn't really give him the chance. So, thanks."

"You didn't seem to need my help." Kiernan muttered, and Fae smiled again. "We better get out of here, just in case someone called the police." Fae nodded and he started jogging down the street. Fae kept up easily, and a block or two down he slowed and she stepped up next to him. He looked over and asked, "Do you want to head back to the apartment, or...?"

Fae shook her head. "No, I haven't been outside in a city in a long time. Can we just walk around?"

Kiernan nodded and pointed down another street. "There's a park that way, we could go walk around there. Just have to be careful drinking the alcohol, it's sort of illegal to drink it outside."

Fae laughed.

"Really? That's ridiculous. Someone would actually arrest you for drinking?"

"Yes. Really." Kiernan watched as Fae rolled her eyes, but hid the bottle under her coat. It only took about ten minutes to walk to the park and step onto the sidewalk that wound through the rolling dark green of the grass.

They walked around mostly in silence. Sometimes Fae would smile to herself as she stared up at the clouds and the stars as they occasionally broke through. While Fae was looking skyward, Kiernan couldn't take his eyes off of her. The ghostly outline of the bands had faded completely, and the moonlight lit her skin up and made it shine. They found a hill in the park and sat down on it and started passing the scotch back and forth. The alcohol was keeping Kiernan warm in the cold air so he shrugged his jacket off.

"I want to ask you a question." Fae's voice surprised him as it broke the quiet that had settled between them.

"Sure." Kiernan held the bottle against his knee, tilting the last few inches of amber colored liquid inside from side to side.

"Why didn't you just tell that guy I was yours? It might have avoided all of that, even though the fight was fun." She hadn't turned to look at him and was still staring up into the sky like she wanted to memorize what the clouds looked like.

"Because I wanted to." That answer made Fae turn to look at him, the place between her eyebrows wrinkled as she tried to decipher what he meant. Kiernan sighed and explained, "When he asked me - I wanted to say you were mine."

"Then why didn't you?"

"First, saying it aloud could have claimed you, in fact, it probably would have, and I told you already that I want you free. Second?" He paused and stared down at the practically empty bottle. "I don't know which part of me wanted to say it. Me, or Gormahn." Fae reached over and took the bottle from him, tilting it to take the last drink.

"Well, at least you're honest." She glanced at him and Kiernan gave her a half smile, but she beamed a smile back at him. What he'd done to deserve *that*, he didn't know, but every time she smiled he felt warm inside. She stood up and extended her hand to help him up, and even though he didn't need it, he took her hand and let her tug him to his feet.

"Ready to head back?" he asked. Fae was looking up at the sky again, but she nodded and her smile was still on her face. It didn't take long to get back to the apartment and walk up the flights of stairs. When they got inside Kiernan immediately went and grabbed one of his pillows and some blankets and came back to the living room where Fae was standing by the battle axe on his wall looking at it. He paused, "Planning to attack me again?"

"Maybe, I haven't decided yet." She turned around, her smile still tugging at the edges of her lips. Kiernan set the pillow and the blankets on the arm of the couch.

"Well, I'd prefer if you didn't kill me in my sleep. At least let me be awake for it." He was only half-joking when he said it. She grinned and he pointed at the stuff on the couch. "Here's some blankets and a pillow, I don't have another bed, but I've fallen asleep on the couch before. It's pretty comfortable, and I figured -"

"The couch is fine, thanks." She cut him off. He nodded and took a few steps back towards the hall to his room.

"So, I'll see you in the morning?"

Fae muttered, "Yeah," and turned to spread out the blankets across the couch. Kiernan headed to his room and shut the door behind him, leaning against it. The clock showed it was a little after three, but he couldn't sleep even with all the liquor.

Fae was in his apartment.

She was here, and she was *safe*, and more brave and beautiful than he had guessed. If she ever wanted to leave he wouldn't stop her, but that didn't mean he wasn't going to do everything he could to convince her to stay.

CHAPTER ELEVEN

SEATTLE, WASHINGTON

WHEN DAWN CAME Fae felt the warmth of Eltera's power flow through her while she was snuggled comfortably in a thick blanket. Turning her face into the pillow she took a deep breath - it smelled *wonderful*. It was a clean smell, a mix of the way the earth smelled after it rained and some kind of spice. Burrowing her face into the smooth pillow case, she suddenly remembered where she was, and whose pillow she was cuddling. Sitting straight up she looked around to find Kiernan standing at the entrance to the kitchen, holding a pan in his hand.

"Morning!" Kiernan's eyes moved over her and he chuckled to himself. "I never noticed how brightly you lit up. You're a regular glowworm." Fae looked down at her skin which glowed gold, the color of her goddess' power. There was nothing to heal in her except for the haze of alcohol still lingering in her blood, which rapidly burned away. Closing her eyes she tried to hold on to Eltera's presence, but it faded away with the light coming from her skin. When she opened her eyes again Kiernan was still standing at the opening to his kitchen.

"Morning..." Fae grumbled, scrunching her face up at him. She had slept in her clothes just in case Kiernan's moral values had a shift while they were sleeping, but he hadn't bothered her at all. She tossed the blanket off and let her feet hit the cool tile floor.

"I'm making breakfast. I wasn't sure what you'd like so I have pancakes made, and bacon, and sausage, and I'm making an omelet, but if you'd rather have the eggs another way I still have half a dozen -"

Fae put her hand up to stop him. "Thanks anyway, but I'm not hungry," she mumbled, rolling her shoulders to stretch. Kiernan's face reflected his disappointment as he looked down at the pan in his hand, the delicious smell of breakfast wafting towards her. Fae felt a brief pang of guilt at refusing him, he looked like a kicked puppy.

"Oh, well, I can get you something else if you want?" He was hopeful for a second, until she dashed that too with a shake of her head. Fae stood up and Kiernan stepped back into the kitchen. Pulling the blanket off the couch she started folding it, and behind her she heard the pan land in the sink and water start running. Fae dropped the blanket over the pillow, turning to see Kiernan at the edge of the kitchen, his arms crossed over his broad chest. "When was the last time you ate anyway?"

Fae thought about it for a moment, and then she spoke quietly, "The night of the party." Her stomach turned thinking about that night, and then her mind leapt to Juliet. Juliet screaming, Juliet beaten and unconscious, ... Juliet dead. *She definitely didn't want to eat now*. Kiernan looked angry for a moment, and his body tensed up for a second at her answer. She wondered how much of that night he'd seen, but he didn't even begin to say anything about it.

"You have to eat. Just tell me what you'd like and I'll go get it." His words were stiff, and she could tell he was on edge.

She sighed, preparing to explain. "It's okay, honestly. I don't really like eating food that people cook for me unless I have to. Why are you up so early?" Kiernan didn't keep arguing with her, but his disappointment and frustration was visible all over him. When his dark eyes flicked up to meet hers, she saw a flash of pain in them.

"Nightmare." He was too serious, this whole discussion was too serious for early morning. Neither of them could have slept more than a couple of hours, but that was just one more advantage to belonging to a god.

Fae nodded at him and hooked her thumbs into the pockets of her jeans. She almost asked him about the nightmare, or if he was okay, but the questions caught in her throat. The ease of talking with him from the night before seemed to have left her when the scotch burned away from her blood.

"Can I use your shower?" she blurted out the question to fill the void in the conversation.

Kiernan pushed a hand through his hair and nodded. "Of course, I'll stay out here and clean up the kitchen. Take as long as you want." He gestured towards the hall and Fae took a few steps back, giving a quick awkward smile before she turned on her heel and escaped to his room. When she stepped inside she turned and shut the door, and after a moment she locked it. Her stomach was uneasy at the thought of locking the door, and him noticing it.

Why was she even concerned about hurting his feelings?

Locking the door was a practical decision; anyone would do it in her situation.

"I am so fucking stupid." Fae huffed out a breath and flipped the lock back. Why she was trusting him, she didn't know, but *this* was his chance. If he crossed the line she'd just – what? Try to kill him again and fail? Fae muttered to herself and looked around the room. His bed was a mess of rumpled sheets and a big comforter half on the floor.

He didn't seem to sleep easy, that was for sure.

His clothes from the day before were on the floor around a dark wicker basket, which was probably his laundry hamper. The door to the bathroom was slightly ajar and she pushed it open and flipped the light switch. The bathroom was larger than she had imagined with a long counter, a huge claw foot bathtub, and a big glass shower. She fumbled around the bathroom for a bit to find a towel, a washcloth, and to verify that there was soap in the shower. Once she had it she slipped out of her clothes and folded them carefully, turning the water to hot. It poured out of a flat rain showerhead, straight down, and she stepped in and almost moaned aloud at how good it felt.

Fae tried to shower quickly, but it was soothing to relax under the water, and the soap he used had the spiced scent that she had caught on his pillow. It was a nice break from the vanilla she had used for the last three years, the one Nikola had been obsessed with. Strange how just being allowed to *smell* different was freeing, and she had to admit his soap smelled amazing.

Standing under the water her mind drifted back to how he had been the night before. He had acted completely normal around her at the bar, almost relaxed. He treated her so normally it was almost weird. He was quick to smile and laugh, and she didn't mind thinking of how he had looked in the dim light of the bar, and the cool light from the moon. She grinned remembering how he hadn't moved to stop her or help her when she'd gotten into it with those guys at the bar – he had just let her fight her own battle.

The only time he'd stepped in was to stop the guy who was responding to the curse, which she was still grateful for.

Even then, had he wanted to, he *could* have just claimed her for himself and avoided the entire situation, but he hadn't. He'd kept her free like he had promised. Now that she was thinking about it he had also rescued her from the guards in the snow, and she'd never really thanked him for that, especially since Butler would have been waiting for her. She hadn't thanked him at all really, for the safe place to stay, lying to his friends, the clothes.

Then on top of everything she'd refused the breakfast he'd made her. If he wanted to have her he didn't need to drug her food, he could have taken any of his numerous chances to make a claim, he could have fucked her when she was pinned to the floor.

Fae rested her head against the tile and cursed. Her father wouldn't have been happy with how she was responding to Kiernan's kindness. He had taught her that whenever she was a guest, she should be grateful for anything they provided. It had just been lifetimes since she was anyone's *guest*, but Kiernan had made it clear that's what she was, and she had been completely ungrateful.

"Way to go, Fae. A couple millennia of slavery and you forget all your manners..." Flipping the water off, she squeezed out her hair and wrapped it up in a towel before drying off. There was a toothbrush still in the package out on the counter, again evidence that he was being thoughtful.

She was such a bitch.

She looked through his cabinets and couldn't find a real hairbrush, or a hair dryer, so she just vigorously toweled her hair and attempted to finger comb as much as it was possible. Keeping the towel wrapped around her she stepped back into his room to find that he had lined her bags up against the wall the night before. Digging through them she found a green sweater, and another pair of jeans. Her hair was still very damp, but she couldn't do anything else about it. Taking a deep breath she opened the door and walked back into the living room to find Kiernan sitting on the couch watching something on TV.

He turned to look at her and stared at her the same way he kept looking at her, like she was some kind of new creature that had walked out of the ocean. It was a little unnerving, but the expression quickly faded.

"Did you have a good shower?" He made a face that reflected how dumb he thought that question was.

"It was fine, and I -, um," Fae came and stood next to the end of the couch picking at the fabric a little. "I just wanted to say thank you for everything you've done so far - the clothes, and trying to make me breakfast, and getting me away from the guards and out of the snow. I'm sorry that I was a bitch, and I'm sorry for trying to kill you before giving you a chance to explain yourself." She forced herself to look up from the couch at him.

Kiernan seemed surprised, and he just shook his head. "You don't need to thank me, at all. I wish I could do more. All of this doesn't even begin to make up for everything that – well, *everything*." He stood up and pressed buttons on the remote and the TV clicked off, then he dropped the remote back on the couch. "Also, I should have known better than to cook when you couldn't even watch me do it - that was stupid of me. I have an idea though, if you'd be willing to come somewhere with me?"

"Okay." Fae was relieved he hadn't made a big deal out of her thanks. Kiernan was dressed in a black sweater that hung well across his shoulders. His jeans were worn and ended in the same shoes he'd worn the day before. He smiled at her, and she smiled back which instantly took some of the awkwardness out of the situation.

"Then let's head out, Glowworm."

"What did you call me?" Fae wrinkled her nose.

"Glowworm. After all, you lit up my living room like one this morning." Kiernan grinned mischievously at her as he opened his front door for her to step through.

"I am *not* a Glowworm." Fae glared at him over her shoulder as they headed to the stairs.

"Too bad, I like Glowworm." At a landing in the stairwell she turned and punched him in the arm, he grabbed it and laughed.

"Don't call me that!" She glared at him, but his grin only broadened as he rubbed his arm.

"You telling me not to call you Glowworm is only going to make it stick. Alright, Glowworm?" Fae rolled her eyes and mumbled some obscenities while jogging down the stairs. Kiernan followed her down and when they came out on to the street he gestured to the left.

"We're going that way." Kiernan told her while trying to keep the laughter out of his voice. Fae headed that direction walking a swift pace ahead of Kiernan. He jogged a few steps to catch up to her.

"Come on, don't be mad, Fae. I'm taking you to my favorite place in the city, you can't be mad once you're there." She glared at him, and he just smiled at her, which made her want to smile despite herself. He had a big grin on his face the entire way while he pointed out some local landmarks. They took a few turns before they arrived at a pair of gates with a sign that read:

'You can bury a lot of troubles digging in the dirt'.

"What is this place?" Fae looked through the wrought iron fencing at the large plot of land where little sheds were placed randomly. The whole thing was surrounded by buildings as if the city had just forgotten to build there.

"It's a community garden." Kiernan pointed at the sign. "That sign has been there for a long time. It's what originally made me come in. I had a lot of troubles to bury."

Fae looked over at his face and he seemed lost for a minute, "It looks... nice?"

He laughed. "It's not going to win any awards for beautification, but it's a place where people from around the city can come and plant gardens, grow fruits and vegetables, and then everyone can take some home."

Fae traced a hand across the worn edges of the sign while Kiernan punched a code into the push button lock and then opened one of the gates. Fae followed him in while he walked along a meandering tiny path between sleeping gardens until he got to one of the sheds. He let her in first and inside there was some stored warmth, and in long troughs were growing vegetables and herbs. Light came through the semi-transparent walls and ceiling so that it was easy to see by. She watched as Kiernan rushed around the little greenhouse gathering gloves and spades and a few clay pots.

"*This* is your favorite place in the city?" Fae shrugged off his coat, and walked up to one of the troughs filled with soil and small, green, growing plants. She traced one of the tender leaves with her finger. It was mint. A little ways over was a section filled with basil, and the scent in the air was wonderful and fresh and earthy. Kiernan stepped up next to her, smiling like a kid with a new toy as he held out a pair of gloves to her.

"Yeah, I told you I was a farmer once. Digging in the soil is what I was meant to do. If I'd had the choice I would have kept my spade over a sword. Anyway, I just wanted to take care of something real quick before we do what I came here for. You can help if you want." Fae took the gloves and smiled at the idea of getting back to a garden as she tugged them on. It had been one of the few joys for her at Ráj Manor. Kiernan moved over to a trough crowded with tomato plants with small tomatoes just starting to appear all over them.

"I wouldn't have imagined you spending your spare time in a place like this." Fae looked over at him, his broad shoulders bent forward as he picked up a spade, digging gently around one of the tomato plants.

"It makes me feel more like myself. It was one of the first things I really wanted to do after I started to wake up from Gormahn's control." Kiernan shrugged. "We need to give these a little more space, the girl that planted them didn't plan very well and they're going to choke themselves. We just want to replant some in that empty section at the back." Fae grabbed the other spade and mimicked him. Kiernan very gently lifted out the first plant, and being careful with its root system, he walked back to the other trough and replanted it.

"How long have you been here?" Fae asked while lifting her own. She was good with plants, her father had taught her everything she needed to know about tending them and she felt confident in moving the little green lives back and forth. They quickly found a rhythm to clean up the crowded bed.

"Maybe ten years, I'll have to move on soon or people will start to wonder why I look the same. I can only say it's *good genetics* for so long. I'm going to be sad to leave this one though, some great locals support it."

"Where were you before Seattle?"

"Denver, Colorado. I like the cooler temperatures. I've never been a fan of hot places, and I wanted out of Europe for a while."

"Did you do this there too?" She asked, and Kiernan nodded at her.

"Yeah, I helped get a community garden started there. I mainly just gave people the money to do what they already wanted to do. I've donated to this one too to keep it afloat."

He spoke so casually, and Fae watched him for a minute as he moved the tender plants, carrying them with care. It made her think of her father, and how he had told her repeatedly that a good man puts his hands in the ground, while others simply walk upon it. Fae wasn't sure what kind of man Kiernan was yet, but this was another tally mark in the 'good guy' category.

"Where did you get all the money for that?"

"You'd be surprised how much money you can gather across the centuries... especially when you've ransacked almost every major civilization in the last two thousand years. Artifacts and gold and jewels are easy to sell if you have the right connections." He pressed the soil down around the last transplant and started to water the troughs of herbs and vegetables. Lifting his head up from a bed of lettuce he smiled at Fae. "We also have some really smart accountants." Fae smiled and tugged her gloves off while she watched him.

"So, if this isn't why we came here, what are we here for?" She crossed her arms and Kiernan turned around and set the watering can down.

"Come on, I'll show you." Opening the door he stepped outside and held it for Fae to walk through. Once he had secured the door he walked across the lot to another little storage house, and Fae followed him, tugging his coat tight around her in the wind. When she got to the door she was surprised to find big baskets of fresh fruits and vegetables stacked on tables inside. A big sign at the back read: '*Take what you need. Leave what you can.*' There was a simple locked cash box under it and a slot to drop in money. Unfolding a cloth bag Kiernan handed it over to her. "Go ahead, pick what you'd like to eat. Then you can cook it at the apartment. I won't touch anything."

"It's fine if you do. Really." Fae rubbed the top of the bag between her fingers looking across the fresh produce. It made her stomach growl to think of all of it, but she was still nervous at the idea. Kiernan hopped up on one of the empty spots on the tables, scooting back until he was leaning against the wall.

"No, it's not. I'm okay with that considering everything they've put in your food. Pick what you'd like, it's the best produce in the city." He leaned forward to watch her, his dark eyes tracking her as she walked slowly up and down the rows. Fae traced her fingertips across the rough wood tables, grabbing a few carrots, a handful of snap peas, several potatoes, and turning down the back she grabbed an eggplant.

"This is good." Lifting the bag a little, Fae gave a small smile.

Kiernan chuckled. "You sure that's enough? You can grab some more so you have a couple of meals." He hopped down off the table and Fae grabbed a few more of each item until the bag was heavy. Tucking a few bills into the lockbox he waited for her to be done.

"Thanks, Kiernan. All of it looks great."

"Of course, now we just need to head to a market for

meat and anything else you might need, or, wait, are you a vegetarian?" He turned around from the door and paused.

Fae had to stop herself from laughing, so she just covered her mouth before she spoke, "Not at all. I used to help with the butchering before everything became so readily available in stores."

"Good to know you're not squeamish." He smiled at her, and then headed back outside. When they left the little garden, Kiernan made sure the gate was secured and then headed back towards his apartment. After a few minutes of Kiernan asking her what she planned to cook with her not having any answers yet, they went inside the market. It was Sunday morning and there were crowds of families walking through the aisles pushing big carts, and single people carrying baskets on their arms. It meant the entire store was crowded. Kiernan placed his hand on her back to guide her to the side of the entrance so they were out of the way. He walked up to a woman at the register and leaned over to talk to her, she turned around and a blush crept across her cheeks as she looked at Fae.

Well, if Fae didn't feel awkward *before* she sure did now.

"Everything's okay. Elsie knows we're bringing in some veggies from the garden so it won't be any trouble when we're done." Kiernan talked to her as he was walking back over, then he turned and pointed, "Meat counter is at the back of the store."

"Got it." She nodded, and Kiernan gave her a big smile over his shoulder as he snagged a basket from the entrance and walked down one of the aisles towards the back. Several women's eyes followed him as he moved, looking at him like *he* was the meat. There was something that itched inside her when she saw the women staring after him, but Fae pushed it away and started to follow him. When they got to the big glass case filled with pre-portioned cuts of meat she watched as Kiernan looked over the little labels before walking over to her.

"Alright, do you know what you want?" Kiernan seemed relaxed and happy. She was amazed that he melted into the population so seamlessly, like it was normal to be in a store where food filled the shelves ready to be picked up. Fae felt like she stood out, because she couldn't relax at all. She expected at any point for someone to show up and ruin everything, discover who she was and drag her back to Butler or some new personalized hell.

Choosing a protein for dinner seemed ridiculously mundane when compared to the majority of her life decisions.

"Fae?" Kiernan's voice broke through her thoughts. He was still smiling, and the man behind the counter was waiting for her answer, he gave her a smile too.

'*There isn't a threat here*', she had to remind herself and take a breath.

"Umm, chicken?" She stepped up to the glass case and looked inside as the guy wrapped up chicken breasts. "Oh! Salmon too?" Kiernan laughed to himself and nodded to the man behind the counter who grabbed a few fillets and wrapped them up too. The man handed them across the case to her and she smiled and muttered a thank you. That had been... easy.

"Geez Kiernan, you can't just come in like this and surprise me!" Fae jumped at the loud female voice that was only a few steps behind her. Turning around she saw that the woman wrapping her arms around Kiernan was the same from the front of the store. When she leaned back from the hug her eyes creased at the edges with the strength of her smile. The woman kept one arm around Kiernan and extended her hand to Fae. "I'm Elsie, and you are...?"

"I'm Fae." She reached forward and shook Elsie's hand who grinned even bigger and turned to look up at Kiernan, who was easily a foot taller than her. She was probably in her mid-forties and had a big mop of curly brown hair on her head, and whoever she was to Kiernan her touch seemed welcome.

"Kiernan, I could smack you for not telling me you had such a beautiful young lady in your life. I thought you said you always tell me everything?" Elsie talked to him like he was a kid, and Kiernan didn't seem to mind.

"I do tell you everything, Elsie. Fae and I just met each other." Kiernan grinned at her and hugged her to his side before letting her go. Elsie gave Fae a onceover, but the glance didn't feel judgmental or threatening. Elsie seemed to be warm and kind, and her smile looked genuine.

"Well, my girl, you shouldn't let *this* one go," Elsie punctuated her statement by tapping Kiernan on the arm. "He's one in a million. Grab on to him and hold on tight!"

"Don't scare her away, Elsie. Fae and I are just friends." Kiernan was blushing slightly but he still smiled at the woman. She responded by throwing her hands up with an exasperated sigh.

"Here now, I've *never* seen you with a girl before so she has to be something special." Looking at Fae, Elsie spoke in a conspiratorial whisper, "Don't let him fool you, you wouldn't be here if he didn't like you, and as beautiful as you are he won't hold out." Fae grinned as Kiernan's blush brightened and he leaned forward to tug Elsie back from Fae.

"Is that right? I didn't expect him to spend his time alone." Fae was enjoying this way too much and Kiernan's embarrassment was obvious. Elsie stepped out of Kiernan's hands and looped her arm through Fae's, and the two of them started walking towards the front of the store.

"Oh, he's *always* alone. Sometimes I go to his place and make him dinner because I think otherwise he would just sit there, alone, staring at the television. I just take care of him like I would my boys." Elsie was pretending to whisper, but was actually talking so loudly that everyone could hear her. Normally Fae didn't like to be touched but Elsie instantly made her comfortable. There were no weird looks, no strange stares, Elsie had treated her like she was an old friend, and Kiernan's obvious discomfort was making it hard for Fae not to laugh. Elsie started talking again, loud and warm, "See, I have two boys about

Kiernan's age, and they're both off at college so I have to spend all my mothering on him."

"And I'm lucky to be mothered by you." Kiernan was shuffling behind them, the blush starting to fade from his cheeks as he watched them both.

"You're right you are!" She wagged a finger at him before leaning back towards Fae. "Has he told you that he helped my boys get scholarships to college?"

"No, he hasn't told me about that." Fae smiled as they stopped at the check-out line at the front of the store, and she glanced back at Kiernan to see him rolling his eyes.

"Such a modest boy. A couple of years ago he heard me talking about saving up to send my boys to college and he suggested they send an application to the company he works for because they do scholarships. He brings me the essay topic and a form and I have them both fill them out." Elsie was talking with her hands, and Kiernan was looking at her like she was a precious stone. "So, I have my son who had already graduated fill it out, and my other son, Timothy, was graduating that year so I made him fill it out too. And you know what?!" Elsie's voice was even louder in her excitement.

"You don't need to tell Fae this story, Elsie." Kiernan had shoved his hands in the back pockets of his jeans, but pulled one out to push his fingers through his hair.

"Hush, Kiernan." Elsie chastised him and turned back to Fae with a huge smile. "They *both* won! Full scholarships! I have never been so grateful for anything in my life, the Laochra Company is such a blessing, and it's all thanks to this boy." Elsie grabbed Kiernan's face between her hands, and he smiled down at her and gave her a hug. When Elsie stepped back her eyes were filled with tears. "He is wonderful. Don't let him fool you, he needs a woman like you. I can tell you're a good girl, and so pretty."

"Thanks for fully embarrassing me, Elsie, I'm sure it will take my pride at least a week to recover." Kiernan was smiling as he said it though and Elsie just waved her hands at him, trying to avoid crying.

"Stop it, just stop it now. I have to go back to work, break time over!" Elsie grabbed Fae's hands and kissed her on the cheek. "You two have a good time today."

"Thank you, Elsie, I'm really glad I got to meet you." Fae was smiling, and Elsie just nodded and wiped her eyes before heading down one of the aisles. Kiernan stepped in front of Fae and let out a breath of air.

"I'm sorry if she was overwhelming. Elsie kind of adopted me a few years ago. I told her my parents were dead when she asked if they'd be visiting one time and she has insisted on feeding me and taking care of me since then." His cheeks still held a touch of color, and it fascinated Fae that such a little woman could have such an effect on him.

"She was lovely. In fact, I think I should talk to her some more, find out more of your secrets." Fae stepped up to the checkout and Kiernan laid the basket with the little packages on the belt. "But... Laochra Company? Scholarships?" He put a finger over his lips and leaned past her to pay the cashier, then they headed outside and Kiernan turned around and started walking backwards in front of her.

"I had to tell her something, it seemed the easiest solution."

"So you paid for them?"

"Yeah, it wasn't a big deal. I just made up some forms, printed them out and had her kids fill them in. She works so hard but would never be able to afford college working there, and the dad died a few years back." He shrugged and adjusted the bag of vegetables on his arm. "Plus, you see how happy it made her?"

"Yes, I did." Fae smiled and stepped up next to Kiernan. "You're a very interesting guy, Kiernan."

"I knew that already, but I'm glad you're figuring it out. Ready to make lunch, Glowworm?" His cocky grin was obnoxiously attractive, so Fae shoved him and he laughed as they turned down the street his apartment was on.

CHAPTER TWELVE

SEATTLE, WASHINGTON

KIERNAN HAD SPENT an hour standing at the entrance to his kitchen with his hands studiously shoved into his pockets while he guided Fae around with words alone. He gave directions to help her find the cutting board, knives, pans, olive oil, and seasonings.

When she grabbed the knife she had cheerfully turned towards him. "Letting me hold a butcher's knife? Bold."

"Well, since you've already tried to kill me with the largest blade in the house, and failed, I feel pretty safe." He'd grinned, and she had scowled at him.

"Asshole," she had muttered under her breath, but then he'd been rewarded with one of her smiles that made his heart race, and it made him want to be in the kitchen helping her instead of standing to the side just to prove he didn't want to hurt her. Just to prove he wasn't trying to drug her with Oblivion. His stomach twisted as he came face to face with the reality she had lived for too long. It wasn't paranoia on her part, it was her *life*.

It made him want to take a midnight trip to that house in Caledon and slit some throats, but that would be a step in the wrong direction. That was the darkness talking.

Fae moved around the kitchen easily once she knew where things were. She cut the vegetables with confidence and laid them into a pan while simultaneously keeping track of the salmon. It was clear she was a lot better at cooking than he was, but she'd probably had more practice. When she was done he realized she had made two plates. She handed him one with a smile, and they sat down to eat in his living room. At first they were silent, but then they started talking over anything that came to mind.

It was so easy to be around her. He wasn't hiding who he was, like he had to with mortals, and since she no longer seemed to hate him, he could see this working out. But there was the issue - what was *'this'* exactly? The chance of Cole or Eryn stopping by definitely wasn't out of the question, and it's not like they ever knocked first. He'd have no way to explain this if they saw her. It was brutally obvious that she was Faeoihn. That would be just about the worst case scenario for whatever this was, because if Gormahn knew she could kill her master he'd destroy her, and he doubted even Eltera could protect her. Beyond the complete possibility of a horrible outcome, he still didn't have a bedroom for her – he didn't even have a bed to let her sleep in – and would keeping her here really be any different than her being trapped in any other house on the planet? Would he be any better than any other person who'd kept her?

"Kiernan." Fae was leaning forward on the couch looking at him, her eyebrows were pulled together and he realized she had probably said his name a few times. He had completely lost track of the conversation.

"YEAH?" He sat up straighter and gave her a smile before picking up his fork and taking a bite of the salmon. It was delicious.

"Do you like it?" She spoke and then her lips were parted just a little and for a second he wondered what it would be like to lean forward and kiss them, but he pushed that thought aside. She didn't need someone else wanting to paw at her, he was better than that.

He had to be better than that.

"It's really good. Actually, I think it's the most the spices in that cabinet have been used since I moved here." He popped another bite in his mouth to prove the point, and the satisfied groan that escaped him wasn't faked. It was seriously the best meal to come out of his kitchen – ever. She smiled again and he was warmed from the inside out, no matter what thoughts crossed his mind he'd never do *anything* to stop that smile. In fact, he'd probably kill anyone who threatened it. Darkness or not. Still smiling she sat back and started eating everything on her plate. Between them talking about more books and authors she ate another plate of food, which he was glad to see. The power in them kept them alive, but it didn't make hunger hurt any less, and he knew she'd been hungry.

When they were done he took her plate from her and cleaned up the kitchen. She watched him from the living room as he washed the dishes and loaded the dishwasher, all with her feet tucked under her on the couch. With her shoes still on. If she hadn't looked so comfortable he would have commented that her shoes were going to mess up the pale fabric, but he didn't have the heart to ask her to move her feet.

If he had to he'd just buy a new couch.

When he put the last of the dishes in the dishwasher and clicked it on he walked back into the living room to find her tracing her hand over the box that held the observation glass. He had left it on the table by his chair, and now he sort of wished he'd hidden it in a closet. Or under the bathroom counter. Or sealed it in cement. Now she'd probably want to check in on one of the Faeoihn, and he couldn't watch her do that again. Just the idea made him nauseous.

"Why were you watching me?" Her voice was calm and quiet, and she flipped the lid open again to look at the glass and then let it fall shut with a clap. That was *not* the question he had expected.

"I don't know."

"Come on, just tell me, what made you look that day?" She looked up at him and her hair fell into her face, and with a delicate swipe she tucked it behind her ear.

"The vines – the ones on my arm – when something happens that shouldn't, they grow and it kind of burns. So I knew something was going on, and -" he took a breath, pushing a hand through his hair, "and I sort of always check on you first. And when I did… I saw you outside in the snow." Kiernan's stomach was in knots talking about this again, the last conversation had been a complete disaster, but Fae seemed calm.

"Why check on me first? Why watch me over the others?" Fae asked it without judgment, and Kiernan sighed and tugged at the sleeves on his shirt. Out of habit he traced his fingers over the black line starting on his palm, and he only glanced up at her for a moment. Her eyes weren't accusing, or angry, and maybe that made it easier to admit the truth to himself. It had been hard to understand why, even when Cole had brought it up, hard to put into words until she was in front of him. Until she was living and breathing and fighting and - *beautiful* - in front of him.

"Because of who you are." He grabbed his hair for a second before pushing his hands through it again, and then he leaned back against the wall. That little wrinkle appeared between her eyebrows and he wanted to smooth it with his thumb. How could he put it into words, without sounding crazy, how she was the most interesting of them all because she was just so strong, how her willful nature was the most beautiful thing about her, and her strength in the face of everything she had gone through made him know that he could live with *his* life, or at least survive it.

"By the gods, Fae," he groaned in frustration at not being able to find words for how he felt. "It's just who you *are* that always made me check on you first."

"Explain." Her voice was still calm, her body still relaxed as she sat curled on the edge of the couch with her shoes tucked neatly under her. That didn't mean she wouldn't dart for the door if he sounded as crazy as he felt. But if he was going to answer her, he was going to put it all on the table, everything he was thinking. No lies, and if the truth made her freak out, he'd deal with it.

He took a deep breath and tried his best to put it into words. "You're strong. Not physically – well, yes, physically, I mean I had a hell of a bruise yesterday to prove that –" he stopped and looked up to see one of her eyebrows neatly raised, so he made himself take another breath to reset and continue. "I just mean that you have this iron will. You don't let any of this shit break you down. I've watched people collapse under much less and you're still... you. You're sarcastic, and funny - you're hilarious when you want to be - and you're brave."

"I -"

"When I first started to come out of whatever haze - whatever *bloodlust* - Gormahn had me under for all those centuries I couldn't imagine getting out of bed and facing the world that I'd done so much damage in. I was overwhelmed by my own actions. I just wallowed in the memories I had, the violence I'd done, the terrible things. It was after a few days of self-pity that I started to actually use that damned observation glass he'd assigned me, and there you were." Kiernan had started pacing as he talked, occasionally looking at her, but he couldn't tell how she was reacting to what he was saying.

"You were there, every day, talking back to your *masters*. Protecting others because you knew *you'd* be okay the next day, because you knew you could survive it. Defying them in the smallest of ways and then taking their punishment and coming right back at them like it didn't faze you at all. And on top of all that you were somehow still *kind*! To mortals!" He sounded exasperated by the idea of her being kind, and he'd always been surprised that she could still manage it after everything she'd been through. "I could see that you didn't want to get close to those mortals but you would anyway, you would care for them, help them, guide them, and then I saw how much it hurt you when you lost them. Watching all of those things - watching you be *human* in the face of the worst parts of this world - helped me to be human again, to feel like I *could* be human again. I wish more than anything I had saved you sooner, that I had stopped it all the first chance I had, but I swear to you, Fae, I swear on my life I'll die before I ever let them take you back."

He finally looked at her, and he didn't know if she was going to respond, freak out, run, or attack him again. Her cheeks were flushed and it brought color to her lips and he caught himself staring.

"You actually like that about me? The defiance?" Fae's voice was quiet.

"It's what makes you who you are. It's – it's my favorite thing about you." Kiernan almost whispered it, afraid he had already scared her off and any minute she'd bolt for the door.

"I think you're the only person in millennia who's *ever* liked that about me."

"People are idiots." Kiernan shoved his hands in his pockets to stop the fidgeting.

"And you're not?" Fae's eyebrows went up again and the ghost of a smile appeared, and it made Kiernan grin.

She was so damn feisty.

"No, Glowworm, I thought you knew by now that I'm a genius." He said it with more bravado than he felt, and she rolled her eyes and threw a pillow at him.

"I hate that name."

"Well, I love it. *Glowworm*." Kiernan couldn't stop grinning. She was still sitting on his couch with her freaking shoes on the cushions, and he couldn't be happier about it.

HE SPENT the afternoon showing Fae how to work the TV with his surround sound system. He brought out the laptop and introduced her to the internet, but she was going to need a typing program to get comfortable with it. Before bed he opened a bottle of wine. Fae told him that she loved wine, but never got to have it, and he decided he'd stock up if it made her happy. The fact that she let him pour her a glass told him more about her level of comfort with him than anything else she could have done.

When it was finally time to sleep he left her in the living room again and went to his room and shut the door. He stared at his bed, but didn't want to lie down yet. Sleep would just mean nightmares, and he'd prefer to avoid them as long as possible. He reorganized his books, this time by genre, cleaned up his clothes and put them in the hamper, shuffled the bags of clothes he had bought her, cleaned the shower and the bath tub – and when he saw it was after two, he knew he had to lay down. Tugging the sheets and comforter back into place he dropped onto his pillow, and clicked off the light. In the dark he took deep, even breaths to let himself fall asleep.

Breathing in, and out, and in, and out - and then there was *fire*.

Fire, and screams, and a sword in his hand. He looked down and he could see the end of the sword was black with blood in the firelight. A woman ran past him, and she turned and started to ask him for help. At first her words were gibberish but his brain slowly started to translate it, it was Italian. The small village they were in was set in the shadow of a small mountain. The countryside was beautiful in the daytime, olive groves filled the area around it – and now it was all on fire. He wanted to react, to grab her and hide her somewhere, keep her safe, but his muscles wouldn't respond to him. She was walking backwards, her hands pressed together like she was praying, and he wanted to tell her that no one was listening, and that if one of the gods did she probably didn't want them to hear her. If Gormahn responded she'd definitely regret it. He heard his name called above the screaming, and his head turned to see Eryn coated in ash, his arms dark with blood. His lips were stretched in a wide grin and his teeth were gleaming white in the firelight.

Eryn crooked a finger at the woman and she was smart enough to be afraid of him, but now she was like the rabbit frozen by fear as it was approached by the hunting dogs. He could hear her murmuring pleas in Italian and he wanted to say stop, he felt his throat working to speak but nothing came out. Then, Eryn grabbed her by the hair and pulled her to make her stand up, he said something to Kiernan but he couldn't hear anymore. The world was a whirlwind of white nose as Eryn shoved the woman at him and he saw her mouth open in shock. Kiernan caught her by the shoulder but he looked down to see his sword in her stomach. He pulled it back, his chest tightening, but the damage was done, the blood was coming out, and Eryn was laughing and everyone wouldn't stop screaming.

Kiernan snapped awake and realized he had screamed in his sleep. He sat up and gripped his hair. It was another memory, a memory he didn't want, that he wished was only a nightmare, but he knew better. He had done that. He had killed that woman. He'd killed so many. His skin was cold from the sheen of sweat that covered him, and he had to reach across the bed to tug the sheets and comforter back over him. He had just covered himself when a soft knock came at his door.

"Co -" Kiernan had to cough to clear his throat. "Come in." Fae pushed the door open and was standing there in jeans and a t-shirt. He needed to buy her pajamas.

"Kiernan?"

"Yeah." He leaned over and clicked on the light, and when he looked back at her she looked genuinely concerned.

"You were screaming."

"Yeah, I'm sorry. Nightmares. I didn't mean to wake you up, or freak you out. Everything's fine." Kiernan pulled the comforter a little higher as he saw Fae's eyes drop across his shoulders and chest. He really should have slept in clothes.

"Want some water?" She had pulled her eyes back to his and he couldn't stop staring at her tangled hair. Even with bedhead she was a vision – a vision of something he didn't deserve. She tilted her head. "It's just, I get nightmares too, of *things*, and when they're bad like that I always wake up and my mouth is dry. I think it's the screaming." He realized she had explained her offer because he hadn't answered, so he nodded.

"Water would be great, thanks." She gave a small smile and slipped out of the room, and a moment later he heard cabinets opening and shutting. He took the opportunity to jump out of bed and grab a pair of jeans. He had just pulled them into place when she walked in with a glass of water. He took the glass and drank, shaking off the acrid taste in his mouth from the memory. He was surprised she'd even offered, that she'd even come to check on him at all.

But then again, she was a much better person than he was.

"So you really have nightmares?"

"Yes." He took another drink of water and then set it on the table, and when he turned back Fae's eyes were somewhere around his waist. It made him grin despite the lingering memory of the nightmare, and he couldn't resist teasing her. "Like what you see?"

"What?! No." Fae's cheeks were on fire and it brought out the red in her hair, he laughed and the tension started to ease out of his shoulders. If she was a cat her hair would have stood up across her back, and he loved it.

"Sure, Glowworm. You've boosted my ego though, so thanks. I'm already feeling better."

"Like you *needed* a boost to your ego, your ego seems fine." Fae crossed her arms and rolled her eyes, which only made him laugh again.

"Well, I'm going to go for a run to clear my head. I probably won't be able to go back to sleep, but you should." Kiernan turned and checked the clock and saw that it was a little after four.

"I'd give you some company, because I'm not going to be able to sleep either, but I don't think I have any running clothes." Fae stepped over to the clothing bags and kneeled down by them, starting to look through. Kiernan winced. He had really not thought things through, no pajamas, no workout clothes, and just one pair of shoes.

"That's it, I'm taking you shopping today, and then you can pick out what you want. It's close to dawn anyway and it would be a bad idea for you to go all Glowworm on the street." Kiernan found himself smiling and it surprised him. Usually after a nightmare like that he'd feel off all day, but Fae had come to him, and brought him water, and it had made the bitter memory fade into the background.

"You don't need to get me anything else, I appreciate the clothes."

"I'm taking you shopping because you *need* the clothes, and you can't get them on your own. Even if you wanted to go get a job, according to this government you don't exist." Kiernan stepped past Fae to get to his closet and walked in.

"Well, then I'll make you breakfast. What do you want?"

"You don't owe me anything." He called from inside the closet as he tugged a shirt on, and then he stepped out. "Seriously, Fae, you don't need to do anything for me. I'm the one who needs to make things up to you, a shopping spree is the least I can do."

"Okay, but I'll still make breakfast. Just because I want to, and then you can take me wherever people buy clothes." Fae made it a statement so he couldn't argue about it, and he put his hands up in surrender.

"Deal." He smiled at her and she returned it before she turned around and headed for the kitchen.

CHAPTER THIRTEEN

Ráj Manor, Caledon, Ontario

"Find her, dammit!" The glass he threw shattered against the wall and Butler took a deep breath trying to regain control. The guard in front of him, Thompson, had flinched. *Weakling.*

"We don't know where to look, sir." Thompson kept his voice even, but his muscles were tensed.

"So you keep saying. If she disappeared into thin air, someone took her who was able to *do* that, because she would have used that particular skill before now if she'd had it." Butler grabbed a new glass from Nikola's collection and poured himself another drink. He threw it back and hissed a breath through his teeth as the alcohol burned its way into his empty stomach.

"Yes, sir, but all we have is a loose description from the

men. She didn't speak to him, or say his name. How can we possibly know where he took her?"

"You keep questioning anyone involved, *that's* how." He took another drink and rolled his shoulders. "Have you tracked down the guest who had such an interest in her? The one who left that night."

"Ah, him." Thompson took out an iPhone and started tapping away. "We found the flight he took out, it was a private jet back to the US. We've sent a few of our guys to *encourage* him to come back and stay with us again."

"Good." Butler was nodding, but he wasn't able to think straight. He still wasn't sure what had happened that morning, only that things were out of control. Nikola was dead and it had happened on his watch, his son was being contacted by the lawyers, contractors would arrive today to start fixing the parlor, and they were missing one smart-mouthed whore. He had to get it all fixed before the heir arrived or he was out of a job, and out of the lifestyle he had become accustomed to. No one was going to take this away from him, not after all the years he'd put in. Especially not *her*.

"Sir, what do you want us to do next?" Thompson was standing at ease and had tucked his phone back into a pocket.

"Where are the idiots who let her get away?" Butler set the glass down and picked up a bottle of vodka, taking a drink from it.

"Evans, Cooper, and Hernandez are currently scrubbing

the entry way tile by hand. Cooper is having a particularly difficult time with the broken arm."

"Good. If they finish that today, send them to me." He took another drink and Thompson nodded to him.

"How long do we have before the new master of the house arrives?" Thompson needed the answer, and the question was a valid one, but it made Butler's blood boil. Nikola had handled the business side of things, but the house, and all those inside it, had mostly been under Butler's control. Nikola should have left *him* the house. Should have left *him* the slaves. He should have passed on ownership of all of it to him. He would keep them under control, and there'd be no more of those little acts of defiance that Nikola had let slide. It would be a new regime. He just had to convince Marik, the spoiled brat who only came home to beg for more money, bed a few girls, and cause a disaster, before launching himself back into the world. If he could convince him to sign control of the house over to him, everything could go back to normal. No, it would be *better* than normal, because he'd be in charge with no one to run his orders by.

"I don't know, a week or so. The lawyers have to track down what city he's set up camp in and fly him back. We need all of this shit settled before then." Butler could feel the buzz of the alcohol humming in his veins and he took another drink to try and calm the rage he felt.

"We will do our best to find her." Thompson took a breath. "Anything else, sir?"

"Finish your interrogations of the girls, one of them has

to know something about Fae's plan, they were all in there with her that morning."

"We will, sir, if there's anything for them to tell, they'll tell it." Thompson was grinning when Butler looked over at him.

"Good. But don't mark their faces, if Marik shows up earlier than expected we still need them to look pretty." Butler set the vodka down, and Thompson saluted him before walking out of the office. It had been Nikola's office, the massive desk and book covered walls reeked of money and privilege. Nikola's father had been the one to start the business, grabbing up mineral rights in Eastern Europe and raking in the cash while the people starved and died in numerous wars and uprisings. Nikola had stepped in and taken the business to new heights through investments, and deals, and bribes to officials in a variety of countries.

All of it done to fund his own personal estate with its collection of slaves. Butler knew it was all about having power, and now it was time for him to be the one in charge. For *him* to be the one with the power.

Butler left the office and walked down the hall where he took a key out of his pocket and opened one of the bedroom doors. When he stepped in he heard her trying to move back and it made him smile.

"So, Caridee, where did we leave off last time?" He tucked the key back in his pocket and turned to find her right where he'd left her the night before – sitting on the floor zip tied to the footboard of the bed.

"Sir, I don't know anything, I told you that, what more do you want from me?" She had her knees pulled up protectively in front of her and was leaning back against the footboard as far away from him as the bindings allowed.

"Tell me what you *do* know." Butler stepped over to the dresser and picked up the whip. Nikola had let him use it on Fae, but he didn't like him to use it on the *normal* girls. He hadn't understood how persuasive it could be. Caridee made a whimpering sound behind him.

"Please don't. I, um, I know she's not human, she's something *else*. She glows like the fires of hell are inside her every morning and she heals from anything because she's a witch of some sort. She even worships pagan gods!" Caridee was pulling on the zip ties, but it was only making them cut into her skin.

"I know she's not human, Caridee, that's what makes her worth lots and lots of money. I also know she killed Nikola somehow, and you're going to tell me what she told you girls about it." Butler uncoiled the whip and Caridee started crying, her dark hair was covering her face and she started muttering in Spanish. It might have been a prayer.

"She said nothing, she was going to ask about Juliet, she said nothing else." Caridee's words came between sobbing breaths and whimpers.

"Well, let's see if you stick to that story, shall we?"

CHAPTER FOURTEEN

SEATTLE, WASHINGTON

AFTER BEING WOKEN by his nightmares, the trip to the garden, meeting Elsie, and listening to the list of reasons for his fascination with her – hating Kiernan was getting harder.

But *that* was its own level of weird.

He was Laochra, the sworn enemy of the Faeoihn. He had literally been created – against his will or not – to destroy her and all of her sisters. To bring Eltera down. She should hate him, despise him, and nothing he did should have been able to change her mind about that. By his own admission he'd done horrible things, and what did it matter if for the last one or two hundred years he had behaved a little better? Did that erase all of the horrible things he'd likely done?

The answer was *no*.

Except when she looked at him, when he smiled at her as they were reading, or as they watched television, he seemed... nice. Kind. He was such a dichotomy between who he was clearly trying to be, and who he had been for almost two thousand years. A constant war of light and dark. And loathe as she was to admit it, Fae knew firsthand the light wasn't guaranteed a victory simply for being 'good'.

'And when he had you on the ground he stopped himself,' her brain piped up and she groaned quietly.

Fae wasn't sure how to feel. Was she betraying Eltera, and her sisters, every time she smiled at him? Every time she enjoyed his company? It had been so fucking long since anyone treated her like she was *normal*. Treated her like a person. Guilt gnawed at her for enjoying it while the rest of her sisters suffered, while the girls back at Ráj Manor still served as slaves. It was like every small moment of happiness she allowed herself was a slap in their faces.

Kiernan had taken her shopping the day before for more clothes and they had easily bantered back and forth about how they'd have to have a rematch now that she had workout gear. He had insisted on giving them to her, on giving her anything she wanted. The mere fact that he had been concerned about buying her clothes, about her being comfortable, about her being *happy* was ridiculous. A Laochra shouldn't care. A Laochra *wouldn't* care.

So, what did that make Kiernan?

As if on cue he stepped out of the kitchen holding a

spoon, and smiled broadly at her. He was so fucking *handsome*. Old world strength in his broad shoulders, his thick arms, and his muscular chest. He was a warrior. A killer.

And he was making them soup for lunch.

'Oh yeah, Fae, he's so evil. Diabolical soup making – you should head for the hills.' Her mind was taunting her, and apparently her subconscious already had an opinion about him.

"Hey, the food is about to be ready. Are you hungry now or should I let it simmer?"

"I am hungry, actually, and it smells great." She forced a smile back and he nodded and turned away. He was bobbing his head to the music, shifting back and forth as he danced his way back inside the kitchen and she hated herself even more for finding him attractive.

Fae pulled her feet up onto the couch and buried her head in her hands, and then she laughed to herself as she kicked her shoes off so she didn't mess up the fabric. He was such a neat freak. He always did the dishes. Wiped down the table when they were done eating. His room was almost always perfect. The bathroom sparkled. She hadn't lifted a *finger* to help him since she'd arrived, and it didn't seem to bother him at all. In the few days she'd been around him he seemed to have no interest in requiring anything from her.

It was like he just wanted some company. A break from the monotony of immortality, and that was something she *did* understand.

"Alright. I can't promise it's anywhere near as delicious as your meals, but at least I know how to make a soup. And I looked up a recipe so I even used some seasonings in it and toasted some sourdough -" he froze mid-sentence as he was setting two full bowls on the table. "What's wrong?"

"Nothing." She wasn't sure what her face had told him, but she quickly wiped her expression with the practice of years and walked to the table. She noticed he had even put the second bowl at the seat she had claimed for herself, and it was just one more tiny kindness piling up in her mind. One more note in the *good guy* column that made everything more complicated.

"Come on, Fae, what is it?" He looked genuinely concerned, but she just dropped into her seat and picked up the spoon.

"Nothing, this looks delicious. Let's eat, okay?"

Kiernan stood there for a second, and she watched the irritation pass over him before he sighed and walked back into the kitchen to return with a plate of sliced bread. When he sat down silently, her stomach flip-flopped. She was about to try and fill the silence when he spoke. "I'm being pushy, aren't I? I keep dragging you out of here on errands, I'm always trying to talk to you, and then I told you all that stuff." He sighed.

"Kiernan, it's -"

"No, it's okay. I'm sorry. I'm going to look for a safe place you can go. Somewhere you won't have to be around me all the time." He nodded as he stared down at his soup.

"Somewhere you won't have to worry about anyone. I'll find it, I swear."

Just the idea of that seemed impossible, but the more she thought of having her own place – a place no one could find her – the more she felt a bubbling warmth inside her. It felt like hope, and *that* was an emotion she hadn't allowed herself in over a millennia. Fae wanted to ask him *why*, wanted to try and dig the truth out of him, beyond his pretty speech about thinking she was strong. None of it made sense in her head as to why he'd risk everything to help her.

After all, no one else ever had.

Instead of arguing, or pestering him further, she just nodded. "That would be amazing. Thank you, Kiernan."

"It's the least I can do." He picked up a spoonful of soup and blew on it a little. "I'll um, give you some space too. I'm sure you're sick of being around me. I mean, why *wouldn't* you be, I'm -"

"Nice." Fae interrupted him and his dark eyes jerked up to meet hers.

"Nice?"

"Yes. You are, Kiernan. You're nice, and I don't – I don't hate your company." She flipped her gaze to the soup and pushed the spoon through it. He was silent to her left, but for all her supposed bravery she was too chicken to look at him again. A blush flushed her cheeks as he stared.

"Well, that's good to know," he said and both of their eyes dropped to the soup.

When Fae finally scraped the last dregs up with a slice of bread, he broke the silence.

"I have an idea."

"Which is?"

"If you want to, I mean if you think it would be better than just sitting around reading or watching television, we could... spar?" Kiernan pushed a hand through his dark hair. "I know you mentioned it yesterday, but if you were joking that's okay too. I just thought it might be nice to spar with someone who could keep up with me. There aren't exactly a lot of options for me since I'm never at Gormahn's keep anymore, and I'd hurt a mortal without even trying."

"So, you're saying I'm a challenge?" Fae tried to bite her cheek to stifle the grin, but it broke through anyway and he laughed and smiled back.

"Well, maybe not a *challenge*, yet, but you could be if you brushed up on your skills."

"WHAT?" She shouted and he shoved back from the table with a wild grin, and she found herself laughing. "I'm going to kick your ass and remind you just why Gormahn had to send almost twice as many Laochra against us to take us down!"

"Such big words from the little warrior. Why don't you show me what you've got?" He walked backwards away from the table, and she noticed, *a little more than she should have*, the way his body moved like a predator's. Strong and powerful.

And she was *definitely* going to kick his ass.

"Don't you want to clean up the table, neat freak? It might distract you during the fight if you suddenly remember there's a bowl not in the dishwasher. A bowl with *food still in it*." She arched an eyebrow at him as she stood up from the table and was rewarded with an embarrassed flush to his cheeks.

"That's fine. The loser can clean up lunch." He kicked off his shoes and pulled off his socks. "Just remember, you need to scrub the pot before you put it in the dishwasher."

Fae yanked her own socks off as she moved around to face off with him in the open space in front of his desk. "Oh, you've done it often enough I doubt you'll forget."

He shifted into a relaxed fighting pose, his hands open at his sides. "Only hand to hand today. No grabbing weapons off the walls, Glowworm."

The name grated on her nerves and she groaned. "I hope your god heals you fast, because I'm going to break a few bones and I don't want to listen to you cry all afternoon."

"Enough talking, show me what you got."

AN HOUR later Fae was incredibly sore, but energized, and doing dishes in the kitchen. Even though she'd lost she couldn't deny that it had been fun to fight against someone that was a challenge. On the few occasions she'd been able to fight against the ones who kept her, it had been ridiculously easy to take them down – that is, until they overwhelmed her with numbers, or used the curse against her.

Kiernan had been gentle with her, and she knew it. He could move fast, and he was incredibly strong, but he had instead only delivered mild hits to show her where her openings were. Somehow she doubted his trainer had been so kind, once upon a time. If he could even *remember* being trained.

That was the other part of her internal debate.

Could she really hold him accountable for the things he'd done when he didn't remember half of them, let alone been in control of himself? It didn't seem right. And he was so unfailingly kind. Not just to her, but to strangers, to *mortals* like Elsie.

For all his darkness, he wasn't doing such a bad job of being human either, and if he could recognize that and respect that in her... she could do the same for him. She could give him a chance, Laochra or not, to be a friend. Hadn't that been what Ebere had asked her to do? To open up and let someone in?

"What sounds better to you – Jurassic Park or Indiana Jones?" Kiernan leaned on the doorframe of the kitchen holding two DVD cases.

Fae laughed. "I have no idea what those are."

"Right, I know, but what *sounds* more interesting? Dinosaurs rampaging across an island or a guy searching for ancient artifacts and getting in all kinds of trouble?"

"Um, dinosaurs?" She looked at him like he was ridiculous, but then he grinned broadly in his excitement.

"Gods, you're going to *love* this. It's incredible! The things mortals can do with computers, I swear, they look real. You won't believe it!" He walked back into the living room and called back towards her, "Hurry up with the dishes, Glowworm. We have pop culture to catch you up on."

"Shut up! I almost had you at the end, you got *lucky*." She knew it was a lie, but it was fun to hear him burst into laughter in the other room. She couldn't wipe her own grin off her face, and she decided to stop trying to fight it.

Fae had promised she'd try to make a friend, and if her friend happened to be an immortal warrior from the wrong side of her pantheon? Well, so be it.

She was going to watch dinosaurs fight things.

CHAPTER FIFTEEN

SEATTLE, WASHINGTON

THREE WEEKS.

Three weeks of living with Fae.

It had started out rough – *no*, it had started out miserably with the attempt to kill him – but it had gotten so much better. There had been a week of awkwardness, of getting her set up for a normal life. A week of showing her pieces of his life, and pieces of the mortal world she had never had the chance to experience.

Since then, there had been nights where Elsie had surprised them with dinner, and when Fae was out of the room Elsie had grilled Kiernan on whether or not she was finally his 'someone special'. No matter how many times he denied it Elsie kept smiling and saying she *knew*.

There were days where they did nothing but lounge

around and read without talking, except to insist that the other person read a particular paragraph. There had been long arguments about characters and plots and whether their choices had been wrong or right. Some nights had been intense conversation about life, the universe, and everything in between. Even when she raised her voice, arguing passionately for her opinion and driving him crazy in the process – he loved it. She kept up with him, and there were times she made points that stymied him into silence. The little victorious grin that would creep over her lips made him groan outwardly, but inside it was like he'd won something precious.

His cleaning lady, Martha, had come twice and both times been shocked by Fae's presence. Their first encounter had been interesting, and had required Kiernan dragging Fae out of the apartment for coffee while explaining clearly that Martha cleaned houses as a *job* and was *not* a slave of any kind. Fae had insisted on watching him pay her, and the sweet woman had repeated his own explanations in the kind of voice usually reserved for the mentally handicapped. Kiernan had just been grateful that Fae hadn't drawn a weapon on him during that particular exchange.

They had also tended the community garden, cooked meals, ate together, drank *a lot* together, and in one ill-conceived plan almost destroyed Kiernan's beloved Land Rover when he thought he could teach Fae to drive in a single afternoon. *That* was going to take a lot more time, and it would be a while before he forgot the frightened little screech she'd let out just before she'd slammed on the brakes. The last time he'd brought it up she'd nailed him in the back with a coaster.

Yeah, it had been three weeks, three amazing weeks where his life wasn't empty. It felt like they were slowly settling into a routine, and that was what worried him. He didn't know how Fae saw the situation, or what they should call each other – *could he even claim the title of friend after all the years he'd left her suffering and alone?*

Maybe not.

He did know that he felt happy, and whole, for the first time in his immortal life, and even if they never named this, he wanted it to go on forever. Kiernan shifted the pan in front of him, then bumped it sharply to flip the pancake. As he was setting it down he saw the faint glow appear on the floor under him just before his legs collapsed beneath him.

"Ha! I got you!" Fae laughed, grabbed his wrist, and twisted his arm behind his back until his shoulder screamed and he groaned aloud. Ah yes, they'd *also* spent a lot of time sparring and Fae was enjoying it profusely. Kiernan was trapped on the floor and his narrow galley kitchen didn't allow for much maneuvering, especially with his broad shoulders. Turning his head to see her grinning broadly above him, the red in her hair lighting up from the remnants of Eltera's power, he couldn't help but smile. Getting his head back into the moment he assessed her stance and her hold on him and quickly kicked one foot into her left ankle. Fae saw it coming and shifted her weight to her right foot, ensuring his strike didn't do much more than bruise her.

"You know, Fae, this is not usually how people say thank you for making breakfast." Kiernan tried to maneuver, but the pressure on his arm and shoulder limited him. Fae had thought this one out. He tapped the cabinet with his other hand, acknowledging her win, and she let go of him and bounced on her feet. She was practically dancing in place with her glee at winning when he rolled over, and she extended a hand to help him up, which he took.

"I had to get you back for ambushing me when I was reading. Not playing fair." Fae raised her eyebrows up, daring him to argue that. He tried to hide his grin by turning back to the stove.

"You *said* you wanted to practice with swords again." Kiernan was struggling to keep his voice level, but the edge of his laughter was creeping in.

"I don't think I ever said I'd like to have a sword tossed at me seconds before you tried to take my head off with one." Fae crossed her arms and leaned against the doorway to the kitchen as the glow of her skin faded.

"Next time be more specific, Glowworm." He couldn't hide his grin anymore and she took the chance to deliver a sharp kick to the back of his right knee that would have sent him to the ground again if he hadn't seen it coming. "You're energetic this morning. I would have thought an eight mile run and all of that wine would have you a little slower today."

"Not a chance." Fae winked at him and looked down at the plate Kiernan had already filled with pancakes. She snagged it and walked over to the table to set it down at the spot that had become *hers* over the last few weeks. With a roll of his eyes Kiernan made himself more, and in a few minutes they had glasses of juice, butter and syrup on the table. He watched Fae slather her pancakes in butter and dig in. Kiernan dumped syrup on his until the plate threatened to spill some over the sides, and then dove in.

Sometimes he didn't even notice how different things had become with Fae there, it was a slow transition to a new normal that felt right. No more sitting alone in his apartment trying to remember the past, or forget it, or – to be honest – watching Fae through the glass. Instead she was here, with him, smiling, laughing, and periodically attempting to kick his ass. He wouldn't have traded it for anything.

"So what's the plan today?" Kiernan was watching Fae devour breakfast while using a ruler to keep the book she was reading open. At the rate she was moving through his library he'd have to go with her to a bookstore soon. She looked over at him, the tiny furrow between her eyebrows appearing as she started thinking of an answer. For the thousandth time he had the urge to reach out and run his thumb over that little wrinkle, or tuck her hair behind her ear, or kiss her. He stopped himself from thinking about it and reminded himself he was happy with how things were, no need to ruin it by thinking with his cock.

"Ummm." Fae swallowed a mouthful of pancake and looked up from her book. "I don't care really, but I do want a rematch on swords today. I still say yesterday wasn't a fair go of it."

"Yes, you're right. All people who want to kill you will politely ask if you have a moment for them to attack you first." He grinned, and she kicked him under the table.

"Jerk."

"Aww, still a sore loser, Glowworm? It's okay, I'd be happy to help you brush the dust off your swordplay some more." That earned him a glare, but she was stifling a smile. She liked the banter as much as he did, so when she lunged for him and he pushed back out of her reach, her frustrated scream just made him laugh.

"I'm grabbing a shower. Don't watch the next episode without me, okay?" She stabbed her fork into her last bite, and then took her plate into the kitchen to set it in the sink. When she walked past him towards his room she smiled at him so he knew she wasn't really mad. He had already showered that morning, so after he cleaned up the dishes he sat down at his desk and opened his laptop. Even though the nightmares were less frequent now, he still didn't sleep easy and was always up before her.

"Four hundred e-mails? By the gods..." Kiernan hadn't even looked at his inbox since Fae had arrived and now he was regretting it. There were e-mail blasts from Eryn who had adopted the basics of technology in order to keep in touch with the Laochra that left the nest – mostly invites for raids in war torn parts of the world. Fifty of the e-mails were from Cole, mostly links to funny internet videos or articles, but a good chunk of them were requests to hang out again. He wouldn't be able to ignore them forever, but a little while longer wouldn't hurt. Between those two there were updates on his portfolios, his real estate holdings, his annual donations to charities, and a lot of spam mail. He was still going through it when Fae stepped out of his hallway, she had black yoga pants on that made her legs look incredibly long and a light green top that hung a little loose on her delicate shoulders. He wanted to jump to attention when she walked into a room, but knew it wasn't what she wanted. Making sure he wasn't staring he tried his best to smile casually. She had called him out for staring too many times.

"On your computer?" Fae's hair was still a little damp and she was using her hands to finger comb it. She hadn't put on make-up or high heels or jewelry - and she was perfect.

"Yeah, trying to check in on the real world and see what I've missed." He clicked on another set of advertisement e-mails and hit the delete key. She walked over to him and leaned on the desk to see his screen. Kiernan studiously glued his eyes to the laptop and not the gentle curve of her back as she leaned forward.

"Are they going to come looking for you again? The others?" Her question made him look at her.

"Cole and Eryn?" Kiernan opened up the e-mail folder he used to keep all of the Laochra communications. "I don't know, I'll have to go see Cole eventually just to calm him down, and if I see him he'll probably keep Eryn at bay."

"When would you need to do that?" Fae stood back up and the furrow between her brows was back as she scanned the titles of the e-mails.

"In a week or so." He slowly shut the lid of the laptop until it clicked. "I don't really want to think about that today though."

"Okay, next episode then?" She gave him a small smile and he nodded. Turning on her heel she dashed into the living room with an agility and grace that would have made mortal ballet dancers green with envy, but Fae didn't even seem aware.

"I KNEW IT WAS HER!" The look of victory on Fae's face was priceless, they had been discussing the series finale of the latest show they were binge-watching. For the last thirty minutes they had argued back and forth, and she *still* wouldn't admit the twist in the last episode had surprised her.

"Sure, you did." Kiernan didn't even care whether she had known or not, but it was fun to prod her. Like seeing if a pup was going to bite you if you ruffled its fur too much.

"I did!" She insisted again which just made him laugh. They were each sitting at one end of the couch where they had taken up watching movies and television shows he thought she'd like. Fae reached behind her and dug around in the drawer of the end table, when she sat back up he saw a flash of silver and caught the throwing dagger on instinct. It would have been a very irritating hole in his shoulder had he missed. Apparently this pup was showing its teeth today.

"Really, Fae?" He waggled the dagger back and forth, and she grinned wildly. "Alright, if that's how you want to play. Let's go with bigger blades, eh?"

"Sounds great." She pushed herself up and grabbed the sword that hung above the couch. Kiernan couldn't help but smile as he got up and went to his room to grab another. Changing into athletic pants so he'd be able to respond quickly if she went hand to hand, he pulled off his socks for better traction. When he came back into the living room Fae had coiled her hair into a bun, and had already moved the TV stand over and pushed the kitchen table against the wall. Her smile was huge as she balanced on bare feet with the sword poised over her shoulder. Of everything about her, *this* was the hottest part. The warrior who didn't show an ounce of fear looking at him. The one who had spit in his face the day he'd brought her here, even when he had her pinned to the floor. She looked him in the eye, and actually smirked at him.

Full grown men had run from him on a battlefield, and this girl bared her teeth.

"Ready?" Kiernan let his eyes wander over her curves, he wasn't so much checking her out as identifying any weak points she may have today, or at least that's what he told himself even as his cock twitched in his pants.

"Ready." She was excited at the idea of a fight. Eltera

hadn't been wrong when she'd chosen Fae for a warrior, it was in her blood to have a weapon in her hands. As he watched her he noticed her gaze didn't stay at his either, and he almost called her out on her wandering eyes but decided to let the sparring session speak for itself. They stepped towards each other and immediately started circling to warm up their foot work.

"Want to start with high or low blocks?" He asked while keeping his sword up and ready to react if she struck first.

"High blocks, your reach is longer than mine and it's good practice." Her eyes were tracking his movements too, every muscle tick drew her eyes to it. She was as fast as he was, as strong as he was, as immortal as he was – and that meant they didn't have to hold back. He shifted right but brought the sword down hard towards her left side. She didn't fall for the feint and reacted by bringing her sword into the side of his and knocking it away. When she spun he kicked out to try and trip her, and she jumped his foot. He almost didn't have his sword back in position when her blade came back at his chest. They were close together for a moment, both of their breathing still even, before they pushed off and stepped back.

Circling again, like predators. This time Fae acted first stepping to the side and then going low for a thrust that would have gone through his stomach if he hadn't jumped back, he brought his sword up to knock hers away and returned with a slash towards her shoulder.

Blocked.

Fae's grin wasn't fading, and Kiernan could feel his

cheeks starting to ache with how hard he was smiling. *This was fun.*

"Enjoying yourself?" He pushed his left hand through his hair to keep it off his forehead while he kept his eyes on Fae. The apartment was warm since the heat was on and he was already starting to sweat.

"Absolutely." Her voice made it clear she was enjoying herself. Next came a side slash that he knocked away before he returned a low strike, and then he shifted it into a high strike when she blocked it. The pace of the fight increased with no more circling and pauses between.

High, low, low, side, high, leg sweep.

Block, block, block, block, block, and she saw the sweep coming.

The clanging of the swords and the swish of the metal coming apart was a sound he never thought he'd enjoy, but he was. He laughed when she moved in close and delivered a sharp elbow to his ribs on his right side, but he returned it with a hard body shot that sent her to the ground. They were both rubbing bruised areas and grinning. Kiernan held his hand up to signal that they would pause, and he rested his sword against his leg to pull his soaked shirt over his head, with a tiny section of dry cloth he wiped off his face.

The apartment was *way* too hot for this.

CHAPTER SIXTEEN

SEATTLE, WASHINGTON

FAE KNEW she should get up, but despite the fact that she had a very bruised tailbone from a rough landing, she really wasn't minding the view. When Kiernan stretched to pull his shirt off, the muscles of his stomach rolled under his skin, the lines that marked them shifting and stretching with his movements. Then it was off and he rolled his broad shoulders to relieve the strain of the sparring session. The dark lines of the vines were a little over halfway up his bicep, and she knew he'd have to take care of those soon because they were much too close to the dark sword shape over his heart.

The mark of Gormahn.

It no longer surprised her that she cared about his safety. After all, he cared about hers. She didn't want him to get hurt. Especially not because he was so busy keeping her safe that he wasn't taking care of himself. Well, unless *she* was the one hurting him, then she didn't mind at all.

Snapping herself back she met his eyes again only to find his cocky grin. He knew where her eyes had been.

Dammit.

"Ready to keep going, or do you need a bandage for your ribs?" Fae taunted him, but he just laughed and pointed down at her.

"At least I'm still standing, Glowworm. You want to rejoin the fight, or should I just bring you a sleeping bag until morning?"

She wasn't going to lose today. Readjusting her grip on the sword hilt she stood up and lifted her blade. She didn't give him a chance to breathe, immediately spinning and delivering a hard strike to his right side, and sure enough it took Kiernan a half second longer than normal to get his sword up. The hit to the muscles on his sword side obviously hurt and it was slowing him down.

Time to press it.

She blocked his returned strike and spun away to attempt a blow at his back. He still blocked it. Again and again they went for any weak spot they found in the other, but each attack was stopped time and again. She was a little more agile, but he had more reach and more weight to put behind his strikes. When he delivered a two-handed downward strike at her shoulder she could feel her teeth vibrate when she blocked it. *Ouch.* An hour passed like that - strikes and blocks, kicks and punches, footwork and taunts.

After a forward block, they ended up almost nose to nose, their swords caught between them. They were both breathing heavily, and Kiernan's brown hair was matted to his forehead and there was a flush in his cheeks, but he still grinned at her like a maniac. This close to him she could see the shadow of facial hair that had come through during the day and she wanted to touch his cheek, wanted to run her fingers through his hair like he always did, wanted to -

"Fae?" When he spoke, his voice was a low rumble in his chest between trying to catch his breath, and hearing her name out of his mouth instead of the annoying nickname he'd chosen made her heartbeat do funny things. "Think you're done kicking my ass today?"

"I can be, as long as you're admitting I won." She smiled at him, catching her own breath. With a groan he stepped back and rolled his eyes, letting their swords slide apart until he could rest the tip on the floor. Fae turned around and slid her sword back into the scabbard, hopping onto the couch to return the sword to its place. Kiernan didn't bother and leaned his blade against the wall before dropping onto the couch, still breathing hard. Fae stepped back to the floor and watched as his chest rose and fell, her eyes following the lean lines of muscle that made up his chest and stomach.

He had dropped his head back and his eyes were barely open, his long lashes fanning out over his cheek bones. Strands of his hair were still matted to his forehead, and his lips were parted just a little as his breathing started to slow.

Maybe it was the adrenaline rush from the fight, his kindness over the last three weeks, the fact that he didn't treat her like she was fragile when they fought, or just the fact that he looked *really* incredible without a shirt on – but she took a step towards him, and then another. And then she found herself on his lap, and he snapped to attention as her knees landed on either side of him. She sat back on his thighs, and tried to catch her breath but her lungs wouldn't work right.

His dark eyes were wide open but he hadn't said a word, and hadn't moved a muscle since she'd touched him. If she thought her pulse had raced while they were fighting, it was nothing compared to *this*. He had to be able to hear her heart pounding against her ribs, had to hear the way her breath hitched with the choice she'd just made. She'd already come this far so she wasn't going to back down now. Fae leaned forward and laid her hand against his cheek, the stubble was rough against her palm and she heard him hold his breath just before her lips met his. His skin was hot from the exertion of the fight, but his lips were surprisingly soft against hers. He didn't move to touch her, but he did lean into the kiss, and his eyes fell closed so she closed hers too.

It was sweet and chaste and gentle, and then it was over.

She sat back and the look of surprise and shock on his face made her smile. She let her hand move to his forehead and she pushed his hair back, her fingertips running through his dark hair like silk. He made a low sound in his chest as her hand found the back of his neck. She'd wanted to do that for *weeks*. Her fingers wound themselves in his hair, and the groan he released was like a big animal's purr.

Fae couldn't resist leaning forward to kiss him again, and *this* time there was heat. Like a spark had landed and the wood was catching, with the promise of fire on the horizon. His lips parted, head tilting back as she leaned over him to deepen the kiss. The fabric of her shirt brushed his chest but there was still an inch or so of space between them. His hands were tucked above him on the couch, and when she opened her eyes she noticed his fists were clenched into the fabric to keep them there. When Fae paused to take a breath he turned his head away and she could see the muscles in his jaw tighten as he clenched his teeth.

"You don't have to do this, Fae. You don't." His voice was low and rumbling and his knuckles were turning white in his death grip on the cushions. "You can stay here as long as you want, no matter what. You don't have to -" His dark eyes met hers and they were full of concern. He was still trying to protect her, even though she could feel hard ridge of his erection through his jeans, which made it clear what his body thought about the situation.

"I know I don't *have* to, Kiernan." Fae ran her hand down the front of his chest and she felt his muscles jump under her touch, then she leaned forward again and placed a light kiss against his lips. "But I've wanted to do this for over a week." Her lips curved up in a playful grin as she watched relief flood his face.

"Oh thank the gods." Kiernan sat up straighter, releasing his grip on the cushions and bringing her closer to him with a hand in the small of her back. As he pressed her into his hard chest she ran her hands down his back, feeling his muscles shift under his skin as he held her to him. He looked over her face like he wasn't sure she was real, and then that cocky, mischievous grin split his face and his right hand came up to cup her cheek, his thumb tracing her cheekbone.

This time when their lips met there was wildfire. The kiss ripped the air from her lungs and she wrapped her arms around his neck to pull him closer. Kiernan's hands slid from her face, over her neck and then down her back. His palms were tracing the curve of her waist and the hollow of her back as he pulled her against him. Lifting up so she was slightly above him, he let his head drop back a little and she leaned down so the kiss continued. For a moment she felt like she was in a position of power, until Kiernan hooked his hands behind her knees and tugged her against him hard. Her hips rocked against his and the low growl in his chest made her smile against his lips – she still had power. Then his hands tightened on her hips, pulling her down against him as his movements matched hers.

A liquid heat flooded her, a delicious thrumming under her skin that was better than any drug on the planet. She was incredibly grateful for the thin fabrics separating them as they rocked against each other, his hard cock rubbing against her clit in a pattern that was setting her on fire from the inside out. Fae moaned against his mouth and he returned with his own, his fingers marking her hips with the intensity of his grip. She rubbed herself against him, desperate for the orgasm coiling up her spine, and he encouraged her.

He drove himself against her, and her skin tingled, her pulse pounded, and then her whole world came apart in his arms. With a cry she shuddered, muttering something unintelligible as her body tensed against his with each wave of pleasure and static joy. Tightening her arms around his neck, she kissed him hard, and he moaned against her lips. There wasn't a sliver of space between them when the kiss broke, and they both gasped for air.

"Wow." Fae whispered against his mouth and he chuckled low, that cocky grin spreading across his kiss-swollen lips.

"That's a good word for it." He reached up behind her and undid the bun on top of her head so her auburn hair surrounded them both in a curtain. His fingers twirled it before he pushed his hands through it and growled a little as he pulled her down for another kiss.

She nipped his lower lip and he grinned against her mouth, which made her smile too. Slipping his fingertips under the bottom of her shirt he brushed the skin of her back.

"Tell me if you want me to stop." He whispered into her ear and then kissed her neck just below it. In small movements he trailed the kisses back to her lips while his palms moved up her back inside her shirt.

"Trust me, I'm good. If I'm not you'll know it." She made a small sound when he laughed against her neck. With a groan he suddenly hugged her tightly against him. Fae replied with a kiss, but he took it over and sent her head spinning.

Who needed to breathe when you could do this?

She started to think of everything he'd done for her over the past few weeks, but then his hands tightened against her hips and he pulled her close again and she forgot what she was thinking. He nipped her bottom lip back and she shoved her hands into his hair to hold his face to hers, to continue the kiss that was boiling her blood again, taunting the still sparkling energy thrumming in her blood. Fae cut off the kiss suddenly and grabbed the bottom of her shirt to rip it over her head. He sat back against the couch again, leaning back from her so he could see her. The black sports bra was a stark contrast against her pale skin, and she held her arms over her head for a second as she watched him react.

His eyes were glued to her skin, tracing every revealed inch with the intensity of an academic. He slid his hands up her arms and took the green shirt from her, dropping it to the couch beside them, then he slowly moved his hands down her arms, across her shoulders and then down her sides. His touch was light, and reverent, and sent goose bumps across her skin. The fire inside her slowed to a steady burn and her rapid breathing calmed as he began kissing across her shoulders, his fingertips tracing behind her and down her spine. He rested his hands at her hips, just above where her pants began. Fae realized she was biting her lip, amazed by how he looked at her as if she was someone precious, important, and deserving.

"I'm not dreaming this, right?" he whispered it and then reached up with his thumb to pull her lower lip from between her teeth. His question made Fae blush, and he gave her a small smile. It was a sweeter smile than his normal mischievous one and made her stomach do a flip. Kiernan's thumb was resting against her lip and his eyes were focused at her mouth. He seemed frozen in the moment until she lightly nipped his thumb and he groaned. Then the sweet look melted away, his lips parted and formed into a grin that was clearly offering a lot more fun than they'd just had. Hopefully with a lot less clothing.

"It's not a dream, Kiernan." She shifted her hips, rubbing against his still hard cock, and he groaned again and she grinned. If he couldn't read that as an open invitation, she'd ask him to get checked for a head injury that Gormahn's power hadn't corrected. When he didn't move forward, her lips landed on his and whatever restraint he had been using collapsed as she pressed herself against him.

His hands moved over her skin, and she ran hers across the ridges of his stomach before trailing her nails lightly down his sides. Breaths came in gasps between their lips and the tension between them kept rising. Fae lifted herself up again and Kiernan took the opportunity to leave a trail of fire down her neck and across her collarbone.

When she ran her hands through his hair and made him

look up at her, she traced her fingers across his lips and he kissed her fingertips. He tugged at her hips to return her to his lap and when she didn't sit back down he laughed low in his chest.

Fae was enjoying having the upper hand when he grabbed her and stood up and she had to lock her legs around his waist to keep from falling. In this position Kiernan's head was slightly above hers, and his cock was firmly pressed against her core, but his hands were trapped holding her up. She wrapped her arms around his neck and kissed him again, and then she felt a wall against her back. He pressed her hard against it, grinding himself between her thighs, his teeth tracing across her shoulder as he dipped his head down.

She couldn't catch her breath, between each roll of his hips that lifted her higher and higher - and then there were stars bursting behind her eyes again. She gasped and his lips were on hers again, his hands cradling her face as another orgasm shook her and left her desperate to have him inside her.

"Please, Kiernan..." She reached behind him and hooked her thumbs into the waist of his pants, but he gently grabbed her wrists and pulled them to his chest.

He was still for a moment, his head bent to rest against her shoulder. When she rolled her hips against him he groaned and lifted her by her waist, stepping back to make her unwrap her legs from him. Confusion washed over her, pushing back the warm glow that the pleasure had left inside her. She opened her mouth to talk but he quieted her with a soft kiss. Now that she was standing she had to look up at him. His eyes were dark and his cheeks were flushed from their efforts, and then the edge of his mouth lifted in a half-smile.

"I want -" Kiernan's voice choked and he cleared his throat, taking her hands in his and intertwining his fingers with hers before he continued, "I want to do this right."

"You are doing it right. *Trust me.*" Fae said it quietly, but couldn't keep the humor out of her voice. He laughed and leaned down to put his forehead against hers.

"You're incredible, Fae." Kiernan mumbled, and she almost spoke but he placed the tiniest kiss on the tip of her nose, and the sweet nature of it surprised her so much she stopped. "And it's because you're so fucking incredible that I want to do this the right way. I want to bring you flowers, I want to take you to dinner, I want to take you on a real date, and – I want to *earn* the right to be with you."

Her heart was fluttering in her chest like an insane bird trapped in a cage. Fae slid her hands around his neck and raised herself to her tiptoes so she could kiss him. He kissed her back, and it was sweet and gentle again, but the strength in his arms when they moved around her and pulled her against him promised that the fire was just calm for now.

"Okay." Her mouth had gone dry, and she couldn't think of anything else to say.

"Okay?" He leaned back from her, his face looking a little confused.

"If you insist on wooing me, you can." She smirked and he grinned back at her before scooping her off the floor into his arms.

"Oh, my lady, if you want to be wooed, I shall woo the hell out of you." He leaned down and kissed her, his cocky grin returning as he carried her down the hall to his room. His bed was a wreck as usual, a giant knot of sheet and comforter but he sat her down on the edge and proceeded to try and even it back out. He paused as he was about to hand her the sheet, freezing in place, "I'm sorry, I didn't mean to – I mean, you don't have to sleep in here, I just -"

"Hush and come here." She took the sheet from him and he smiled as he sat down on the bed next to her. Fae shifted over and Kiernan reached to the side and clicked the lamp off. He didn't touch her at first, but she shifted in the bed and pressed her back against his chest.

The pillow she had been sleeping on for the last few weeks had always smelled amazing, that heady mixture of spice and earth that she had connected with him. His bed was even better, the same scent on overdrive, and she turned her face into the pillow and took a deep breath. Kiernan's arm slid around her waist and he pulled her tighter against him.

"Thank you…" His voice was such a quiet whisper into her hair that she wasn't sure she had heard it right. She waited on him to keep talking, but it was clear he wasn't going to. He was taking steady breaths as they both tried to calm down. To relax and get some mental space from everything that had just passed between them.

Fae started to count her heartbeats, an old trick that had always worked when she was too wound up to sleep, and *fuck* was she wound up. For once being wrapped in the warm heat of another person didn't feel claustrophobic; it felt soothing.

Just before sleep came over her she realized that the bands had *never* activated. In all the intensity he'd never claimed her, never even thought about it because their ghostly tingle had never shown up. If she hadn't felt completely safe in Kiernan's apartment before, tonight had made the last question in her mind fade away.

She was finally safe.

CHAPTER SEVENTEEN

Seattle, Washington

Kiernan's bed was a warm cocoon and he really didn't want to get up yet, but the light coming through the blinds was too bright to stay asleep. He stretched and his hand bumped into something and his eyes snapped open onto golden light. Fae was curled up in a ball next to him and the sheets were gathered down around her waist.

Her porcelain skin was glowing bright enough to have woken him up from a dead sleep. In all the weeks she'd been there he'd never seen so much of her skin exposed when Eltera's power came to her. His eyes moved over her face and he was surprised once again by how beautiful she was, *and she was in his bed.*

Propping himself up on his elbow he looked down at her and lightly traced a finger down her arm through the light. He could feel the faintest tingling sensation like her skin was humming. Fae's lips parted and she took a deep breath and Kiernan noticed that the air smelled like rain, clean and earthy. A few strands of her auburn hair had fallen into her face so he reached forward to tuck them behind her ear. Her eyes opened and she gasped, grabbing his wrist and jerking back from him. He watched as her face shifted from surprise, to a brief flash of anger, before relaxing as she recognized him.

"Kiernan?" She sounded so sleepy and confused, and that little wrinkle had appeared between her eyebrows again. He wanted to touch her again, but knew it had to happen on her time. Fae's fingers were tight around his wrist, and although he didn't try and move his arm away she noticed and released him. "Sorry, I didn't know – I mean, I didn't remember I was *here*."

"It's okay. You surprised me too to be honest." He smiled at her and she smiled back, releasing the tension in her shoulders as she let her head relax back onto the pillow. Fae was staring up at him and he was still in shock that it was real, that the night before had not been some wonderful dream. Now that she was relaxed he grinned down at her and traced his finger between her eyebrows to smooth the little wrinkle away. She crossed her eyes to look at his finger and then she took his hand to place a kiss on his palm.

"I slept *so* well." She let go of his hand and stretched out like a cat. Her back arched off the bed, the curves of her body outlined by the faint golden light on her skin. When she lay back down she turned towards him and gave him a wicked smile that had dangerous effects below his waist.

Tease.

He grinned back and leaned over her, bringing his lips almost to hers. He heard her breath catch as she waited for the kiss, but instead of letting their lips touch he slid a hand over her stomach and around her waist. Kiernan smiled down at her as he ran his fingers over her skin, resting his hand on the delicate bend of her waist.

"Last night was more than good. A better word might be... incredible." He pulled her hips sharply towards him and a small gasp escaped her. He felt the movement of air against his lips, but other than his hand their bodies weren't quite touching. It was making her start to fidget, and he loved the desperate little movements she made to get closer.

She squirmed and shifted forward, trying to kiss him, but he evaded her and smiled while shaking his head slowly. Two could play at the teasing game, and her frustrated little growl gave him a huge sense of satisfaction. Her blue eyes caught his and she pushed her hands into his hair, her nails trailing across his scalp, and *dammit*, it almost made him crack.

Her touch sent chills down his back, and made heat rise in his stomach. He wanted to make this linger, to drag out each of these precious little touches with the only person he'd been able to be himself around in two thousand years. Looking down the narrow gap between them, his eyes trailed down her body. Fae's breathing was picking up, her pulse jumping at her throat, and he tilted his head against her touch. Then her fingertips moved to the back of his neck, and she pulled his mouth to hers, and he caved. Their lips touched first, then her chest met his, and then their legs were intertwined as he let his body press hers into the bed.

If he'd thought for even a moment that last night had been a one-time event, he had been wrong.

"Kiernan..." Fae breathed his name against his ear and he could feel his hold on his control slipping. His hand was at her hip and his fingertips were toying at the edge of her pants, their breaths were coming in gasps again and he wanted her. By the gods, he wanted her so much that his cock ached, but he wanted – he needed – her to know what having her in his bed meant to him. He needed her to know that he knew how precious it was that she *let* him have his hand on her skin, and how lucky he was for her to *want* it there.

He felt a growl rumble in his chest and then he pushed himself up and off her. The glow in her skin had faded, but she still looked unreal lying in his bed.

"You're making it very difficult to be a gentleman right now," he grumbled.

She trailed one hand down his stomach, and her fingertips dipped under the waistband of his pants. Every inch of him wanted to feel her hand wrap around the steel of his cock. He wanted to push her thighs apart and drive himself inside her, hear those little gasps and murmurs that she'd made the night before. He wanted to drown in those little sounds, but he couldn't, *not yet*. Supporting himself on one arm he took her hand away from his pants like he had the night before, and brought it to his lips to kiss her knuckles.

"Kiernan... It's *okay*. I swear." The edge of frustration in her voice made him groan.

If he admitted to her just how much he wanted her he knew there wouldn't be any more waiting, there'd be no patience, no reason. They'd be naked in an instant and fucking a moment later, and it would be amazing, but it wouldn't be *right*. Kiernan let go of her hand and sat up next to her, and she kicked her legs in frustration with a little tantrum. He stifled the smile that almost took over his mouth and looked up at the ceiling, leaning his head back against the headboard as he tried to convince his cock to give up. Fae whined and looked over at him. "Why on *earth* are you fighting me on this?"

Because I'm a complete fucking idiot, he thought as he stared at her stretched out on his bed. He trained his eyes back on the ceiling and forced a deep breath.

"Because I just - I don't even know how - *why* this happened, Fae. I don't know what I could have possibly done to deserve –" he waved his hand in the air and then at her, " – *this*." He gritted his teeth and focused on bringing his pulse down and trying to regain some control over his body.

His brain knew this was right, but his body really disagreed with him. Fae huffed and pushed herself up, crossing her legs to sit next to him. He wanted to go into one of his closets, find his coat, and make her wear that, because having her next to him in nothing but a sports bra and those yoga pants wasn't helping him calm down. It was just making his balls ache.

"Fine. You really want to know?" Fae had tried to run her hands through her hair and found it in knots, so she started working on them with her fingers as she shot him an exasperated look.

"Yes. I do." Kiernan locked eyes with her to keep his gaze from wandering south, and she tilted her head and sighed to herself before she spoke.

"You said you watched me in your observation glass, because of who *I* am, right?" Fae asked, and he nodded. "Well, same thing, that's why I wanted to kiss you."

"Because I watched you?" Kiernan knew he looked confused, and she just rolled her eyes.

"No, idiot. It's because of who *you* are. At least, who you've proven yourself to be these last few weeks." Fae mumbled the words while she messed with her hair, but he wasn't letting her off that easy.

"You made me explain myself, it's your turn, Glowworm." Kiernan grinned at her and she smiled a little before she started talking.

Fae tore through a few more knots in her hair, biting her lower lip for a minute while she had some kind of internal debate about what to say. He wanted to push her, to press her for an answer, but that would just make her refuse to tell him because she was feisty, and defiant, and wouldn't do a damn thing if she didn't *have* to.

Hadn't he said he loved her defiance?

Maybe he really was an idiot, because now was a terrible time for her to dig her heels in when he was so close to learning what on earth had made her kiss *him*.

"It's a lot of things, Kiernan." Her voice was quiet, and he froze against the headboard, not wanting to stop whatever she was about to say. A blush crept across her cheeks, and then she started talking again, "You're just so – so relaxed. You just accept me, and all my stuff, and somehow you make me feel *normal*. I have never, ever felt normal around anyone. There's always this huge space between me and them, this gap that I can't cross for anything... and that's not there with you. You know *exactly* who I am, my whole history. All of it. But you don't treat me any differently." She had started to braid her hair, having given up on unknotting it, and she stared at the ends of her hair instead of him.

"I don't think I can explain to you how incredible that is, how incredible that *feels*. To be treated like a person instead of a freak, or a thing that can be used and bartered and sold." Her shoulders caved forward while she spoke. It all made her look so small, and it reminded him of how young she'd been when Eltera froze her life.

"I wouldn't -" Kiernan started to explain that he'd never hurt her, or let someone take her, or let her be sold, but she shook her head and he stopped.

"I thought you were a liar. That first day, the day you took me out of the snow, I was convinced you were a liar. It didn't matter that you held back, that you didn't pick up a weapon when you had the chance, that you didn't take advantage when you had me on the ground. You're Laochra, and that meant you were a liar." He tried to suppress the flinch that her words caused, but it was difficult because it hurt to hear those words from her lips. "When you apologized, when you swore never to hurt me again, when you touched those little bruises on my wrists with so much shame – I thought it was an *excellent* act. I kept waiting for you to change, to spring some trap on me when my guard was down."

"You were waiting on the darkness to show itself again." Kiernan said what she was obviously dancing around, and it felt like a knife to the gut to think of the fear she'd felt just being around him. He wanted to leave, to disappear, and let her feel safe again. He was about to stand up, fighting the ache in his chest, when she looked up and her blue eyes stopped him.

"I was... for a bit. Even when I had fun talking to you, even when you were kind, or funny, I was terrified it was just a really, really good act. I've never had someone be around me, in a position of power, and *not* take advantage, Kiernan." She finished the braid, and with nothing to tie it off she just stared at the end, twisting it in her fingers. "You made a promise to me, but I wasn't ready to hear it. The words didn't mean anything to me, no matter how earnest you were, no matter how much it sounded like the truth. It wasn't the words that did it at all, it was everything you've done *since* the promise."

"Every time you protected me, and every time you let me fight my own battles. Every thing in your life you shared with me, every time you joked with me, laughed with me, like it was the most natural thing in the world to you. Every single time you fought with me and didn't treat me like I was fragile, but actually pushed me, challenged me. It was because of every moment that you could have touched me, that you could have tried something, or honestly, just laid a claim to me – and you *didn't*. That's when I started to think that this could be real, that you could be real, and I wanted it. I wanted to have something real for once in my life." She shrugged, and he could see tears in her eyes when she looked up at him again. "I wanted you."

Kiernan's heart was racing, he wanted to speak but he was afraid to break whatever had come over her. Her eyes stayed on his for a long moment, their ethereal blue all the more vibrant as she held back the tears he could see brimming. "Fae..." He whispered, and she broke the eye contact and let go of her hair, letting her hands fall back into her lap.

"It wasn't a light decision, Kiernan. I didn't kiss you because I thought I had to, or because I just thought it would be fun – although it really was." She glanced up at him and offered a small smile before she stared at the bed again. "I kissed you because I wanted you, I *still* want you."

"I know, I just -"

"It's okay, I get it. You want to handle this differently, but I'm just woefully unprepared to deal with this – with *you*.

You have to understand, I was never the type of girl who dreamed of a family one day. That was all my sisters, they were hunting boys in the village as soon as they had breasts. While they were off flirting, my father was teaching me everything that he knew about nature and the worship of Eltera, about caring for the earth, about plants for healing. I believed *that* was my future, following in his footsteps and caring for people in our village and in others. I never even thought I'd find someone who would be okay with that, especially since my father really wasn't *allowed* to teach a female those things."

She shrugged to herself and said, "and then Eltera took me, and I felt like I belonged with *her*, with all of my new sisters, and I never even thought about having more, about having someone in my life, because I was perfectly happy." Fae stopped talking and swallowed, her fingers pulling at the sheet in a nervous pattern.

Kiernan's stomach took a dive and he suddenly felt sick because he knew what event had happened next in her life, and he wanted to stop the conversation and return to the things she had said that had given him hope, but she started talking again.

She spoke so quietly that if they hadn't been silent he might not have heard her. "Then all those potential choices were taken away from me, and it didn't matter."

It hurt him to see her in pain, and he wanted to grab her and hug her and swear to her that it would never be like that again, but he wasn't even sure his touch was still welcome right now. After all, he *was* Laochra. He had been on the battlefield the day her life was torn apart, and he'd done nothing to stop it. In fact, he didn't even really remember that day.

He wasn't sure it would have been possible to feel sicker, but he did.

Fae took a breath suddenly and his eyes moved back to her, but her gaze stayed down. There were tiny drops on the sheet she had pulled into her lap. "After all that? After this life I've lived? I didn't think I had that as an option, I didn't think anyone would think I was worthy of that. Ever. And no one ever has."

Kiernan's jaw clenched tight, and part of him wanted to find the people who had made her feel this way, the ones that were still alive anyway, and beat them into the ground. He would prove to her she was worth more than anything else on earth, no matter *what* he had to do. She rolled a shoulder and glanced up at him before continuing.

"I focused on protecting as many people as I could, and not caring about myself. It was easier if I didn't care what happened. Easier to feel good about myself if I was shielding someone weaker, because at least I had a purpose. But then *you* tried to protect me. You cared enough to try. You came and got me out of the snow, took me away from those guards, and Butler, and that house. And I can't stop thinking about the girls I left there. I keep having nightmares about them, about what's happening to them – but I can't go back. I feel horrible, but I don't *want* to go back." She sighed, "I couldn't help them anyway, and you –"

His eyes widened and she flinched as if her words hurt her.

"You're so kind to me, and it's been so long since anyone treated me like this. You bought me clothes, and insisted that I eat, and you still understood all of my paranoid concerns. You didn't push me to do anything, you agreed with every idea I had – you even let me try to drive your *car*." A smile flitted over her lips and the relief from it made him let out a quick laugh at the memory of her almost crashing his Land Rover into the building. Her eyes lifted and met his and he could see they were shining, but her smile didn't slip this time. "You took care of me, but you didn't treat me like I was breakable... and you're a good person, Kiernan." That made him pause, a few weeks of being good hardly made up for lifetimes of wrong.

"Fae, I'm not –" Kiernan stopped when she reached forward and grabbed his hand.

"Our circumstances aren't what I'm talking about. We've had two thousand years of bad circumstances. I'm talking about who you are at your core. I'm talking about the person who starts gardens, and gives kids scholarships, and helps people load their cars at the store. The kind of person that risks his life, and everything he's known, to save one of the only people in the world he should have never, ever saved." She shifted her legs underneath her and kneeled so she sat a little higher than him. Their fingers were intertwined and they squeezed each other's hands. "*That's* the guy I decided to kiss last night, the guy who I really wish would relax his gentlemanly qualities for a few minutes – or for an hour or two." They both laughed and she leaned closer to him. "*That's* what you've done to deserve this, Kiernan, and I'm trying to deserve you too."

Kiernan leaned forward and kissed her, and she kissed him back, but it was like a seal on their conversation and not a kiss that stoked the fire between them. The kiss was an agreement that they had both laid it all out on the table and they were both still there, still in it, and he had no plans of going anywhere, because as much as he made her feel normal, Fae made him feel *human*.

"You know, I'm really trying to deserve you too, to deserve all of this, because I feel the same way. Which is why I'm taking you to dinner, and maybe a movie. That's what the mortals do these days."

"A date?" Fae brushed a hand under one of her eyes, before she sat back on her heels and smiled at him.

"Yes, Glowworm, a date."

CHAPTER EIGHTEEN

RÁJ MANOR, CALEDON, ONTARIO

THE HEIR to the manor had arrived with absolutely no notice the evening before. Nikola's only son, Marik, had shown up in a hired limousine that almost hadn't made it up the main drive through the falling snow. He hadn't called ahead and hadn't warned anyone.

Butler had carefully planned how the introductions would go with Marik. He had spent the last *two weeks* working out how to make it as perfect as possible, to show the new master of the house that Butler was indispensable.

Things had *not* gone to plan.

When Marik had walked through the front door he had unfortunately been seen by one of the guards who hadn't worked at the manor the last time Nikola's son had visited – so the idiot actually asked Marik who he was. Apparently, Marik had laughed. Then he had looked in on the parlor where the contractor's men were still finishing repairs, and when he went to walk up the stairs Annika had almost run into him carrying a basket of laundry. Thankfully, he had sidestepped her without incident and headed up the stairs.

Annika would have earned more than a few cane stripes if she had upset the new master of the house. It was only after that disastrous arrival that Butler had been able to respond to the message over the radio that the man who had come through the front door was, in fact, *the heir*, the new master, Marik.

The expletives Butler had streamed from his mouth as he'd rushed from the guards' quarters towards the front of the house were harsh enough to peel paint. He found Marik with his feet propped up on his father's pristine desk, smoking a black cigarette, and flicking ash directly onto the smoothly polished wood.

Marik had grinned and acknowledged Butler, but as soon as Butler had launched into his rehearsed welcome speech Marik had stopped him with a raised hand. He had refused to listen to any *business talk* and just wanted to know where the twins were, and which bedroom he could use. Butler had begrudgingly shown him both and promptly had the door slammed in his face.

So, Butler's evening had been spent with his now constant friend – whiskey. A lot of whiskey. And at some point, enough whiskey that he'd passed out.

It was after eight the next morning when Thompson woke him up, but he was smart and was well out of arm's reach while yelling Butler's name over and over. When he finally woke up he had thrown something across the room at him, which had unfortunately missed. A shower, a shave, a handful of pills knocked back with more whiskey, and a change of clothes later and he was ready to check on the house.

Contractors were finishing the parlor, today should be the last day. Lena was keeping the girls on their chores and keeping them on the mend from their *interviews*. And there was one sleeping prince.

Around one o'clock Butler heard over the radio tucked in his ear that Marik was awake, and waiting in Nikola's, no, now it was just *the* office. This time when Butler stepped inside he did a double-take that Nikola wasn't the one sitting there poring over documents with a laptop open on the corner, and papers spread across the lacquered top. It was Marik's black cigarette being tapped into an empty coffee cup, that reminded Butler who was sitting in the chair that had almost been his. Then he looked up and grinned at Butler as he raised his hands, stretching them behind his head.

"Morning, Butler." Marik's dark brown eyes were daring him to correct him about the time, but Butler wasn't taking the bait.

"I thought you might tell us when you were ready to start the day so we could talk to you about the house and catch you up to date." Butler let the door click shut behind him before striding forward to the chairs tucked neatly in front of the massive desk.

"Are you referring to updating me on the parlor repairs? They seem to be almost complete by my check yesterday. Or potentially the girls? I'm quite sure *Lena* is the one keeping that section in hand, as always. Could you be referring to my father's death? Between the lawyers, the autopsy report, and a little fill-in-the-blanks session with Sobeska and Zofie last night – I'm quite aware that he was murdered, likely through supernatural means. And, speaking of that, you might be referring to the girl who is currently missing in action? Fae? Well, it seems no one knows anything about *that*. So, perhaps you *could* catch me up to date on that little detail." Marik smiled calmly, his voice had stayed flat and professionally cold, just like his father's always had. Despite his party-boy persona, his extravagant spending patterns, and his less-than-tasteful free time preferences, he was still Nikola's son.

Butler's fist clenched as he gripped the back of the heavy chair and pulled it back from the desk. He twisted it at an angle before sitting down heavily. His jaw creaked with the strain of his clenched teeth and he forced himself to relax.

"You seem quite well informed for someone who spent the last few weeks moving so quickly through Eastern Europe and South Asia that the lawyers almost gave up reaching you." Butler forced himself to smile, not wanting to lose the game before it even started, but it felt more like a grimace through the tension of his face.

"I got the first message when they sent it, and every one

after that. I just wasn't ready to return quite yet." Marik allowed smoke to trickle out of his mouth as he spoke and punctuated the statement by blowing a stream into the air. Nikola had never smoked outside of the parlor.

"You're here now, that's what matters. As far as the missing whore, we have a lead in the house right now – a guest from the night of the Winter Dinner who had quite an interest in her. Even went so far as to attempt to purchase her from Nikola that night." Butler felt a sense of smug satisfaction settle the acid that was roiling in his stomach.

"And who is that?" Marik laid the cigarette on the small plate which held his coffee cup before flipping through a few papers on the desk to pull out a single manila folder, which he flipped open.

"Andrew Clark. I spent the day yesterday interviewing him about why exactly he left in the early morning hours after the Winter Dinner, without even a goodbye." Butler leaned forward and watched as Marik flipped to a page in the folder that was filled with text and had a small picture of the man in question stapled in the corner.

When Marik lifted his eyes to Butler they were darker, and glittering with a predatory excitement that caught Butler off-guard. Nikola had looked at everything with a sense of boredom, his interest only piqued when he found a new girl he wanted to acquire for his collection, even then there had never been this level of fierce intensity in his eyes.

"Well, this *is* news. I think we should go meet Andrew

together, don't you?" Marik pushed himself up, his hands flat on the desk as he waited for Butler to stand as well.

"Of course, he's downstairs in a storage room." Butler stood up and Marik grabbed his cigarette and walked around the desk with a bounce in his step.

The quick walk to the storage room was silent except for the consistent puff and exhale of Marik's incessant chain smoking. When Butler unlocked the door and pushed it open they were greeted by a rough gasp and immediate coughing. The room was pitch black but Butler stepped confidently inside and pulled the string that turned on the bulb in the center of the room.

The floor was plain and shelves lined three of the walls. Various outdoor tools like rakes and shovels were hanging from racks on the last wall, and zip tied to one of the metal shelving units was their guest – a larger man in ruined suit pants and a stained gray button down. His dark, curly hair was matted to his head with what Butler guessed was blood, but he couldn't remember giving the man a head injury.

When the man's eyes adjusted he finally looked up at them both, and he didn't look good. The split lip had been the result of the man threatening Butler with police action. The darkening black eye had been from trying to fight the men Butler had sent to retrieve him. Maybe *that* was where the head injury had come from? Not that it mattered.

"He-help me, please. You have to get me out of here. I can pay you, I can pay you a lot of money. Please, this guy is insane." Andrew was talking fast, looking past Butler to Marik who stepped around and crouched down in front of the whimpering man.

"You're Andrew, yes? Andrew Clark from Connecticut?" Marik grinned as he blew cigarette smoke into the air again before letting the cigarette hang between his knees while Andrew nodded slowly. "The same Andrew who used to be a politician, but now focuses more on land and real estate dealings?"

Another slow nod from him.

"Wonderful. Then I'd love to continue the business relationship you had with my father." Marik waved his hand back and forth, the smoke trailing from the lit end as he watched Andrew's eyes widen with realization. "That is, after we clear up this little mess."

"I've already told Butler I had nothing to do with her disappearance. I would have gladly taken her with me, but your father was completely unreasonable -" Andrew stopped as Marik scooted forward, the cigarette suddenly much too close to his skin for comfort.

"My father was a collector, like a curator at a museum. He treated these girls like artwork, never let anyone play too rough with them, watched them with careful consideration, appreciated them like no one else." Marik talked smoothly, his words gliding inside Andrew's ears like water across the edge of a blade. "And much like a museum, when you're invited to one, you don't point at pretty pictures on the wall and ask to take them home with you. That's *rude*."

"You - you're right, it was rude." The cigarette was hovering less than an inch above Andrew's arm.

Butler found himself watching in fascination as Marik talked. His fingertips tingled with the urge to have Marik press the black cigarette down, but he could only hold his breath as Marik continued.

"Yes. That was rude. After all, what was your plan had you taken her? Play house with her? Do you think she'd have melted into your arms as some kind of savior when you wanted the same things from her that my father did?" Marik brushed the cigarette against the fabric of the shirt and it melted away from the heat leaving a crisp little hole in the pale gray.

"I... I don't know what I thought. I just wanted to help her. That's it." Andrew was sweating. It was rolling across his forehead and down his cheeks, and gathering against the collar of his shirt.

Marik laughed, it sounded mechanical and automatic, like a recording, and it made Andrew jump. "See what helping people gets you?" Marik took a long drag on the cigarette, before blowing the smoke directly into Andrew's face, who immediately scrunched up his nose and coughed. Marik's post laugh grin disappeared in an instant and he leaned forward suddenly, his hand gripping Andrew's face tightly. He increased the pressure, forcing his mouth to pucker and his split lip to start bleeding again. "Listen to me very carefully. To win in life, you have to be the wolf among the sheep. You have to slit their throats before they even notice the claws underneath the fleece. You're a sheep, Andrew, and I'm a wolf. And sheep that want to live help the wolves get the other sheep. You want to live don't you?"

Andrew nodded, but was unable to talk with the pressure on his face.

"Good. Then tell me everything you remember about Fae and the night of the Winter Dinner."

CHAPTER NINETEEN

SEATTLE, WASHINGTON

KIERNAN WAS INSANE.

He had spent the whole day running around the apartment planning like he was arranging a party for a hundred people instead of a simple date. He had asked her at least a hundred questions about her favorite foods and what she liked, and after each set of questions he would return to his computer or start making phone calls. It had been tempting to tease him, mock him for how serious he was being, but instead she'd just nested in his bed with a book and left him to it.

Now they were in a dimly lit Italian restaurant near the water, tucked into a private corner at a small table, and everything coming out of the kitchen smelled *amazing*. It felt both completely natural and surreal to be across from him. If she didn't think about it - about who they were and what the future might hold - she could almost pretend she was just a mortal girl, and he was just a mortal guy, and they were just on a normal date.

Almost.

Fae's eyes traced his jaw. It was clenched again, and his brow was furrowed under the edge of his dark hair. His moods changed faster than she could keep track. One minute Kiernan was grinning at her, and the next he was brooding and silent. *Like this.*

She didn't understand why he couldn't just live in the moment, enjoy the bit of happiness they were having *right now*, and stop stressing about the someday, about the myriad ways that things could go horribly wrong. It's not like she didn't have anxiety, or fears, but she wasn't going to let them ruin the good things.

You have to find your happiness where you can, she'd said that to so many slaves over the centuries, and it was the truth. Acknowledging the anxiety seemed to let all the bad thoughts in for a moment. Her mind was suddenly whirling with possibilities, that someone would take her from this bit of happiness and lock her away again. That some beautiful mortal girl would make Kiernan realize how stupid and dangerous it was to get involved with a Faeoihn. That –

"There are times I still can't believe you're here." Kiernan was smiling at her again, another shift in the winds and he wasn't dark anymore. This was the light side of him, and she tried to stifle the grin that wanted to appear at the sight of his smile. "I keep thinking that if Gormahn wanted to punish me, there'd be no better way than to make me think I could be happy, that I could begin to redeem myself for everything I've done – and then he could just take it all away. Wake me up from this dream. I think that would finally break me."

"You're not dreaming, Kiernan." Fae felt the burn of a blush in her cheeks, and she reached forward to take a sip of her water.

"Isn't that what you'd say if I *were* dreaming about you?" He arched an eyebrow and she laughed, acquiescing.

"Well, yes, I guess that's true." Fae leaned back, looking up at the intricate designs carved into the ceiling. "But if it *is* a dream, Kiernan, you've got to stop waiting for it to end. Bad shit could happen at any moment. You could wake up, *hell*, I could wake up. Maybe the whole thing with Nikola's death, and my implausible escape, and finding you is *my* dream, *my* fantasy of what I want to happen."

"You forget that *I* knew what you looked like before this dream, you didn't know I existed."

"Okay, maybe I just imagined a hot guy, a warrior that could keep up with me, someone that I could respect, who was also from my own people *and* immortal - and dreamed him up." Fae tilted her head at him, and his grin grew wicked.

"Did you just call me hot?"

"Calm down, your head is big enough."

"Noticed that too, did you?" He laughed and she threw her napkin at his face.

"You're ridiculous." Fae rolled her eyes, and he reached across the table to take her hands. She was hypnotized by the rhythmic movement of his fingertips across her skin, which seemed to make the rest of the world fall away.

"So, you're happy?"

"Yeah. Very happy." Fae ran her fingernails lightly over his palm and grinned.

Kiernan's dark eyes flicked up to hers and she saw a boyish excitement flash through them. "Then who cares if it's a dream?" He shrugged and leaned forward across the table to kiss her. When their lips met Fae felt the heat spark between them again, a burning rush under her skin that reminded her of what it had been like to climb onto his lap the night before. Brave and fearless. Moving her hand to his cheek, and then into his hair, the kiss changed from a chaste press of lips to a dance of tongues, his teeth grazing her lips. When her fingertips brushed the back of his neck she could feel the rumble of his groan against her mouth as his hands cupped her face and held her firmly.

There really had been no reason to leave the bed this morning.

No. Reason. At. All.

"Umm, I'll come back." The waitress standing next to their table was wide-eyed and blushing bright red when they broke apart. Fae flashed her a smile, but Kiernan leaned back to his side and was staring at the table as she heard him take a slow breath. In and out. He raised his gaze to Fae and the look in his eyes held promises for her that sent a shiver down her back that settled between her legs with liquid heat. When he turned those dark eyes on the waitress her blush went scarlet, and Fae understood the way the woman's mouth dropped open. She wouldn't be surprised if her own was hanging open too.

"No, it's okay, we'd like some wine." Kiernan's voice was a notch lower than normal, and he grinned to himself when he looked down at the wine list. He ordered a bottle and the waitress retreated from the table in a daze.

"Are you *sure* you want to have dinner?" Fae arched an eyebrow and grinned. Kiernan's eyes traced the neckline of her sweater, and he tightened his jaw for a second before responding.

"Temptation, thy name is Fae." His smile broadened when he brought his eyes back to hers. "Let me do all this, please, it makes me feel better about everything."

"Okay, Kiernan, a date it is." Fae replied quietly, giving him a secretive smile as the waitress returned with their wine and the glasses. She sat up, prim and proper, no more sultry glances or suggestive dialogue which had Kiernan pouting for a few minutes.

Be careful what you wish for, warrior boy.

When they ordered food from the menu, Kiernan kept adding new things he wanted her to try if she even glanced at them. The girl left with a dizzying list of items that Fae knew would be impossible for them to eat. He just shrugged and said if she only tried a bite out of each, it would be worth it. "I have a confession, by the way." He smiled at her, so the nervous flutter in her stomach at those words abated a bit.

"Alright..."

"I've seen you naked before. Quite a few times, actually." Kiernan was blushing, *really* blushing, and Fae burst out laughing. She hadn't thought about all he'd seen in the glass, but as rare as it was for someone to even give her clothing it didn't surprise her.

"Kiernan, if that's the worst thing you saw in the glass, you really didn't watch very often." She had meant for it to be light-hearted, but his face turned down, a shadow passing over his features. "Wait, I didn't mean to accuse -"

"I always shut the box." He spoke quietly, cutting her off, but she wasn't sure she had heard him right.

"What?"

He sighed and kept his eyes away from her, dancing between the glasses on the table, the bottle of wine, the silverware. "I always shut the box, whenever one of them would – I always shut the box. I watched the punishments usually, just because I was mesmerized by how strong you were, I admit that, but I didn't watch them -"

"Fuck me?" Fae finished and he flinched.

"Yeah," he mumbled.

She sighed, grateful that the wine was at the table

because she needed a drink to have this conversation. "I wouldn't have cared if you did, Kiernan. Honestly. It's kind of a relief that you know everything, that you *understand*. I came to terms with my curse a very long time ago."

"But you shouldn't have to!" The anger in his voice made her frown a little, and he pulled himself back.

"Well, tell me the truth, did you think I was hot?" She smiled, and the rage fled in the wake of his surprise.

He laughed, and shrugged, the blush on his cheeks darkening a bit. "Um, yes. *Hot* would be a good word, so would beautiful, gorgeous, incredible, brave – I mean, you're extraordinary, Fae." Kiernan smiled up at her and it was her turn to blush. He really knew how to make her feel like the only woman in the room, like someone valuable and precious.

"I think I'm supposed to say thank you," she muttered. He shrugged, and she leaned back from the table. "If we're having confession, I have one too."

"Do you?" He leaned forward on the table with a much lighter expression on his face.

"I'm pretty sure Eltera killed Nikola." Fae said it softly.

"WHAT?!" He shouted and nearby tables looked over, a few patrons glaring.

She leaned forward and hissed at him. "Holy shit, be quiet, Kiernan." Fae pushed a hand through her hair and sighed, she'd already said the worst of it, now she had to explain. "I wasn't sure at first. I really wasn't. When you first took me to your apartment and interrogated me over it, I was still in such shock that any of it had happened that I wasn't thinking clearly... but it's the only thing that makes sense. I know I don't have that kind of power in me, she just used me to channel it like she does whenever she heals me in the morning. I glowed with the power of the gods, just like in the mornings, and like you said – I've never been able to control fire like that before."

"But Eltera is a goddess of nature." Kiernan said the thought aloud, his forehead wrinkling in concentration. Fae nodded and he blew out a breath. "That's really the only solution, but she *shouldn't* be able to do that. She's bound by Gormahn, she has the actual manacles on her. She shouldn't be able to use any of her power -"

"And yet, somehow, she's always been able to heal us. Even the morning after the battle." Fae shrugged, picking at one of the plates of food. "Maybe you're not the only one Gormahn's power is waning with."

Kiernan's eyes widened. "Maybe."

"Listen, I didn't want to talk about this tonight. Dates are supposed to be fun, right?" She forced a smile.

He shook himself and nodded. Then they started talking about lighter subjects and the crowded restaurant, the stress of their predicament, *everything* seemed to fade away. He was so passionate and animated when he spoke about the things he cared about. His plans for the garden, a hiking trail he wanted to go on with her, an insta-trip to the Galapagos for a day on the beach in the middle of winter. As he talked about the future he insisted that the world was open to her, and that they could go anywhere.

"I want you to be happy, I want to give you a good life more than anything." Kiernan was looking down at their hands again, still intertwined on the table. "And I'll stay with you as long as you'll have me, Fae."

She ran her fingertips across the dark line that started in his palm and trailed up his wrist and then under the cuff of his shirt. She watched him shiver before he smiled at her, and she forced a smile back.

She hated that they had kind of flipped roles on the positivity front, now he was the one being hopeful and wonderful – and all her mind was giving her was the fact that nothing good ever lasted long in her life. She was able to be happy in the moment, to find the good in the present, but the future? He was making plans for a future that may not even *exist*, and she wanted to get excited about them. She wanted to do all of that, but the future had always been a dark place, a doomed place, full of new masters and potential cruelties and lost friends.

"What is it?" His brow furrowed, and she shook herself.

"It's nothing, keep going. I want to hear more about all the places in the world we can see since we have Air Laochra to travel with."

"Fae... if you don't want to go to those places, we don't have to, and... if you're not sure you want me there for any of it –"

"Stop." She shook her head. "That's not it, Kiernan. These

last few weeks are the happiest I've been since before – well, since before. I just kind of feel like I'm waiting for the other shoe to drop. You said you feel like you're dreaming and you're afraid you'll wake up? Well, I have the same feeling, except I'm waiting for something to ruin *this*." She gestured between the two of them and then took a hearty drink of wine. "I'm all about celebrating the good in the now, but I usually try not to think about the future."

"I'm sorry, it's just hard not to think about the future when I finally want one." His shy smile made her want to kiss him again. She wanted to ignore the mortals in the restaurant and climb onto his lap and kiss him slowly, let the warmth build between them until it erased all their doubts and concerns.

He said he wanted a future with her.

A future with someone who cared for her, who understood her, who respected her – and someone who wouldn't die on her.

"It's okay, I like listening to you talk about it. It's hopeful, it's... beautiful."

"I do have one more plan, but it's something I have to show you and I can't do that here, so let's change the subject. Something lighter. What's your happiest memory? The *truth*, and while it may be difficult, don't just say something with me in it. I already know how awesome I am." Kiernan grinned, and she laughed. He could be so freaking arrogant, but she knew that right now it was a show to lighten her mood. His eyes reflected the dim light around them and it made his face look softer, less stressed and concerned than he had in the weeks prior.

"Umm, something without you? Now won't *that* be difficult." She grabbed her wine, resting her lips on that glass as she brought her mind back to the question. When had she last been really happy?

Her father's face flashed into her memory and it felt like a punch in the stomach.

She wished for a moment he could be there to see this place in her life, this good and peaceful place. He would have approved of Kiernan, someone who worked in the soil and had a respect for things that grew. Someone who was brave even though he was damaged, still good even though he'd been made to do terrible things, someone who was still able to care even when he'd lost everything. Her father had always said she'd find someone who respected her for her strengths, and protected her where she was weak, and Kiernan seemed to fit the bill. Which was both exhilarating and terrifying.

"My father is my happiest memory." Fae smiled a bit, and he nodded to encourage her to elaborate. She took a breath and let the door of her memory open wide, and she was flooded with the incredible childhood she'd been given. Her eyes started to burn with tears, but she pushed them down and started talking. "There's so much of who he was that made me who I am, it's hard to even put into words."

"He gave me a childhood to envy. I can remember one

time, when I was maybe ten, it rained so hard that the village almost flooded. Tiny rivers were flowing through the paths. Everything was coated in slippery mud, and pools of filthy water clogged with branches and leaves and dirt were sitting in all the low spaces. I was *amazed* by it, by the power of it all. But my mother didn't want us going out in it because if we ruined our clothes she'd have to mend them or make new ones. My sisters listened, but I stood at the entrance to our home watching the rain pour down as if one of the gods was emptying a giant bucket over us. My father had been grinding herbs into poultices, listening to my mother berate me for standing in the doorway, and he suddenly just got up, grabbed my hand, and dragged me out into the rain. My mother started screaming at him, but he just pulled me farther away into the storm until her voice faded into the thunder and the rain."

"We were soaked in seconds, our legs were coated in mud, but we laughed and celebrated the power that nature, *Eltera*, was wielding in that moment. We ended up slipping and falling in the mud, and my hair was coated with it and matted down, and he helped me up. I remember starting to cry and being terrified of what my mother was going to do and he shook me and said, '*Clothing can be fixed, but you should* never *tame yourself.*' And then he just hugged me. He hugged me even though both of us were filthy, and soaked to the bones from the downpour. I just – I felt perfectly, unconditionally loved in that moment."

"He sounds like a great man." Kiernan was watching her with a thoughtful look.

"He was." Fae smiled into her glass. "I think you two would have gotten along. He always had his hands in the dirt too, and he always liked my attitude."

"We could have commiserated on how we dealt with you, Glowworm." Kiernan grinned and Fae threw one of the bread rolls at him. He caught the projectile, and laughed before taking a bite and setting it on a plate of mostly untouched lasagna. "You know, Branna was feisty too, and such a temper. She was never afraid to speak her mind to me, never afraid to slap me upside the head if I did something foolish. I think Lann would have been just as defiant given time."

"So you're saying you have a type?" Fae laughed and he joined her, nodding.

"I guess I do have a type."

"Your turn. Happiest memory."

"That's easy, I think about it all the time. It's the day Lann walked for the first time." His smile faded a little as his eyes focused on some point in the middle distance while he reached for the memory. Fae tried to picture what a little boy with blond hair and Kiernan's features might have looked like, then he started talking again. "It was a gorgeous day, I'd been digging up the soil to plant some things in our little garden, and as I walked back towards our house Branna was holding his hands so he could take steps with her. Then, all of a sudden, he just let go, eyes on me, and waddled towards me. I felt like my chest was going to burst with pride. Pride in him, and for how much I loved Branna for giving him to me. As soon as he got to me he just started laughing, and then Branna was cheering for him. 'A leanbh na páirte', *my dear child*, she said, over and over. It's a good memory, and I'm glad to have it of them."

"I'm glad you didn't lose that memory." Fae finished her glass and set it down.

"Me too." He had a wistful smile on his lips, and Kiernan's glass was empty as well as he twirled the stem between his fingers. There was a pause in the conversation as they both pulled themselves back to the present, leaving their memories in the dust of the past.

"So what's next? I think the kitchen has been thoroughly exhausted by your orders." Fae grinned, and Kiernan looked around at all the plates and shrugged.

"I don't think the kitchen will mind the money, and this place donates food to the local shelter." He stood up and extended his hand to help her from her chair. "Ready for the second half of the date?"

"Absolutely." Fae took his hand and he pulled her up. "What's the second half?"

"Trust me, it's better to see it." He didn't release her hand as they walked out of the restaurant, and only broke it for a moment to pull on their coats. Once outside he gripped her hand a little tighter, but he didn't lead her towards the parking lot. Instead, he moved them around the side of the building. Fae raised an eyebrow as they stepped under an old metal fire escape. His hands cupped her face and then his lips found hers and the fierce kiss burned her lips. The heat between them built and she clenched her fists into the lapels of his coat as her back hit the brick wall. She could feel the chill of it through her coat, but she didn't care. His hands were moving down her side and they pressed against the curve of her waist as his body leaned against hers. Her heart was racing as she wrapped her arms around his neck and pulled him down to her. When they finally separated, they were both gasping, breath intermingling in clouds between them in the cool air.

"I've been wanting to do that all through dinner." Kiernan smiled down at her, his thumb tracing her cheekbone before moving down over her lips.

"No complaints here." Fae smiled, trying to calm her heart rate and ease the blush in her cheeks. "Is this where we go to the movies?"

"We're not going to the movies, I have something much better. You have to close your eyes though, so the surprise isn't spoiled." Kiernan placed another kiss on her lips and she closed her eyes as he wrapped his arms around her. "Hold on to me, okay?"

CHAPTER TWENTY

Badenoch, Scotland

Kiernan leaned forward and breathed in the scent of her hair; he loved how she smelled. He never wanted to wake up without it, without her, ever again, and depending on how she reacted to his surprise that might be possible. Fae's arms tightened around his neck again and he focused on their homeland. The odd tugging sensation filled him as they shifted, and he had to take a deep breath to push back the temporary dizziness before he opened his eyes.

The sky was still dark in the early hours of the morning, and there was a fine mist falling that made the chill in the air a little stronger. Her blue eyes opened as she swayed in his arms from the aftereffects, but he shook his head down at her.

"Not yet, just a moment more." He smiled when she

closed her eyes again. Twisting his head around, Kiernan tried to pinpoint the place he had visited only a handful of times before, usually when she was sleeping, but he had studied it on maps carefully.

He turned Fae in his arms so she was facing the craggy mountains where the paler gray of the coming dawn made their outline evident. There were trees nearby but they were mostly in a wide open space that smelled as green as it was. It was even more beautiful in the daylight.

"You brought me somewhere wet." Fae was smiling when she said it, but he could see that the mist was starting to make her hair stick to her skin and droplets were gathering to slide across her cheeks, down her chest and beneath the neck of her sweater. He pulled his eyes away, reminding himself why he was there.

"Yes, it's raining a little, but I thought you might remember how much it rained in our homeland." Her eyes snapped open and he felt her body tense against his. She shook slightly as she leaned down in front of him, and put her hands on the ground. He stepped away to give her space, and she pressed her fingers into the earth.

"This is our land?" Her gaze turned up to him and he could see the tears forming at the edge of her eyes. All he could do was nod. "I haven't been back. I never got to come back. No one ever..."

"I know... I was thinking, if you want, this could be where we move next, since I need to move on from Seattle before people start noticing I look closer to twenty than thirty. I actually bought the land last week. I was trying to think of somewhere you'd want to live that's a little less populated, less encounters with mortals, but there's still a village a few kilometers away for things you might want or need, or for a little social interaction."

"I used private funds through some shell organizations, the Laochra have no way to track it as mine, and as far as Cole or Eryn or any of the others popping in – they couldn't get here because they won't know about it. We have to have to be able to see a place, to picture the space to appear there. So, you'd be safe here. I promise." Kiernan cleared his throat as he finished his ramble. She was looking at the ground again, grass springing from between her fingers. Then her eyes started to bounce between the mountains, the trees in the distance, the hazy sky, and the earth under her hands.

"Also, I, uh, I had a local contractor draft up some plans for two cottages on this land, although there's more than enough room for an entire village. I just didn't want you to feel trapped with me. Ever. And I can still build two if you want." He was trying to talk but her eyes found his again and locked on, and in the dim light of the night sky it was hard to see her expression.

"You don't need to build two, Kiernan." Fae stood up again, stepping so close to him that her chest brushed against his. "I've actually grown quite comfortable being cramped into a small space with you."

"Is that right?" He wanted to reach out for her, his hand twitched with the urge to tuck the damp hair behind her ears, but he knew he had to let her take the lead. He couldn't push this.

"Yes. Even if you build two, I have a feeling we'd only use one." Her fingers nimbly shifted the buttons of his coat until it was open and she slid her arms inside to hug him. Kiernan gave in and brushed her hair back before returning the hug. For a moment, this gentle side of her made her seem so fragile. He wanted to protect her from anything or anyone that would even think about hurting her. In an instant he felt the dark one that he kept at bay surge inside him as he thought of someone laying a hand on her again, and he had no doubts about the lengths he'd go to protect her, to give her the life he'd promised. There were flashes of blood coating his hands, of a sword clenched in his fist, of an unquenchable rage burning inside him and he jerked himself back from the edge.

No. There was no room in this moment for the dark one. There wasn't any more room for that person – he *never* wanted to be that person again. He cleared his throat and made himself smile as he pressed a kiss against her hair.

"You can choose everything for it. We might both live there, but it will be yours. Floor to ceiling. I just ask that you let me bring my TV?" When her laughter rang out it seemed to vibrate against his chest and the sound pushed the darkness back.

"Deal." Fae looked up at him, slid her hands around to the back of his neck, her fingers moving into his hair as she pulled him down to kiss her. Her lips were surprisingly warm in the chill of the air and his body reacted instantly as she pressed herself against him. He poured his anxious energy into the kiss and she responded with a hunger that pushed him to keep up.

When his hands moved to her waist again he tugged her towards him, and she made a sound of surprise that was so small and feminine he felt himself growl in response.

By the gods, he wanted her.

Fae wasn't shy though, and she untucked his shirt to slide her hands underneath the fabric and across his stomach. He gave in to the urge to hold her, picking her up so she wrapped her legs around him. The way her gasp for breath sounded in his ear, he knew he had to start counting backwards from, oh, ten thousand, or all of his well-meaning restraint was going out the window.

"Your choice, Glowworm. Stay here or go back to the apartment?" He spoke the words quickly, and she kissed him again.

"Apartment. Morning will come too quickly here." She smiled at him and moved her hands underneath his shirt, around to his back where her nails trailed down over his skin.

"Hold on then." He growled out the words as he tried to hold his concentration on his apartment, the mist disappeared and for a second he didn't quite know where they had ended up until he tried to take a step to balance himself and bumped into the bed. He'd appeared in the bedroom.

Not like he had certain things on his mind at all.

Fae recovered more quickly from the shift this time, noticed their location, and immediately shifted her body weight higher so he would lean back onto the bed. When he did she was neatly straddling his waist, and he didn't mind that at all.

"Nice landing." He grinned up at her, and he was grateful for the streetlights coming through the windows because he could see the smile on her face as she looked down at him.

"Thanks." She leaned down and placed a kiss against his lips, and he could feel her fingers against his stomach as she started unbuttoning his shirt. He held his breath and clenched his fists to his sides. He wasn't going to rush her in this, after all, they had forever. She pushed his shirt open and placed small kisses across his chest, even over the dark sword mark that represented Gormahn's hold on him.

When she pulled at the arm of his jacket he sat up and slipped the shirt and jacket off and threw them both over her shoulder to the floor. Her grin was wicked as she dragged her nails lightly over his chest and down his stomach. Then she pulled her own jacket away dropping it behind her, and he heard the distinctive double thump of her shoes hitting the floor. He kicked his Converse off and laid back down, watching her reverently as her fingertips dipped under the bottom of her sweater and she slowly pulled it over her head.

Inch by inch her skin was revealed until it passed over her head and her auburn hair tumbled back over her shoulders.

His breath caught in his chest. "You are beautiful, Fae..."

Instead of the smile he had expected, she flinched, and fear swirled in his stomach that she'd changed her mind.

He was about to stop everything when she spoke softly. "Neala."

"What did you say?" Kiernan propped himself up on his elbows to be closer to her, and she crossed her arms over her bare stomach.

"My name isn't..." She winced and brought her eyes back to him. "My name isn't Fae. It's Neala."

"Neala?" He repeated and she nodded slowly, looking away from him again. He grabbed her chin gently and made her look at him. "You got the name Fae from a master, didn't you? Because you're Faeoihn."

"Yes, and I just thought before we did anything else, you said you wanted to do this right, and -"

"I'd love to call you Neala. Neala is perfect," He smiled at her. Neala meant *female champion* and he couldn't imagine that her parents could have chosen a better name. "I feel incredibly honored that you told me."

"Can you say it again?" She smiled back at him, and he laughed quietly.

"Neala."

"By the gods, it's been so long since I've heard that." Fae, no, *Neala* leaned over him, her auburn hair a curtain around them. "And it sounds better than I remember from your lips."

"Oh really?" He tried to play it casual, but that was

practically impossible with his hard cock pressing against the juncture of her thighs, still wrapped in tight fitting jeans. She leaned down and her hands moved up his sides, over his shoulders and into his hair. He could feel her nails on his scalp as she tilted her head and kissed him deeply, and he returned the kiss with every ounce of wanting he'd experienced since he'd first laid eyes on her. Kiernan's hands slid up her waist and he suddenly appreciated their stop to buy the dark green lace bra that met his palms. His mind flipped back to earlier in the evening, to several days before, to the hundreds of years before that, and he was still in awe that she was there in his arms and her lips were pressed against his.

She pushed herself up, her hands splayed across his chest and she smiled down at him. "Yes, it really does..." Her hands moved down the muscles of his stomach to the waist of his pants, and his stomach tensed underneath her touch, his cock kicking against the zipper that confined it painfully.

"I am trying so hard to be a good guy right now." Kiernan rested his hands on her hips, and she took that moment to grind herself against him. He groaned, and she grinned at him.

"Stop trying, Kiernan." Neala took his hands, sliding them up her sides to cup her breasts. He took the invitation, rolling his thumb over the nipples pressing against the lace. He growled and sat up, sealing his mouth over the little buds through the cloth. Her back arched forward and she shifted in his lap, another growl escaping him against her skin as he was unable to keep quiet with her there.

"Little minx, you are about to make me stop playing nice." He grinned as he sat up, pinching her nipple lightly between his fingers.

Her mouth spread into a smile. "I don't need you to play nice with me." Neala's fingers slid into his hair, but this time she tightened her fist, making his scalp light up with a sting that had him hissing air through his teeth.

He growled and lifted her into the air again when he stood. She let out a surprised yelp as he dropped her back onto the bed and her hair fell around her in a halo. Her cheeks were already flushed making her blue eyes vibrant, and lips darker. He paused to let his eyes move over her, but he didn't miss that she was doing the same. In moments they were naked and Neala moved back across his bed, and he followed her, climbing onto the bare sheet. He caught her thigh in one hand and yanked her back towards him, ending up under him as he leaned forward. Pushing her thighs apart, he growled low as her pussy was bared to him. Before he'd even thought about it he'd bent his head down and licked up her slit, parting her lips to let him taste her.

Neala gasped and arched off the bed. "Holy shit, Kiernan!"

He had to fight the urge to laugh as he settled down on his stomach, trapping his hard cock against the bedding because he was going to be here a while. When she tried to snap her thighs shut around his head, he grabbed her knees and spread them wide. There was no way she was going to keep him from doing this, from hearing her scream his name in pleasure as she came, and this time he wasn't just going to feel her in his arms, he was going to taste her.

CHAPTER TWENTY-ONE

SEATTLE, WASHINGTON

NEALA GASPED as his tongue found her clit and her hips lifted against his mouth, a stream of muttered curses leaving her lips as her fists gripped the bedding.

Holy fuck, he's good at this.

Her body was tense as she fought the urge to press her thighs against the sides of his head in an effort to stop the overwhelming waves of pleasure, or hold him exactly where he was so he could push her over the edge. He moaned against her skin and it made her moan back. It had been years since someone had done this, and she wanted to press her hips harder against his talented tongue, but then it would suddenly be too intense and she'd jerk back. His fingers tightened on her thighs hard enough to leave bruises, but she didn't care. She was close, so fucking close.

"Please, please, Kiernan..." Neala was begging, and she never begged, yet somehow with Kiernan it was good. The growl it summoned from his chest was hot enough, but then he thrust two fingers inside her, curving them to brush against that bundle of nerves that had her lifting off the bed. His mouth followed her though, concentrating on her clit as his fingers worked their magic. She was begging, whimpering nonsense into the air above her as she arched her back and felt that delicious tingling covering her skin, making her shiver. Another tug on her clit and a crippling wave of pleasure crashed through her, and she screamed his name.

Then, she shattered.

Behind her eyelids was a fireworks show in the darkness, and her body was caught in the riptide the orgasm had brought her. Then he was on top of her, his cock brushing against her, and his dark eyes were asking.

She nodded, spreading her legs, "Please?"

Kiernan kissed her and then thrust himself inside her in one hard movement that sent a ripple through the both of them. She could taste herself on his lips, and their moans met against their mouths, warm and vibrating as his weight dropped over her. His hips began to piston between her thighs, and she let herself fall into the heady pleasure of feeling full and fulfilled.

She was so wet, and every thrust stretched her, aching as he bottomed out, a small cry escaping her each time. He broke the kiss and kissed down her neck towards her shoulder, his teeth scraping her skin, and she held his head to her letting him know it was okay. He thrust even harder and bit down on her shoulder, pinning her in place with the powerful grip on her hip, and his teeth pressed to her skin. She moaned, arching under him as the sensations compounded one on top of the other.

He relaxed his bite and whispered against her skin, "Neala," and she felt like she was glowing, but for once she actually *wasn't*. He knew her real name, and he was saying it. He was calling her Neala, like she was a real person, like she was a lover. It had been centuries since she'd even thought of herself as a person, and hearing her own name in her head was like accepting she was different. *Free.*

She wrapped her arms around his neck and his lips met hers, the kiss difficult to maintain as he continued to drive himself deep. She broke it and raked her nails down his back, grinning at the way his breath hissed just before he dipped his head and trapped a nipple between his teeth. The searing ache combined with the pleasure to make her scream, and he laughed against her skin as his tongue soothed the pain he had created.

He was perfect.

No one had ever treated her like this.

Like it was on cue, his kisses moved up and across her shoulder blade, his tongue flicking out against the skin of her neck until he was hovering over her lips again. "Is tusa an leath eile díom".

You are the other half of me.

Neala felt her heart ache at hearing their language, and what he meant with it. She bit her lip against the next cry that tried to escape her lips, the pleasure beginning to overwhelm her again. That delicious tension coiling at the base of her spine to leave her gasping and whimpering in his ear, and it was clear he loved it as he growled and picked up the pace, and switched back to English. "Think you can come for me again, Glowworm?"

She grinned and dug her nails into the skin of his back, and he bit down on her shoulder in retaliation. The thrill of him pinning her to the bed beneath his weight, her thighs spread wide for him, for someone she cared about, who cared for her, was too much – the orgasm hit like a tidal wave, drowning her in sensation and he moaned against her skin and spread his knees on the inside of hers to thrust harder, deeper.

Then he joined her, his seed spilling inside her with a warm rush and a low groan against her ear as he collapsed over her. He mostly caught himself on his elbow, but he was all muscle, and she wasn't bothered at all by the way his hard chest pressed against hers. They were both catching their breath, and she laid gentle kisses across his shoulder hovering above her, whispering between each one, "Is tusa a rún mo chroí."

You are the secret of my heart.

He turned and kissed her hard, his tongue meeting hers as she wrapped her arms around his neck, deepening the kiss as they poured out the things there were no other words for at the moment. Then he placed one more gentle kiss to her lips and slid from her, moving to lie next to her.

Heavy breaths filled the silence in the room as he shifted them to lay the right way and he pulled her to his side, his arms hugging her tight. "I'm not sure how I survived without you," he whispered against her hair, and it brought tears to her eyes.

She turned her head to kiss him again and then laid her head on his chest, facing him and twining their legs together. His heartbeat was still fast, matching hers, but as his chest rose and fell more steadily it evened out. "Thank you, Kiernan."

A soft laugh came from him and he kissed her hair. "I should be thanking you, álainn." *Beautiful*. Neala smiled, and he squeezed her tighter against him.

They lay there for a while, her head spinning with the magnitude of what had happened in the span of a day or so. Everything that defined her existence was upside down. Two thousand years of beliefs flipped on their head because she was in bed with a Laochra, he hadn't summoned the bands to claim her even when they slept together, and she was pretty sure she was falling in love with him. Her damaged, sometimes light, sometimes dark, warrior.

He fell asleep first, his breaths quieting and his grip on her slackening. She stayed cuddled against him, reveling in the heat from his skin. Looking up at his face, she smiled at the relaxed expression on his face – completely at peace. Neala grabbed the sheet with her foot and pulled it up over them, cuddling down next to him and breathing out slowly. Somewhere between one hypnotizing beat of his heart and the next, she fell asleep.

Her dream was vivid, loud, and overwhelming. She was in a market somewhere in the Middle East and people were pushing their way past each other in brightly colored clothes. They spoke a hundred different languages, ones she had heard in her long life, but oddly she had no fear among all of the people. She didn't give a second glance to anyone she passed, male or female, because she was searching for someone. It was claustrophobic having to push through them, but she finally came to a small square that had a few inches of breathing room.

A fountain stood in the corner, tumbling crystal water that shone in the sunlight, and standing in front of it was Eltera. It was actually her! The goddess, in all her golden glory, in the same dress she'd worn the night Neala had become a Faeoihn.

"Eltera!" she cried, and tried to push towards her, but Eltera shook her head slowly and pointed to a different place on the square.

Standing at the entrance to another long row of stalls was Kiernan, bare-chested and smiling at her. He looked incredible in the sunlight, and she found it was easy to get to him through the crowd, but just before she got to him his face changed, contorting in pain. He put his hand to the dark sword over his heart and when he pulled his hand away there was blood.

So much blood.

He raised his dark eyes to hers and they flickered, black, then green, then black again, and his lips parted like he was going to speak. She reached out for him, trying to scream his name over the din in the market – but then he collapsed to the ground.

She gasped herself awake, knocking Kiernan back from her when she jerked to a sitting position. When she looked over at him he was wide awake and scanning the room for what had woken her up, his body tense. Once he was sure they were alone he ran a hand down her back as she hugged the blankets to her chest.

"Fa- Neala? What's wrong?" He sat up before gently touching her chin and turning her head towards him. She faced him and saw the dark vines that were coiled all the way up to his shoulder, a hand's width away from the dark sword over his heart. She reached out and traced the end of the vines and then laid her hand over the sword, disbelief crippling her that she hadn't noticed it the night before.

"I had a nightmare. I think Eltera sent it to warn me since *you* hadn't said anything. The vines are too close to Gormahn's mark, Kiernan. Why didn't you tell me?" Neala could feel the worried tension in her face, and he smoothed the wrinkle between her eyebrows with his thumb.

"I have a few days yet, and I didn't want to leave you alone." He gave her a reassuring smile, but it didn't quell the sick turning of her stomach. "Plus, I think we've used the last couple of days quite well, don't you?"

"Be serious for a minute." She frowned at him, tracing the end of the vine closest to the mark. It was like her eyes were playing tricks on her, because it almost seemed to be growing by millimeters before her very eyes. "You have to fix it. Promise me."

"I'll contact Cole in a day or so, I promise." He smiled at her and leaned forward to kiss her, but she stopped him, pushing him back.

"*Today*. Contact Cole today." There was an ache in her chest as she remembered the lost and pained look on his face from the dream. Eltera was sending her a warning and she had to listen to it. Nothing she had dreamed had ever felt so viscerally *real*.

"It's not an emergency, I swear. I still have time and I'd like to spend another day with you." He brushed her hair back from her face and then laid his hand against her cheek.

"And what if you don't? You're not going to be able to protect me, or be with me, if you're dead." Neala pulled away from his hand. She wasn't going to drop this, or let him distract her. Not with his gorgeous body, and not even with the fact that he somehow pulled off bedhead like he'd done it on purpose.

"Okay, you win. I'll call him today... but later. Can I kiss you now?" Kiernan grinned at her and she stopped him again.

"Message him now. Please."

He sighed and leaned back to grab his phone from the bedside table. As he stretched his muscles shifted under her skin, and she forced a breath to remind her why it was important that she wasn't under him again already. Kiernan tapped away on his phone and then the edge of his mouth tilted up in a cocky smirk. "There. Happy?"

Fae looked at the phone as he held it up: *Want to go bar hopping again?*

"Yes. I am," she mumbled, and he leaned forward to press his lips to hers. His kiss was like a balm on the ache in her chest as it simultaneously eased the turning of her stomach. Neala climbed onto his lap, straddling him, which snagged his attention because they were both still very naked.

"Listen to me, Kiernan, this whole thing between us only just started. We haven't even had a *chance*, I just don't want you to –" She stopped talking when he leaned forward and pressed another soft kiss against her lips.

"Nothing will happen. I've avoided Cole's messages enough anyway, he'll be ecstatic I want to go out with him again. I promise I'll take care of the vines." Kiernan started kissing her neck, speaking between each touch of his lips to her skin. "I really don't regret a minute that I've waited though."

"Oh, really?" Neala grinned as he kissed across her shoulder. His attitude this morning was infectious and she felt a lightness bubble up in her chest with his promise sealing her concerns away. When her eyes moved down to look at him she realized she had been so distracted by the memory of the nightmare that she hadn't even noticed she was still glowing from Eltera's touch, and the light was reflecting on his skin, lighting up each little line of muscle and making him look delicious.

"Not a single moment, Glowworm." He pushed her backward onto the bed, slipped between her thighs, and spent the rest of the morning erasing any lingering negative feelings from the dream.

HE KEPT HIS PROMISE. By late afternoon he had already talked to Cole on his cell phone and reassured him that he'd been just fine, that he'd just needed some time to himself, but that he was ready for more guy time. Kiernan had then spent the next thirty minutes reassuring *her* that even though he was having 'guy time' with another Laochra he still wouldn't hurt the defenseless, and he had asked her over and over if she was okay with him going.

"You're sure it's okay? Really? I promise it's just a bunch of bar fights." His duffel bag was sitting by the TV and he was fidgeting with his phone, putting it in his pocket and taking it back out to check the time over and over.

"I don't care how many fights you have to get in to get the vines back under control. Just don't kill anyone." Neala was curled up on the couch in a dark blue shirt and jeans, trying not to fidget too badly at the idea of him going off to pick fights. Fights could be dangerous though; she knew that better than most, so she quickly added, "Unless you have to, obviously."

"Thanks, but I don't think it will get to that." His face changed and he pushed his hand through his hair. "Oh gods! I'm an idiot. I forgot something really important. I'll be right back." One second he was standing there and the next there was empty space. It was so sudden that it kind of hurt her head, and she had to rub her eyes. Hopefully mortals didn't catch him doing *that* trick, it would be impossible to explain. She waited, but after fifteen minutes she got up and grabbed juice from the kitchen. Another five or so minutes passed and she had flicked the television on when Kiernan reappeared near his desk.

"You have an issue with 'be right back', has anyone ever told you that?" She smiled at him so he'd know she was playing and walked over to him. He looked flushed like he'd been running, and she arched an eyebrow.

"I'm sorry, I just wanted to give you this before I left." He pulled a strand of leather from his pocket and held it out to her. She took it and hanging from the center of the leather was a silvery disc with the words 'mo ghaol', *my love*, hand carved into it.

"It's just a little gift so you don't forget that I love you –" Kiernan's face froze and he clapped his mouth shut. "So... I said that, but you don't need to say anything back. I just wanted you to have it, and I should really go, he's called twice."

"It's okay, Kiernan, it's beautiful." Neala's stomach was somewhere around her ankles, and she opened her mouth to respond to the declaration with *something*, but he leaned down and kissed her. It started out rushed but slowed into a long, gentle kiss until he finally pulled away from her.

"I really have to go. Tomorrow and the next day should be all I need. Be careful, please? Oh – and design books should start arriving from the contractor for the cottage if you want something to do." Kiernan ran his thumb across her cheek and all she could do was smile at him and then, *poof*, gone again. It kind of made her dizzy when he did that. She'd have to remind him to step back next time so she could maybe close her eyes for a second, or look away.

She had been gripping the silver disc in her palm and she forced her hand open, it really was beautiful. The metal had been hand hammered, and cut, and then he'd somehow carved the words into the disc.

My love.

Did he really love her? He'd said it, but they'd only known each other about four weeks. Well, he had been stalking her with his creepy observation glass for a few *centuries*, so maybe it made sense he'd say it.

Perhaps the better question was did *she* love *him*?

Neala groaned. The dream had wrecked her night's sleep and she was exhausted, she could deal with all of the feelings the last few days had brought up after a nap.

Taking the two ends she put them around her neck and tied the leather together letting the disc slip under her shirt between her breasts. She turned around to the living room and sighed, she could entertain herself for a couple of days. She'd just stay inside, avoid people and catch up on movies and finish reading Kiernan's books, and plan a cottage.

Time would fly by, and first? A nap.

CHAPTER TWENTY-TWO

SEATTLE, WASHINGTON

TIME WASN'T FLYING BY, but at least she was being productive. Sleeping in Kiernan's bed without him had been weird and she'd found herself back on the couch, with his pillow, sometime in the early morning. When she woke up, she'd quickly realized how lonely it felt to wake up to an empty home. She'd *never* been alone and it was odd to have no one to talk to or even observe. It had left way too much time to think, and contemplate, and consider – reflect – mull over – ponder ... *why the hell had he dropped that bomb on her and left?*

Her fingers kept finding their way back to the little metal disc that rested against her chest like it had always been there. When she traced it, she could feel the grooves of the letters against the pad of her finger, *mo ghaol*. So, he loved her, or he believed he did – believed it enough to carve it into a gift for her – but she didn't know what to say back. Even after a day of thinking about it, she couldn't figure it out. She knew she cared about him, Laochra or not, and he was *good*. Whatever he had done in his past under Gormahn's influence, it wasn't the person at the core of who he was, a funny, gardening, neat-freak, warrior.

Even thinking about him made her smile.

As Kiernan had promised, huge design books had started arriving and she was careful to wait until the deliveryman left before she'd step out the front door to grab them. There were books of floor plans, examples of kitchens, floor and wall colors, a book of fabric swatches, and others discussing *styles* of homes.

It was overwhelming.

She had left the television on for noise, but had ultimately set up at the kitchen table around lunchtime so she could spread out. In an empty notebook she was writing down various things she liked along with page numbers and book titles. It was a complete fucking mess. At this rate she'd have a modern country façade with a rustic kitchen, an ultra-modern living room, and an airy, nature-driven bedroom. Deciding on a single theme for a whole house was challenging, but *that* was not what Kiernan had asked her to do. He'd asked her to pick what she liked, so she decided to just make the list of what she liked and deal with everything else later.

It had already been almost twenty-four hours since Kiernan had left and her chest ached with how much she missed him, she kept turning to show him something that made her laugh only to scan the room and remember he wasn't there. She wanted to call him and make sure he was okay, but knew it would be impossible for him to explain to the other Laochra. She wanted his opinion on shutters, and what the hell linoleum was, and whether or not he'd hate the idea of doorless cabinets in the kitchen.

She wanted him back.

She missed him so much that it hurt, like a physical ache under her ribs. A girl had once told her that she was *heartsick* for the boyfriend she'd had before she was taken and sold. The girl had refused to eat, refused to do anything – she had disobeyed simply by refusing to move or react. Neala couldn't remember what had happened to the girl, but she suddenly understood the idea of heartsick too well.

Maybe she did love him.

As she filled a glass of wine the realization settled over her like a cloud and she stepped away from the table to take a break from decorating plans. It really seemed to physically hurt to be away from him, and she wondered how people could stand to be away from their loved ones, if this was what loving someone felt like. The ache in her chest spread wider and grew sharper and she reached her hand up to rub the place it sprang from – and light caught her eye. She held her hand out and saw that bands of light were ghosting around her wrists, slowly growing brighter and more solid by the second.

"*No.*" Neala tried to draw a deep breath and the pain doubled in her chest, making her drop the wine glass, which shattered and splashed red wine across the tile floor. Panic clutched her, and she shook her head, trying desperately to wipe the light away from her. "No, no, no, no, no..." The bands of light became solid, immutable, and pain was steadily moving up her arms like there was glass in her veins. The pain from her arms was reaching towards the sharp ache in her chest, trying to connect it – she was sure it would kill her. She suppressed the urge to scream as the bands pulsed again and she collapsed to the floor. It was impossible to breathe now. She felt like her ribs were broken into shards and fire was filling the space where her lungs had been.

This was what a god's rage must feel like, this was the end.

She tried to focus on Kiernan, on Eltera, as the edges of her vision started filling with black and she forced her eyes tight against the glow of the bands. The last thing she saw was *not* going to be the curse that Gormahn had placed on her. If she was going to die, she was going to die thinking of Kiernan; his playful grin, the way he always stepped too far when lunging with a sword, the way he called her Glowworm, and the way he kissed her.

Her body was humming underneath all of the pain, and she wished for the void of unconsciousness, she prayed for it.

Then, there were voices.

At first they sounded far away, and then it was as if

someone cranked up the volume. They were shouting, someone else was trying to shout over them, and she realized the pain had backed away from excruciating to merely terrible. A raw gasp for air inflated her lungs for the first time in minutes, but someone kicked her hard in the stomach and she quickly lost the breath she had gained.

"Holy shit, it *worked*." A man's voice. Gleeful, but not close enough to be the one who had kicked her.

Where the fuck was she?

Neala placed her hands against the ground, which was covered in a beautifully patterned, thick carpet. She pushed herself up as the pattern came into focus, and her stomach dropped. When she lifted her head she thought she saw Nikola striding towards her from the massive desk in his study, but no, Nikola was dead.

It was his son. *Marik.*

"Oh, gods. No." Neala could barely speak through the raw feeling in her throat and chest, the air still felt like fire in her lungs and another gasping breath came as she tried to stand up.

"Oh, *yes.*" Marik stopped a few feet in front of her and smiled.

This could not be happening. She had to get away from here. Someone reached for her arm and she immediately stood up and broke their hold. Another grabbed her from behind and she twisted the man's hand to slip out of it. Her time without oxygen still had her dizzy, but she reacted on muscle memory when one of the guards threw a punch. She blocked it, brought her elbow into his face, and returned a kick to his stomach to knock him back. A windmill swing came at her and she let the arm extend past her so she could grab it and just as she was about to bring her elbow down to break it – Marik's voice rose up again.

"Fae. *Kneel.*" His voice almost seemed to echo against the walls of books. The bands reacted violently, the pain immediately spreading up her arms and spider webbing across her skin like someone had poured hot oil over her. The arm she'd been about to break swung back, and somewhere in her head she registered the guard had backhanded her. It was *nothing* compared to the pain of the bands, and she wondered if they'd always hurt this much, or if this was punishment for being free of them so long. Once she'd collapsed into a kneel the pain ebbed, but the bands glowed fiercely bright at her wrists as if they were celebrating their new master. *She had a new master.* Marik's eyes were glittering as he stepped forward towards her.

"How?" Neala choked out the word before gritting her teeth as she fought the urge to cry. She was looking straight at Marik, but she took notice of the two men in suits that had their backs to Nikola's desk. They both looked shocked and terrified, and she didn't know who they were, but they had clearly *not* expected her arrival. In her peripheral vision she knew there were at least two guards.

"It was easy, whore. You belong to this house." Butler's

voice came from behind her, and she clenched her jaw against the urge to scream, or throw up. She felt her muscles lock up as he stepped past her. "And this house belongs to Marik now." He stepped up next to the heir who glanced over at him before returning his cold eyes to her.

"Officially, it does. See – I just signed the paperwork taking control of my father's estate. We had the lawyers draft up a special page to accommodate all of the *living property*, such as yourself, that he left me." Marik took a few steps forward and he crouched down in front of her, running his hand over her cheek. Neala started to move her face away, but he grabbed her chin hard. "Once I signed the paperwork, I just demanded that you return. Looks like you heard me, wherever you were hiding. Didn't you, cunt?"

"Fuck you." Neala spit into his face, and his only reaction was to close his eyes, and then wipe his face slowly. Butler yanked her back by her hair, making her cry out.

"Where do you want me to put her until you're done?" Butler's voice was filled with excitement, and the way Marik smiled when he stood up filled her with dread.

"This shouldn't take much longer. Keep her with our guest for now." Marik turned back to the lawyers, who were gawking at her, and spread his arms to gather the men back towards the desk. Butler forced her to the floor and she contemplated fighting, but the guard on her right, who she now recognized from the fight in the snow, was already there. He twisted her wrists behind her back with vicious jerks that strained her shoulders, before using zip ties to bind them together.

"Alright, Fae, let's go meet your friend." Butler grabbed her arm and yanked her up, before pushing her out of the study and into the hall. He walked quickly, taking every opportunity to jerk her off balance as they moved down the stairs and toward the kitchen storage area. Neala still knew every inch of the house, and being back in it was like a weight settling across her shoulders. Butler came to a storage room door and opened it, pulling her after him as he stepped in to turn on the light. "Remember *him*?"

She tried to pull her arm out of Butler's grip, but his fingers were digging into her skin, and she knew she'd have bruises before it was healed in the morning. On the floor was a man in a dirty suit, his hands zip-tied to the storage shelves. He blinked against the light, but eventually looked up at her. At first she didn't recognize him at all, and then the sad look in his eyes struck a chord. She remembered him from the night of the Winter Dinner.

Anthony, or something like that. The failed knight.

"He's been here a few days, if you were wondering where he'd gone. No need to keep up the lies anymore, Andrew. She's here." Butler's voice was filled with bravado, gloating over them in his perceived victory. Andrew, *that was his name*, sighed and leaned his head against the wall.

He looked rough, one eye swollen and bruised, and a split lip. He seemed weak, they probably hadn't fed him much. Neala raised an eyebrow at the man, and he only met her eyes for a second before he looked away. The absurdity of the idea that this mortal had been who she was with for all these weeks made a laugh burble up in her throat. When it burst out, it sounded hysterical and quickly stopped.

"You're an idiot, Butler." Neala looked at him, knowing the laugh and her comment were going to incite violence. The hard punch to her stomach sent the air out of her and he let her double over to the ground, letting go of her arm. She dragged in air, and pressed him further. "You think this guy helped me get away? You think he's good enough to do something like that?" Her eyes lifted to Andrew, and she forced a smile for the show of it. "No offense."

"We know he did. He tried to buy you off Nikola that night and then left when he refused. The next morning you killed Nikola and you left to meet him!" Butler's voice was booming in the tiny room, the concrete walls keeping most of the noise in. Neala felt her brows knit together as Andrew's cheeks blushed in embarrassment and he looked away from her.

He had tried to buy her?

"I haven't seen this guy since the party, and he wasn't even the one who took me upstairs that night, Butler. He had *nothing* to do with my escape, which you'd know if you'd been one of the ones who'd had the balls to try and catch me." She started to laugh, but Butler's boot caught her in the ribs, and she landed on her side unable to stop herself with her hands bound. Two more swift kicks to her stomach and he was raging above her. His breath coming in quick bursts, and as she tried to focus on getting air back into her own lungs he paced quickly beside her.

"Just wait. Just wait for Marik to get a hold of you, slut. Then when he's done with you, you're mine. He promised. You'll regret every smart mouthed thing you've ever said to me. This house is under a new regime, whore, you'll see." Butler was fuming, speaking through gritted teeth as he stomped across the small space. She looked up at him, waiting for him to hit her again, but he just walked out the door and slammed it behind him.

"You shouldn't have done that." Andrew's voice was quiet. He sounded almost the same as he had that night, but there was no lightness to it, none of the jovial attitude that had made her see him as a safe bet before she'd ruined the night.

He had given up. *Weakling*.

"They're going to do whatever they're going to do." Neala rolled so she could sit up. Her ribs hurt, a lot, but when she took a deep breath she was pretty sure none were broken.

"It'll be worse, because you said those things. Butler's insane, and he encourages Marik to be the same. Although Marik isn't exactly sane either." Andrew wasn't looking at her; he was talking to the metal frame of the shelving.

"I think I'm more aware of Butler's psychosis than you are, but thanks." Neala said it matter-of-factly. The bitterness she felt at some privileged ex-guest of the house trying to educate her on living under Butler's power was obvious.

"You're right, I'm sorry." He clipped the words short and then clapped his mouth shut. For a few minutes they sat in silence, and Neala shuffled herself back against a shelving unit and leaned back. She didn't want silence at the moment, her adrenaline was still pumping, and she wanted answers. She wanted to know how the *fuck* she had gone from planning a cottage with her – whatever Kiernan was – to being on her knees in Ráj Manor again.

"So, Andrew... you tried to buy me?" Neala tried to consciously drop the hostility from her voice, and his eyes jumped to meet hers as the blush crept back up his neck.

"Yes, but it -" He cursed under his breath and yanked the zip-ties back against the shelving causing it to shake a little. "I was trying to help you. After they – after he *hurt* you, I just wanted to get you away from them."

"What was your plan?" She noticed his eyes dropped, but he seemed to steel himself for the conversation and looked back up at her.

"I hadn't exactly thought it out. It's not like I have some big estate. People would notice if I brought you home. Maybe I would have tried to free you, maybe I'm not as good as I think I am and I would have kept you. I don't know. I never had the chance to find out." He sounded ashamed, but he kept his eyes on hers and she had to respect the honesty.

"I knew you were trying to be some knight at the party,

but I'm sure you've noticed I'm not the damsel you should pick if you're feeling heroic." Neala's sarcasm took over as the constant humming pain of the bands began to fade. The curse seemed happy to have a master again, and the bands were responding to Marik in a way she'd never seen.

"Yes, I noticed." Andrew had his own bitterness, and looking at his injuries, knowing that before now he'd led a life of privilege, she could imagine that this was beyond horrible to him.

"Well..." Neala swallowed her anger, her hidden fears of the situation, and the leftover frustration she had at his active participation in the Winter Dinner, and spoke again, "Thanks for trying to help, and I'm sorry you got dragged into this. Do whatever you have to do so you can go home. You can't help me."

His head snapped up. "What do you mean?"

"Tell them whatever they want to hear, Andrew, and go home." She sighed, trying to find a comfortable position.

"They'll –" he was struggling with the words. Some sense of propriety stymieing his vocabulary, but he seemed to find some balls when he looked up at her again. "They'll do horrible things to you, Fae."

"My name isn't Fae, and yes, they will. They're going to do horrible things to me either way, so do what I said. Save yourself."

"I –"

"Save yourself, Andrew." She locked her eyes with him,

and he looked like he was about to speak again but he stopped himself. Defeat washed over him like a wave, and he turned to face the shelving. That was the last time they talked, after all, there really wasn't anything more to say after that.

CHAPTER TWENTY-THREE

Ráj Manor, Caledon, Ontario

After about twenty minutes of uncomfortable silence, the door clicked and a young guard opened it. She hadn't seen him before and Neala tensed, but the brown haired man just moved over and gently helped her to her feet. "I need you to come with me."

Dread pooled in her stomach, but part of her was relieved to not have to sit and watch Andrew spiral further into his self-loathing; she just didn't have the energy for it. The man led her out of the storeroom silently, keeping his touch light on her arm as they walked. Thoughts swirled in her head – of Kiernan, of the life they'd almost had, and of what waited for her now that she was back in this house.

Suddenly the guard stopped near the entry to the hall of master suites and his grip tightened on her arm before he let go completely and stepped away from her. "Fuck, fuck, fuck…"

"What?" Neala snapped at him, and he shook his head, laughing bitterly. She rolled her eyes and stood in the middle of the hallway, waiting for the idiot to get himself under control. There was too much on her mind to worry about some asshole's personal issues. She'd already done that with Andrew.

Honey brown eyes turned to her and he gripped his hair at the root, looking her over. His voice was tired when he spoke, "I thought you got out for good."

The words felt like a slap and she fought the urge to flinch against the memories of Kiernan's couch, of Elsie, of Kiernan's bed. "Why do you care, guard?"

"Hills."

"What?" Neala glared at him, jerking against the ties on her wrists, but his eyes wouldn't meet hers anymore.

"Nothing." The man reached forward and pulled her down the hall again. They were in the shorter west wing that *had* held Nikola's bedroom, but the guard stopped in front of a different door. He lifted his hand to knock, and his knuckles went white with the hard grip of his fist. "Just be careful."

"Like that's fucking possible…" Neala muttered and he sighed and let go of her arm. Then his knuckles landed on the door in a quick series of loud knocks.

Butler opened it.

Neala regretted for a moment that she'd pushed him, because his anger was simmering just behind his eyes and she knew he could snap at any moment. When he suddenly smiled at her she unconsciously took a step back, but the other guard was right behind her and she bumped into him.

"So glad you could join us, Fae." Butler grabbed her arm to pull her inside, and then nodded at the guard with her, "Stay outside, Hills."

The guard, Hills, gave her one last look and she couldn't figure out why he'd said anything to her. Why he had even bothered. Then he turned away and leaned against the wall outside the door. Butler turned her around and when the door clicked shut behind her, her pulse started racing as panic rose up inside her. The curtains on the windows were drawn against the cold, and there wasn't much light in the room to see by. Butler dug his fingers into her skin again and pulled her forward into the room, towards the bed. She planted her feet on the carpet and jerked to the side, breaking his hold on her so she could step away from him.

If he thought she was going willingly to whatever he had planned, he was wrong.

"You really are this defiant all the time, aren't you?" Marik's voice, smooth and calm like his father's, came from her right. He was lounging in a chair against the wall and she saw his face when he flicked his lighter to light a cigarette. "We'll see how long you keep that up." Out of the corner of her eye Butler lunged for her, but

Marik raised his hand and Butler stopped short. He grumbled to himself and moved to flip on a lamp.

"I have some questions for you, and I encourage you to answer them honestly," he paused, "Well, just to be safe, Fae, I order you to tell me the truth." Marik leaned forward in the chair, and Neala rolled her shoulders as she felt the warning hum in the bands. "Butler has told me you said Andrew Clark had nothing to do with your escape, is that true?"

"Yes." Neala clipped the word short, leaving off any honorific he may have been hoping for. Marik didn't seem surprised by her answer, or the lack of a painful response from the bands.

"Alright. Butler, release him. I'd rather have him out making me money than taking up space in my house. Make it clear to him that if this little incident were to damage our business relationship I'd be very *disappointed*." Marik gave a smile as Butler passed by and opened the door to talk to the guard in the hallway. "Next question, how did you kill my father?"

"I don't know." Neala waited for the bands to react for the vague answer, but they didn't respond at all. She breathed a sigh of relief, grateful that her *guesses* had not counted as knowledge to the curse. Marik's eyes narrowed slightly as Butler slipped in silently and returned to standing behind her.

"You *don't know* how you killed him?" He was clarifying to give the bands another chance to respond, and she could feel Butler's rapt attention on her as he caught on to the current line of questioning.

"No." She rolled her shoulders trying to adjust the tight ties on her wrists. Out of the corner of her eye she saw Butler shaking his head at Marik. No, the bands were not responding.

"How interesting..." He sat back in the chair, resting his ankle on his opposite knee. "Now, for the question of the hour - who helped you escape the guards?"

Neala clenched her jaw shut. She wasn't going to name Kiernan. She wouldn't reveal who he was or where he lived because she knew Butler and his men would track him, and Kiernan would fight for her, and it would all be pointless. She'd still be claimed, and he would still be Laochra. If the curse was dragging her back, she wasn't letting it drag him down too. She wouldn't give him the opportunity to ruin his life. The bands pulsed against her skin and the aching pain started to crawl up her arms, digging into her shoulders like claws.

"You're really not going to answer me?" Marik seemed a little surprised, and he watched her with a fascinated expression as the pain suddenly doubled and she clenched her teeth to suppress a gasp.

"No." Neala spit out the word, and his eyes widened slightly before he masked his face with a smile.

"You *are* feisty. I like it, it makes things interesting." Marik took a long, slow drag on the cigarette as he trailed his eyes over her, letting the smoke trail out as he spoke.

"Well, if you don't want to answer any more questions, undress."

Neala's stomach flipped and she pulled against the zip-ties unconsciously. Butler laughed to himself and stepped up behind her. She felt his hands pull her wrists back, a quick movement and the zip-ties were cut. Neala stood there, rubbing her wrists while a smile settled on Marik's face. Her discomfort seemed to be what was making him enjoy the moment so much, so she had to make herself not care. The bands were glowing brightly as they hummed another warning against her skin. *Undress.*

She'd had a month of freedom, of being in control of her own actions, and for a moment she contemplated letting the bands do their worst just to spite him. Maybe she'd black out from the pain, and then none of it would matter. Marik rolled his eyes, done with waiting, and stubbed out the cigarette in a small tray beside him.

"You can either do it yourself, or I'll have Butler help you. Your choice." He gave her a look that dared her to call him on the bluff, and she saw Butler move closer.

"No, wait." Neala held out her hand towards Butler, the idea of him touching her made her sick. She wanted to put off being near him for as long as possible. Being back in the house already made her stomach turn, and right now she wished she had Kiernan's power to just disappear with a thought. She'd go back to the spot he had picked for the cottage, and see it in the daylight.

Gray skies, and craggy mountains, and lush green grass.

"Now, Fae." Marik's voice broke into her thoughts and

yanked her back to reality with the name that had always been a synonym for *slave*. Neala took a shuddering breath, trying to calm herself enough to become as detached as she'd been before. She grabbed the bottom of her shirt and started to pull it off over her head, but Marik's voice interrupted her, "Slow."

Butler was an arm's length away from her, and she knew he'd jump at the opportunity to humiliate her, so she slowed down. Shirt first, which she dropped to the floor, and then she slid the jeans to the floor, revealing skin inch by inch. She could see red marks on her sides from the hits she'd taken earlier. If they had enough time they'd bloom into bruises, but she'd probably heal before then. She pushed the clothes to her side with her foot and Marik clapped his hands together loudly.

"Lovely. Keep the bra and panties. I think this is a much better uniform than the dress, don't you Butler?" Neala focused on the wall past Marik's head, if she could just ignore him she'd halt the blush creeping across her cheeks. She tried to remind herself that she was basically in a bikini, and people wore those for fun; she'd seen them in the store with Kiernan.

"Of course, sir." Butler's voice didn't sound convinced, but he'd never been interested in the girls' clothes. When it came to his entertainment, he preferred force and violence, not pretty clothes.

"Okay, Fae, on the bed." Marik stood up and Neala moved backwards from him. She shook her head, and felt the hum of the bands pick up, and a sharp pain began between her shoulder blades. The first sign of irritation appeared on Marik's face and he sighed. "Fine. You want it that way? Butler, help her."

Neala had lost track of Butler when she was focused on Marik and suddenly Butler's arms went around her, pinning her arms to her sides. She kicked back into his shin when he lifted her off the ground and he cursed.

His words growled in her ear as he half-dragged her backwards, "You never listen to me, but now you'll see." When he got to the bed he picked her up and dropped her onto it, and she immediately sat up to try and get away from him. Butler just grabbed her arms and pinned them above her head, his tight grip making them ache even through the pain from the bands.

Then, Marik was suddenly above her, straddling her waist to keep her there. "Butler is going to let go of your arms, but I order you not to move them, got it?" Marik's voice was still calm, and Neala felt the bands hum against her wrists. The urge to cry rose up suddenly and she clenched her teeth against it, but Marik must have seen the tears welling in her eyes. "Oh, don't be upset yet, we haven't even started! I wanted our first encounter to make it clear to you who's in charge here. As long as you obey me, I won't have to hurt you, and while these bands of yours are interesting I'm a lot more *hands on* when it comes to punishment. Understand?"

Neala felt taut as a bowstring, and she was holding her breath because she was worried if she breathed it would come out as a sob. She tried to release her mind to wander like she used to do so easily. She didn't want to be here right now. If she could detach and be somewhere else it wouldn't matter, none of it would matter. That morning she'd been planning a future, a real one, where she'd be happy and now she was back, but she could picture that open green space at the foot of the mountains and her unique little design-confused cottage.

Marik grabbed her face hard and leaned down over her, breaking the fragile vision she'd been building. "Hey! Come on now, you have to look at me. Don't lose focus. Answer me when I ask you a question, or I'll hurt you. It's very simple. Do you want me to hurt you?" Marik's calm façade was slipping a little, and the bands pulsed a wave of pain down her arms. It collided with the tension in her chest and she winced and glanced over at Butler. She knew he was enjoying this, and that he'd take any opportunity Marik gave him to hurt her. He was just waiting for Marik's order.

"No. I don't." She hated how her voice cracked when she was on the verge of tears, and Butler just smiled down at her. Marik tightened his grip on her face and made her look at him.

"Why are you looking at Butler? *I'm* the one you need to focus on. *I'm* the one in charge." Marik's eyes were fierce, and she realized that underneath that cool exterior was a rage she had never seen in Nikola. It made her stomach drop. A muscle in Marik's jaw ticked and he suddenly reached over towards Butler, and when he leaned back he had Butler's knife in his hand. Neala stilled as he pressed the edge against her neck.

"I understand that my father didn't like to get his hands dirty." Marik started to trail the knife down her chest and towards her stomach, but he wrapped his other hand around her neck and squeezed lightly to keep her from lifting her head. "I am *not* my father. I think a level of fear creates a healthy respect, and I believe *you* should fear me." There was a blinding pain in her side and she started to cry out, but Marik's hand tightened on her throat until she couldn't breathe.

The knife. He'd actually cut her.

He was smiling when he leaned down to her face again, and she was starting to panic from the lack of air, but when she tried to shift she realized the knife was *in* her side. She felt dizzy, and nauseous, and Marik was watching her face as the edges of her vision started to go dark. Then she heard a knock at the door. Marik removed the blade and released her throat in one swift movement, and she gasped from the pain of the knife being torn out of her. She tried to move her hand to her side, but the bands sent a jolt of pain through her bones.

He'd ordered her not to move her hands.

Except now she was bleeding, and she couldn't tell how much, she could only feel the pain that washed over her in cold sweeps. She was definitely crying now. How could things have gone so wrong so fast?

"Sir? The lawyers are saying they can't leave until you finish signing the documents." Hills was at the door speaking. Marik twisted at his waist above her, blocking her view and looking at the door.

"I already signed the estate documents." Marik growled

out the words, but the calm mask was slowly descending over him again.

"I'm sorry, sir, they asked us to find you. They said they can't process your requests without your signature."

Marik's head turned back to face her, and he brushed a thumb across her temple wiping the tears that had gathered there. He looked completely disappointed at having to leave her now, and that made her sick.

He had wanted fear, he had it.

In a swift movement he was off her and back on his feet, a nonchalant calm settling over him. He wiped the knife across the front of his white shirt, leaving two swipes of bright red, before he handed it back to Butler.

Apparently he wanted to make it clear to the lawyers that they had *interrupted* him.

"Well, then, let's go tend to business. Have Fae taken to the girls' quarters, I'm sure they would love to see that she's back." Marik took a few steps towards the door and turned around. "You can move your arms now, Fae. I'll come get you later so we can continue our discussion. For now, you should think about trying to keep me in a good mood."

Neala winced when she sat up and swallowed the scream that caught in her throat when she applied pressure to her side. She glared across the room at him, asking quietly through clenched teeth, "Why?"

"Because, Fae... this is me in a *good* mood." Marik turned

and left the room, and Butler started to follow him. He was practically glowing when he looked at her.

"Hills, take her to the girls' quarters. Marik will get her from there later." Butler grinned and slapped the guard on the shoulder before he followed after Marik.

CHAPTER TWENTY-FOUR

Ráj Manor, Caledon, Ontario

NEALA WAS HOLDING her hand against her side as hard as she could, but the blood was leaking through her fingers, and she was really only succeeding in smearing it over her skin. A good mood? He was insane. Andrew had been right about the explosive combination of Butler and Marik. Butler was straightforward with his violence, but Marik obviously craved it too. It was just hidden under the surface with him. Together they would only feed off each other until every girl in the house was dead.

He'd actually stabbed her.

She was shaking with the shock of it. Gods, what had she walked in to? What on earth could she do against someone who could stay so calm while being so violent? There was no end to what he might do with her, every morning when she healed -

"Fae?" There was a light touch on her shoulder, but it made her jump and turn quickly, which caused blood to pour through her fingers, and she hissed from the pain of it. Hills was staring at her side with an open mouth. "Holy shit - he, he *stabbed* you? He's never... what the -" the guard cut himself off with his hand over his mouth and he suddenly ran into the bathroom and came back with a towel.

He held it out to her and Neala sighed and took it from him so she could press it to her side.

"I can't believe he actually stabbed you. You're really bleeding. Are you okay?"

"Did you seriously just ask me that?" Neala choked out the words as she slid off the bed, holding the towel to her side.

"You'll heal, right? That's what you do, isn't it?" The guy seemed sincerely worried.

"Yes. That's what I do." She said it bitterly, and Hills snapped back to himself.

"Can you walk to the girls' quarters? I can carry you if you need me to." The guard looked like he was trying to be helpful, but she wanted away from him. She wanted away from this room more, so she started walking to the door and he followed. They walked in silence up the north stairs to the girls' quarters and the guard there gaped at the blood as he opened the door. Hills stayed outside as she walked in, clutching the towel to her side.

When the door clicked shut there were gasps and

screams and yells as a few of the girls saw her. Neala took a few steps forward, but they surrounded her. Sobeska and Annika and Mei-Li and Irena and Zofie and Ebere and *all of them*. Their faces swam in front of her, and she felt claustrophobic until Ebere raised her voice.

"Get back! You're freaking her out." Ebere clapped her hands and Sobeska helped to pull Irena and a few girls away. Ebere grabbed a big pillow for Neala and she helped her sit. When she bent to sit down she felt blood run down her side, and the sensation made her nauseous. Once she was sitting her other hand came up to brush across the silver disc which still rested against her skin, and she bit her lip against the urge to cry again. When would Kiernan discover she was missing? If he stuck with his original plan it would be at least a day before he was even going to come home. The pit of anxiety in her stomach opened further. What if she never saw him again?

Everyone was talking at once asking too many questions. Where had she been, if she was okay, why was she bleeding, what had happened – and Neala couldn't bring herself to answer any of them.

"Are you kidding me?!" Caridee's voice was shrill, and everyone stopped talking as she pushed one of the girls out of her way. "You're all asking if *she's* okay? Have you all forgotten that she left us here? She is the one that caused all of this and she just *left*. She left Butler in charge, and now *Marik* is here and in control of us?" She was hysterical, her breathing was ragged and her eyes were so wide that Neala could see the white all the way around her brown eyes.

"I'm sorry, Caridee, I am. I know it's worse. I've already had the pleasure of meeting Marik." Neala peeled the towel back and Irena pushed forward with a sob, her hands gently touching the edge of the wound. Irena was murmuring about how she'd help Neala get better, how she missed her, and Neala touched Irena's hand and forced a smile for her. It only made things worse as Caridee started yelling again.

"You're *sorry*? *Sorry*?! You've spent, what, an *hour* with Marik? You don't know! You don't know anything! Where have you been all this time? Where have you been while we've been here, while we've been suffering?" Caridee was throwing her arms out, moving closer to Neala while others stepped back to give her room.

Neala smiled bitterly, trying to adjust the towel to staunch the bleeding as much as possible as she pictured Kiernan's apartment, his cozy couch, the beautiful view of the bay.

"I was somewhere good, Cari, somewhere really *good*, but it doesn't matter now. When Nikola died I couldn't get back inside to help you, and I didn't have a way to get back here to help you." Neala talked calmly, and she glanced over at Ebere before she was caught by a stinging blow across her cheek. She turned and lifted her arm on instinct, blocking Cari's second slap. Cari tried to pull her arm back to try again but Neala grabbed her wrist. "You got *one*, Caridee. Now, stop."

"You don't know - you don't know what you did - what he did. He *whipped* me, he *hurt* me, they hurt us. They hurt us, and this whole time you've been *somewhere good*?" Caridee wasn't stable, that was clear, and Neala let go of her because she was screaming and starting to pull at her hair. The other girls were trying to get Caridee under control, but based on their expressions most of them had just grown used to the outbursts.

"Butler whipped Fae too, Cari, or did you forget that?" Mei-Li spoke softly, reaching out to try and calm her down.

"She heals! She *heals*, dammit! You're all freaking out about the blood? She's fine, she'll be fine. It'll be gone tomorrow! Everything goes away for her!" Caridee was sobbing, tears were streaming down her face, and Neala felt sick. This was not the strong willed, fiery woman she had known when she left. Cari was broken.

"And we all know that when the marks fade, even if they take us longer, we feel perfectly fine about it. Right, Cari?" Ebere asked the question pointedly and stepped between the two of them. Caridee started crying harder and turned around, and Mei-Li put an arm around her waist and guided her to the little nook where Caridee slept. When Ebere turned back around, Neala looked down and realized she was trickling blood onto the cushion beneath her so she redoubled the pressure against her side.

"I'm sorry about that, Fae. Cari hasn't been right since Butler interviewed her about you." Ebere said it softly, but it struck home in Neala's chest as if Ebere had pointed at her and said it was her fault. She had caused this, and as she looked around the room she could tell the small happiness they had been able to create with each other when Nikola was in charge was gone. Even in their space there was no relief from the darkness that loomed over the house.

"What do you mean *interviewed*?" Neala asked, knowing she didn't want the answers, but she had to listen to them. She owed it to them to hear what had happened while she was sleeping peacefully in Kiernan's apartment, while she was eating clean food, and living in safety with someone who apparently loved her.

It took hours for Ebere, Mei-Li, Irena, and a few others to fill her in. It had been worse than she had imagined. Sometimes, in the middle of the night when she had woken up at Kiernan's she had wondered if they were okay, and falsely convinced herself it wouldn't be so bad for them. That they were better off without her there.

She had been wrong.

The entire time they talked to her Neala was waiting for the door to open for Marik to take her back, but he never did. Late in the night Ebere convinced her to change out of her bloodied underclothes and into a dress.

She hated being back in that dress, almost as much as she hated listening to the name Fae again when she'd just started to hear her true name again. Neala just didn't have the energy to explain it all to the girls. Together Ebera and Neala wiped the blood away, and she formed a new towel into a bandage before curling up to sleep in an empty nook.

THE FAMILIAR TINGLE of Eltera's power knitting the skin of her side back together woke her up. Neala sat up and removed the towel that was soaked through and she noticed she had bled onto the dress too. Standing up so she could shower and change, she heard a voice across the main space. A male voice.

"Get up. Now." It was a quiet whisper, but it sounded angry.

"No, please." One of the girls was responding quietly, and she sounded like she was crying. Neala walked towards the noise and even though it was dark she could see the crouching figure of a guard. The guard moved suddenly and she heard a quiet yelp from the girl on the cot. Neala lunged forward and grabbed his arm pulling it back and away from the girl. The guard turned on her and tried to grab for her but she jumped back, quickly moving backwards into the main room.

"You're going to regret getting in the middle of this, girl." He growled, but as he stalked towards her Neala reared her leg back and kicked him in the stomach sending him falling backwards. When he tried to get up she delivered a downward punch that knocked his head against the floor.

His groans woke someone up because the light clicked on at one end of the room. Pushing himself off the floor he tried to grab Neala but she side-stepped him and slammed her forearm into his neck, which sent him to the floor choking. Once the light hit his face she remembered him from before, but he'd never been so brave as to come into the girls' quarters and try and take one of them. He was the guard you did your best to avoid being alone around or he'd drag you into a corner – but the female quarters? Guards *never* came in here.

"I know I've been gone for a while, Evans, but I figured after our fight in the snow you'd at least remember not to try and hit me." Behind him Neala saw Blithe leaning against the wall, her nose and eyes red from crying. Blithe was quiet and sweet and it made Neala even more angry that he'd tried to hurt *her*, not to mention what he'd probably gotten away with while Neala was gone.

"I'm going to tell Butler and Marik that you interfered, whore. The rules have changed, I can do what I want and you *can't* stop me." Evans wasn't even trying to be quiet anymore. He was almost yelling and several of the girls were awake now and standing at the entrances to their nooks wide-eyed.

"Go for Blithe again and see what I can and can't do." Neala spoke with the kind of confidence only raw anger can give someone. Evans turned around to look at Blithe, and then he turned back to Neala.

"You're suicidal if you think Butler and Marik will let this slide." He was furious, and she could see he wanted to hurt her, but he didn't make another move for Blithe, or her.

"Marik actually *missed* our last appointment, you should mention that when you tattle on me." Neala said it loudly and someone behind her gasped. Evans laughed at her and stomped towards the door.

"I'll be back soon, you can count on it." He ripped the door open and slammed it back. The sound of a key turning in the lock was the only noise for a moment in the silent room. When Neala turned back all the girls were standing around staring at her. She was still so angry that he'd come for Blithe in the early hours of the morning, whether Marik was okay with it or not.

That wasn't going to happen with her here.

"Fae?" Irena walked forward, and Neala noticed what she had missed last night. She looked thinner than she had when Neala had left, and her wings weren't fluttering in their normal energetic way. Irena was keeping them close to her body and Neala hated that. That had been how Irena had acted for months when they'd first arrived until she'd finally started to break out of her shell. "He's going to hurt you, Fae. The guards *are* allowed in here now, Marik doesn't stop it and Butler doesn't care."

"Well, they're not allowed in here now." Neala's heart was racing after the confrontation with Evans. She pushed her hand through her hair and looked around at them. "I'm back. I'm sorry I left, but I'll do whatever I can to protect you."

The lock turned in the door again and Neala groaned, sure that Evans couldn't be back already. The door opened a crack and a woman slipped in. When she turned around, Neala's anger ratcheted up another notch.

Lena.

"You." When Lena saw her she spit out the word like venom and walked swiftly towards Neala screaming at her the whole way. "You ruined *everything*! You took him from me!"

"Are you fucking kidding me?" When Lena got close Neala grabbed her arm and twisted her wrist sharply and Lena cried out. Neala just stared down at Lena who was bent to the side trying to ease the pressure on her arm. "*You* don't get to yell at me. Ever." Neala pointed behind her, "Caridee can yell at me, *any* of these girls can yell at me, be mad at me, even *hate* me for leaving them. But you don't get to, not after everything you did for Nikola."

"Don't say his name! Don't you *dare* say his name!" Lena tried to reach up and claw at Neala's face with her other arm, but she just twisted her arm a little more until she cried out and stopped.

"Nikola did not care about you, Lena. He *used* you to spy on us, to keep the girls in line, and no matter how much you loved him you were never more than property to him." Neala's voice was raised, but she was talking slowly and clearly.

It was a last ditch effort to reason with the woman; because Neala had never understood *why* Lena sacrificed the girls she was supposed to watch over just to make Nikola happy. Lena was shaking her head and starting to cry, and for a moment Neala pitied her. Thinking the tears were because her arm hurt, Neala released her wrist.

"You should have died! Not him!" Lena's hands were quick and around Neala's neck in an instant, but Lena was no fighter. Neala just brought her arm down across Lena's to break her hold and then kneed her in the stomach. Lena hit the floor gasping and choking, and Neala's momentary pity disappeared.

"You know what, Lena? Shut up." Neala was furious, remembering every horrible thing Lena had ever done to her or the other girls. "*You* made this place hell long before Marik arrived. *You* turned girls in to Nikola any chance you got. Anything to make him *smile* at you, anything to make him say *thank you!*" Neala's rage had her on a rant, and when Lena tried to get back up Neala pushed her back down with a foot. "No, you stay down. *You* should be the one suffering right now, not these girls. You have betrayed them more times than I can count, and you say *I* should have died?"

"Yes," Lena hissed bitterly, glaring up at her.

"Do the girls even know everything you've done to them? Or have they all been too afraid to tell each other because Nikola protected you? Did you ever admit that *you* were the one that turned in Mei-Li for breaking that dish two months ago?" Neala was leaning over Lena as she listed her crimes. She had never been able to call Lena out on all her actions, but nothing was stopping her now.

"You know, Fae actually took credit for that, Lena, when

the dish broke? And she took the punishment meant for me." Mei-Li spoke up from a few steps behind her.

"Lena was the one who told Butler that Annika was keeping bread in here, I think she spent two days with the guards for that." Ebere said it from against the wall, her own rage leaking into her voice. Then she spoke again. "What about when she told Nikola that I hadn't finished two loads of laundry? Or when Caridee didn't mop the back hall? I think Fae tried to protect us for those too."

"But she -" Lena sputtered, but another of the girls spoke up and Neala pinned Lena back to the floor, holding her there with a foot on her chest.

"Fae was the *only* one here who tried to save Juliet. She volunteered to go in Juliet's place when Nikola ordered it, she even tried to get sent to the guards at the party when I asked her to help – and that's why she got whipped. And then, the morning Juliet died, Neala was the one who went to ask for a doctor, not you, Lena, *you* ran away." Irena was crying again, but she was shouting at the matron from across the room. Other girls started muttering.

There were so many times when Lena had betrayed them.

"You aren't protected anymore, Lena. Marik doesn't care about you at all, and he won't save you." Neala stepped back from her and continued, "I will do everything in my power to protect these girls from Butler, and from Marik, and the other guards, but I won't lift a *finger* to help you."

Lena looked terrified for a moment before she pushed herself up. She looked around at the girls, starting to cry, her perfect façade cracking in a hundred places. As soon as she realized no one was going to stand up for her she ran back out the door, leaving it open behind her.

The girls were all looking at Neala now, but she didn't say anything as she tried to calm her breathing and slow her pulse. She was fighting her urge to go after Lena, and the guards, who had done so much damage in this house. But she wouldn't get far if she went after them and she knew it. Her mind was racing. It was pointless to try and fight the regime of the house, but those little individual fights? Like with Evans and Blithe? She could win those. She may not win the war of control in this house, but she could make it miserable for them to fight it – no matter what it cost her. Lifting her hands to her neck she untied the leather string and held the beautiful silvery disc in her hand as she walked over to Ebere and handed it to her.

"Will you look after this for me? I know I'm going to have to pay for this morning and I don't want to lose it." Ebere was stoic as she took it from her and just nodded. When Neala looked around the room a few of the girls gave her weak smiles, but Neala really just wanted to shower off the blood and to get into a clean dress.

"Fae? I need you to come with me. Now." There was a male voice at the open doors behind her. It was the young guard from the day before, Hills, and he looked worried again. A chill rushed down her spine, but she shoved it away. Neala sighed and gripped Ebere's hand that held the only item in the world she cared about right now, and then she let go and walked towards the door.

"I guess Marik is keeping his appointments today?" Neala tried to sound brave, because she needed to give the girls back some hope or they wouldn't last much longer. Without hope there would be a room full of girls like Caridee, broken and gone. The look on Hills' face at her sarcastic question made her stomach drop, but he didn't say anything. He simply stepped back from the door to let her walk into the hallway, and then locked the door behind her.

CHAPTER TWENTY-FIVE

Tazewell, Virginia

Cole let go of Kiernan's shoulder as they appeared behind his cabin. They were both laughing so hard that they couldn't catch their breath. Cole looked up at the sky, shouting, "Holy shit! Let's sit down!" The snow crunched under their feet as they stomped up onto the back porch and dropped onto chairs.

"That was crazy, Cole. I can't believe you broke a chair over that guy's back!" Kiernan was still laughing but as he propped his feet up on the railing of the porch it was winding down. Cole was still loudly laughing, even with a split lip.

"He bet me I couldn't take him! *Technically* he owes me fifty bucks – maybe I should go ask for it?" Cole raised an eyebrow, standing back up. He wiped the back of his hand across his mouth and chuckled a little when he looked down at the blood.

"I think the cops are already there, probably a bad idea for us to show back up." Kiernan leaned his chair back and grinned at him while Cole pulled open his back door and started to step inside.

"Yeah, yeah, yeah... want a Coke?" Cole was still smiling even though he had to dab at the blood on his lip with his shirt. Kiernan nodded and relaxed back, looking out over the snow covered landscape. Dense trees surrounded Cole's cabin, keeping the world hushed and quiet around them. It was nested amidst the over fifty acres of land he owned. Just a single road heading up, and no neighbors for miles – Cole's bit of paradise.

"Here." Cole tapped the side of Kiernan's chair with a can and then sat back down taking a drink from his own. "Man, I have missed this. Eryn is way too serious to go out like that and just have fun. He's down for either total destruction or nothing." Cole leaned over and slapped Kiernan on the arm, laughing again. "You knocked that one guy out! I bet you the fifty bucks that other guy owes me that he'll be sleeping until tomorrow."

"These last few days have been ridiculous, but fun." Kiernan smiled, watching the last rays of sun filter through the trees, leaving deep shadows in the woods around them.

"Yeah, maybe you shouldn't avoid me so hard in the future, eh?" Cole leaned back, appraising Kiernan as he tilted his own chair onto two legs.

"I know. I just needed some time to myself, some time to adjust to life away from Gormahn's keep." Kiernan mumbled, knowing it had probably hurt Cole to be ignored for so long. First, because he couldn't *find* Kiernan. Then, when he had found him Kiernan ignored the letters. Later, the phone calls. And for the last couple of decades he'd been ignoring letters, and e-mails, and cell phone calls. Cole hadn't given up though.

"I get that. And it seems like the time away fixed whatever was wrong with you. You actually seem happy." Cole wasn't looking at him. He was staring out into the woods and the lack of eye contact made it easier to talk about the damage Kiernan had done to their friendship. They'd been like brothers once, and it seemed Cole was willing to be like that again.

"I am happy. And I'm sorry about avoiding you, when I left the castle I broke off from everything, but I shouldn't have ditched you too." Kiernan pushed on his side where he'd taken a series of punches earlier that night, and smiled. The ache would fade in a few hours, but for now it was a nice reminder of getting to fight side by side with Cole again. Even after centuries they didn't have to talk to work together in a fight, it was as easy as breathing.

"Don't worry about it. It's all in the past. So, what finally made Kiernan the Brooding happy? Even back in the day when you were all-warrior-all-the-time and hanging with Eryn you weren't what I'd call *happy*." Cole finished the can of coke and got up to set it just inside the door. He grabbed his guitar and came back out while Kiernan was debating how to answer. If he brought up Neala, even if he didn't say her name, Cole would never drop it until he knew who she was, so that answer was off the table completely.

"I don't know, maybe I'm finally settling into life. I'm just happy." Kiernan finished his own drink and put it next to the chair, enjoying the chill in the air and the darkening woods. He could understand why Cole lived out here, where he could be himself and not worry about anyone intruding on his space. It was a different kind of quiet than in the city, an old quiet.

"It took you two millennia to settle into life?" Cole was grinning at him as he started to pluck on his guitar, but Kiernan just rolled his eyes.

"Maybe it did, what do you care?" Kiernan threw the can at Cole, but he dodged it and laughed while he plucked the earliest notes of Heart-Shaped Box by Nirvana.

"You don't have to tell me what it is. Whatever it is, I'm glad you have it, because it woke you up. And I've missed this – having you around, I mean." Cole stared down at the guitar, and Kiernan just nodded.

"Me too, brother, me too." Kiernan said it and then let the silence return, the guitar the only noise around for miles and miles. Out of the corner of his eye he could see Cole smiling, but there was no need to talk more about it, they were good again. Like there hadn't been almost two hundred years of silence.

After an hour or so Kiernan started to get antsy. He wanted to go home, and he wanted to see Neala again. It wouldn't be so late in Seattle and he was sure she'd be up, and just the idea of having someone waiting for him at home made him feel light and warm. The more he thought of Neala, of getting to wrap his arms around her again, the more anxious he got to leave. He didn't want to ditch Cole so quickly, but he didn't have the patience to wait anymore. He stood up and stretched, looking over at Cole who seemed to already know what was coming. Cole sighed and leaned the guitar behind him on the wall as he stood up. Then he pulled open the door and reached inside, grabbing a duffel before dropping it at Kiernan's feet.

"You heading back home?" Cole asked with a smile.

"Yeah, I have stuff to handle, but this was good. Maybe we can keep this a regular thing? We just might want to expand into other bars." Kiernan grinned and Cole laughed, making his lip split again.

"Agreed." Cole said it loudly, and they clapped each other on the back. "So that means I'll see you soon, yeah?"

"Yeah." Kiernan stepped back from him and Cole nodded as he gave him his sarcastic salute. Focusing back on his apartment, he felt himself shift and the warmth of his apartment hit him like a welcome home.

"NEALA!" He turned around and set the duffel bag against the wall. An uneasy feeling unfurled in his stomach as his eyes scanned the apartment. Something wasn't right. It was too quiet, and too still. He'd expected Neala to come out as soon as he got there. Slipping off his coat he took a step forward and glass crunched under his shoe. There was a broken wine glass and a dried pool of wine under it.

No.

Panic ran through him as he turned around and shouted her name into the dark. He ran to the bedroom and flipped on the light, then the bathroom, the closet. He was tempted to check under the bed.

Nothing.

Running back to his living room he saw all the design books laid out across the kitchen table and a notepad. *Maybe she'd left a note?* He moved around to the side and traced his fingers over the smooth script of her handwriting. It wasn't a note, just things she'd liked in the books. Things for the home they were going to build.

She hadn't left on her own.

The realization became a hole that was tearing open inside his chest and all the darkness was leaking out of it, filling him up. He walked over to his desk and slowly pulled the wood box for the observation glass towards him. His stomach was turning as he flipped it open, and he tightened his jaw as he thought of her and touched the glass.

It flared to life under his hands and he saw her figure, her arms extended above her, head down. The hole in his chest grew, the dark one she had kept at bay just by being near him filled him up like a bitter wind. He forced himself to run his fingertip counter-clockwise and images flashed through the glass on fast-rewind. She was back in that house, she was hurt - *they'd dared to touch her* - and then he got to the moment when she'd been pulled there. He let it play and couldn't bring himself to touch the wood, to hear her screaming when the bands lit up and she was yanked back to that house. The silent film version was torture enough. His hands went into his hair and he pulled at it as the truth set in.

Someone had claimed her; someone in that house had claimed her without even knowing where she was.

Panic and disbelief gave way to anger as the images he'd seen flashed through his mind. He had sworn he'd protect her, and he had failed. He roared as the rage swelled inside him and he slammed his fists down on the desk, the glass top shattering into a million pieces. The box for the observation glass, his laptop, and other things hit the floor amidst the sparkling fragments. He roared again and picked up the box for the observation glass, hurling it against the wall. It rebounded off and the glass flew out and slid across the floor, undamaged. Looking down Kiernan saw the black lines on his arm. The vines were between his wrist and his elbow now, much shorter than they'd been when he left, and now he knew that part of that retreat - part of his pushing the poison back - had been Neala being returned to a master. His chest hurt from the pain of failing her, his stomach was roiling with how much he wanted to tear Butler's head off.

He had to do something to fix this. He had to fix it *now*.

He felt himself losing it, losing himself. He was moments from a complete blackout like back in the days of

Gormahn's control. All because his neglect had sent her back to hell. He roared again trying to maintain some semblance of control, and kicked the frame of his desk. It skidded backwards before toppling into the remnants of the glass top.

That was not controlled.

He tried to breathe but his lungs wouldn't inflate, his chest burned and the urge to destroy rose up and filled every thought. He had tunnel vision as he looked across the broken glass, the spilled wine, and he fought with the side of him that was Laochra, the side that urged him to let go of civility and take back what was *his*. The thought bobbed to the surface in the violence of his mind, all those times he had worried he would claim her for himself... it was this voice he'd been fighting. And now none of it mattered, because they had taken her, and she was in pain. His ribs threatened to cave in from the ache. The images had moved fast but he had watched them hurt her. They had hurt her. Again and again.

His.

Kiernan felt himself shift again and he was disoriented for a second as his eyes ran across metal shelves full of weapons, and boxes of bullets. His hand traced the black metal grip in front of him, lifting the gun from the rack. He turned around to see trunks of clothing and realized where he was – the weapons vault at Gormahn's keep.

Kiernan knew he wasn't in complete control of his thoughts at the moment, but some part of him had a plan and it involved a need for a lot of weapons. Whatever the plan was, he was on board. He could feel the old bloodlust rising in him like a fog, obscuring the pain he felt, and focusing him on a single need to get to Neala no matter who he had to get through to do that. He wanted her back, he wanted her because she was *his*, and they had no right to touch what was his.

Hate pulsed inside him, smoothing the jagged edges of his pain, rolling away his shame and regret at failing her. Kiernan could feel the growl work its way through his chest until it vibrated his teeth. This was the version of him that Eryn had loved, the version of himself that Eryn had smiled at before they charged an opposing army. This was the dark one.

This was not who Neala wanted.

Kiernan put his hands against the wall, forcing himself to breathe. He thought of her, and of everything good she said she saw in him. If he was going to get her, he had to still be worthy of her when he got there. The buzzing in his head slowed a little with each deep breath, and with the easing of the bloodlust came the return of the pain in his chest – but her safety was the only thing that would heal that.

Kiernan let himself get to the edge of that bloodlust, teetering over the edge where the clarity of battle meant he wouldn't give mercy to those who had harmed her, but he didn't let himself go where he couldn't come back. He wouldn't be some mindless killing machine, some puppet for a god of war, not ever again. With a steadying breath he moved quickly, changing into combat gear and using the various straps on the clothing to arm himself. He grabbed the smallest set of clothes he could find and shoved them into a bag that he put across his back, crisscrossing the sword peeking over his shoulder. He palmed two Beretta handguns and thought of that house, focused on it even as his pulse ramped up, and then he felt himself shift again.

CHAPTER TWENTY-SIX

Ráj Manor, Caledon, Ontario

It was dark. Kiernan crouched to look around, he could hear breathing all around him but it was much darker than the weapons vault and his eyes were still adjusting. He took a step backwards and heard a feminine yelp as he stepped on someone. They scrambled away from him in the dark, *not a threat*, and then a light clicked on.

Kiernan swung one of the guns toward the source of the light and he saw a small framed girl of Asian descent, with dark, pin-straight hair. She stared at the gun, but her face didn't register fear, just a resigned acceptance. Someone else was scared though and he heard a few suppressed screams around him. He lowered the gun and scanned the room looking for Neala's auburn hair, the curve of her waist, her pale blue eyes.

"I'm looking for Neala... *Fae*." Kiernan's voice rumbled out of his chest, lower and more strained than normal as he said the name he'd promised himself to never use again. As jumbled as his head was at the moment, he was impressed he'd strung together an entire sentence.

"She's not here." The smooth, calm voice came from his left and he spun to see a dark skinned young woman step out of a nook, a soft yellow dress clinging to her curves. She was beautiful, and although her eyes showed fear, she didn't back down from talking to him.

"Where is she?" He tightened his grip around the guns, feeling his knuckles grind under the strain.

"Downstairs. Has been all day." It was the girl by the lamp that had spoken this time, a soft voice slightly tinted by an accent. Chinese, if he had to guess.

"How do you know?" Kiernan didn't feel like chasing ghosts, and he didn't know why his focus had brought him to this room instead of right to her.

"We could all hear her screaming." A very young sounding voice that made Kiernan's stomach plummet. *Screaming?* He turned around to see a waif thin pixie, very rare on this plane of existence. Her light blue skin and tuft of unruly hair would have been enough of an identifier, but those iridescent wings springing from her back would have made it obvious even to a mortal.

"Gods..." Kiernan whispered to himself as he turned away from the pixie, not wanting to let his brain bring up all of the images of what had made Neala scream loud enough to be heard through the floor. He rubbed the grip of the gun against his temple, clenching his teeth against the urge to let loose and scream again.

"Are you the one she was with? The good place?" The dark skinned girl took a step towards him and he couldn't even process what she was saying. She extended her arm and from her hand hung a silvery disc on a dark strand of leather. It was like a punch to Kiernan's stomach, he'd *just* given that to her. The girl winced when he moved towards her suddenly, but she didn't step back. His nausea increased as he imagined what it would take for a girl to react that way to any man approaching her, and what kind of bravery it would take for her to stand her ground.

"She was with me." Kiernan didn't respond to the other question, but he grabbed the disc between his fingers and traced his thumb over the letters he had painstakingly carved into the metal.

"Then after you get her, after you help Fae," the girl let go of the necklace and he watched her swallow and take a breath, "will you help us too?" Her eyes were wide but she straightened her back, making herself be brave. Kiernan respected that in her, the strength it took to ask for help from a stranger, just on the faith that he had helped Neala. He turned his head to look over his shoulder at the assembly of women around the room, all staring at him and waiting. It looked like someone had walked through all the major cultures of the world and picked a beautiful girl or two from each of them, and they were all afraid.

He couldn't say no. Neala had carried more than enough guilt for leaving them.

"Yes," he said, and several intakes of breath around him showed their surprise, "but I have to get to Neala, I mean Fae, first. Tell me where she is, and I'll come back for you. I swear it."

"Right under us." The soft spoken girl near the light talked again, but when he turned to look at her there was a faint smile on her lips. His words had made her smile, his words had sparked hope. Kiernan nodded and focused on moving to the floor below him, his pulse was racing, his stomach twisting at what he'd find, but he tucked the silvery disc in a pocket, gripped the handle of the gun and moved.

Another dark room. This time he wasn't going to move so foolishly, instead he closed his eyes and counted in his head, waiting for his pupils to dilate. With his eyes closed, the sound of his pulse in his ears was deafening, and he made sure to breathe carefully so as not to alert anyone. Even the swish of his clothes moving seemed loud. When he opened his eyes he could see he was in a large bedroom.

The faint glow underneath the door showed the outline of a huge bed, a chair, an open door opposite him that likely led to a bathroom. He scanned the room until he saw her, and it looked like she was still suspended by her arms. He holstered the gun and slid a combat knife out, walking quietly to the bed. He leaned over it, and saw no one. Moving past the bed, Kiernan checked the rest of the room and found it empty.

Why would they leave her alone? Unless –

Kiernan ran across the room, storing the knife as he grabbed her face, his hands lifting her head up so he could see her. She made a tiny sound as she took a sudden breath, and it was the best sound he had ever heard. His eyes stung and his chest ached; she was alive. Everything would be okay. He brushed his thumb over her cheekbone, whispering, "Neala? Neala, are you awake?" Her head lolled against his hands and he gently let her chin rest back against her chest. She was out cold, completely naked, hanging only by her wrists. *Assholes.*

Tracing his eyes up her arms he could see the rope around her wrists, and that it was looped over a metal hook that could have been a light fixture at one point. He wrapped his arms around her and tried to lift her off the hook, and she gave a weak scream. Kiernan immediately let go, and she dropped slightly.

"No, no, no..." Neala muttered and lifted her head, whimpering, "I won't. I won't." Kiernan reached forward and touched her face, leaving a smudge of red behind on her pale cheek. Looking down at his arms he could see a dampness on his gear, and his hands were smeared with swipes of blood.

Her back.

"Neala, it's Kiernan. I'm here, *mo ghaol*, I'm here." He tried to wipe his hands off on his pants before he touched her face again, lifting her chin so she'd look at him. When her eyes opened she started crying and he thought his chest might implode from the pain of it.

"Are you really here?" Neala's voice cracked as she spoke.

"Yes, Glowworm, I'm here, and I need to get you down." He used the nickname and it worked, she woke up a little more. His feisty Faeoihn.

"I hate that name." She growled the words out and it made him feel lighter inside, to know she still had the strength to be irritated with him.

"I know. I can't touch your back, so I want you to wrap your legs around me and I can lift you that way." He spoke with a smile, and a breathy laugh came out of her.

"This is the lamest excuse to get me against you I've ever heard." She was smiling, and although she sounded dazed she let out another soft laugh. A tension in his chest broke when he heard her laugh, only *she* would be able to joke while bleeding and hanging from a wall.

"I'll try to come up with even lamer excuses when we're out of here. Come on." Kiernan placed his hands at the backs of her thighs and he watched her arms tighten a moment before she swung her legs around his waist, and he held her there. He shifted her higher and secured her while he reached up and unhooked the rope. When she was loose he felt her arms go over his head and she buried her face against his neck, hugging him tight with her whole body.

"You really came for me," Neala whispered it against his neck and he turned his head to place a kiss into her hair, taking a deep breath as the soft rain smell of her skin engulfed him.

"Did you think I wouldn't?" If he wasn't so elated to be holding her again, he would have been insulted.

"I thought you *couldn't*." Neala's voice cracked again and he heard a sniffle. He brought one hand up to the back of her neck, trying to hold her as best he could without touching her back. Speaking of which...

"Nothing could have stopped me." Kiernan squeezed the back of her neck, and tried to stay calm as the darkness rose in him again. "Now, tell me, how bad is your back?" She stilled against him, and he leaned his head away from hers. Neala still had her arms around his neck, and when she leaned back he could see bruising around her neck. It made his heart hammer harder in his chest. "Neala, tell me."

She swallowed, looking down at the zipper of his jacket and not at his eyes, "Marik, Nikola's son, the new master, asked Butler to show him how to use the whip. So, he did, and they used me for practice."

"I know, I – I saw. I just need to know how bad it is." The darkness in him that had temporarily abated on finding her alive grew and overwhelmed the joy he'd felt a moment before, because all of the images he'd seen in the glass were back in full color.

"It's fine, I promise."

Kiernan didn't respond to her obvious lie, he didn't think he could without screaming, so he lifted Neala and she dropped her legs from him. He leaned down and pulled her arms over his head. Underneath the rope he could see her wrists were raw and he walked with her to the window where he tugged the edge of the curtain back. Slipping out his knife again he sawed through the ropes and dropped them to the floor, clenching his teeth hard against the things he wanted to say. He cradled her wrists in his hands, a bitter bile rising in his stomach. Then he moved a hand to her elbow and started to turn her around so her back would be to the faint light from outside, but she stopped him. "You don't want to see, Kiernan."

"I need to." He could hear the self-loathing in his voice; she'd been hurt because he'd been careless, because he hadn't checked in. The images he'd seen in the observation glass, even moving fast, had been bad enough. Now, he felt like he should have watched it all in real time, so he would *know* what he had cost her.

Her hands cupped his face and she kissed him hard – he totally didn't deserve it, but his hands slid into her hair as he kissed her back. She was brave, and strong, and so incredibly beautiful.

She was redemption.

"You don't need to do anything. Dawn is a couple of hours away, I'll be fine." Her lips moved against his as she whispered and he wished he could hold her to him as tightly as he wanted.

"Neala, I need to see."

"Kiernan –" she started to argue again, but he pressed a finger over her lips and turned her around. Her back was a bloody mess, and it was impossible to count the number of lashes. He bit down and tried to breathe through the rage inside him. It washed up like a cold tide, tugging at his feet, wanting to drown him in the darkness where it promised blood and vengeance and power and control.

"I'm going to kill them." His voice wasn't his own. He could hear the tremor of his rage in it and she turned around slowly in front of him, her wide blue eyes looking up at him. That little wrinkle appeared between her eyebrows, and he knew all of her senses had to be telling her to run from him. She should run from him. He was tainted, ruined, a failure. He didn't deserve –

Neala slowly slid her hands around his waist and pressed herself against the front of him, squeezing him in a gentle hug that diffused the rage inside him like it was nothing. She was pure light, and as much as he hated himself for it, he let it swallow him. He wrapped his arms around her shoulders, staying high on her back, as he felt her nuzzling against his chest. *By the gods, he loved her.*

"Let's get you out of here." He whispered against her hair. "Hold on tight."

"Wait! I can't leave the girls again, you don't know what they did to them because I left. I can't do that to them again!" Neala talked quickly, a slight panic filling her voice as she leaned back from him.

"I already met them upstairs, and I swore I'd get them out. But, only *after* I got you out. I'll come back right after you're safe and secure." Kiernan forced a smile, and she nodded and leaned her head against his chest. He took another breath against her hair and thought of his apartment. He focused and started to shift, but light suddenly burst in front of him and his grip on Neala slipped.

CHAPTER TWENTY-SEVEN

Ráj Manor, Caledon, Ontario

Explosive pain rocked her, and the bands were lit up so brightly that Neala had to close her eyes against it. Her lungs filled with a gasp and she bit down on her tongue to stifle the scream she had started. She realized when the pain first started to ebb that she was on the floor, and she was on her back, which was likely why the pain was still so vicious. Rolling to her stomach she pushed herself up and shuddered as another surge came from the bands. Dark boots came into her vision and she looked up to see Kiernan gripping his left arm at the elbow where the vines were moving slowly up his skin.

"Apparently *that* is why we're not allowed to remove Faeoihn from their masters." He looked sick as he spoke and lowered himself to the floor next to her, all his weapons shifting around him.

"I get it now." Neala almost choked on the words, and she felt sick with worry as she looked at the doorway, knowing at any moment Marik or Butler could reappear. Over the next few minutes her bands faded into a ghostly outline, and then slowly disappeared completely. Kiernan's eyes traced her back and he winced while she maneuvered herself into a sitting position with her legs tucked to one side.

"I'm going to kill them, Neala." Kiernan's voice was so matter-of-fact, so cold, that she almost didn't respond. When she looked at him she saw the pain in his eyes and knew it was pointless to argue, to ask him to leave her there and keep himself safe. He'd never do it.

"Alright, but I'm going to help." She tried to straighten her back but a muscle spasm underneath her skin stopped her.

"You can't do anything right now. We'll wait for you to heal, and then we'll leave the old fashioned way." Kiernan had made a decision in his head, and he was determined. He wasn't thinking clearly, not with his eyes glued to her back and that look of pain and rage in his eyes, but he *was* determined.

"Old fashioned?" Neala arched an eyebrow at him.

"The old fashioned method of just killing everyone in our way before we walk out the front door." Kiernan slid one of the guns out of a holster and pulled the top of the gun back until it clicked and slid forward again. "I'm getting you out of here, Neala." He leaned forward and kissed her again, and she couldn't put into words how safe she felt next to him, despite their circumstances. He ended the kiss by running his thumb over her lips, and then he moved next to her and let her lay her head in his lap. She was still exhausted from the day, from the pain, and the bands, and as his fingers slid through her hair sleep slipped over her like someone had flipped a switch inside her.

Neala wasn't sure how much time had passed, but she felt Kiernan lift her head as he suddenly moved out from under her. She started to ask him what he was doing but he quickly covered her mouth, and it was then that she heard the click of a key in the door. He stood next to her and tugged the curtain closed so the room fell into darkness again, and then he was moving towards the door. Neala tucked herself behind a chair near the window and waited. Since he was in all black she struggled to track Kiernan against the wall, and then the door opened spilling dim light from the hall into the room.

"You awake, Fae?" A male voice asked, filled with a sinister laughter. It was Evans who had pushed the door open, slipping the key back in his pocket, and he seemed to pause to wait for a response. "Doesn't matter. Butler said to make up for your behavior this morning I could have some fun with you before dawn, and that means we've still got plenty of time."

Neala's stomach tightened as he laughed to himself, and she clenched her fists as anger overwhelmed any fears she had. Before she could move, Kiernan stepped like a shadow out of the darkness to the right of the door. One of his hands went over Evans' mouth while the other brought a knife to his throat. Kiernan kicked the door shut and Neala couldn't see them anymore, but she could hear them wrestling for the upper hand.

Desperate to see what was happening she twisted and reached up to rip the curtain back, yelping as she strained her back. She turned to see Evans struggling against Kiernan's grip, but Kiernan was taller and stronger and clearly not exerting much effort to control him. She saw him lean forward to say something in Evans' ear and the guard struggled even harder, but then Kiernan dragged the knife across his throat and dropped him to the floor. As he stood over the man and watched him bleed out she knew she was looking at Kiernan the warrior, the Laochra, the cold-blooded killer. He didn't waver, his breathing was even, and he hadn't dropped the knife yet.

Neala stood up behind the chair and the edge of her shadow passed over Evans on the floor. She wanted to speak, but she didn't know what to say. Kiernan stayed still when he spoke, "I'm sorry. I should have killed him slower."

"He's dead, it's -"

"He was going to -" Kiernan made a frustrated growling sound in his chest, " - he deserved a slower death." Kiernan spoke through gritted teeth and Neala walked over to him slowly, watching him carefully before placing her hand on his arm.

"It's okay, will you come sit with me? I'm still tired." She slid her fingers down his arm and interlaced them with his, tugging him back toward the window, away from Evans. The distraction of needing to care for her worked, and although his other hand tightened its grip on the knife, he let her lead him over to the window where it was brighter.

"I'm sorry, Neala, that I let this happen." As they sat down Kiernan let the knife drop out of his hand to the floor next to him, and then he shoved both hands into his hair. She didn't think he noticed the blood he swiped across his temple and into his dark hair.

"You didn't *let* anything happen. Marik did this. When he signed that document his lawyers drew up to transfer the estate - he *owned* me. It was over. Everything else was the curse, and you couldn't have stopped that even if you'd been standing right next to me." Neala winced as Kiernan smacked his head hard back against the wall.

"I should have been there, I should have been *here* the second it happened." He looked over at her and her heart hurt with how pained he looked; she wasn't going to be able to convince him otherwise.

"You're here now." She squeezed his hand and he dropped his head back against the wall again, even harder. Neala sighed trying to distract him again. "What did you say to Evans?"

"That was his name?" Kiernan's eyes found the body across the room and the muscles in his jaw ticked as

Neala nodded, "I told him he won't be lonely in death, because the rest of them would be joining him soon."

"That would explain why he struggled so hard." Neala muttered, and felt a sick sense of pride that Kiernan had done it. *Her warrior.*

"My turn for a question." He pulled his eyes to her, tightening his hold on her hand for a second. "When you were waking up, you said '*I won't*'… why? What were they trying to make you do?"

"They wanted your name." She looked down at their hands.

"Why didn't you just give it to them? You could have avoided -"

"They wouldn't have stopped with that." Neala interrupted him and spoke matter-of-factly, "Once they had your name they would have wanted where you lived, how you got me away from here, details of our time together. They would have wanted all of it. And if I was going to be stuck here, I wasn't going to let them hunt you and ruin your life."

"I would have enjoyed killing them as they came for me, trust me. But, like you said, I'm here now. You're safe, and I won't let them touch you ever again." Kiernan pressed a kiss to the side of her head and she leaned against his shoulder.

They were quiet for almost an hour as she dozed in and out, until the glow on her skin started. Like always, at first it was as if she were under a spotlight, but then it was obvious that the light was coming from inside her skin. The glow steadily increased, fading smoothly from deep amber to bright gold. It lit up Kiernan's blood stained hands, bounced off the weapons and clasps on his gear and made his eyes look gold as they reflected it back. A humming ran through her whole body as Eltera's power touched her – it healed the skin of her back, wiped the bruises away and renewed her energy better than a cup of espresso. Kiernan had a look of wonder on his face that made her smile.

Now that it didn't hurt to move, Neala climbed onto his lap and pulled his face to hers to kiss him the way she'd wanted to when she first woke up. His arms went around her and he held her tight, pressing her against him. For a while she had thought she'd never get to kiss him again, never be held by him again.

That would have been a crime.

His fingers pressed against her freshly healed back, but she groaned a complaint into the kiss when her hands met the harsh fabric of his combat gear. No easy buttons, just layers and layers of cloth between her and him. Neala pressed herself against him, rocking her hips against the erection she could feel straining his pants. He groaned as well and leaned back from her, cradling her face. The light from her skin was fading, but the sunlight outside the window had already started to paint the sky a myriad of colors. It was time to go.

"I swear, as soon as we're safe and alone, we'll continue this."

"Kiernan, please?" She grinned at him, the warm pulse between her legs was growing and urged her to strip him, and push him onto his back, and ride him until the orgasm wiped away everything that had happened since she saw him last.

"Glowworm, trust me, I want to fuck you. I want to spread you out and lick you until you're screaming my name and begging me to stop." He kissed her again. "But I want to do that when neither of us are covered in blood, and when our enemies are dead."

Neala's mouth had opened when he'd described what he wanted to do, a blush burning in her cheeks as memories of the last time he had held her thighs apart as he'd done *exactly* that. "I'm going to hold you to that promise, Kiernan."

"You do that." He grinned and shifted her off his lap, tossing her the little bag of clothes he'd kept on his back. "Those were the smallest we had, hopefully they fit, and," he reached into a pocket and pulled out the silvery disc he'd made her, "I have this for you as well."

"Ah -" Neala bit her lip, her eyes welling up and threatening to spill tears down her cheeks again. Her voice cracked as she spoke again, "Thank you, I - I'd given it to Ebere to keep it safe, before they took me." She smiled and tied it around her neck again, her fingertips tracing those beautiful words once more. Clearing her throat and tearing her fingers through her hair she shook off the emotions that wanted to overwhelm her. "So, what's the plan?" Neala dressed quickly, tightening the gear with straps and attaching one of Kiernan's knives to her thigh.

"We head upstairs for the girls, and then we head outside. We kill anything between us and those objectives." Kiernan gave her a wild smile that made her think of battlefields and war cries. This wasn't going to be a sparring match, this was real. He unhooked one of his guns and held it out to her, but she didn't take it, arching an eyebrow at him.

"I don't know how to use one of those."

"Really?" Kiernan looked surprised, and she laughed.

"Oh yeah, Kiernan, my masters have always thought it was a great idea to not only give one of their slaves a gun, but to *also* teach them how to use it."

A light blush moved across Kiernan's cheeks. He finally laughed and holstered the gun, and instead slid a scabbard over his head and grabbed the hilt to draw a very sharp sword. "Well, I know you can use this, and I'm quite sure none of the guards here know how to defend against it." He said it with such pride that she felt a bubbly warmth in her chest. The smile on his face wasn't fading, in fact the wildness of it was spreading to his eyes, and making him pulse with energy. Neala took the sword from him and grinned back slipping the scabbard over her head to lie against her back. With a sword in her hand she had the same feeling she'd get before her and her sisters would take the field for battle. All trash talk and cheers and bets and challenges – *pure excitement*. That same chaotic buzz in her blood came to her now.

"Let's go." Neala grinned and moved towards the door to the hall.

"I think you should wear this more often, Glowworm." His eyes moved over her as they walked towards the door, leaving Evans on the floor.

"I thought you'd prefer me naked, but if you like this so much I'd be happy to. Every day. Once we're back home." She paused with her hand on the doorknob, because Kiernan pressed his hand to the door holding it shut a moment.

"I like you in anything, *mo ghaol*." He leaned down and kissed her again, quickly, before stepping back and palming a gun in one hand, and a dark knife in the other.

Neala smiled and yanked the door back, but the hall was empty. Stepping out, Kiernan walked next to her and they both headed toward the north stairs. Her eyes were trained on the space in front of them when two of the guards passed across the end of the hall. Kiernan crossed the distance between him and them in a matter of seconds, thrusting the knife up through the jaw of one of the guards, cutting off a shout of warning. He used him as leverage to kick the other guard back. Neala caught up an instant later, and brought her sword across the belly of the second guard. Then she quickly covered his nose and mouth to keep him quiet as he collapsed to the floor.

Her body sang with the rush of battle again, and the way Kiernan looked at her made her feel radiant, powerful – all of the things she'd never felt in this house.

"Upstairs?" Kiernan whispered as he wiped the knife off,

and she nodded. Thus far they had made it through the morning unexposed, but it was going to be a lot more difficult with fifteen girls to move with. Near the top of the stairs, Neala stopped Kiernan.

"When we hit the top of the stairs, the female quarters is all the way to the left, and there's no cover between us and the door. Whoever is at the door is going to see us coming." She whispered it, adjusting her grip on the sword. Kiernan slid his knife back into its sheath and checked the gun.

"Then we silence him as quickly as possible." He muttered it and started up the stairs again. When he cleared the top he took off at a dead run, and she could hear the shout of surprise from the guard at the door. As she raced after him she saw Kiernan stop and level the gun as the guard started shouting.

"CODE BLACK! CODE BLA-" The guard's voice echoed down the hall before a loud pop came from the gun in Kiernan's hand and the guard dropped. Kiernan cursed and continued down the hall. Neala stepped up behind him to find him tugging a small plastic bud out of the guy's ear, pulling the wire from under the guard's collar.

"He got that out. We have to move faster." Kiernan said it as he ripped a key off the guard's belt and passed it to Neala. In a click the door was open and Neala saw them all standing around, gaping at her. She looked down at herself, black combat clothes, a swipe of red across her sword, a wild gleam in her eyes – they'd never seen her like this, never seen her as anything other than a slave like them, never seen her as anyone other than *Fae*.

Neala's eyes came up and Ebere was smiling at her. She wanted to tell them all that this is who she was, who she was always meant to be, but there wasn't time - and Ebere knew her story anyway.

"You really came for us." Ebere smiled and clapped her hands. Irena ran at Neala from her right and almost knocked her over in the bear hug she delivered. Her wings were flicking madly again, and it made Neala want to cheer because she hadn't lost her to despair. Neala squeezed her back with her free arm and then let go.

"Of course I did. Now, everyone listen up, we have to move *fast*. We're going to go down the north stairs, and to the storage near the kitchen where they keep the winter clothes. Once you're dressed for the snow, we go out the back doors and move away from the house towards the tree line. Stay behind us, okay?" Neala waved a hand to encourage them to hurry up as they all rushed forward to bunch together near the door. She noticed Mei-Li was pulling Caridee towards them but that Cari was wide-eyed and struggling, digging her heels in to the carpet.

"No! No, they'll punish us! They'll hurt us, we have to stay in here! Please -"

"Neala, I don't know how long we have with the alarm that guard sent out, we have to move now." Kiernan spoke under his breath to her, his eyes watching Caridee.

She growled and walked towards the frantic girl, moving Mei-Li out of the way. Neala took a breath and spoke in flawless Spanish. "Cari – *Cari* listen to me."

Caridee was stunned into silence, and Mei-Li jerked her head back as well as Neala spoke.

"I know you're afraid, and I know it's my fault that bad things happened to you. I know that you have *no reason* to trust me, but I need you to. I need you to trust me so I can get you out of here."

"You speak Spanish?" Cari's mouth hung open, and Neala grinned.

"Fluently. And before you ask, *yes*, I did understand every mumbled comment you've ever made about me. Now, will you please come with us? Will you please come with me so you can be free?"

Caridee stared at the floor, her body visibly trembling, but from the tangled curtain of her hair Neala heard a soft, *"Yes."*

Mei-Li moved in and wrapped an arm around her again, guiding Cari towards the group and Neala walked back to the door with a deep breath.

Kiernan turned to look at her and tilted his head. "Is she good?"

"She's good. The men's quarters are in the other wing, there's only three of them, but we can't leave them either." Neala clenched her jaw for a moment as she argued internally between what was right and what would *feel* good. Somehow, morality won out. "There's also one more slave. Lena. I have no idea where she's sleeping now, but it's not in the female quarters."

"Let's get the girls out first, then we can go for the others if we have time." He kissed her cheek and flashed a brief smile, and then Kiernan stepped ahead of her into the hall.

"Stay quiet, okay?" She spoke to the group and several girls nodded, then Neala moved into the hall as well. They could all hear shouting downstairs and Neala jogged ahead to catch up to Kiernan. As soon as they reached the north stairs they could hear heavy footsteps starting up. He looked at her with a calm that only experienced warriors had. There wasn't a trace of doubt in him about who would win and who would die.

"Don't let any of them get back up, they all stay down. Permanently." Kiernan locked eyes with her and she nodded. Neala turned and held a hand up so the girls stopped in the hall. They were all huddled together with their eyes wide with fear, sitting targets. She really wished she had time to make them at least hide against the walls, but then the first guard rounded the bend in the stairs and she and Kiernan both stepped backwards to lure him up the whole way.

Three more came behind him, and they seemed surprised when Kiernan lifted the gun. He fired three shots, hitting each of them in the chest, and they tumbled back down to the landing. The first guard made it to the top of the stairs and he tried to rush Kiernan, but Neala stepped forward and brought the sword across the back of his thigh. The blade sliced through fabric and flesh like it was nothing, and he went down hard with a guttural scream. She put a foot over the cut in his thigh, pressing down until he screamed again, writhing on the floor.

"You, bitch!" The guard screamed, slipping a knife out of a sheath on his hip, but she saw it and slammed the tip of her sword through his hand, pinning it to the floor. He screamed again, and Neala heard a few of the girls gasping and whimpering behind her.

Kiernan just watched her, and then tried to bite his cheek to stifle his smile before he spoke. "Tell me what a code black is." Kiernan crouched in front of the guy, tapping the gun against the side of the guard's head.

"Go to hell." He spat, and Neala brought her foot down hard on the back of his thigh drawing another sobbing scream from him, a stream of profanity tumbling from his lips until she eased the pressure.

"Code black?" Kiernan repeated.

"AGH! It's a code that tells everyone there's a lethal threat on the premises." He groaned as Neala applied more pressure to his leg again, "God! It means - It's when we get the master of the house to a safe room and neutralize the threat. That's it!"

"Thanks." Kiernan stood up and fired the gun once, putting the guard out of his misery. Neala arched an eyebrow and he looked at her, then past her to the girls. "Let's go."

They moved down the stairs fast, and at the bottom Kiernan took the guard position while Neala shuffled everyone down the back hall towards kitchen storage.

She didn't want to leave the girls unprotected, but letting Kiernan out of her sight made her stomach twist. He looked back over his shoulder at her and forced a smile, giving her a nod to encourage her.

She gave a quick smile and nodded back, running down the hall to get ahead of Annika who was at the front. As soon as she passed her, a guard turned out of another hall in front of her. She grabbed his shirt and slammed him into the wall, holding her sword to his neck before she got a look at him.

"No, Fae!"

"He's nice, don't –"

"Wait, don't hurt him!"

A chorus of cries came from the girls behind her, and it was the only thing that kept her from slitting his throat. His eyes were wide, and in his relaxed hand was a handgun, his finger way off the trigger. It took her a second, but she recognized him as Hills, the one who had told her to *be careful* as he'd escorted her after she'd first arrived, and who had brought her *back* to Marik and Butler the day before.

For that alone she wanted to kill him.

"Please! Fae!" From the same hall stepped Alec, the tall, blond cook of the house. He looked horrified, his hands reaching for the guard. "Please, don't hurt him. He's good, he's with me."

Hills swallowed and she watched as his Adam's apple grazed the edge of the blade. Alec was her friend, and she liked him, but Hills was a guard. Weird, and strangely concerned for her, but still a guard. He'd handed her over to them knowing they were going to hurt her, he'd probably even seen the array of whips laid out on the bed when they'd sent him to her. Neala's hand shook with the urge to hurt him back, to make him feel even a fraction of the pain they'd put her through – but the girls had asked her not to, and there were tears in Alec's eyes as he pleaded with her.

Dammit.

"He's a good one, Fae, he's been helping us." One of the girls behind her said it, but she didn't move the sword yet.

Then others spoke up saying he had brought them food, taken them from the guards' quarters, helped protect them, given them first aid supplies. Alec really looked like he was going to cry. All their pleas finally pushed her decision over the edge and she dropped the sword from him. Then Alec pulled Hills towards him - and kissed him. Neala's eyes went wide, watching as they held each other tightly.

Oh. He was *with* him.

Their kiss broke and they leaned their foreheads together, whispering soft words for a moment. Then Hills turned towards her. "I want you to know, I am so, so sorry Fae." He was almost as tall as Alec, but where Alec was all blond hair and light eyes, Hills was brown hair, freckles, and honey brown eyes. He seemed sincere, and everyone had vouched for him, and he *had* been gentle with her as he was leading her to those bastards. He'd urged her to be careful. She sighed and nodded.

"Do you know how to use that?" Neala gestured at the gun in his hand and he kept his finger off the trigger, but adjusted the weapon back into his grip.

"I spent four years in the army. I know how to use it." Hills kept one hand on the gun, and the other interlocked with Alec's. It suddenly made a lot of sense to her that Hills would volunteer to serve as escort - he had no interest in the girls. It ensured that none of the guards got too much alone time with one of them, and it let him check on them. There was a chance he had chosen to escort her to keep the other guards away from her as well, even though the result with Butler and Marik was predetermined.

She was suddenly glad she hadn't hit him, or worse.

"Good." She cleared her throat. "I need you to lead them to the supply room, get them dressed for the outdoors, and get them outside through the back. Ebere can help you." Neala gave the command and he didn't flinch, didn't even give her a side eye for ordering him around. He just nodded and moved down the hall. It was odd, but she trusted him.

Neala jogged back towards the stairs, and she heard some kind of commotion. Panic filled her as she turned the corner to find Kiernan fighting two guards, but then she froze in place.

He had *definitely* held back when he had sparred with her.

She watched as he spun, all power and grace as he delivered a hard kick to one of the guards, knocking him down. Then Kiernan blocked a punch from the other, returning with his own, and following it up with an elbow to the guard's solar plexus and a knee to the stomach in such a fast sequence that the man had yet to react to the first strike when Kiernan stepped back. Fluid and smooth, and each hit delivered with way more power than he'd ever used with her.

The guard on the floor started to get up and it broke her out of her trance. Neala slid the sword into the sheath on her back with a grin. He didn't even see her, which made it relatively easy to grab his arm, twist it into an arm bar, and drop her elbow to break it. When he screamed and lunged at her with the other one she pulled the knife and sliced his forearm open. Kiernan stepped up next to her, the gun back in his hand, and the other guard was dead on the floor. The guard was cursing at her between sobs, his blood pooling on the floor under him, and then she stepped behind him and snapped his neck. It was quick, and it was better than he deserved. They both heard shouting in the foyer and nodded at each other in silence, moving towards it slowly.

"YOU?!" The roar came from the figure who had turned the corner into the hall they stood in. Neala felt her muscles tense as she immediately recognized Butler's voice. Kiernan saw the change in her and walked forward, the white-knuckled grip on the guns in his hands showing his rage. Butler raised his own gun at Kiernan and Neala screamed as she heard gunfire.

CHAPTER TWENTY-EIGHT

Ráj Manor, Caledon, Ontario

One. Two. Three.

Kiernan watched as Butler collapsed in front of him, the man's gun sliding across the smooth tile as a look of shock came across his face. As he got closer he saw that the shots had hit home, above the knee on both legs, and one in the shoulder of the man's firing arm. Kiernan had seen the muzzle flash from Butler's gun but he assumed it had gone wide, or his body hadn't informed him of where it hit yet. He was sure he hadn't heard a cry from Neala, so the bullet hadn't hit her.

Either way? He was going to make him hurt.

Kiernan brought the butt of his gun into the side of the man's skull. Butler's head snapped to the side, and when he brought it up he wasn't even looking at him, he was staring straight past him to where Neala stood. "I knew it, I knew it was you. It's always *you*, you worthless whore!"

The darkness flooded his chest again, begging him to let go and destroy the trash in front of him. To drag him out front and stake him to the earth and make the death slow and painful. Butler had hurt Neala, not just once, or twice, but *over and over*. He had been the organizer behind so much pain and horror for her, and he needed to pay. Kiernan's hand itched to pull the trigger, shoot him in the belly and let him die slow, but he settled for a second pistol whip into the man's teeth for what he'd called her.

A stream of curses came out while Butler spat blood and part of a tooth onto the floor. Kiernan crouched in front of him, pressing the gun into one of the wounds on Butler's leg. The man half-screamed before he cut himself off.

"I heard you wanted to know my name." Kiernan growled out the words, and Butler's eyes were matte discs, a steel blue color that showed the rage inside him. "It's Kiernan." Switching the gun to his other hand, Kiernan delivered a hard punch to the other side of Butler's face.

More blood. Another spit onto the floor.

"So you're the one who came for the slut? You think she cares about you? That she's *capable* of that?" Butler's words were garbled, almost unrecognizable as they passed through what remained of his mouth. Kiernan responded with a kick into Butler's stomach as he stood.

"What is it with you? You think it makes you a man to

hurt women?" Kiernan was trying to steady his breathing, but he could feel the fog of his bloodlust swarming his mind. He wanted to hurt him, to have a week or more to make him suffer. To have him begging for death long before he gave it to him.

"Butler is nothing more than a shell filled with hate." Neala interrupted his thoughts with her voice. She was next to him now and in some ways it brought him back from the edge, and in others it reminded him of why he wanted to kill Butler in incredibly slow and creative ways. "There's nothing left in him that would make him a man by any standard."

Despite his injuries Butler still lunged for her, and Kiernan kneed him in the face to stop him. He was practically foaming at the mouth, his eyes boring into Neala and completely ignoring Kiernan. Butler was cursing, raging about Neala and what he thought of her with a single-minded ferocity. Kiernan temporarily entertained the idea of cutting his tongue out and feeding it to him, but he wasn't the one who deserved to choose his punishment.

"You don't get to talk anymore." Kiernan stepped behind Butler and clamped a hand around his throat, cutting off his tirade. "Neala, I wish we had the time to make him suffer as much as he deserves."

"I know." Neala held up a hand, her blue eyes were somehow calm as she drew the sword from over her shoulder. In that moment she looked like a goddess come to deliver final justice. Breathtakingly beautiful, and unforgiving, and deadly.

She pressed the tip of the sword over Butler's heart and he jerked his body away from her, but Kiernan pressed his knee into the man's back to hold him still and Neala realigned the sword as the man sputtered for air.

"This is for Juliet," the blade slipped past the fabric of his shirt and pierced his skin, "and Caridee," she pressed it further and Kiernan could feel the scream in the man's throat. "And for me." The blade slid farther, and it must have pierced his heart because the blood flowed fast down his front. "And every other woman you've ever laid your hands on." Neala put her hand on the hilt of the sword and shoved it *through* him; Kiernan moved his knee fast to avoid the blade.

In a matter of seconds Butler had stilled and Kiernan let go of him. As he slumped to the side Neala planted her foot in his chest and wrenched the sword free. She held it to her side, the blood dripping onto the pale gray tiles, and she just stared at him.

He couldn't really remember seeing the Faeoihn fight, he barely remembered random images of the epic battle, but he imagined it had been incredible to watch them. Her eyes snapped to his and it surprised him, he wanted to do something – hold her, kiss her, dedicate himself to her, kneel at her feet and swear he'd protect her for the rest of his life – but he stayed still.

"Thank you for letting me kill him." Neala's voice was feather soft, and he could only nod. A crash came from the hall the girls had gone down and Neala took off before he had thought to react. He followed after her, keeping up so he wouldn't get lost in the twisting back halls. There was a guard holding a gun on a tall blonde girl, most of the other girls were already in winter gear. Huge coats, boots, and pants. Another guard, brown haired, was pointing a gun at the hostage taker. Neala seemed to know what was happening because she stepped up next to the brown haired guard.

"All of you, get back to the slave quarters! Do it now and the punishment won't be as bad." The guard shouted, holding the blonde in front of him and looking panicked.

"Butler's dead. Let Annika go." Neala spoke clearly. She wasn't moving towards him because she couldn't do much with a sword that wouldn't potentially hurt the blonde. Her flat comment about Butler made everyone gasp with shock.

"Liar!" The guard moved to point the gun at Neala and Kiernan reacted instantly, when he fired the gun he heard screaming and the blonde girl turned away. He hoped he hadn't hit her, but he couldn't let the man fire at Neala. *She was his priority*. When he rushed forward he saw the bullet had gone in on the right side of the guard's forehead, and Kieran breathed a sigh of relief.

"Fuck this! This is insane!" The brown haired guard was wide-eyed. He turned around and a tall blond guy, not in guard gear, wrapped his arms around him.

"Is everyone dressed, Hills, yes or no?" Neala took charge and it made Kiernan smile a little to watch them all turn towards her, and hustle to respond, even in the stress of the situation. She had no idea the power she had over people, how others latched onto her strength to make themselves stronger. He loved her, utterly and completely, plain and simple.

"We need to wait, Fae." Hills, the guard, was talking again, and rubbing the hand with the gun in it against the side of his head. She turned towards him and arched an eyebrow, letting him speak. "I, uh, called the police. I've kind of been working with them for a few months, undercover, trying to gather enough evidence for them to do a raid on this place, to shut it down. They know there are armed people here trying to get the girls out, and I didn't name you guys, but they're coming."

He and Neala *were* the armed people, and in general police forces didn't care what your reasons for walking around with weapons and killing people were. They preferred to lock everyone up and sort out details, and jail sentences, later. Not good when you were immortal and cursed. Things got incredibly complicated very quickly.

"Hills. That was *not* helpful." Neala spoke through her teeth, her frustration evident. "How long do you think we have?" she asked.

He shifted his weight from side to side as he thought, before finally dropping the gun to his side. "I called about ten minutes ago, we're pretty far out here, but maybe another ten to fifteen? Less if they use air support." He grimaced, and the blond guy squeezed his shoulder.

"You and I *cannot* meet the police." Kiernan spoke in hushed tones to Neala as he pulled her to the side. She nodded along with him as he spoke, her eyes scanning the group of girls.

"We can go out the side now and start moving, if we get to the woods before they arrive they'll be too busy with everything here to track us." Neala looked up above her, and then scanned the halls to either side for any hints of guard activity. Kiernan nodded, and Neala moved back to the girls.

"Help is coming, I think the police will protect all of you." She glanced to Hills and he nodded to her. "Stay with Hills, arm yourselves with whatever you can, and do not give mercy to *any* of the guards left. Be strong, you all deserve to be free."

"You're leaving?" It was the dark skinned girl, and she looked like she might cry as she came forward and hugged Neala. Watching Neala hug her back he knew they'd made the right choice in getting the girls, even though it had resulted in violence and chaos when they probably could have slipped away mostly unnoticed.

"I don't think the police would quite understand." Neala said it with a half-laugh and the girl nodded against Neala's shoulder, and let go. Then his Faeoihn was overwhelmed as almost every one of the girls hugged her, whispering thanks, over and over.

It was wonderful, but they really didn't have time for extended goodbyes.

"I'll miss you, Fae, I mean *Neala*." The pixie had stepped in front of her, blushing a little. "That's what he called you."

"It's my name, Irena."

"Well, mine is -" a burble of sound came from the girl that resembled a bird chirping and the sound of rushing water at the same time. It hurt Kiernan's head to hear it. The pixie laughed. "I know you can't say it, but at least you know it now." The two hugged hard again, but a thought struck him.

"Wait, you'll have to come with us I think. Mortal police don't know about your kind, they won't handle it well." Kiernan spoke up, knowing that it was going to be that much harder to move with the other girl, but he couldn't leave her to become some science experiment. The little pixie looked confused a second and then closed her eyes. It almost seemed like the edges of her skin blurred, as Kiernan tried to focus it gave him a headache and he had to look away and blink. When he turned back there was a tiny, pale girl with short blue hair and the pixie's features, but no wings.

"I'll be fine. We know how to hide, they just never let me." The girl smiled and grabbed Neala in a bear hug. "I'm going to try and get home."

"I had no idea you could -" Neala was flabbergasted as she hugged her back. "You're full of surprises, Irena. Have Kiernan give you his cell number, then you can call us if you need us."

Kiernan sighed, his muscles tense with worry that the mortal police would show up, but he took the pen that Hills offered and wrote his number on a scrap of paper and she tucked it into her pocket. Neala turned to him and he forced a smile, trying to show that he was confident her plan would work.

"Good luck." Kiernan nodded at the group and then turned to head down the hall Neala had indicated. As they moved he reloaded his gun, tracing a path he hadn't walked before. At the end was a door, and they picked up the pace so they could get outside and out of sight before the police arrived.

The click of a door opening stopped him, and Neala froze too. From a room to one side, just in front of the door, came three men. Kiernan lifted his gun and fired on the first, he hit him somewhere in the chest and he dropped. He aimed at the second who was lifting his own gun, and Kiernan fired twice, still hitting center mass and that guy slammed into the wall. Adjusting to aim at the third guy, Kiernan started to pull the trigger and a surge of pain like he'd never felt bolted up his left arm, sending his shot wide and bringing him to his knees with a shout.

"Kiernan!" Neala was a few steps behind him, but right as she spoke the man at the end of the hall raised his voice.

"Fae, get on your knees! And drop the fucking sword, it's not like you're going to use it." Kiernan felt the hum in his words.

Shit.

He was the master. Marik.

When Kiernan looked behind him he saw the bands on her wrists, the pain in her face as she knelt and the sword fell from her hand. She had her teeth clenched shut, and he saw fear in her eyes.

"Good girl. Push the sword away from you now," Marik commanded. The bands flared, and she did.

"Leave her alone." Kiernan growled it out and stood for a moment, but when he tried to lift the gun again to shoot him he felt the vines spread, burning through his skin and sending a sickening pulse through his body. He dropped the gun as a sharp stab almost made him buckle. Without the gun the pain abated somewhat, but he still struggled to take a breath.

"I don't know who *you* are, but apparently you can't hurt me either, which is perfect." Marik spoke clearly and calmly as he leaned down and took a gun from one of the dead guards. "As far as leaving Fae alone? She's *mine*, and always will be." It happened fast. Marik raised the gun, Kiernan heard Neala scream something, he heard the shot, and then he looked down to see blood coming out of a hole in his chest. He felt light headed, probably from shock, but then his instincts kicked in and he applied pressure to the wound.

Any minute Gormahn's power would kick in and stop the bleeding.

Any minute.

Neala was crying, he could hear her behind him shouting his name, he had to do something to reassure her, but it was impossible to get the breath for it. The bullet had hit his lung, if he tried to force the air he was going to choke on the blood. *Where the fuck are you when I actually need the power, Gormahn?*

"Stop whining, Fae. Be silent." Marik walked towards them, and Neala's voice choked off. "I'm assuming he's the one who helped you escape before? Well... I think we should show your friend *exactly* who you belong to."

Marik opened his mouth to give an order, the hum in the air resonating in Kiernan's ears as the power of the bands waited to act. Kiernan put a hand on the floor next to him and touched the edge of the sword. *Yes.* Just as Marik stepped next to him Kiernan grabbed the blade, the sharp edge digging into his palm, and then he shoved it up into Marik's chest, under his ribs. A white-hot pain seared through Kiernan's chest, over his heart, but he forced himself to grab the hilt of the sword and push it deeper. Marik looked down at him with a look of confusion, the gun thumping to the floor as Marik crumpled.

Then, everything went dark.

CHAPTER TWENTY-NINE

RÁJ MANOR, CALEDON, ONTARIO

NEALA COULDN'T PROCESS what she'd seen, and it took her a moment to realize she was frozen with panic and shock. Marik had *shot* Kiernan, and he was bleeding, but then Kiernan had run Marik through with the sword. He'd *killed* him. She had to get to Kiernan, she had to stop the bleeding. When Neala tried to stand up the bands reacted instantly, sending pain arching across her back, and then her attempt to scream only doubled the pain.

Tears burned the edges of her eyes as she folded forward, stifling her urge to cry out so that the bands would stop. She lifted her head when the pain finally faded and she heard a slight rattle of breath come out of Marik.

He was still alive.

His breathing was weak, he wouldn't live - but what about Kiernan?

Her mind flashed back to their first real conversation, the one where he'd explained why he had never helped one of the Faeoihn. He'd said he *couldn't*, that it would kill *him* to kill a master. Which was exactly what he had just done. For her.

No, no, no, no, no.

Neala slapped the floor next to her, unable to speak, or move from the spot, as long as Marik still lived. Kiernan didn't react at all. Bending forward as far as she could while staying in the kneel, she found that the tips of her fingers could brush Kiernan's boot. She tapped it, over and over and over.

Nothing.

Sitting back up she pulled at her hair. Her hands were streaked with blood and she was sure she had wiped some of it on her face when she had brushed her tears away. She mouthed Kiernan's name and slammed her palms on the floor again. Still no response, and the bright glow of the bands on her wrists mocked her by pulsing a steady ache as they ticked away the last seconds of Marik's life – and maybe Kiernan's.

Neala tilted her head to the side, trying to still herself so she could look for a rise and fall of Kiernan's chest. Bracing her hands against the ground she held her breath. Was he breathing? Had she imagined the faint movement of his clothes? Was that rattle in his chest or Marik's? She felt a hitch of breath in her own chest as she cried silently. He had come for her, to save her. Even when he couldn't just use his power to disappear with her, he had stayed, he had fought for her and killed for her. Not just her, but all the girls. Complete strangers to him, and he had saved all of them. *And for what?*

If Kiernan was gone, she'd just end up in some new hell. Alone.

Her hand gripped the disc on the necklace, and a pit opened in her stomach. *She'd never said she loved him.* Another sob welled up in her throat, coming out in a silent gasp of breath as tears ran down her face. She was so stupid, so fucking stupid. She'd had him with her for *hours*, why hadn't she said it the moment she saw him? Why hadn't she screamed it at the top of her lungs the moment she was awake and in his arms?

The bands disappeared.

The constant humming ache they had supplied disappeared with them, and the first sound that came out of her was a sob. She moved towards Kiernan, rolling him gently onto his back. His face was pale, his eyes closed, and Neala laid her cheek against his lips to check for breath. She waited, and waited – no movement of air against her cheek. Another sob rolled out of her as she pressed her fingers to his throat, digging her fingertips in, desperate for a pulse that she knew wasn't there.

"Kiernan, please, Kiernan, wake up! Wake up. GET UP, DAMMIT!" She shook him, but he didn't move. Her hand found the bullet hole and she started to rip at the clasps and zippers that held the jacket on him. When it was open she grabbed the knife at her side and simply cut the shirt open. The bullet wasn't the problem, it was about three inches below his heart, and survivable, especially for an immortal. No, the problem was the dark sword mark over his heart, completely wrapped in the vines that spread from his shoulder.

His curse. Gormahn's guarantee of obedience.

"NO! This *can't* be happening, Kiernan, I fucking love you! I *love* you, I love you, please, you can't leave me... this didn't mean anything if you leave me!" She was screaming at him, hitting his chest, even though he couldn't hear her anymore. Tears burned paths down her cheeks as her mind filled in what would happen next for her – she could run, but eventually someone would find her, claim her, and she'd be trapped again. No hope for freedom, or anything good ever again.

Always with the memory that she'd lost the only person to ever love her.

She couldn't do that. She wasn't that strong.

Reaching over Kiernan she picked up his gun. She was no expert with it, but she understood the basics. Point, pull trigger. She lifted it and put the still warm end against her temple. She probably, *hopefully*, wouldn't survive a headshot. Closing her eyes she gripped the gun harder, her finger pressed to the trigger, and guilt swelled inside her as she tried to get the courage to pull.

Eltera.

"DAMMIT!" Neala screamed, dropping the gun to her

lap. She sobbed, screaming with futile rage. Then she looked up at the ceiling, her chest a hollow wasteland that the goddess had to be able to see. "Eltera, if you're still there, if you still see me and know me, if you have *ever* loved me like a daughter... release me from this! Release me from my pledge to you! Please, just let me go, because I can't, I can't do this anymore." She gripped the gun in one hand, her other hand moving down Kiernan's arm until she could interlace their fingers. Neala squeezed her eyes closed and lifted the gun to her temple again, breathing in, and out. She was shaking, a lot, or – no, *she* wasn't shaking at all. A boom of thunder cracked over the house, and it made her take her finger from the trigger as the floor shook beneath her.

"Oh, Neala, of *course* I still love you." That voice. Neala's eyes snapped opened and she looked up to see Eltera towering over her, a look of sadness etched into her impossibly beautiful features.

"Eltera?!" Neala's voice cracked with disbelief.

"Yes, my daughter?" She reached forward and her hand pressed against Neala's cheek, a humming sensation filling her as the golden light that radiated from the goddess touched Neala's skin.

"I -" she started sobbing again, the pain in her chest too overwhelming, "I can't keep going. Not without him. I can't do this for another two thousand years, or more. I'm sorry, I want to be strong for you, I've tried to be strong for you, but I *can't* go on without him."

"I had never planned for you to be without him." Eltera

removed her hand from Neala's cheek and leaned down to rest it on Kiernan's chest. "But I had to know if he was the right one, if he would, in fact, sacrifice everything for you. I had to know he deserved you."

"What?" Neala sat back, confused. "You - you *knew* about this? You knew he would kill Marik? You knew he'd *die* trying to protect me?!"

"I sent you a warning to prepare you." Eltera's speech was calm and straightforward, which infuriated her even as Neala's mind jumped back to the dream of blood pouring from the mark on Kiernan's chest. Of course the goddess would send her a jumbled, confusing, abstract message, and assume it was clear. She couldn't just show up in her head and say '*Hey, Kiernan is going to kill Marik when he steals you back*', that would be too easy, too literal.

"But why didn't you *stop* it?!" Neala screamed, and when Eltera's eyes lifted to hers they glowed gold and fear quivered in her stomach, reminding her to be respectful. Adopted mother or not, Eltera was still a goddess, and her tolerance for insolence was practically non-existent. "I love him," Neala whispered meekly and the short-lived irritation on Eltera's face melted back into compassion.

"I know you do, and it took so much effort to bring you two together." Eltera was glowing more brightly, the light diffusing the edges of her so that Neala had to blink against it. "I had to kill your last master, *not* an easy feat when I had to use you as a conduit and make sure my power didn't kill *you* as well. Then I had to send the right idea, at the right time, for Kiernan to check on you so he would have the urgency to go to you and rescue you. So many moving parts when working with mortals, so many decisions to affect."

"So you *did* kill Nikola?" Neala asked, still a little surprised to have it confirmed even though she'd guessed it herself.

"We both did in a way, Neala." Eltera's voice echoed in the hall, lyrical and powerful. "I may be locked away, I may be Gormahn's slave, but I have *never* abandoned any of my Faeoihn. In a way I am always with you. I love each of you, and my plan is to give you all the happiness you deserve." The light grew blinding, and out of it came the echo of Eltera's words, "Starting with you, Neala."

The light disappeared and Kiernan gasped. He sat up straight, coughing and wheezing, and his eyes were wide – and *green*. Neala let out a sob of disbelief, and when his head turned he immediately cupped her face and kissed her hard. Neala's heart was pounding, the tears on her cheeks suddenly happy ones as she thrust her hands into his hair to hold him against her.

He was alive, he was alive, he was *alive*. She pulled back, and though she probably looked like a wreck from the fighting, the blood, and the crying, she smiled and let the words tumble from her.

"I love you! I love you, Kiernan, and if you *ever* try to leave me again I'll beg Eltera to bring you back again just so I can kill you." Neala laughed through most of it, so overwhelmed by the joy of having him with her again that she couldn't even say the threat seriously. His wide grin took her breath away before he kissed her again;

their lips pressed so hard together it felt like they might bruise.

"I love you too, Neala." He spoke the words against her lips, and then he looked down at his chest, running his hand over the place where the bullet had gone in. That was when she noticed the ouroboros, a serpent eating its own tail, surrounding the dark sword on his chest. A symbol of ends and beginnings, of the power of nature and life. Eltera's symbol. The vines were still crowding the sword, but Kiernan was breathing – he was alive. He had seen the new symbol as well, tracing his fingers across it. "But... *how*? How am I -"

"Hello, Kiernan." Eltera cleared her throat and smiled down at them both, and when Kiernan turned and saw her he almost choked. He scrambled to get into a kneel, bowing his head.

"Goddess, I -"

Eltera waved a hand at him, cutting him off. "It's okay, Kiernan. Relax, we have some things to discuss and I do not have much time."

He took a deep breath, but the tension didn't leave his shoulders as he slowly lifted his gaze to Eltera's face. "Goddess, Eltera, I, ...did you bring me back?" His voice cracked as he asked the question, and Neala reached over to grab his hand as emotion swelled in him.

"Yes, I did." Eltera smiled at him. "Neala called out to me for you."

Neala smiled when he looked at her again, and she was

still shocked by the vibrant green of his eyes. "I couldn't live without you." His smile lit her up from the inside, pure joy filling her up like a balloon. She brushed her fingers across his temple. "Your eyes are green."

"What?! How?" Kiernan looked back up at Eltera and she smiled.

"A side effect of placing my mark on you. By blocking the poison from the Ebon Oak, I've also blocked you from Gormahn's control, apparently that means your eyes have reverted back as well."

"*That* is what this does?" Kiernan laid his hand over the ouroboros, looking to Neala in shock before turning back to the goddess. "He can't control me? He can't kill me?"

"No, Kiernan. He cannot. Although you were doing a fine job resisting him all on your own." Eltera winced, and the ghostly outline of the manacles appeared on her wrists, linked by an ethereal chain. She took a shuddering breath, not even acknowledging them as she raised her eyes again. "I brought you back, and I have placed you under my protection, but it was not *just* for Neala. There is a deeper purpose."

"Of course." Kiernan straightened his back and cleared his throat, "Eltera, I will do anything you ask of me, my life is yours."

"Hmm, well it *has* been a long time since I have heard a pledge like that." Eltera's smile broadened, and her eyes flicked back to Neala. "He is delightful, my daughter. I wonder though, would he be willing to leave *you* if I asked?" Kiernan twitched and looked over at Neala. His eyes were wide, tense with the painful idea, and her chest ached too because she had no idea why Eltera would even ask that after everything they had been through.

Then he grabbed her hand.

The moment their hands touched Neala gasped as the bands appeared again, blindingly bright for a moment, a dull ache burning up her arms until the pain settled back around the bands.

"No!" Kiernan stood up, and even as big a guy as he was, Eltera still stood half a head taller. That didn't seem to phase him though as he looked her in the eyes, and started shouting. "This can't happen! She's supposed to be *free*! She's supposed to be -"

"*Yours*." Eltera arched a delicate eyebrow at him, and tapped a finger on the exposed sword mark on his chest, zapping him slightly to make a point that he had no chance to fight her, and that respect was still required.

"*Mine*?" Kiernan looked confused, and Eltera reached down and took Neala's hand, placing it in his again.

"Yes, Kiernan, yours. You just claimed Neala for yourself." Eltera smiled, looking quite proud of herself. "Just as my mark, and your pledge, has made you mine."

"But, I wanted her free..." Kiernan mumbled as he gripped Neala's hand tighter, helping her as she stood. Eltera closed her eyes for a moment, the bands becoming more solid by the minute, and Neala knew there had to be pain. The manacles on Eltera's wrists were glowing vibrantly, but the goddess took a slow breath and then looked at them again.

"None of my Faoeihn, not even Neala, can be free. For they are bound to me, and I am not free." Eltera tilted her head slightly. "But you will keep her safe, will you not? You will love her? You will take care of my daughter and protect her while still allowing her as much freedom as possible? You will make her happy?"

"I would do anything for her. I love her." Kiernan gripped Neala's hand and she felt like she was glowing, her chest was full to bursting with how happy she was, and for once the sight of the bands on her wrists made her feel *good*. She belonged with Kiernan, Eltera had said it. His eyes met hers. "I need to know, are you okay with this?"

"Don't order me to clean your house, and I think we'll be just fine." Neala laughed and he smiled and kissed her.

"We both know I'm the neat one, if you had your way the house would be a mess." He grinned and touched his forehead to hers, squeezing her hand as she kissed him again, not wanting to admit the truth of *that* out loud.

"Just remember, Kiernan, if you ever *did* hurt her, you do belong to me of your own volition. And while Gormahn's power is still inside you - and it will continue to keep you immortal and heal you – *mine* is the power keeping his poison from killing you." Eltera's smile remained calm and serene, which almost made the threat a little more frightening. With a snap of her fingers his ruined shirt and jacket disappeared leaving him shirtless and suddenly clean of blood. Gormahn's vines were pushed back below his elbow, and Neala's eyes widened with the incredible power it must have taken Eltera to do that.

"Yes, Goddess." Kiernan bowed his head, and Eltera nodded to him. But as Neala watched, she saw the goddess go pale, a tremble rushing through her, and the bands pulsed a vicious golden light.

"I wish I could stay, my daughter." Eltera moved forward, cradling Neala's cheek before she placed a single, soft kiss to her forehead. "Yet, I am bound by my own pledge, and it has taken a great deal of energy for me to come here. I know you will do what I need you to. I know that together, both of you will."

She stepped back shakily, and Neala spoke up fast, "Thank you, Eltera. Thank you for this, but what do you need us to do? What can we do to repay you?" Neala gripped Kiernan's hand tighter in hers.

Eltera looked impossibly sad for a moment, her features still beautiful but so full of sorrow that Neala's heart almost broke for her. Then she spoke softly, "You can save your sisters."

Then there was a rumble of thunder, and a flash of golden light, and she was gone.

EPILOGUE

1 MONTH LATER

SEATTLE, WASHINGTON

"No. I already said no, and I mean it, Neala." Kiernan had his head in his hands, his elbows propped up on his new desk.

"You're so stubborn, what happened to us having an equal partnership? You not abusing your power and all that?" She sat down on the edge of Kiernan's new desk and smiled down at him, running a hand through his hair. He looked up at her through his fingers and grumbled quietly. "Come on, let's try it."

"No." His answer was muffled against his palms and she sighed in frustration. Neala pushed his chair back and knelt in front of him, grabbing his hands to pull them away from his face. His gorgeous green eyes settled on the bright bands of light circling her wrists and he tried to turn away from her again.

"I know you hate them, I hate them too, so can we please at least *try* to get rid of them?" Neala was on the verge of begging; it had been a rough few weeks. After Eltera had disappeared, Kiernan had tested whether he could take her with him if he popped somewhere else. Once he knew it worked they had reappeared on top of the house. There they had watched as the Ontario Provincial Police had arrived and swarmed the premises. Several vans had appeared to take the girls away, and Neala had watched Lena climb into one of the vans as well. The guards had been stripped of their weapons and carted into various police cars. Coroner vans had arrived for the dead.

Ráj Manor was being shut down.

Once they were sure everyone she cared for was safe, they had returned home. The first few days had been blissful, and they'd spent ninety percent of that time in *bed*. Kiernan had refused to leave even to go shopping, and they had enjoyed every form of deliverable food the mortals had. It had been perfection.

Everything had been perfect, but the bands were always there. Bright and shining, even though their dull buzz against her skin had faded into the background of her life with him. They never hurt, but she couldn't go *anywhere*. If the mortals saw them it would bring too many questions, draw too much attention, and attention could bring the other Laochra. So they were at home. *All the time*. And Kiernan hated himself for being the cause of it, hated that she was still bound by Gormahn's curse, and lately any time his eyes landed on the golden light of the bands they seemed to sap him of any joy he had.

Neala was over it. It was time to see if he could order them to disappear.

"*Mo ghaol*, I couldn't stand it if I hurt you. I've seen what they can do to you, and I – I just can't be the one that causes that." His thumbs brushed through the light, cradling her wrists.

Neala brought her eyebrows together as she asked, "Shouldn't that be my choice?" That caught him, and she knew it. He groaned and looked up at her, and she knew he was tortured by the idea he would hurt her, but being trapped in his house dealing with his guilt was torture for *her*.

"Okay." Kiernan sounded so defeated, but Neala bounced up with renewed energy. *Finally*. A chance to get rid of them. He spoke again, "What do I need to do?"

Neala held her arms out in front of her, so used to the bands on her wrists that she wondered how it would feel for them to fade again. "Just demand that they don't show. Make it a command."

He leaned back in his office chair, looking miserable. "I don't want to do this."

"I know you don't, but you have to. Come on." Neala grinned at him, but he didn't return the smile. He took a steadying breath and blew it out, and looked somewhere near her sternum, unable to meet her eyes.

"Don't let the bands show, Neala." His voice shook as he

spoke, and lilted up at the end as if he were asking a question. Nothing happened.

"It has to be a *command*, Kiernan. You have to mean it. Talk to me like you do when I make a mistake in a sparring session!" Neala stomped her foot on the ground and he finally looked her in the eye. She continued, "Don't you want to be able to go out? To the community garden? Meet with the contractors *together*? Let Elsie come over? She's going to break down the damn door the next time you try to turn her away!"

"Yes, I do. Yes to all of it." Kiernan was resigned, but the guilt he was feeling came out in his voice.

"Then don't do it for us, do it for *me*, because I want to go see the cottage they're building in the daylight, not in the middle of the night, alone. I want to be able to walk down the street and hold your hand, and let everyone see us together. I want to go on another date." Neala smiled and leaned back against the wall, stretching so that the shirt she was wearing pulled up to reveal some of her stomach. Kiernan's eyes followed the edge of the fabric and a hunger quickly replaced the guilt there. "I want everyone to know who *I* chose."

"Neala?" Kiernan's voice had an edge to it, his eyes moving over her curves. She smiled and answered with a questioning sound. His voice was dark and intense, the kind of voice that made heat coil between her thighs. "I never want to see those bands again. Ever. Do you understand?" The bands hummed. "Make them disappear."

Neala gasped as a sharp pain rocked up her arms, and Kiernan was in front of her holding her arms before she'd opened her eyes again. She looked down just in time to see the bright bands wink out. The pain faded instantly, and the relief and the joy made her grin. "Do you see?!" She screamed, bouncing with excitement. Kiernan shouted a cheer and picked her up against him, swinging her around.

"By the gods, you're beautiful." Kiernan said just before he pressed his lips against hers, and then they were wrapped in each other. Her back hit the wall and she wrapped her legs around his hips to hold herself there.

The darkness and the guilt between them was gone, and all that was left was the brightness of hope and the heat that flushed her every time he touched her. Neala reached for the bottom of her shirt, but he got to it first, shoving it up her ribs to get his hands on her skin. His lips trailed down her neck, grazing her skin with his teeth as he groaned, "I want you, please tell me -"

"Yes, yes, yes, I want you too." Neala grinned, and pressed herself harder against him. His guttural growl made her shiver as he turned and laid her out on his brand new wooden desk. Papers crinkled underneath her, but she ignored them as he grabbed the top of the yoga pants she wore and ripped them off, with her underwear, in a single sweep. Kiernan groaned as he pushed her thighs apart, his eyes feasting on her spread out before him.

"So. Fucking. Perfect." He trailed his mouth up the inside of her thigh, and her hips lifted unconsciously, seeking the contact she knew would bring her delirious pleasure.

Kiernan paused, hovering over her mound, the warmth of his breath sending a shiver over her. She propped herself up on her elbows to look down at him, and he locked eyes with her just as he dipped down and trailed his warm tongue between the lips of her pussy. Neala moaned and arched against his mouth, but he pulled back before he made contact with her clit.

"Kiernan!" She complained, but he stood up and reached for her, yanking her up to a sitting position so he could kiss her. She tasted herself on his lips and felt the hard steel of his erection rubbing against her. *Would she ever get tired of his incredible body, or his unreal skill at turning her into a warm puddle version of herself?*

There was no way.

"You're so damn impatient." He grinned at her, ripping her shirt over her head, and then sliding his hands around to her back to flick the clasp of her bra so she was suddenly, wonderfully, naked in front of him.

"I waited two thousand *years* for you, and you're calling me impatient?" Neala arched an eyebrow and he laughed and spanked her ass lightly.

"Shouldn't you be speaking to me respectfully or something? Isn't that in the curse somewhere?" Kiernan was teasing her, taunting her to get her wound up, but the way his eyes moved down her body felt like an electric tingle and it was deliciously distracting.

"You're the stalker, you should know better than anyone that respect has never been a strong suit of mine..." Neala reached between the two of them, stroking him through his pants, and she delighted in the way his breath caught and his jaw clenched as he fought to maintain control. "What I really think you should do, is take off all these clothes."

"No respect, and now you're giving me orders?" Kiernan's voice was unfocused as she continued to stroke him, his hips moving in time with her movements. Then, she pulled her hand back and his eyes snapped open on her. "Neala!"

"Now who's being impatient?" She grinned and he flipped her over, face down on the desk. Immediately pressing himself against her, grinding as he leaned over her.

"Such a feisty Faeoihn..." he nipped across her ribs, brushing kisses across her back that had her squirming. He pressed a hand between her shoulder blades to keep her still and she loved it, loved that it was him, loved that she had teased him into taking action – and *gods* she wanted him inside her. "Stay absolutely still, please." He was careful with his words, ensuring they weren't an actual command, but she still grinned.

"Such a bossy Laochra." She barely got the words out before he brought a hand across one of the globes of her ass, and she jumped, then he repeated the same stinging spank on the other cheek.

"I asked you to stay still, Neala." His voice was a rumble from behind her, and she almost responded, but then he traced his fingers through the ample wetness that had been gathering between her thighs and all she could do was moan. "So, you want to go on another date with me?"

"Yes..." she mumbled, rocking her hips against the desktop as he found her clit and began to roll it slowly, sending jerking waves of pleasure through her. The warmth of his bare skin pressed against her as he leaned forward.

"And you want to have dinner with Elsie again, even though she's going to do *nothing* but brag about how she knew we were meant to be together?" There was laughter in his voice, but it held the edge of his restrained passion as he dragged it out. He suddenly thrust two fingers inside her and she cried out, trying to keep her focus through the pulse that he was drumming between her thighs.

"She was right, she deserves to know that, Kiernan." Neala moaned as he found that bundle of nerves inside her and stroked it, his fingers curving over her pubic bone to bring her right to the edge.

"True. What about the contractors? You really want to meet with them? Help with planning our home?" He continued the devious movements, and her pussy was so wet that she wanted to beg him to stop tormenting her, but his words woke up something even better inside her than the pending orgasm.

"I want all of it, Kiernan, I want all of it. I want to plan our home, I want to plan our future – I want *you*." Neala said it through shaking breaths, and he removed his fingers and she felt his cock press against her. *Finally.*

"I love you, Neala, and trust me – I want to plan our future too, because you don't have to want me, you *have* me. Forever." Then he thrust inside her, filling her and stretching her to make her moan and grab onto the other side of the desk. His hands landed on her hips as he started to move, and each hard slap of his body against hers was punctuated with a wave of pleasure that crashed through her.

Neala let go, letting herself ride the incredible intensity of his body moving against hers, that liquid heat building into an overwhelming need to break through to the other side. Her legs shivered, her body tensed, and he kissed her ribs, moaning against her skin as she tightened down on his hard cock. Then the tension inside her snapped and sent her sparkling into the kind of orgasm that left her nerves shimmering. He moaned her name, and a moment later she felt him come, his body weight pressing her harder into the desk under him.

She couldn't wipe the happy grin off her face. Post-orgasmic bliss, and the kind of wholesome joy that came from being loved completely by another person. He pressed kisses to her skin, murmuring about how beautiful she was, how lucky he was, and how much he loved her. The words filled her up and she wanted to turn over and wrap herself around him, she wanted to lock her heels behind his thighs and hold him to her. She wanted to be with her perfectly imperfect warrior, her lover who walked between the light and the dark, the man who could kill without flinching and the man who gave scholarships to boys he didn't know just to make their mother happy. He was complicated, but so was she – and they had each other.

"I love you so much, Kiernan." She breathed it against the wood under her cheek, and she felt the satisfied rumble in his chest. Just as she was about to open her mouth again to elaborate on the myriad ways he was perfect for her, Kiernan's phone went off. It was an irritating, loud song that blasted some choice words into the air.

"Dammit, really?" he groaned, and she laughed.

"Cole is calling again." Neala turned her head to look at him and he slid from her, helping her to stand up so he could kiss her again.

"He can wait? For after round two?" The hope in Kiernan's voice made her want to laugh.

"No, you've put him off for a month, and I thought you promised you weren't going to ditch him again?" She smiled up at him and he grumbled, but she knew he cared about his best friend. He leaned over and grabbed the loud, buzzing phone and answered it.

"Hey man – yes, I'm still coming – no, I'm not cancelling – I'm just.... wrapping things up. Twenty or thirty minutes? Deal." Kiernan pressed the screen of the phone and looked back to her. "I'd rather be here with you, Glowworm."

Neala pinched the back of his arm and he yelped. She smiled, "You're not the only one with a promise to keep, Kiernan. I have my own plans for the next three days."

"I know, I know. I guess this means we have to put clothes

on?" His eyes trailed over her and she returned the favor, taking in the hard planes of his body, the strong cut of his jaw, the five o'clock shadow she'd felt brushing against her skin – and his vibrant green eyes.

"Yes, we have to put on clothes and *you* need to put in your contacts. Remember? You need your creepy Laochra eyes to go see Cole." She grinned and he faked a pout.

"You thought my eyes were creepy?"

"Oh, by Eltera's grace, don't even try to pout right now." Neala grinned and he returned it, picking her up in his arms to walk towards the bedroom.

"Fine, I won't pout, but I'm going to enjoy every *single* minute I have with you until I have to leave, and I'd prefer if you'd get dressed really, really slowly." He leaned down and kissed her, and she laughed against his lips.

They got dressed, probably much more quickly than Kiernan would have preferred, and he stepped out of the bathroom. It was a strange sight to see the irises of Kiernan's eyes black again, but there was no way he could see the other Laochra without the costume contacts he'd ordered. As Neala moved closer she marveled at how perfectly they covered the green, and she found herself tilting her head to try and see the edges.

"Well, how do they look? Is Cole going to run me through with a sword when he sees me?" Kiernan tried to make it light, but they both knew there was a lot of risk with him going back, but it would be worse if he ignored his friend again. Until Neala was able to stay in their new, hidden home – Kiernan had to keep everyone away from his apartment.

"From what you've told me, Cole would never hurt you. But they look perfect. You look like you did when I met you."

"I don't look happier?" He grinned and she laughed as he wrapped his arms around her.

"So smooth."

"You say that like it's a surprise, when we both know how awesome I am." He said it seriously, but Neala just laughed again and shoved him back a bit.

"*You* made me a promise, Kiernan, now go fulfill it before your head is too big to travel, and do *not* make that a joke!" She smiled up at him, her own excitement catching up with her. "Please go get her?"

"Of course, *mo ghaol*. Kiernan grinned and stepped back from her, swooping into a deep bow that she was sure he had *actually* perfected during the Renaissance. Then he shifted, and she had to rub her eyes to let herself refocus. It wasn't five minutes later when she heard a high-pitched squeal from the living room.

"NEALA!"

Neala rushed into the living room and was almost tackled to the floor by the force of the five-foot ball of energy. A puff of blue hair was tickling her nose when she squeezed Irena back. The pixie hadn't wasted any time calling Kiernan once she was settled with an organization that helped to get women back on their feet and out of the slave trade. Right now she was using a glamour to hide who she really was, but she was still Irena.

"I'm so glad you're here!" Neala couldn't hide her own excitement, and they hugged again and jumped up and down. Kiernan was trying to hide his laughter behind them.

"So, I brought a *list* of movies we have to watch. And I'm thinking our meals should revolve around sugar and pizza, and you said we would go shopping if you -" Irena was buzzing and talking fast like she always did when she was happy, but she stopped silent and let out an ear piercing squeal. "THE BANDS ARE GONE!"

Neala grinned. "Yes, I finally convinced him to try -"

"That's amazing! It means we can go out, and *you guys* can go out, and I'm just so happy for you!" Irena let go of her glamour and her figure blurred for a second until the whir of pixie wings was audible, and then Neala saw the friend she knew so well. Blue skin and all.

"With so much fun planned, I guess you don't need me around then?" Kiernan faked a wounded look and Irena just rolled her eyes and jumped over to the couch to drop herself on it. Neala walked over and wrapped her arms around him.

"I will *always* need you." She kissed him softly, and she could feel when his lips spread into a smile.

"It's only three days, right? And this time nothing will happen." Kiernan whispered into her hair as he hugged her tight against him.

"I'm yours, and you're mine. Forever. Eltera promised us that. Three days is nothing." Neala whispered back.

"I love you, Glowworm." He kissed her, and she grinned.

"I love you too." With one last kiss he stepped back and grabbed his duffel from near the wall. Neala crossed her arms over her stomach and waved a little. Kiernan winked at her, and then shifted, but she wasn't worried. She knew he'd be back.

She'd spend the next three days being as normal as it was possible to be when 'normal' included an orphaned pixie and a Faeoihn trying to figure out modern day Seattle.

Then he'd be back, they'd start the journey to save her sisters, *however the hell they were supposed to do that*, and the time they had spent apart wouldn't matter.

It wouldn't matter because they really did have forever, and for once the future was something Neala really wanted to think about.

THE END

ABOUT THE AUTHOR

Cassandra Faye lives in Texas where she's done nothing but fantasize about other worlds her entire life. Constantly daydreaming about ancient powers, faerie realms, old gods, and how seriously dangerous unicorns would be if they existed, Cassandra writes the stories she's always craved. Taking paranormal and fantasy worlds, mixing them in with modern day, and adding a dash of darkness.

So, if you enjoy those fairy tales that were a little more *grimm*, or if you ever wondered just how bad the villains could be as you held on for that happily-ever-after, then you might be just the person she's writing for.

https://www.fayebooks.com/

Don't miss a release! Sign up for the newsletter to get new book alerts at: https://www.fayebooks.com/newsletter

Cassandra also writes dark contemporary romance as Jennifer Bene. You can find her online throughout social media with username @jbeneauthor and on her website: www.jenniferbene.com

ALSO BY CASSANDRA FAYE & JENNIFER BENE

Daughters of Eltera Series (Dark Fantasy Romance)

Fae *(Daughters of Eltera Book 1)*

Tara *(Daughters of Eltera Book 2)*

The Thalia Series (Dark Romance)

Security Binds Her *(Thalia Book 1)*

Striking a Balance *(Thalia Book 2)*

Salvaged by Love *(Thalia Book 3)*

Tying the Knot *(Thalia Book 4)*

The Thalia Series: The Complete Collection

Dangerous Games Series (Dark Mafia Romance)

Early Sins *(A Dangerous Games Prequel)*

Lethal Sin *(Dangerous Games Book 1)*

Damaged Goods *(Dangerous Games Book 2)*

Fragile Ties Series (Dark Romance)

Destruction *(Fragile Ties Book 1)*

Inheritance *(Fragile Ties Book 2)*

Redemption *(Fragile Ties Book 3)*

The Beth Series (Dark Romance)

Breaking Beth *(Beth Book 1)*

Standalone Dark Romance

Taken by the Enemy

Imperfect Monster

Corrupt Desires

The Rite

Deviant Attraction: A Dark and Dirty Collection

Reign of Ruin

Crazy Broken Love

Appearances in the Black Light Series (BDSM Romance)

Black Light: Exposed *(Black Light Series Book 2)*

Black Light: Valentine Roulette *(Black Light Series Book 3)*

Black Light: Roulette Redux *(Black Light Series Book 7)*

Black Light: Celebrity Roulette *(Black Light Series Book 12)*

Standalone BDSM Ménage Romance

The Invitation

Reunited